Quintin
Jardine

SKINNER'S ROUND

<u>headline</u>

First published in 1995 by
HEADLINE PUBLISHING GROUP

First published in paperback in 1996 by
HEADLINE PUBLISHING GROUP

First published in this paperback edition in 2009 by
HEADLINE PUBLISHING GROUP

2

Cataloguing in Publication Data is available from the British Library

ISBN 978 0 7553 5773 4 (B format)
ISBN 978 0 7472 5041 8 (A format)

Typeset in Electra by Avon DataSet Ltd,
Bidford-on-Avon, Warwickshire

Printed in the UK by CPI Antony Rowe, Chippenham and Eastbourne

Headline's policy is to use papers that are natural, renewable and
recyclable products and made from wood grown in sustainable forests.
The logging and manufacturing processes are expected to conform
to the environmental regulations of the country of origin.

HEADLINE PUBLISHING GROUP
An Hachette UK Company
338 Euston Road
London NW1 3BH

www.headline.co.uk
www.hachette.co.uk

Hello, Mother

Acknowledgements

The author's thanks go to:

Harry Abernethy, for his advice on international
communications technology.
Jack Arrundale.
D. M. Robertson.
The Royal and Ancient Golf Club of St Andrews.
Sue Scarr, shy and retiring.

Sunday

One

'Looks just as if he'd drowned in Lambrusco, doesn't it, sir?'

'Remember who this is, Neil. If this bloke went under in anything, it'd be pink champagne.'

'Aye, I suppose so. But what a way to go, eh. There's something . . . what's the word? . . . something Romanesque, about it, isn't there?' Detective Sergeant Neil McIlhenney beamed with a shy pride at the description dredged up from the silted depths of his vocabulary. 'If those boys fell out with the old Emperor they'd just jump into the bath and open an artery. But to jump into a Jacuzzi, now that's style.'

The other man chuckled grimly, in spite of himself. 'Ha! The Emperor Michael! From what I've heard of the man, he'd have had a laugh about that one. He was a bit more modest than that.' He paused, examining the tiled exterior of the raised oval tub.

'I dare say he'll have a funeral fit for a Caesar, though, when the time comes. For now he's just a stiff in a bath-tub, buggering up our quiet Sunday.' He looked around the tiled walls. 'Where's the switch for this damn thing, d'you think?'

'Could this be it, sir?' McIlhenney tugged at a long cord which hung from the ceiling, by the doorway of the cubicle. The gurgling of the Jacuzzi, and the whirr of the extractor fan set into a panel in the frosted window, each came to a halt in the same second.

The two policemen peered into the big bathtub as the bubbles settled and the bright pink water cleared. Only the body's right knee broke the surface. Despite the steaming warmth its skin was a waxy yellow. The man's head lolled on his left shoulder, exposing fully the great gaping gash in his throat, which smiled up at them like a misplaced mouth.

'D'ye think he *is* dead then, sir?'

'Very funny, Sergeant. Were you all that East Lothian CID had to offer when the shout came in? Jesus, I asked for you to be posted down here, too.'

'*Aye*,' thought McIlhenney, '*and if I'd known what a miserable arse you were going to turn into, I'd have asked to stay with the whores and the druggies.*'

Aloud, he said: 'Sorry, sir. I'll remember to keep a serious tongue in my head from now on.'

The other man softened at once. 'No, I'm sorry, Neil. I shouldn't be getting at you. It's just this bloody uniform. It gets itchy in this heat.'

McIlhenney grinned back at him. 'Tell me about it; so does this Marks & Spencer double-breaster.

'Look, sir, since we're not going to give poor Mr White the kiss of life, why don't we step outside till the doc gets here.'

The man in uniform nodded, and led the way out of the cubicle into the changing room. 'Which doc did you call?' he asked, as McIlhenney closed the door behind them. There was an edge to his question.

'Nobody. I told young Keiran to do it. With it being Sunday, there was just the two of us on duty. That's why I came on my own, that and the fact that the call said it was a suicide.'

The senior officer grunted. 'Suicide? Not unless he's hidden the blade in a very unusual place . . . AFTER he's cut his throat. As far as I could see when the water began to clear, there's no weapon in the tub. There's nothing else in the room either, and the old steward swore he didn't touch anything when he found the body.'

'I'd better let my higher-ups know,' said McIlhenney, taking a mobile phone from his pocket. He pressed a short-coded number, then the send button, and waited. The call was answered, by a woman, on the third ring. 'Superintendent Higgins? Neil McIlhenney here. Sorry to bother you at home on a Sunday, ma'am, but this is a serious one. We've got a suspicious death out here in East Lothian, in the clubhouse of the new Witches' Hill Golf Club.'

On the other end of the line, Alison Higgins whistled. 'That sounds like quite a setting. How suspicious is it? Are we talking about murder?'

'Not much doubt.'

'Any identification?'

'Yes. The victim is Michael White; you'll have heard of him, I'm sure. He's one of Edinburgh's big players, a multimillionaire. He made loadsamoney in the rag trade, then after he sold out he made some more backing property deals. He was part of the consortium that developed this place.'

'I'm on my way, Sergeant. Remind me, where is Witches' Hill?'

'It's just at the back of Aberlady. Take the road to Drem, then turn left at the roundabout. You can't miss it after that.'

'I know where you are. Give me half an hour.'

McIlhenney pressed the end button and looked across at his

companion. 'Should I call the Big Man, sir? I mean this is nearly on his doorstep . . . or on one of them, at least.'

'You've told your area head of CID. That's your chain of command.'

'But sir . . .'

'You heard me. That's it.'

McIlhenney looked across, his appeal against the decision written in his eyes. The other man shook his head and turned away. He was facing the door to the changing room when the soft knock sounded and it opened.

'Hello Andy. Might have guessed I'd find you here.' She stood framed in the doorway, tall and tanned, with auburn hair, verging on golden. Her fawn trousers were close cut and emphasised the curves of her hips, while her floppy white cotton shirt, even hanging loose, could not mask the heaviness of her breasts. The square medical bag which she clutched in her right hand looked incongruous against the informality of her dress.

She smiled. A sudden, open smile. Its warmth filled the room and broke the tension. McIlhenney, in the background, exhaled loudly. Professor Sarah Grace Skinner laughed aloud. 'Hi, Neil. Good to see you too.' She paused, registering the uncertainty in the Sergeant's expression. 'Don't worry, guy. I don't have a problem here.'

Lending weight to her words she stepped across to Andy Martin and kissed him on the cheek. 'Missed you,' she said softly as she brushed against him.

'I didn't think we'd see you here,' he said. 'I thought you'd be all wrapped up in getting ready for that new job of yours at the University.'

'No, not completely. I don't start until next month, and

even then, I'll still be on the roll of Force Medical Examiners. Today I'm on call, and as luck would have it, we'd decided to spend a week or so in the Gullane cottage, so I was only two or three miles away.'

'Is . . . ?'

She cut off Martin's hesitant question with a shake of her head. 'No. He's back at the cottage, looking after Jazz, and catching up with the DIY. I've finally persuaded him to fix that shaky shelf in the kitchen, before something falls off it and lands on the baby!'

She paused. 'Aren't you going to ask how he is?'

'I don't need to,' said Martin. 'I know how he is. He made himself pretty clear, remember, to both of us. I still don't know everything that he said to Alex that morning, but whatever it was, it had its effect. I haven't seen her since, and I'm still inclined to blame Bob.'

'If it's any consolation, we haven't seen her either. We tried to contact her through the people she's with, but there was no response, until I had a call from her around a month ago, from Milan, asking how her halfbrother was doing.'

'Did she ask about me?'

'No,' she said, with a shake of her head; 'nor about her father, either.

'Don't blame Bob entirely, Andy. From what Alex told me, all of you could have handled it better than you did. In your case, Alex expected you to support her, without question. Sometimes you have to choose sides, even when it hurts. Sometimes you just can't have it both ways.'

'And how about you, Sarah? Whose side are you on?'

'D'you need to ask? I'm on his, right or wrong. He may be a stubborn, short-fused old bear, but he's MY bear, even when he's facing ass-backwards! But Andy, it isn't a question of sides any more; it never was, really. We all want the same thing, and that's to have Alex back home.'

Martin sighed, in exasperation. The Superintendent's badges on his shoulders reflected the ceiling spotlights for an instant, as his broad shoulders sagged. 'Yes, Doc, of course you're right. I made a bollocks of it, as per bloody usual. See me, see women? Will I *ever* get it right?'

Sarah grinned at him and punched his chest, lightly, with her left hand. 'Maybe, when you learn to stop thinking everything through, and just do what instinct tells you.'

He looked at her sharply, with an old hurt in his eyes. 'I did that once, remember?' he said quietly.

'Yes, so you did. Stupid of me to say that.

'Look, enough of this. I take it that our customer's through there, where Neil went.' McIlhenney had withdrawn tactfully to the Jacuzzi cubicle almost as soon as Sarah had entered.

Martin nodded, and led her through the empty changing area, past the navy blazer, white shirt and grey slacks which hung on three separate hangers from a frame in the centre of the room, past the casual sports clothes which lay crumpled on the floor beside a gaudy pair of white and tan leather shoes, and a blue sports bag, gaping open.

Sarah paused in the doorway. 'He's in the tub,' said Martin, pointing. 'Big wound to the throat.'

She nodded. 'So where's the blood?'

'None. Only what's in the bath and the splash down the side.'

'Got a theory?'

Martin pointed to his left. 'See that shelf. His car keys, house keys and some loose change are there, but there's no wallet or wristwatch. Looks like murder associated with theft. White comes in here, puts his gear on the shelf beside the towel-rail, gets into the Jacuzzi. Neil checked: it was made ready for him by the steward. This changing suite was Michael White's private facility. The steward told us he didn't like showers. Someone follows him in, does him as he's lying in his bath, and makes off with his watch and wallet. Apparently the watch was a gold and diamond Rolex, and his wallet was always stuffed.'

'That's your thinking?'

'What else fits? The shelf's just inside the door, behind the tub. Maybe the guy hoped to sneak in and get out without White hearing him, only it didn't work out that way.'

'Mmm,' said Sarah, thoughtfully. 'I've met this man, you know. The Whites were at the Prouds' party last Christmas. And Bob knew him reasonably well through the New Club.'

She walked over to the Jacuzzi and looked down at the late Michael White. She shook her head sadly for a second or two, but then her expression changed, becoming completely professional and dispassionate. She put down her bag, opened it and took out a pair of disposable latex gloves, which she snapped on. 'Just for the record.' She reached into the bath and held the right wrist for a few seconds. 'What's the time, Neil?'

'Two-twenty-seven, Doctor.'

'OK, better note that down as the moment when life was declared extinct.'

She grasped the jaw and raised the head for a closer look at the wound. 'Big knife did that. No weapon found?' She looked up at McIlhenney, who shook his head.

Wisps of brown hair floated up as she let White's head sink back down to his shoulder. Idly she stirred the water, from which the crimson blood had begun to separate. 'He must have

9

died very quickly, otherwise there'd be even more blood than that. A single cut, almost to the bone, yet hardly anything splashed outside the bath. What d'you think guys?'

Martin stepped over beside her. 'He's lying with his back to the door. He hears the thief, but before he can pull himself up the guy takes two steps across and does him.'

'Yeah, but even at that . . . Come here, Neil. Down on your knees with your back to me.' McIlhenney, puzzled, did as he was told.

'Now look, to do that, our killer, having stepped across that tiled floor, would have had to grab his man by the chin with his left hand, and pull him round . . .' she took hold of McIlhenney and pulled his head up and to the left '. . . to expose the neck so that he could make the cut.' The sweeping movement of her right hand left nothing to the imagination. In her grasp McIlhenney paled.

She released the big detective. 'What's wrong with that?' she asked him as he stood up.

He shrugged his shoulders. 'Dunno.'

'What's wrong with it, colleagues, is that if it had happened like that, even if it was so quick that White had no chance even to struggle, when he hit the artery, the blood would have gone halfway up the wall on the right there. Yet there isn't any, apart from that smear over the edge of the tub. There's no knife, so no attempt to make it look like suicide. And there's been a theft. So if it happened the way you say, why would our killer wipe the wall, so carefully as not to leave a trace? And if he did that, why would he leave that one smear?'

Martin smiled. He knew Sarah Skinner, née Grace, from many crime scenes. He was in awe of her eye for detail. 'So tell us, why?'

'He didn't. That's not what happened.' She knelt beside the tub and reached into the water once more, with both hands this time. She took hold of White's head firmly, moving her fingers around the skull. The two policemen watched in fascination. Eventually, she nodded and hissed, 'Yes!! Got it!' She looked up at them, still holding the victim's head.

'There's another injury! Above the hairline, on the right temple. He has a depressed skull fracture.' She let the body go and stood up. 'No one followed him in here. Someone was waiting for him. Behind the door, I'd say. White opens the door right-handed and comes in. Even as it's closing, he's putting his gear on the shelf, standing naked and with his back to the man who's waiting.

'Whack! The attacker beans him with something, on the side of the head. He goes down, and from that blow he's out, believe me. Our guy could have taken the money and run. But he doesn't do that. Instead he hauls White, a dead weight, across and heaves him into the Jacuzzi. Then he outs with a long-bladed knife and cuts his throat, in the tub. When the artery shoots, only the first spurt breaks the surface.'

'Why should he do that?' asked Martin, but it was more a prompt than a question.

'So that he wouldn't get blood on him. This guy didn't come in here to steal from White. If he took his watch and wallet it was only to make you dumb coppers assume that was the motive. This man, our perpetrator, came in here to kill White, and to walk away quietly afterwards.'

'Hi Pops.'

She stood in the doorway. The peach-coloured towel trailed on the hallway floor, hanging loosely from her right hand. Her long dark hair, its natural waves dampened down by the shower, was ruffled from vigorous rubbing. The blue satin bathrobe, tied firmly at the waist, clung tightly to her, its 'AM' monogram featured by the swell of her left breast.

Bob Skinner stared down at his daughter, in his best friend's hallway, in his best friend's robe. His eyes were wide with astonishment. His mouth began to form words, but no sound came out. He shook his head, as if to clear it.

Alex frowned suddenly as she noticed the lump on his forehead, and the cut, with its two stitches.

'Oh pops. Your head! Andy told me, but...'

The sudden narrowing of his eyes cut her off short. 'Never mind my head.' His voice, recovered, was hard and grim. 'Is this what it seems?'

'What do you mean?'

'Don't give me that!' he snapped, with a coldness that shocked her. 'You know bloody well what I mean! How long has this been going on? You and Andy. Shacking up!' He slammed the flat of his right hand against the blue-painted front door, sending it flying back on its hinges.

For the merest instant alarm showed in her face, and then it was gone as she flared back at him. 'Just what has that got to do with you? What the hell happened to belief in me and trust in my judgement . . . or in Andy's for that matter?'

'Trust in your judgement! Don't make me laugh. I did that once before. Remember him? And as for Andy, he's a walking disaster when it comes to relationships. I have a fair idea of the number of women that have stood in that doorway – and probably worn that dressing-gown too – and none of them stayed around longer than a couple of months.

'Is that what you want to be? Another notch on the headboard?'

The girl's eyes flared and her jaw thrust out aggressively – in a way, although neither realised it, which mirrored his own. 'God damn you, Pops!' she spat. 'You think I'm some sort of bimbo? Some easy lay? Maybe you've got your notches the wrong way round. Maybe Andy was my pushover.

'You're insulting me as a person if you suggest that I'm a victim here. I chose Andy just as much as he chose me. We . . .' She stopped short.

'Fuck it, I am twenty-one years old. I will NOT explain myself to you!' She stepped back and slammed the door in his face.

Hot rage erupted and engulfed him. He pounded the blue paintwork with his fist. 'Open up, girl!'

Her shout was muffled by the door. 'Don't "girl" me! I'll talk to you when you're ready to listen. Now piss off to your new family. You've just blown this one.'

He raised his fist to pound the door again, but a firm hand caught his elbow. 'Bob, easy!' said a soft voice behind him. He shook his arm free and spun round, ignoring the pain in his damaged right foot. Andy Martin stood there on the landing, unshaven, in jeans and teeshirt. He held a newspaper and a white paper bag in his left hand.

Skinner seized him by the shirt front and slammed him back against the half-tiled wall. Martin let himself ride backwards on the force of his shove, only tensing his powerful shoulder muscles to protect the back of his head. The vivid green eyes looked back at Skinner, calm and unblinking.

'Let me go, Bob, and cool down. We were going to tell you, but the time wasn't . . .'

Skinner's hiss of anger cut him off. 'You treacherous bastard, Andy. You didn't tell me because you couldn't summon up the bottle. *You were ashamed of yourself. She didn't tell me because she knew exactly how I'd feel. I trusted you all these years, treated you like a brother, and all that time you've been . . .' He paused as if to steady himself.*

'*Christ you've known her since she was a wee girl! Did you fancy her then, in her school uniform? Are you that bloody sick?'*

Martin shook his head. 'No, Bob. I'm not. And neither is Alex. And neither are you. But you have had a bang on the head, and you have been up all night. So why don't you cool it and go back to Sarah; get some sleep and do some thinking.'

Skinner snarled. 'Thinking! If I really start . . .'

Martin put the flat of his free hand on his chest. 'Look, man. If you were going to take a pop at me you'd have done it by now. But you're too much of a straight arrow polisman for that. So do what I say. Head off home and rest up. Unless you want to come in and talk this through over breakfast.

'*It's the last chance you'll have for a fortnight, for we're off to Florida in about three hours. What's it to be?'*

Skinner stood there for a second, staring at him: then he released his grasp and pushed himself backwards, away from Martin, but without blinking or breaking eye contact. 'Breakfast, Andy? You can stick your bacon rolls up your arse, boy.

'*No, I'll head off and do my thinking. And while you two are off in your holiday paradise, you can do some too, about your career path. For that's what I'll be mulling over.*

'*You've betrayed my trust, Detective Superintendent. And if you think you can do that and stay on my team, then . . . No, no one could be that naive!'*

Two

Detective Superintendent Alison Higgins looked around the impressive area. 'As plush as any five-star hotel,' she murmured to herself. The hexagonal foyer of the Witches' Hill Golf and Country Club was carpeted throughout in a dark brown wilton, matched by the light flock pattern of the wallpaper. Portraits hung on two of the walls. One depicted a middle-aged man in Highland dress, sitting ramrod straight in a high-backed red leather chair. The face was strong, with a piercing gaze above a prominent, sharp nose, and iron-grey hair which seemed to rise from the temples like wings on a Viking helmet. The other showed an altogether more conventional figure, standing beside a desk. He was dark-haired, and wore a double-breasted business suit. Higgins had difficulty in coming to terms with the fact that this assured, smiling figure was the man she had just seen, waxy-hued and grotesque, in the Jacuzzi tub, newly emptied on Sarah's instruction.

A tartan-blazered receptionist was seated behind a mahogany counter, near the smoked-glass entrance. The young man wore a slightly stunned expression. Every so often he would glance fearfully across at the three police officers, his eyes lingering on Alison Higgins, blonde and trim in her dark jacket and skirt, with authority in her bearing.

She was one of the highest-ranking woman police officers in Scotland, in day-to-day charge of criminal investigation in a sector which took in East Edinburgh, and a rural area which stretched through East Lothian and down to the border at Berwick.

She looked up at the two men. 'Sailing's my sport, lads, not golf, so humour me by explaining exactly what this place is, and what the rich man in the bathtub had to do with it?'

Martin glanced at his watch. 'No point in asking Neil. He wouldn't know a golf club from a walking stick. Briefly, you are standing in the clubhouse of the newest, swankiest golf course in Scotland; no, scratch that, in Europe. Witches' Hill is a championship-standard eighteen-hole course, built to attract the highest of the high rollers. Golf is an international game now, with huge money involved – dollars, yen, Deutschmarks, you name it – and Scotland is still recognised universally as its ancestral home.

'The land on which the course is built belongs, like much of the rest of this area, to the Marquis of Kinture. That's him on the wall over there.' He nodded towards the portrait of the man in the chair. 'By the way, the reason he's sitting is because he's wheelchair-bound. A few years back he landed a light aircraft rather harder than he had intended, and broke his back. Before his accident the Marquis was a scratch golfer – that means he was very good, Alison. Since then he's been involved in golf administration, as a member of the R. and A. Committee.'

'Eh?' said Alison Higgins.

'The Royal and Ancient Golf Club of St Andrews, the ruling body of world golf.'

He paused, glancing at his watch again. 'Anyway, in his

wheelchair the Marquis began to take a closer interest in his estates than before. One of the first things he found was that, in common with many other landed interests, his liquidity wasn't what it used to be. To succeed in farming today it takes foresight, good crop selection, and substantial investment, plus a good slice of luck.

'So he looked at all of his assets and tried to figure out how to make them work harder for him. Eventually, he focused on the triangle of land where we are now. It's never been much use for agriculture apparently. It's all bumps, hollows and ponds. But looking at it on the map one day, inspiration hit him. The biggest of the bumps has a name – Witches' Hill – and one of the ponds has too. It's called the Truth Loch.

'The Marquis knew that in medieval times East Lothian was a notorious centre for witchcraft and the black arts. Not only that but Witches' Hill was right at its heart. In the sixteenth century, it was said that the biggest of the covens met there, a gathering of crones from all around – from Longniddry, North Berwick, Dirleton, all around here – and that they held their ceremonies on its top, casting spells, calling down curses, and sacrificing livestock to the Devil.'

He paused. Higgins and McIlhenney were staring keenly at him. Even the young man behind the reception desk was listening. He grinned.

'The tales were all just rumour and folklore, and no one took them too seriously, until something happened near the village of Longniddry. I can't remember what it was, but suddenly every sudden death, every epileptic fit, every deformed baby was blamed on witches, until the whole county was up in arms. No one knew for sure who these people were, but as usual, there were plenty of fingers to point.

'Eventually the craze found its victims. A woman called Agnes Tod was accused and, so it was said, put to the torture. Names were named; two other local women, her friends. Agnes's confession was enough. The Earl of Kinture, the present Marquis's ancestor, pronounced the three women guilty. They were rounded up ... and can you guess what happened?'

Martin chuckled at his colleagues' rapt expressions. 'Better than bloody *Jackanory*, this bit, isn't it!

'OK, time's up. The good Christian folk took the three of them off to Witches' Hill. They tied each one to a tree on the top, doused them with grease, and piled kindling around them. Then they were all strangled, and the pyres set alight. It was said that the whole county turned out for the burning of Witches' Hill.'

McIlhenney snorted. 'Ah'll bet it did! What about the other place, the Truth Loch?'

'I was coming to that. After Witches' Hill, persecution really took hold. A ducking stool was set up at the Truth Loch. If some old body was accused, they'd bring her along to the loch and tie her into a chair on the end of a long shaft. Then it was lowered into the water, and the suspect was immersed, completely. After a while, they brought her up. If she had drowned, she was innocent. But if she was still alive ... '

'Let me guess,' said Alison Higgins. 'They dried her off and burnt her!'

'Got it in one, Ali. That's why you're an ace detective, and I'm just a humble uniform!'

'So that's what the Marquis had on his estate.'

'Yup, and with that knowledge came a great idea. He decided to take his useless, lumpy land and to turn it into a brand-new, high-class golf course, with the very best of facilities, with Witches' Hill and the Truth Loch as its highlights. It would cash in on Scotland's position as the home of golf by targeting wealthy players from all around the world.'

Higgins raised an eyebrow. 'But that's what Gleneagles does. Isn't it a bit of a risk?'

'Yes, but the Marquis reckons he's got an edge, even over them. His stately pile's just up the road. Bracklands, it's called, and as part of the top package on offer to visitors, they're put up there. Four-posters, servants, deer and pheasants in the grounds, the whole works. The business plan must have been solid enough, for Michael White put up most of the development capital, and one of the top-dog course architects came in as the third man in the consortium.'

'How are the bookings going so far?'

Martin glanced at his watch for a third time. 'I don't know. The next couple of weeks will tell.'

'Did you notice the stands behind the clubhouse as you came in, and that big tented area away over on the right?'

Superintendent Higgins nodded.

'Well, you being a non-golfer – which, incidentally, in East Lothian is another word for "atheist" – you won't have heard of the invitation tournament that begins here on Thursday. It marks the opening of the course. The Murano Million, it's called . . . backed by the Japanese car company, hence the name. The world's top eight golfers, playing four rounds' medal play for a prize of one million pounds sterling. They go round in a pro-am format, each pro with three invited guests.

'That's what the stands are for, and the tented exhibition village. The consortium's gamble is that the event will get so much cover worldwide as a result that it'll get Witches' Hill off to a flying start. I doubt if this morning's event will be a help to them, though. A murder inquiry in the middle of a million-pound golf festival.'

He put a hand on Higgins's shoulder. 'So that's the background to your investigation, Ali. I don't envy you. Now I must go. I'm responsible for policing the event, and I've got a meeting with the PGA Secretary in about thirty seconds.'

'Thanks a lot, Andy!' She grinned at him. 'But you don't really think this is going to be my investigation, do you? It's right on the ACC's doorstep. Do you think he'll just let me get on with it?'

'Did you call him?'

'D'you mean you *didn't*? Christ, I knew you two'd had a bust-up, but I didn't think it was that serious.'

Suddenly Martin glared at her, uncharacteristically, and she was startled. 'ACC Ops is my line commander, not Bob Skinner. And if he's out of touch, then I call the Chief. That's what I did this afternoon.'

'Don't tell me Sir James is coming down too!'

He shook his head. 'No. He's doing something useful instead. In fact he's got the worst job of all. He's going to see Michael White's wife. She and Lady Proud are good friends.

'So you've called ACC Skinner?'

'Don't be daft, Andy. Of course I did. He's coming down as soon as he can.'

Martin shrugged his shoulders. 'Good luck to him. I'm off to my meeting. See you later. Let me know if you need any back-up from my people.' With a nod of farewell he turned on his heel and disappeared through a door, marked 'Changing Rooms and Course', at the rear of the foyer.

Alison Higgins glanced up at her sergeant. 'What's the real story, Neil?'

'What d'you mean ma'am?' McIlhenney's gaze was angelic in its innocence.

'Gaucheness doesn't suit you, man. You know what I mean. The bust-up between Andy and Bob Skinner. I know that the official story is that Andy's move out here is a temporary thing that the Chief decided on, to help prepare him for an ACC post. And I've heard the grapevine version that it's disciplinary, because Andy piled up his car on the way to a crime scene and left the Boss exposed.

'I don't believe either of those. Only Bob Skinner moves people into or out of CID, everyone knows that. As for the accident version, he's walloped people for sloppy work or stupidity – remember those two guys from Gayfield – but never for an honest mistake or an accident. And Andy was his protégé, too.

'There's more to it. You were in that car with Andy. What do you know?'

McIlhenney looked at her with complete candour, and with none of the irony of which he was an acknowledged master. 'Superintendent, I know that I never doubt the word of my Chief Constable. And I know that caught in the middle of a battle between Bob Skinner and Andy Martin would be absolutely the last place where I'd want to find myself.

'And if you'll take the advice of a humble flatfoot, that's all you'll want to know too.'

You can wind your neck in right now, Bob, unless you want another battle on your hands! Yes, I knew about Alex and Andy, and no I didn't say anything to you. I didn't because Alex asked me not to, she wanted to tell you all about it herself. Remember that couple who were coming to dinner the other night, before you cancelled it?'

Skinner nodded, thunderclouds still gathered on his furrowed brow.

'They were our mystery dinner guests, and that's when Alex was going to tell you.'

'Then it's just as well we had to cancel, otherwise there'd have been chicken bloody chasseur all over the walls!'

Sarah smiled at him. 'No, I was going to do a nice green salad, just in case.'

For once her humour was lost on him. 'Did Alex ask you what you thought?'

'No, and why should she?'

'Suppose she had asked you, what would you have said?'

'I'd have asked her how serious it was, and if she'd said that it was only a fling, I'd have advised her to put a stop to it.' As she spoke she poured two mugs of coffee from the filter machine, and handed one to her husband.

'When Alex told me they were together I wasn't too surprised. It occurred to me round about the time that Jazz was born that they were getting, not intimate . . . how do I put it . . . comfortable with each other in a way they'd never been before. But I didn't pay too much attention. I had other things on my mind just then, and for a while afterwards!'

Skinner grunted and stared into his mug. 'And I, of course, didn't see a bloody thing. My best mate takes my daughter into his bed, and I, the great detective, I hadn't a clue.'

'Bob, you have got to get this in proportion! If it works for them, you should be happy!'

'And if it doesn't, I should be understanding. When Andy

says "Thanks for the memory," like he always has in the past . . .'

Sarah looked at him sharply.

He held up his hands, splashing coffee on the kitchen floor. 'OK, save that one time. But when it breaks up, when Alex finds out it isn't all sunshine, who picks up the pieces for her?'

'But why should it break up? They've known each other for long enough.'

'Don't remind me! No. It'll break up for the same reason Andy's other flings broke up; because sooner or later, usually sooner, he lets his women see where they stand in relation to the job. That's his mistress, and as long as she's around he won't have room for a wife . . . especially one as demanding as my, sorry, our daughter!' He took a sip from his mug, and Sarah, looking into his eyes, saw for the first time the concern behind his anger.

'Look, Bob, I know you think that Alex lights up the ground behind her as she walks, but she's a big girl now. She's got big girl rights, and that includes the right to make her own mistakes . . . which I don't think this is.'

'What about father's rights, Sarah? I'll tell you what they include: the right to be told when something like this happens within the family. That's why I'm steamed up.'

'Did it ever occur to you that Alex might have made Andy promise not to tell you before she could?'

'Doesn't count. I'm old-fashioned that way. Andy was family, almost as much as Alex. When their relationship changed, even when it began to change, he had a duty to speak to me before things went . . .' he paused, '. . . too far. He abused his position.'

'What, falling for Alex is an abuse?'

'No. Forming a relationship with my daughter and passing up on every one of the many opportunities he had to tell me

about it: that is. You're family, you play by its rules. Andy didn't,
so he's put himself outside the wigwam.'

'And Alex?'

'Even now, they'll be packing to catch their holiday flight.
Alex has made her choice.'

Three

'I'm sorry, sir, but the clubhouse is closed.'

'What's your name, Constable?' The man was tall, around two inches over six feet, wide-shouldered, lean and powerful. His steel-grey hair, which matched the colour of his slacks, seemed, in a strange way, to emphasise his vitality. There was a look of authority in his blue eyes which made the young officer gulp involuntarily as he answered.

'PC Pye, sir.'

'Well, mine is Assistant Chief Constable Skinner.'

The young man sagged so suddenly that his smart new uniform almost seemed to lose its creases. Then, a second later, he snapped to attention, red-faced. 'I'm sorry, sir, I didna' recognise you . . .'

'Out of uniform?' said Skinner, reassuring the boy with a quick smile. There was a strange sadness about it. Something about PC Pye reminded him of another young officer from a few years before. 'That's all right, son. I didn't recognise you either. How long have you been with us?'

'Since May, sir. I'm stationed at Haddington. I really am sorry, sir.'

'Don't be. The way I'm dressed, I look more golfer than polis . . . and I'm sure there are those who'll say that's always the case. You've reminded me to wear this.' He took his photographic warrant card from his pocket and clipped it to the open pocket of his shirt, above the Gullane Golf Club crest.

He nodded towards the impressive cream-clad clubhouse building. There were no windows on either side of the wide entrance. Instead the doors were flanked to the left by a huge brass coat of arms, and to the right by the legend, 'Witches' Hill Golf and Country Club', spelled out in tall letters. 'Superintendent Martin inside?'

'No sir, Mr Martin came out a few minutes ago, with another gentleman. They went off down there.' PC Pye pointed vaguely to his right.

'Probably walking the course,' said Skinner.

'Sergeant McIlhenney's inside though, sir, and a lady superintendent.'

'Thanks, Constable. You haven't seen a gentleman in a wheelchair, have you?'

'The Marquis, sir? Yes, sir. He arrived just after Mr Martin left. He told me to say that anyone who wanted him would find him watering his Iron Horse. Those were his exact words, sir,' PC Pye added.

'How did he look?'

'He seemed really upset, sir. A lady brought him, in a Range Rover with a tail-lift thing, and as she was lowering it down he kept swearing at her.'

Skinner grunted. 'Sounds about right.' He was aware that the Marquis of Kinture had accepted his paraplegic condition with an ill grace.

'How about the press officer, Alan Royston? Is he here yet?'

'Not as far as I know, sir.'

'Damnit. The Edinburgh press are a bit sleepy on a Sunday, but they'll show up sooner rather than later, and *en masse* too, for this one. When they do, tell them that I'm here, and marshal them in that area of the car park to the left. I'll send another officer out to join you as soon as I can. Once the hacks realise what's happened here, it'll be Bedlam.

'Right, son, keep up the good work.' The young constable snapped a smart salute as the ACC stepped through the automatic doors.

Skinner glanced around the foyer. It was empty, but for two middle-aged uniformed officers, sergeant and constable, who stood, chatting and looking bored. They came to attention as he entered. 'Afternoon, sir,' said the sergeant.

He nodded a brief acknowledgement. 'What are you two doing? Crowd control? You should know better, Sergeant Boyd. That lad shouldn't be on his own out there, however keen and smart he is. Get outside and keep him company. And you, Constable Roe, you take yourself off to the end of the driveway, and stop every car turning in off the road. Tell the press as they turn up to report to Sergeant Boyd.

'Sarge, until Royston or someone from his office arrives to take charge of them, you make sure that any camera people that arrive are kept together in the car park. I don't want them running all over the place taking snaps of the Marquis, or any of the players that are here. Now, where is everyone?'

'Miss Higgins and Neil McIlhenney are through in the changing area, sir,' said Sergeant Boyd. 'The Marquis, two of his guests and some players are together in the big bar. The caddies, green-keepers and the men working on the stands are all in the caddy shed. There's a uniformed officer with each group.

27

'My gaffer's gone out to walk the course with the man from the PGA. He left me in charge.'

'Is that so? Well next time he leaves you in charge of anything, don't let him down. Make sure you're out front where you can be effective, not hidden in a quiet corner talking about yesterday's football. Get on with it, both of you.'

He jerked a thumb towards the main entrance and strode off towards the changing area.

The dressing room door was open. Alison Higgins was seated on a bench, and stood up as he entered. McIlhenney, his back to the door, identified the newcomer from the Superintendent's expression, and turned with a smile.

'Jesus Christ,' barked Skinner. 'Is everyone here just standing around?'

Higgins was flustered, momentarily. 'I didn't want to begin till you got here, sir. The Marquis looks like the type who needs careful handling, and some of the others gathered in the bar seem pretty high-powered too.'

He looked back at her. 'When will you get it through your head, lady, that you're high-powered too? You're a Superintendent of Police, and in the new structure that's one grade below me.

'That said, all I can see here are chiefs and warrant officers. Where are the CID foot-soldiers?'

'On their way, boss,' said McIlhenney. 'Mario's on his way out, and Alan Royston's bringing three Detective Constables with him. We'll have a right few statements to take.'

'Has anyone been told what's happened?'

'Williamson, the steward, found the body. He ran into the manager's office, blurted it out, then collapsed in a faint. Mr Bryan, the manager, used to be one of us. He verified

28

Williamson's story, then he phoned us. But other than that, he's kept the detail to himself.

'He told the people waiting in the bar that Mr White had been taken ill. When we got here, Mr Martin told them that he had died, but that's all they know.'

'How about the Marquis?'

'Mr Martin told him the same when he called him.'

'We'd better not keep them waiting much longer then.'

He glanced at the door of the Jacuzzi cubicle. 'I saw an ambulance outside. That means the body's still here?'

Higgins nodded. 'Yes sir. We thought you'd want to see it.'

Skinner shook his head. 'Thanks, but no thanks. I've seen enough stiffs to last me a lifetime, and I knew this one. Sarah described the scene, and I'll see the pictures. So if the photographer and the scientists are finished, you can take him off to the morgue.'

He looked across at McIlhenney. 'See to it, Neil, will you. Then tell everyone in the bar that we're nearly ready to speak to them. We'll need at least two separate rooms for interviews, so set that up with the club manager. Once that's done, let us know. We'll be outside.' He paused, then an afterthought struck him. 'Oh yes, ask Sergeant Boyd to contact Mr Martin on the radio and tell him that I want to see the PGA man when he's finished with him.'

'Sir.' The bulky Sergeant moved towards the door.

Skinner motioned to Higgins, and followed him out of the room, but instead of returning to the foyer, he turned to the left and followed the corridor until he came to another door, he opened it and stepped out into the open air.

The afternoon was sunny and warm, but the Witches' Hill golf course was still scented by the last mowing of its greens and fairways, dampened by overnight rain. They were facing the wide first tee, and beyond it, a beautifully manicured green, which sloped away to the right.

From the rough on the far side of the first fairway, a conical hill rose sharply. Its flanks were wooded but the summit was clear, giving it a strange, tonsured look. Skinner pointed towards it. 'That's it, Ali,' he said. 'Witches' Hill; it gave the Marquis his idea and the course its name. The local legend has it that the witches were burned at the bit on the top, and that nothing's grown there since. If you go up there, on top you'll find the vestiges of some tree-stumps and bugger-all else.'

'Had you heard of it before it was made into a golf course, sir?'

Skinner nodded, a soft smile flicking the corners of his mouth. 'Yes, years ago. Myra, my first wife, was a teacher. When we moved here she researched the local history for her class work, and she came upon the story of Aggie Tod, Witches' Hill and the Truth Loch.

'I'd forgotten all about it until the Marquis announced his project.' He looked down at Higgins. 'It's not an everyday topic out here, you see. The tourist people are happy to sell this county on the back of its golf, beaches and sailing, but they keep quiet about the bloodshed and persecution for which it was famous before that.

'On the whole the locals take a dim view of the Marquis's venture. And the golfers tend to look down their noses at his course. It's parkland, y'see, not links, so they look on it as a bit of an Ugly Duckling. But I've played it, and I can tell them, it's a swan all right; I found it a really good course, very mature and ready for play.'

The Superintendent looked up in surprise. 'I thought it wasn't open yet?'

'It isn't, officially, but the Murano people have played here, and Michael White took a few of us out one Sunday last month.'

'So you knew White, sir.'

'Sure. Not that well, not as well as the Chief, but we knocked into each other every so often. He was a member of the New Club, and a real man about town.'

'How did you find him? What sort of a man was he?'

Skinner smiled. 'Are you interviewing me, Superintendent?' Higgins flushed.

'That's OK. You should be. I knew the man, I have insight. Michael White was a very successful man. He made his money in the retail trade, with a chain of mid-price, good quality clothing stores, for C1, C2, customers and he got it exactly right. Sold out around ten years ago, in his early forties, for a right few million quid. He invested successfully in sure-thing property developments until the slump started, but he's done nothing much since then . . . other than play golf.

'When the Marquis came up with his project, he didn't have the cash to fund it himself, so he gave Michael first refusal. Golf was his great passion, so, probably for the only time in his life, he took a business decision on emotional grounds and said "yes".

'As a man, Michael White was friendly, generous, ethical, honest, in love with his wife, and well-respected; and no, I cannot think of a single reason why anyone would want to lie in wait for him and cut his throat. Any other questions, officer?'

Higgins hesitated. 'Couldn't theft have been the motive, sir?'

'Sarah says that's unlikely, the way it was done, and I'm with her. The watch and wallet were nicked as a red herring. Christ, his golf clubs were worth more, and they'd have been a hell of a lot easier to steal!'

He shook his head. 'No, Alison. Michael White was assassinated, executed, killed out of malice; choose your description, but it was premeditated murder.'

He slapped his hands together. 'Now, do we know who we've got in the bar?'

'Yes sir, Mr Bryan, the manager, gave me a list.' She produced two pieces of A4 paper from the right-hand pocket of her jacket, unfolded them, and scanned them quickly. She held one up for Skinner's inspection.

'Six of them, including the Marquis. According to this the other five are all his guests.' She read quickly from the list.

'Bill Masur, Chief Executive Officer, Greenfields Management, Mike Morton, President, Sports Stars Corporation, Andres Cortes, Tiger . . . that's what it says here . . . Nakamura, Paul Wyman, and the Marquis himself. Mr Highfield from the PGA is here too, but Andy Martin took him off to discuss policing for the tournament.'

'He's assuming it's still on,' Skinner muttered. Alison Higgins looked at him in sudden surprise. 'Well . . .' he said and shrugged his shoulders. 'We may have to consider that. But let's cross that bridge later.

'That's quite a list. SSC is the biggest sports and entertainment management company in the world. It's American based, but it goes everywhere. Until fairly recently it had no challengers, but Greenfields has been making big strides in the last few years. Masur's an Aussie, and typically aggressive, by reputation.

'The other three are all golfers. Cortes is Spanish. He's the leading money-winner in Europe, just as Tiger Nakamura is on the Far East circuit. Paul Wyman's a Yank. He's been their top money-winner for the last two years. They'll all be playing this week.

'Did Bryan give you a list of staff present?' Higgins nodded, and waved her second piece of paper.

'Yes, sir. Three of them in the clubhouse. Joe Bryan himself, Tommy Williamson, the steward, and Laurence Bennett, bookings and reception. There's a fourth member of the permanent staff, Iris McKenna. Mr Bryan described her as his assistant. She does the book-keeping. She's off today.

'The other full-time staff here are Jimmy Robertson, the club professional, Archie McCubbin, the caddy-master, and three greenkeepers, all named Webb. Brothers, presumably.'

Skinner grinned. 'Not necessarily, half the greenkeepers around here are Webbs. I take it that they're all over in the caddy-shed, with the scaffolders and the caddies.'

Higgins nodded.

'In that case,' he said, 'let's hope there's no booze over there, or we'll have to wait a while to get sense out of some of them.'

'Sir!' McIlhenney's voice sounded from behind them. 'Everyone's here now, including this one.' Skinner and Higgins turned. The Sergeant was standing just outside the doorway. Beside him was another man, as powerfully built as McIlhenney, but narrower in the waist. His black hair and fine features lent him a slightly Latin appearance, which was accentuated by his pearly smile.

'That's it,' said Skinner. 'I know we've got trouble now. McGuire's here.'

Detective Sergeant Mario McGuire's grin widened still

more. 'I can't speak for you, sir, but I know Miss Higgins and I are in the shit all right. DI Rose and I had an appointment with my parish priest this afternoon. Now she's having to go on her own. You can imagine how pleased she is.'

Skinner laughed. Detective Inspector Maggie Rose, McGuire's fiancée, was his personal assistant. She was a redhead, with a temper to match. Their wedding was thirteen days away.

'Don't worry,' he said. 'I'll write you a note. Good to see you anyway, Mario. Neil's briefed you, I take it.'

McGuire nodded. 'Yes, sir.'

'Right, let's get to work. You three take one of the DCs each, to take notes and write up witness statements. I want individual interviews to establish the exact location of everyone here at the time Michael White went into his dressing room. Most of all I want to know whether anyone else was seen going in there. At this stage, I don't want any mention of murder. All that you say is that Michael White has been found dead. The natural assumptions are heart attack or suicide. Let's see whether anyone assumes otherwise.

'Mario and Neil, you two get across to the caddy-shed and interview everyone there. Alison, you and I will give the common folk in the bar the kid glove treatment . . . I'll start with the Marquis.

'Right, let's get this investigation on course.'

'All I'm saying, Alex, is that maybe Bob has a point.'

'What! About us, you mean?'

'No . . . well, yes . . . well, no, not in that way. He can't expect to pick your partner for you, but he's got a right to disapprove, if that's the way he feels. I'd hoped that he would be

happy about you and me, and I'm disappointed by the way he acted, but you know how he thinks somet . . .'

'Just hold on a minute. If we're talking about rights, I've got a right to expect his support, come what may. Yes, and I've had it in the past, even when he guessed I was way in the wrong. Yet now, when any reasonable person should see this as something that we've both taken a long time to come to, and should be happy for us, he throws a hundred-megaton wobbly.*

'And you can stand there and take his side! He's supposed to be your friend. D'you know what he said about you?'

'Yes, I was coming up the stairs then. It hurt but it's the truth, and you know it. Since I've been on the force I've had upwards of a dozen girlfriends, none of them long-term. He's seen that. Christ, he used to get their names mixed up! Isn't he entitled to be worried about that, as your father?'

'No, he bloody well isn't!' She hissed the words. 'I suppose he was right about this dressing-gown too.'

'I suppose he was!' he barked back. 'But what the hell's that got to do with it?' It was as close as she had ever seen him come to losing his temper.

She glared at him, then, slowly and deliberately, untied the sash, peeled off the blue robe and threw it at him, across the bedroom. He caught it in mid-air, and there was a sudden, pleading look in his eyes. 'Look, honey, I'm sorry. I just reckon he's got a point about being kept in the dark, that's all.'

She stood naked before him, and he could see the tension gripping her body. 'Rubbish!' Her stomach muscles bunched as she shouted at him. 'How many times did we try to get to see him? God knows! But he never could make the time for us, tearing around everywhere chasing all those bad people!'

He shook his head. 'But I had a dozen chances to tell him, and I passed them all up.'

'Yes, because you knew it was important to me that we told him together. Because I made you promise.'

'OK, and you were wrong . . . and I was wrong to agree. It was something between Bob and me, before Bob and us. Now he thinks that I've betrayed him, and if you don't know how he'll feel about that you don't know your father.'

'Oh no? Well I don't think I've known you either, until now. Tell you what I think, Andy. I think you're more worried about your bloody job than about me. You're wondering, "How can I square it away with Big Bob and save my career?" Well, Superintendent, I'll make your choice simple.' She knelt down beside a big, soft hold-all, which stood, unzipped, on the floor. Delving into it, she found a pair of white cotton panties.

'What're you doing?' he asked, as she pulled them on and reached for her black denim jeans draped across the bedroom chair.

'Can't you even figure that out? I'm off!'

'Aw, come on, Alex. Get a grip of those knickers, and calm down! We're off on holiday in an hour or two.'

'Like hell we are! You can go, and take my ticket. You've got from here to Glasgow Airport to find someone else to use it. That shouldn't be too difficult for you, given your track record.' She pointed to the blue bathrobe, which he held still, loosely, in his hand. 'You'd better take Old Faithful too. It could come in handy.'

'Alex!'

She fastened her jeans, and drew a sweatshirt over her head, shaking her damp hair as she adjusted the garment to her body.

'Look, Andy, it's simple. You're either on my side of the street,

or you're not. You had a choice a few minutes ago, and you stood right in the middle of the road. Well, guess what? You just got run over!' Tugging on a pair of low-heeled fawn suede shoes, she picked up the hold-all, slung it over her shoulder, and took her small black handbag from the dressing table.

She was in the doorway when he called after her. *'Know what? You're just like him. There are no shades of grey in the Skinners' world, only black and white. Ayes or Nos.'*

She turned back to face him. *'Leave my values out of this. This is about you, Andy, and yours. They're all "maybes". He insulted me, he insulted you, and you took it. Then he threatened your career, and it's "Oh maybe he's got a point."*

'You know what? I reckon you'd shoot me if the boss told you to!'

The silence which fell on the room was palpable. His tanned face, suddenly bloodless, looked yellow. He gasped, and for a second she thought he would spring at her. But then his green eyes moistened, and swam. She turned away from the hurt she had caused, and left the room.

A few seconds later he heard the front door close, quietly.

Four

'About bloody time too. Skinner, isn't it?'

'That's right, My Lord; Assistant Chief Constable, Edinburgh.'

He walked down the room, past the polished board table, towards the man in the powered wheelchair, his hand extended. The Marquis of Kinture reached up and shook it, with the affected ill grace which Skinner knew was his frequent manner. They had met on several occasions, and on each one the crippled nobleman had greeted the policeman in exactly the same way.

The wheelchair, and its occupant, sat in the bay window of the Witches' Hill boardroom, which faced out over the wide eighteenth green looking down the fairway and across the Truth Loch. 'Had enough of those Johnnies in the bar. Nothing but business talk, even from the golfers. Decided to withdraw in here.

''S all right, isn't it?'

'Of course, sir. I wanted to speak to you in private anyway.'

The Marquis shook his head. 'Poor old Mickey gone to meet his Maker and all those buggers can talk about are rights and bloody royalties. No sensibilities, these people, none at all.' He looked up at Skinner, with a faint, surprising grin.

'He finished with a par, so Cortes told me. Safe drive to the middle landing area, good three wood to the green, two putts. Spaniard put his tee shot in the water.' The Marquis chuckled. 'Teach the bugger! Damn good hole that. The pros'll think they can carry the corner of the loch, but they'll find that it's nearly always into the wind . . . even, sometimes, when you wouldn't think there was a wind blowing!'

Skinner nodded. 'You're right. And not only the pros. Your loch owes me a Top Flite.'

'You've played the course?'

'Indeed. Michael invited me a few weeks back. The poor bloke had a par up the last then too.'

'So you knew Mickey. Real shocker, this, eh. Seemed so fit, too. Talk about life's bloody ironies. Here's me stuck here in this damnable thing, and there was he playing three or four rounds a week. Yet which one of us is floating in the bloody Jacuzzi?

'What'd they reckon it was? Heart attack? Stroke? Bryan just said he'd been found dead in the tub.'

Skinner sat down in a red leather chair and looked across at the Marquis. 'None of those, sir, I'm afraid. I've got some even worse news for you. Michael bled to death. His throat was cut.'

The Marquis shook his head violently. He swung his chair, first left, then right, then turned to face Skinner. 'You mean he committed . . .'

'No, sir. Not that. I'm sorry, but he was murdered.'

'Oh by Christ, how awful! Murdered! Right here in the club. Who the hell would . . .' He glared across at Skinner. 'Well, who the hell *would*? Do you have a suspect?'

'It's early days yet, sir. My officers are just beginning interviews with everyone who was here when Michael was killed. Once they're complete we'll see if anything leaps out at us. Just for the record, sir, when was the last time you saw him?'

The Marquis raised an eyebrow. 'This morning. We had some stuff to go over, to do with the tournament. He came out to Bracklands early; ate breakfast with Sue and me.'

'I take it that Sue is Lady Kinture?'

''S right.'

'How did he seem?'

'Full of beans. He was very excited about playing with Cortes. Went on about it just a little too much, in fact. Most difficult thing about all this for me is having to watch all these damn fellas playing my course. I helped design it, you know. Gave O'Malley the architect some ideas. Insisted that he use all the existing features, but create nothing new, except bunkers. My baby, but I'll never hit a shot on her.'

Skinner looked at him, touched by the sadness which had broken through the crusty exterior. 'There's no movement in your legs at all, then?'

'Not a bloody twitch. Been everywhere, tried everything. When something like this happens, they're never quite sure how it'll work out. Sometimes a little movement can come back after a couple of years. Not with me, though. On my arse for the rest of my life.'

'So Michael was a bit insensitive. Did you quarrel over it?'

This time both noble eyebrows shot upwards. 'God no! Chap didn't mean anything by it. Frankly, even if he had, I couldn't afford to fall out with him. Needed his dough in the venture. I'd be in the shit if he pulled out. Have to go into business with the banks, God forbid. So no, officer, we did not have words. Mind you, I was grumpy all morning. Took it out on poor Sue, I'm afraid.'

'You needed White's money, you say. Mind if I ask how the venture is structured.'

'No point in my minding. It's a matter of record. We're incorporated as Witchhill plc. The company has three shareholders; the Kinture Family Trust has forty-five per cent, White Holdings has another forty-five and Ryan O'Malley, the course architect, was given the balance as part of his fee, with the proviso that if he ever wants to sell he has to offer Michael and me five per cent each.'

'No one else with any form of interest?'

'Nobody. Had plenty of approaches from people wanting in on the action. Everybody and his brother – in one case quite literally – were keen to have a part of what's going to be the finest golf development on the planet. Mickey and I turned them all down. We were pretty certain that we didn't need anyone's cash or reputation to make Witches' Hill a success.'

The policeman nodded. 'What's the effect of the death of a shareholder?'

The Marquis smiled. 'Good question, Skinner. In the event of my death or that of O'Malley, there's no effect. But as far as Michael is – or was – concerned, the company has a term policy on his life which will put it in funds to buy out his share. So, as Mr Morton is fond of putting it, how do you like them apples, Assistant Chief Constable?'

It was Skinner's turn to smile. 'They look very tasty, sir, for you and Mr O'Malley. Your respective holdings should double, virtually, as a result of Michael's death. Gives you each a prime motive.'

The Marquis glanced down at his captive legs. 'Don't think I'm up to cashing in on it,' he grunted.

'Ah, but you must know, sir,' said Skinner, leaning back in his chair, fixing the Marquis with his easy grin. 'You don't have to do the killing to do the crime. I investigated a case a few months ago in which a man was responsible for a murder even though it was committed after he was dead.

'But on balance I think you're a bit too obvious a suspect actually to *be* a suspect . . . even if we ignore the fact that whoever killed White didn't do it from a wheelchair.' He paused. 'Still, we must cover all the angles. Where's Mr O'Malley right now, d'you know?'

'I rather do. Nowhere around here, I'm glad to say. Fella's in the pokey in Australia.'

'In jail!'

''Fraid so. Wild bugger, O'Malley. Got into a fight in a bar in Sydney two weeks ago and broke a fella's jaw. Wasn't the first time, so the judge gave him sixty days to cool off. So that's your Theory Number Two down the Swanney.'

Skinner pushed himself from the chair and looked out of the window, across green, fairway and loch. 'And there were no problems between Michael and O'Malley as far as you know?'

'None at all. Nor, I say again, between Michael and me. Been friends for years, since long before this business.'

'Right, but do you know of anyone who might have had a down on him?'

The Marquis looked blankly at Skinner for a few seconds, then shook his head. 'None at all. If you knew him you'll know that he wasn't the sort of bloke to go around collecting enemies.'

Skinner nodded. 'That's what makes this so odd. The man was impeccable. Christ, the New Club'll be in turmoil. A murder victim among the membership!'

The Marquis grunted in agreement, so loudly that Skinner hardly heard the knock on the door. It opened, slowly. A woman's head appeared, blonde and tanned. The Marquis looked round. 'Susan.'

'I'm sorry, are you still busy?'

The Marquis looked up at the policeman, inviting him to answer. He shook his head. 'No, Lady Kinture, we're done.' The heavy oak door swung open wide, and she stepped into the room; suddenly it seemed smaller. Susan Kinture was tall indeed, at least six feet, with a handsome oval face, crested by a mass of perfectly arranged blonde hair. Skinner guessed her to be in her early forties, perhaps a year or two younger than him. The slimness of her build, allied to her height, made it easy to accept that before her marriage she had been one of Europe's top models, and she carried herself with a confidence which made her even more striking. She was dressed casually, but in style, in a beautifully cut golden trouser suit. Probably silk, the policeman thought to himself.

She stared at him as recognition dawned. 'You're Bob Skinner, aren't you? Yes, of course you are. You have that brilliant American wife. I met her a few months ago at an event for disabled charities. Hector and I have done our bit for them since the accident. We feel we have to give a lead.'

She paused, and her right hand went to her chin in a gesture of habit. 'I seem to remember she was pregnant. Has she...'

Skinner smiled. 'Yes, last May. We have a wee boy called Jazz. Getting bigger by the day . . . and louder. That's his American half, of course.'

Lady Kinture smiled. 'Give her my best, then. Sarah, wasn't it?'

'That's right.'

'This is terrible news about our friend Michael. I can hardly believe it. He had breakfast with us. What happened?'

Skinner hesitated. 'I'll let Lord Kinture explain, I think.'

She frowned at him, questioning. She might have pressed him, but they were interrupted by a loud knock on the window. Skinner looked down and saw the Marquis close to the glass, beckoning and nodding to someone outside. 'It's the PGA chap,' he said. 'I want a word with him.'

'Yes,' said Skinner. 'So do I, but if you don't mind I'd like to speak to him first.'

The Marquis frowned. 'Well, I suppose. Tell you what, when you're finished send him up to the house. Susan, let's go home, and I'll tell you all about poor Mickey.' He pushed a lever on the arm of the wheelchair. It hummed into life and swished its passenger towards the open doorway, with Lady Kinture following, like a golden outrider.

'Superintendent, if you think I'm going to let a family squabble deprive me of one of my very best officers, you're kidding yourself. I will NOT approve your request for transfer to another force, AND I will make it clear to my brother Chief Constables that any one of them who takes you on will be on my shit list.'

'I appreciate your confidence, Sir James, but I am really serious. ACC Skinner said I should consider my future career, and that's what I've done.'

'Look Andy, most of us say things in the heat of the moment, then back off from them when the temperature goes down. Bob spoke to me yesterday, after our Tuesday meeting with the Police Board. He told me that he'd surprised Alex at your place last Friday morning, first thing.

'He said that he'd exploded and that there'd been a huge barney on your doorstep.'

'That's a pretty accurate summary of our last meeting.' Martin's voice was heavy with irony. Sir James Proud looked at him, kindly. He had seen the younger man through one or two bad times, but could not recall him ever being so downcast.

'OK, but there's more. He said that when he got home, Sarah had given him a going over, and had made him calm down a bit. He sees now that maybe he did go over the top. I wouldn't say he's completely happy. He really feels you both let him down.

'But all the same, I think that if you went to see him and talked it through . . . Maybe, as a gesture, if you apologised, even.' He angled his great silver head, looking tentatively at Martin. The younger man's green eyes flashed.

Sir James went on quickly. 'What I don't understand is that you and Alex are supposed to be away on holiday. Bob told me you flew to Florida on Friday. So why are you sat here, now?'

Martin smiled for the first time, but without humour. 'That's the nub of it, sir. The ACC doesn't know the damage he's done. You tell me to talk it through with him. I tried to do that last Friday morning, and Alex accused me of taking his side, to protect my career! So I had an even bigger fight with her than the one with Bob, and she packed up and left. I went through to Glasgow after her, but she wasn't there. Eventually I cancelled the flights and told Henry Wills, up at the University, that we wouldn't be using his place after all. I called her number all weekend, but no reply. It wasn't till Monday, when her flatmate came back from a weekend at home that I found out where she'd gone. Remember that band she sang with last year, after the Festival show? Square Peg, they're called.'

'Vaguely. Square Pegs and the like are beyond me.'

'Well, Alex had told me that they're going on a tour of Europe and that they'd asked her if she would be one of their backing singers. She'd turned them down, but she called their manager last Friday morning and asked if the job was still open. It was. She left her flatmate a note telling her that we'd had a bust-up and that she was off, there and then, to join the band for rehearsals in Dublin.'

His jaw tightened. 'So, sir, I don't see me apologising to the ACC. I've spent the last two days thinking about this. He told me that I'd betrayed him. All I can see is that he's broken up the best relationship I've ever had in my life. You know, I was hoping that Alex would come back from Florida with a ring on her finger. Then Bob steps in and we don't even make it to the airport.

'The last thing that he said to me was that I had no future under his command. So I've taken him at his word. I've considered my career path, and I've come to the conclusion that it has to lead me away from him, and right now.'

Sir James pushed himself to his feet and walked over to the window. He looked out across the playing field, seeming to be lost in thought, as a tense silence hung over the room. After almost a minute, he seemed to nod slightly. Then he turned back to face Martin. 'Look son, I'm not going to take anyone's part in this. You are all my friends and I will always be available to every one of you. All I'd say to you is that Bob and Alex have always been closer than any father and daughter I've ever known. Now they've blown up at each other, out of the blue. As for you and Bob, you've been the best of friends for years. This conflict between the three of you . . . it's so sudden and unexpected that none of you knows how to handle it.

'Maybe you never will sort it out. I don't know. But I do know *that if, as I could, I were to phone Jock Govan and get you transferred into Willie Haggerty's job in Glasgow Special Branch – it hasn't been announced yet, but he's been made head of CID – I wouldn't have done any of us any favours.*

'No Andy, this is what I'm going to do ... and this is the Chief Constable speaking now.' He moved back to his chair and sat down again, facing Martin across the coffee table. 'I've got a problem in East Lothian. Charlie Radcliffe told me yesterday that he's going into hospital. He's going to be off for at least four months, and that's only if everything works out OK. That's too long for an area to be without its commander. You're equivalent rank, and a spell in the uniform branch will be good for your career development. The decision is made, Superintendent. You're going to Haddington, on a temporary basis, as area commander. You'll report to ACC Operations, and through him to me. The only time Bob'll be in your chain of command is in my absence, when he deputises.'

'What about my job as Head of the Drugs and Vice Squad, sir?'

'That'll be Bob's problem. Serves him right in a way.

'No more discussion. Your leave's cancelled. Report to Haddington tomorrow. Charlie goes under the knife next Monday, so you won't have much time for a handover!'

Five

'You're not going to tell me to cancel the tournament, are you?'

Arthur Highfield, the Secretary of the Professional Golfers' Association, looked at Skinner apprehensively. They stood in the middle of the practice putting green, set before the wide arc of the conservatory, which opened out from the clubhouse bar, doing double duty as sitting area and viewing gallery.

The big policeman shook his grey mane. 'No, Mr Highfield. No need for me to do that. No point either. I'll want to keep the VIP changing room and the Jacuzzi cubicle sealed off, in case our scientists want a second look at anything, but otherwise you can have the place back.' He paused. 'You don't anticipate any trouble with your sponsors?'

'Murano? They're tied into a pretty tight contract, drafted by Greenfields; even if they wanted to they couldn't break it. I'll tell them right away, of course, but they've got lots of arrangements made. They're putting one of their top eight people in each of the pro-am teams – that's part of the deal – and some of them will have left Japan for Scotland already.'

'How many other VIP guests are you expecting?'

'Another sixteen, apart from the golfers. I've given Superintendent Martin a list. I'll give you a copy too, when we're finished.'

'What about the pros?'

'Well, as you know, Cortes, Wyman and Tiger Nakamura are here already. The other five are playing in this week's tour event in England. They are Deacon Weekes, the US Masters champion, Ewan Urquhart, the Open champion, Sandro Gregory, the Aussie – he just won the US PGA – Oliver M'tebe, the young South African lad, and of course Darren Atkinson, el Numero Uno Mundial. He's the current US Open Champion, of course, so that means that we'll have all four of this year's major winners.'

Skinner laughed quietly. 'With a million on offer, I'm not surprised. It's the biggest golf prize ever, isn't it?'

'That's right. There have been other "million" events, but they've all been in US or Aussie dollars. This is the first in sterling.'

Skinner shook his head. 'I was third in our club medal last month. Won a tenner in the sweep. By the time my wife came to collect me, I'd spent that much in the bar!'

He looked back at the clubhouse. A bulky Japanese man in an outlandishly colourful sweater was looking out of the window. Skinner pointed. 'That's the Tiger, yes?'

'Yes, that's right. Leading money-winner on the Far Eastern Tour. He's never won in America or Europe, but Japanese sponsors always insist on at least one of their countrymen in any invitation field, and of course he's a Mike Morton client.'

'What does that mean?'

Highfield smiled. 'It means that doors open for him. SSC organised this event. The European tour has nothing to do with it. I'm here as the PGA rep, and I've got a say in the running of it, but this is the Mike Morton show. White and

Hector Kinture brought them in two years ago to set the thing up, and, I have to say, they've done their usual awesome job.'

'Hold on a minute,' said Skinner. 'If it's an SSC project, what's Masur doing here? I thought they and Greenfields were deadly enemies.'

'Oh they are, make no mistake. Originally there weren't going to be any Masur men here, but then Deacon Weekes won the US Masters, and Paul Wyman signed with Green-fields in the spring after his contract with SSC expired. Even then Morton wouldn't have had either of them. He was going to introduce two more from his stable.'

'Why'd he change his mind?'

'Michael White had it changed for him. He asked him very politely to book Weekes, and to keep Wyman in the field as the top US money-winner. Morton told him, very impolitely, to get stuffed. So White took a week's holiday in Tokyo and went to see the President of Murano Motors. A two hundred and fifty million yen prize fund buys you a lot of influence. Morton hated it, but he had to back down.'

'So he had a down on White?'

Highfield looked at him in surprise, hesitating. 'Well yes, I have to say that he did. He was reasonably courteous to Mr White's face, but behind his back, "Interfering son-of-a-bitch" is the politest term I've heard him use.'

'You know Morton well?'

'God yes, in my job it's inevitable.'

'What sort of a guy is he?'

Highfield hesitated again. 'Well . . .'

'Look Mr Highfield, this is a murder investigation. I need people to tell me things. But don't worry. I keep them to myself, unless I'm under oath.'

'Well, in that case. Morton is the worst enemy a man could have. Vicious, can be petty, completely ruthless, and of course very powerful. He hates competition and in the past he's fought it off. But Masur's a different kettle of piranhas.'

'In what way?'

'Well for a start, he's as big a shit as Morton. But he's not the only competition. There's Darren's company too. It manages him, and Andres Cortes . . . and young M'tebe.'

Skinner looked at him, taken aback. 'I must start paying closer attention to the golf magazines in the club. I didn't know that Atkinson had moved into management.'

'Oh yes,' said Highfield, 'about a year ago now. It caused quite a stir at the time. He's been self-managed all through his career, and it's done him no harm. Not long ago there was a rumour that he was going in with Greenfields, but he wrong-footed them all and set up his own operation with his brother. He's a very smart guy, is Darren. He thinks long-term. He's in his mid-thirties, so he knows that it can't be too long before he's knocked off the number-one-ranking spot.

'He's a charismatic chap, as well as being a brilliant golfer. He attracts followers like no one I've ever seen, not least because he is what he seems, genuinely likeable. At the moment his overriding aim is to win every pound, dollar or yen that's available to him. But he's very ambitious in other ways, too. He told me that he doesn't want to become another middle-aged legend, touring the Sunshine States and competing with other has-beens for obscene pots of money. The management company is only a first step; he's looking for other golf-related investments. Basically, he wants to become as powerful in Europe as SSC is in the States and Greenfields is in Australasia. He says that he isn't interested in anything beyond that. He simply wants to make sure that there's a strong European management operation available to European players.'

Skinner laughed. 'And get even richer himself in the process.'

Highfield shrugged his shoulders. 'Don't quote me, but rather him than either of those two corporate carnivores in there.'

'I'll watch with interest. Does he have any partners? Cortes, for example?'

'No. Cortes only wants to play. Andres only thinks about his game. It's all that matters. Why, he won a Ferrari in an Italian tournament a few months back, and gave it to his caddy. "I only want to drive golf balls," he said to the press. He likes Darren and he's happy for his people to be running his business. When he signed up, all the Spaniards followed, and most of the young Brits. Quite a few of the older tour guys have signed letters of intent, in advance of their existing contracts expiring.

'Young M'tebe was the real catch, though, after Andres that is. Ever seen him?'

Skinner nodded. 'Yes. I had a day at the Open. He's quite a talent.'

'Wonderful player,' Highfield agreed. 'The next superstar, everybody says . . . and they're right. Once he gets used to Northern Hemisphere conditions, he'll be hard to hold.'

'Atkinson's holding him this week, though. He had a six-shot overnight lead down south, had he not?'

'Oh yes, make no mistake, Darren will stay on top for two or three years yet. He's still a class above the rest. He's due in tomorrow to begin practice. If you're here, I'll introduce you.'

'I'd like that,' said Skinner. 'I'm pretty sure I will be here. I've no idea what our interviews will produce, but even if we make an early arrest there will still be things for my team to do. Normally I try not to become over-involved at crime scenes now, but Michael was an acquaintance, and a very good friend of my Chief, so I'll be giving this one special attention.

'Now I must go. I've told my troops to report to me in the boardroom once the interviews are over. Perhaps you could drop that guest list in there?'

'Bob, just let it lie. We've got a police force to run as best we can, and I don't think that you want it to be deprived of Andy Martin, any more than I do.'

'No, Jimmy, I don't. That doesn't mean that I think Andy's an innocent victim. But I wish I could play that scene over again.'

'And how would you handle it differently?'

'I'd bite my tongue, turn around and walk back down those bloody stairs.'

'Like hell you would, man. Your fuse is too short. As for Alex, she's your double in every respect. You tried to come the heavy father once before, I seem to recall, and she reacted in just the same way.

'Just spare a thought for Andy Martin as the catalyst for an explosion between you two. There he was feeling guilty about saying nothing to you, yet leaned on by Alex to keep his mouth shut. Now his friendship with you is damaged, and Alex has buggered off and left him.'

Skinner leaned his forehead against the cool glass of the Chief Constable's office window. It steamed over as he spoke. 'You're right, of course. Something came to me the other night. I once said that Andy was the one man I'd trust with the lives of my family. When I think about it, that's still true.'

He turned, smiling ironically. 'Best of it is, Jimmy, now that I've had a chance to think about it, they're probably dead right for each other. The boy Andy's relationships have been short-term because he's never found anyone who's interested him more than the job. It was Florida that made me realise it. Florida for a fortnight! I don't remember him ever taking a woman further than Portobello Funfair . . . and even then it was a quick whirl on the Waltzer and back up the road!

'Chief, what you have explained to me in your usual tactful way is dead right. I've been a stupid arse! I'll go and see Andy, and sort it out.'

But the Chief shook his head. 'Careful about that, Bob. You don't realise the effect all this has had on him. He might not be ready to sort anything out yet, and when he is, it might be Alex he wants to see first, not you.

'Transferring him is the right thing to do in the circumstances. And there are good man-management reasons for it too. It's time Andy stepped out of your shadow. He's a young Superintendent, on the fast track, and he needs to broaden his experience. So a spell as an area commander, reporting to Jim Elder, will do him good.'

Six

'If you thought Morton and Masur were high-powered, Alison, wait till you take a look at this lot.'

He brandished the list of celebrity pro-am competitors which Arthur Highfield had given him, as promised, a few minutes before.

'Listen to these. Manuel Ortiz, the Spanish Ambassador, Toby Bethune, the Sports Minister, Frankie Holloway, the movie actress, Norton Wales, the singer, Emerich Neumann, a German car-maker, Everard Balliol, an American billionaire, Arnie Harding, an ex-baseball player turned actor . . . and that's only half the list.

'The rest are the great and the good from the European business community, all from big organisations with the potential to make a lot of use of this place. Andy Martin's going to have his work cut out looking after that lot.'

He leaned back in the big chair at the head of the board table and looked around him. 'So what have we got? Alison, you go first.'

'I don't have very much, I'm afraid, sir. I interviewed four of the five who were waiting in the bar, Morton, Masur, Cortes and Wyman. Nakamura's English consists of three words, so Morton said . . . dollars, whisky and jig-a-jig. What's jig-a-jig, sir?'

Across the table, McIlhenney bit his bottom lip. Mario

McGuire spluttered and broke into a coughing fit. Skinner threw them a look.

'Don't ask, Superintendent. So what *did* you find out?'

Higgins glowered at the two Sergeants, then turned back to face Skinner. 'Well, sir. All five of them, plus White, played this morning. They went out in pairs, White and Cortes first, Masur and Wyman second, and finally Morton and Nakamura. They were playing something called Stableford, whatever that is, and they all had caddies with them. Cortes was still in the main shower room when Masur and Wyman came in. That was just before one o'clock. He told them that White had gone to take his usual Jacuzzi, and that he would meet them all in the bar for a pre-lunch drink. They were due to eat at Bracklands at two, and Lady Kinture was to pick them up at one-forty-five.'

She paused. 'There doesn't seem to have been much conversation in the bar, sir. The way they all described it, Masur and Wyman sat at one table, Morton and Nakamura at another, and Cortes practised his putting on the carpet. Eventually, just after one-thirty, Morton said, "Mickey must have drowned in that bath", and sent Williamson the steward, to find out what was keeping him.'

'And that's how Williamson came to find the body, poor wee bugger.' Skinner shook his head slightly, as if in sympathy. 'Sarah said she had to give him a sedative. D'you know what sort of a shape he's in now?'

'He's steadied up a bit, sir.'

McGuire leaned across to look up the table at Skinner. 'Excuse me, sir, but is there a chance that Williamson might be our man. I mean he's the steward. He probably set the Jacuzzi room up. Could the shock all be an act?'

The ACC smiled grimly back at him. 'You obviously haven't seen Tommy Williamson. I have. He used to be cocktail barman in the big hotel in North Berwick. He's a skinny wee bloke, about five feet two on his tip-toes, and he must be nearly seventy. He'd have trouble picking up my new son, let alone heaving a dead weight into a bathtub.'

He turned back to Higgins. 'The Famous Five are still waiting for me in the bar, yes?' She nodded. 'You still haven't told them that White was murdered?'

'No, sir, as you ordered.'

'That's good. I want to look in their eyes when they find out.'

'You suspect one of them?' asked McIlhenney .

'Of being involved? We have to. They knew that White would be here this morning. That Jacuzzi was his private fiefdom. It was the one place you'd be sure to find him alone.'

He switched his attention to the two Sergeants. 'What did you get out of the caddy-shed?'

'Nothing, sir,' said McIlhenney. 'The professional and his assistants were all together in the shop, pricing stock for sale during the week. The three greenkeepers Webb were working on various parts of the course this morning. They knocked off at half-twelve and met up with the scaffolders and joiners in the caddy-shed. The steel-workers had brought a load of beer in. They were all out on the piss in Aberlady last night, and they needed a wee pick-me-up, like. The caddies joined them too, when they came in. They can sniff out drink anywhere.'

'So they were all there when White died?'

'Apart from anyone who went for a slash in the main building, boss.' .

Skinner glanced up in surprise. 'What about clubhouse security?'

'Security, boss?' said McGuire. 'Insecurity more like. The place was wide open. The temporary urinals on the course aren't available yet, so the scaffolders and joiners have been allowed to use the clubhouse toilets.'

'So there have been guys coming and going all day along the corridor leading to the course?'

Mario McGuire nodded his head. 'That's right, gaffer. Any bugger dressed like a workman could have walked in there.'

'How many men were working today?'

'We didn't count them, but I'd say around a dozen steel-workers, and four joiners. That right, Neil?'

McIlhenney grunted his agreement. 'Uhuh. The joiners are all local guys, but the steel-workers are specialists. They work full-time with the contractor, and travel around. Fearsome characters, they are.'

'Are they still there?'

'Aye, sir. We left the DCs to finish taking names and statements, and them to finish their beer.'

'Right. You two get back over there, and find out if any of them were away from the caddy-shed, for any reason, between one and one thirty-five. And find out if anyone saw anyone who shouldn't have been there, or anyone they didn't recognise or who looked out of place. Meantime, Superintendent, you come with me.' He rose abruptly from the table and led Alison Higgins from the room and through to the bar.

Two of the five men rose to their feet as they entered, but not out of courtesy. 'Christ, another one!' said the taller of the two, in a broad Australian accent.

Skinner looked at him, unsmiling. 'You'll be Mr Masur,

then?' The man nodded. He opened his mouth to speak again, but Skinner cut him off.

'I'm sorry to have kept you all waiting, but there's been a lot to do. I'm Bob Skinner, Assistant Chief Constable. I'm here because we are not dealing with sudden death or suicide, but with murder. Just after he left you, Señor Cortes, Michael White was attacked. His throat was cut and he died almost instantly.'

The colour drained from Masur's tanned face. The other man who had stood as the two police officers entered sank back into his chair. He was a few years older than the rest. The ACC recognised him as Morton from newspaper photographs.

Skinner looked at all five, making eye contact with each, weighing them up. 'You've all spoken to Superintendent Higgins earlier, but there are just one or two things I'd like to ask.'

He glanced towards the swarthy Spaniard. 'Señor Cortes, how did Mr White seem as you played. What was his mood?'

Cortes thought for a few seconds. 'He was good. He was very pleasant, very polite. He was very happy with his golf, too. After that finish at the eighteenth, he was . . . how you say . . . pleased as Paunch.'

'He didn't seem worried about anything?'

'Not at all.'

'Thanks.' He looked once more around the room. 'How many of you had met Michael White before this morning?'

Only one man raised a hand. 'I had. I'm Mike Morton. My company is running this event, so I've had some dealings with Mickey.'

'How did you get on together?'

'Like a house on fire. Mickey was a most charming man.

He and I hit it off from day one. Christ, this is terrible. Poor guy!'

'Did he say anything to you about a problem that he might have had?'

Morton shook his brown-toupéed head. 'No. Mickey was filthy rich and happy about it. He didn't have any problems.'

Skinner grunted. 'That seems to be the general view. One other thing, gentlemen. Did any of you see anyone today who looked out of place. Mr Morton, can you translate for Nakamura-San; tell him what's happened?'

Morton nodded, then spoke quietly to the Japanese. A bewildered look spread across his broad brown face, then he shook his head vigorously. In turn, Masur and the other two golfers did the same.

'Tiger says "no", Mr Skinner,' said Morton, 'and I guess that goes for the rest of us, as well. Other than the course staff and the steel riggers, there was no one around here. Tomorrow is set-up day for the exhibitors in the tented village, and for television. It'll be crazy then, but today, peaceful. That's why we played our little Stableford.

'God, and poor Mickey never knew he won the money.'

Morton stared out of the window for a second or two, then turned back to Skinner. 'Say, what will this mean for the Murano Million?'

'Put the gate up, I should think,' said Skinner.

'You're not gonna tell us to cancel?'

'I don't think that's practical or necessary. It'd cause chaos. We can keep the key area sealed off. No, Mr Morton, you can have your tournament.'

He looked up again. 'Well, gentlemen, I thank you again for your patience. You may all go now, but if anything does occur to any of you, anything at all odd or out of the ordinary, please get in touch.'

He led Alison Higgins back out into the foyer. A well-dressed, slightly-built man in his early thirties stood there alone. He turned as they entered. 'Hi, Alan,' said Skinner. 'What have we got outside, then?' Through the smoked glass of the entrance doors he could see a crowd of people. Two of them carried television cameras on their shoulders.

Alan Royston, the force press officer, nodded a greeting. 'Afternoon, sir. Afternoon, Alison. The tip-off industry's done its work. They all arrived, mob-handed, around ten minutes ago. I have a statement ready for them.'

He handed Skinner a sheet of A4 paper. The ACC scanned it and nodded. 'That's fine, Alan. Tells them what they need to know. You call Edinburgh and have it issued on our press distribution network. I'll see the people outside.'

Royston looked up at him. 'Are you sure, sir? I could do that.'

'That's OK. I'm off to salvage my family Sunday, and I'm sneaking out the back way for no one. I'll deal with them as I leave.'

He turned back to Superintendent Higgins. 'Alison, you get things tidied up here. You can set up your Inquiry HQ here, or in Haddington, wherever you think best. As far as this place is concerned, I want the technicians to go over every inch of that dressing room and the Jacuzzi cubicle, then I want them sealed off and guarded round the clock by a uniformed officer. If our killer has left any trace of himself, that's where it is.'

He stopped short. Suddenly he remembered his own time as a rising CID officer, and his frustration when his ACC would arrive at the scene of one of his investigations. Skinner had christened the man 'Seagull'. 'Why's that?' Andy Martin, then a Detective Constable, had asked him. 'Because he flies in from far away, makes a lot of noise, shits on you, then flies away again.' For the first time in his short career at Chief Officer rank, he saw himself spreading his wings, and realised how difficult it was *not* to become a seagull.

His smile took Superintendent Higgins by surprise. 'Look, I'm sorry. I don't mean to put my big feet all over this investigation, but there's going to be pressure on us to solve this thing and I don't want to expose you unfairly. So I'll keep a personal involvement, and I'll carry the can if we don't get a result. You're the supervising officer, same as usual with a crime in your area, but on this one you report to me at every stage. Right, any thoughts on how we should go ahead?'

Higgins' cheeks were flushed with what Skinner hoped was pleasure. 'Well, sir. It seems to me that the only avenue we've got for the moment is the known antipathy felt by Morton towards White. I thought of asking Brian Mackie to make enquiries in the US about Morton's background, to see if there are any other skeletons in his business dealings.'

'Good idea. You do that; I'll be in the office tomorrow. Look in sometime and give me a progress report. Unless, that is, you get lucky and make an arrest. Mind you on the basis of what we have so far, that'll take a *lot* of luck.

'Now, I'd better go and speak to the press. See you later.'

He stepped through the automatic doors, out into the afternoon sunlight, with Alan Royston following behind. In addition to the two television operators, there were around a dozen reporters and three photographers assembled in the car park. He strolled slowly across.

'Afternoon, ladies and gentlemen. I'm going to tell you as

much as I can. We are dealing with the murder of a man. He suffered a fatal cutting injury some time after midday today, and we do not see the possibility of suicide. Enquiries are under way, and you will be kept informed of their progress.'

'Who's the victim, Bob?' A husky voice came from the rear of the group.

Skinner glanced across in surprise. 'Hello, John. Didn't expect to see you out here on a Sunday.'

John Hunter, a veteran Edinburgh freelance, and one of Skinner's oldest journalist friends, laughed ironically. 'You're kidding. Wi' all these new tabloids opening up and wanting copy, I don't have a day off any more. Come on. You can tell us. Who is it?'

Skinner shook his head. 'Sorry, chum. Not until I'm sure that the widow's been informed.' He nodded towards Royston. 'Alan'll give you a name as soon as we know that's happened.'

''S no one of the golfers, is it?'

'Certainly not. Just be patient for a few minutes more and we'll have something for you.'

'Anything else you can tell us, then? Like, is anyone in custody?'

'No, I'm afraid not. The victim went off to take a bath after playing golf, and the body was found by a member of staff half an hour later. We're still taking statements from everyone who was on the course at the time.'

'Aha,' said John Hunter, dramatically. 'Golfing, eh. That tells us it's no' the Marquis, anyway.' He paused as a thought crossed his mind. 'Here, it's no' Michael White, is it?'

'See you later,' said Skinner, poker-faced, as he left the group and walked back to his car.

*

'How's Andy? From what I hear, he's settled in OK. Roy Old has moved big McIlhenney out to East Lothian, and I expect that he's behind that.

'Jimmy's appointed himself as a sort of unofficial emissary between us, sounding me out, sounding Andy out. He tells me that Andy isn't in the mood for any olive branches. Says he never wants to see another Skinner as long as he lives!'

'So I shouldn't invite him to supper just yet?'

'I don't think that would be a brilliant idea. More to the point though, have you had any joy in tracking down that daughter of ours?'

'No. Her band's management company gave me a list of venues, but they wouldn't go any further than that. I pushed them, but eventually the girl there got rude and told me that they weren't there to act as a contact service.'

'Cheeky sod! Give me the number, and I'll ruin her day.'

'No, my darling. You've done enough of that. I'll write to Alex at each of the venues on the list, just asking how she's doing. Just letting her know that I'm thinking about her. Don't worry, honey. She'll get in touch.'

He looked at her mournfully. 'What makes you so sure?'

She laughed. 'She might have fallen out with you; with me even; but before long she'll realise she's missing her kid brother.

'Just be patient. We'll hear from her. And when we do . . . we'll just take it from there.'

Monday

Seven

'How did she take it?'

'Just about as you would expect of Myrtle White. Very calmly, at first. Then as it sank in she began to shake. No tears, just this violent shivering as if the room was very, very cold.'

Sir James Proud gave a slight shudder himself, as the memory chilled him, too.

'Of all the jobs I've ever had to do in the police service,' he said quietly, 'breaking bad news is the one which I've hated more than any other.'

Skinner nodded. 'You and me both, Jimmy.'

'But that's the first time I've had to face the widow of a friend.'

'How close were you and Michael White?'

The grey-haired Chief Constable reflected for a moment. 'Fairly close, but not confessors, if you know what I mean. But Chrissie and Myrtle have been best friends for years. They'd come to us for dinner on occasion, and we'd go to them. Then we'd see them at parties. Michael and I didn't socialise without our wives, but they went shopping together so often that they had their own table in Jenners' tea-room.

'Chrissie volunteered to come with me yesterday. I was glad of her presence, I tell you. I let her get on with the task of comforting, while I called the doctor in to give Myrtle a sedative. Then I phoned their son-in-law, Gavin, and gave him the job of contacting the rest of the family. I arranged for him to go into the mortuary this morning too, to make the formal identification.'

'Yes, that's good. I suppose you or I could have done it, but it's better if it's a family member. Neither you nor I should be called as identification witnesses when this gets to trial . . . if it gets to trial, because we've got next to bugger all to go on.'

Skinner glanced out of his office window. It was still a few minutes before 9 a.m., and several members of the expanding army of the force's civilian staff were striding purposefully up the steep driveway which led to the police headquarters building in Fettes Avenue. As he watched, Chris Whitlow, the Management Services Director, pulled his car into one of the six reserved parking spaces below the window. There had been one or two confrontations between Whitlow and Skinner during the first few months of the new Director's tenure, as the pure disciplines of financial control struggled to adapt to meet the unpredictable needs of operational policing, but recently the ACC had been forced to admit, if only to himself, that his new colleague was a quick learner and, after less than a year in the post, was proving his worth.

He turned back towards the Chief. 'I don't suppose you asked her any questions yesterday.' Proud shot him a quick glance and shook his head.

'Not a chance. She wouldn't have heard a word I said, even before the sedative took effect.'

'You know we have to talk to her?'

Proud Jimmy leaned back in his chair. 'Oh yes. I haven't been behind a desk so long that I've forgotten that. And I know we can't leave it any longer than today.'

Skinner grunted agreement. 'That's right. Look, I've told Ali Higgins that I want her to run this investigation as far as possible, but this is one instance where it's down to us. You know Myrtle White, and I've met her too, so what d'you say we go to interview her together?'

The Chief Constable picked up a biscuit from the plate on Skinner's desk, and pushed himself to his feet. 'Aye, that's fine by me, Bob. Just give me a call when you want to go.' He turned to leave the room, but Skinner stopped him with a call. 'Hold on, hold on. There's something else.' Proud turned back towards him, puzzled.

The ACC sat behind his desk smiling. 'I should really interview you too, shouldn't I?'

'Christ, I suppose you should at that! Fire away then.' Proud Jimmy lowered himself back into his seat.

'Well, as a good friend of the Whites, have you heard anything that might make you think someone had a fatal sort of grudge against the man? What do you know of his business dealings?'

Proud's ruddy face was serious as he considered Skinner's questions. 'Not a lot, really. The retail business, where he made his millions, was all high-flying corporate stuff. I don't remember him ever really talking about it. His later activity, on the development side, was more *ad hoc*. I think he did it for fun as much as anything else.'

'Did you ever hear him talk about the Witches' Hill project?'

The Chief searched his memory. 'Yes, I did, as a matter of fact. He brought it up one night when we were at their place for dinner, a few years back. He said that Hector Kinture had just come to him with the proposition, and asked me what I thought. I remember telling him that the only thing I'd heard about investing in sport was that you shouldn't do it unless you could afford to lose every penny you put in. And I remember him saying that he could, and that since the thing sounded like fun, he probably would put up the money.'

'How much was it?'

'Three million, he said. Half equity, half loan.'

'Was that the only time he discussed it with you?'

'No. I asked him about it at our party last Christmas. Just before you arrived, as I recall. Asked him how it was going. Very well, he said. So much so that all sorts of people had approached him wanting to buy into the project.'

'Mmm,' Skinner murmured. 'But he turned them all down?'

'Yes. He said that he and Kinture had decided that if they let one in it'd be open season, and that before they knew it it wouldn't be their course any more. So they thanked everyone for their interest, but very politely they refused them all.'

'Did he mention anyone in particular?'

The Chief paused again. 'Yes, he did mention one name. That big promoter fellow. What's his name again? Like a football club . . . Yes! Morton, that was it. He told me that they had asked Morton to set up their tournament, and that he had said that he would only do it if they would give him – give him, mind you – twenty-five per cent of the equity.

'Michael said that he and Hector had told him, politely as ever was, to bugger off, and had said that they would find someone else to arrange their event. At that the chap came back, with a very ill grace and said that he would do it for his usual percentage of all money taken in from spectators, sponsors and exhibitors.'

A broad smile spread over Skinner's tanned face. 'Generous of him. He's a regular winner of the "Nae Luck" award, is our Mr Morton. Here's another interesting tale for you. It seems that the same Morton tried to bend the rules, and stuff this week's event with his own golfer clients. He might have got away with it, only Michael White went to the sponsor and cut the legs from under him.

'And the guy looked at me yesterday and told me, wide-eyed, that he thought White was "charming". According to him they were practically blood brothers.'

The Chief Constable leaned forward in his seat. 'Were they now! I think we ought to find out a bit more about Mr Morton.'

'Too right,' said Skinner. 'That's already under way. Higgins has got Brian Mackie checking him out on the international network. I've got another button I can push too.'

Proud smiled. 'That other job of yours comes in handy at times, doesn't it?'

'It can do. I've thought about packing it in, letting the Secretary of State find himself a new part-time security adviser, then something like this crops up and I decide it's worth it after all.'

He stood up; Sir James followed his example. 'Look Chief, why don't you go and empty your in-tray and I'll speak to Brian Mackie. While I'm doing that I'll have Maggie Rose check that it's all right for us to see Myrtle White.'

'Aye, fine. Come to think of it, we'll take Maggie with us. I'm a plain coward when it comes to coping with grief!'

Eight

Detective Chief Inspector Brian Mackie sat hunched over his desk as Skinner entered his office at the rear of the Special Branch suite. His jacket hung over the back of his chair, and his tight-cut shirt emphasised his bony shoulders, making him look even thinner than he was.

Mackie was serious – bordering on the mournful at times, in Skinner's private view – but his manner flowed from the tightness of his self-control. He looked up as the ACC entered, a shaft of stray light reflecting from his shiny bald head and making his sudden surprising smile even brighter.

'Morning, sir.'

'Christ, Brian, but you look cheerful. Did you win the Lottery or something?'

'As a matter of fact I did. A tenner to be exact, and the Hearts won as well, so my cup of joy runneth over.'

'Come on, Hearts winning just makes you less miserable, that's all!'

'Not when they beat Hibs!'

Skinner laughed. His disrupted weekend had made him forget all about Edinburgh's soccer derby. His predecessor as the Chief Constable's deputy had regarded attendance at a football match as a regular Saturday duty. He might have followed that precedent but for the greater attraction of spending all his available time with his wife and his baby son.

'So when Superintendent Higgins called you yesterday it didn't spoil your Sunday?'

'Not a bit, boss. The truth is I really enjoy international enquiries. Contact with other forces broadens the mind.'

Brian Mackie had been moved into Special Branch as commander in the wake of Andy Martin's promotion to head the drugs and vice squad. Like Martin he had acted for a spell as Skinner's personal assistant. Recognising that changes in the world's political structure would have implications for the internal security work of Special Branch, the ACC had given Mackie added responsibility for international liaison, making him the officer through whom enquiries were extended, when necessary, into other countries. He had taken to his new job to such an extent that he had made himself an authority on the structure of police forces in most Western Hemisphere countries.

'How are you doing with Morton?' Skinner asked, seating himself on a table facing Mackie's desk. 'I want you to report to Superintendent Higgins as requested . . . it's her investigation . . . but, what the hell, I'm here and I'm curious!'

The DCI's face lit up once more. 'I've just had feedback from the States on that, sir. Sports Stars Corporation . . . that's Morton's company,' Skinner nodded '. . . is based in Miami. Since the early eighties it's been the dominant company in its field, and Mike Morton has been one of the most important figures in world sports. Its strength lies in the number of sportsmen and women they have under contract, and the muscle that gives them.

'They're involved in far more than just golf.'

Skinner raised an eyebrow. 'What d'ye mean JUST golf?'

Mackie looked discomfited for a second, but, deciding to ignore Skinner's jibe, he went on. 'Golf is a very important part of the company's business, certainly – in fact that's where it started – but really, sir, now SSC gets everywhere. It's a major promoter as well as manager.

'It has a boxing division, with a string of world champions, recognised by an organisation of which Morton's son-in-law is president. It owns an American football franchise, an ice hockey team, and a basketball side. Morton has a baseball team of his own. Then there's tennis. The company has agreements with most of the leading players.'

'OK,' Skinner interrupted. 'That's all a matter of record, but what sort of a business is it, and what sort of a bloke is Morton?'

'The message I'm getting, boss, is that they're both squeaky clean. I spoke to my opposite number in Miami. He said he knows Morton and reckons that if he ran for Mayor out there, he'd win hands down. He put me on to a contact in the State Attorney's Office and she told me the same thing. Mike Morton is a very respected businessman without a blemish to his name.'

Skinner pushed himself off the table. 'No, Brian, I don't buy that. He's got one blemish that I know of, for a start. He tells lies to the police.' He took a small address book from the pocket of his jacket, and looked up a number. Then he picked up Mackie's telephone and dialled.

The call was answered before the third ring. 'FBI.'

'Christ, Joe, don't you have a secretary yet!'

There was a laugh on the other end of the line. 'No chance, my friend, I couldn't keep one busy. Anyway, there's a view in the Bureau that secretaries are a security risk.

'So how're you doin', you Scottish SOB. It's been a year now, since you made my phone ring.'

Skinner had known Joe Doherty, the permanent UK representative of the FBI, since he was posted in the late eighties. The two men had an informal friendship which had proved valuable on more than one occasion, yet in the main it was conducted by telephone. Doherty was in a high-risk post, and was careful about going out in public.

'Cuts both ways, Joseph. As for how I'm doing, you and I are almost related. I've got a half-American son, now. Didn't you know?'

Doherty laughed again, but there was something behind it this time. 'Yes, I knew. There's very little happens to an American citizen resident in the UK that I don't find out about eventually. Listen,' he went on, 'I've been planning to come up to Scotland to surprise you and meet your new Special Branch guy.'

'Great idea,' said Skinner. 'Tell you what, I'll even give you an excuse. I'd like you to do me a favour. I'm looking for all available information, known or suspected, on one of your lot. He was sat in the next room to a very bloody murder yesterday, a real cool job. The victim was Scottish, and I know that he had crossed your man, seriously, on at least two occasions. Yet when I interviewed the guy, he told me that he and the victim were bosom pals.

'Our international man checked this guy out in his home state, Florida, and they gave him a character reference that makes him sound like Mickey effing Mouse. I'd like to know what your chums think of him. Can you find out?'

There was silence for a second. 'What makes you think we'd know him?'

75

'Ah, I don't know. There's just something makes me think you will. He's a very big wheel. His name's Mike Morton.'

'Morton!' Doherty exploded. 'Then I know the murder you're talkin' about. All over last night's news and today's paper. The golf club. Mike Morton was there?'

'Uhuh.'

'Well, I'll be . . .'

'Look, Bob, I do remember being briefed about this fella, way before I came here. I'll need to update. Leave it with me and I'll be in touch soon as I can.'

Nine

P roud Jimmy stood, nervously, behind the big cream sofa, head bowed and hands clasped together, almost like a worshipper at prayer.

In complete contrast, Myrtle White sat stiff-backed and upright. She was as pale as a ghost, and her eyes were noticeably bloodshot, yet as she looked across at Skinner, seated opposite her in an armchair, she was calm and fully in control of herself. As Detective Inspector Maggie Rose handed her a cup of tea, Skinner noticed that it was his assistant's hand which trembled slightly, not that of the widow.

They were seated in the main drawing room of the White villa in Whitehouse Loan. It was a big, bay-windowed apartment, expensively decorated and furnished, with heavy curtains and a thick Axminster carpet, not fitted but surrounded by varnished wood. There was no television set or hi-fi anywhere in sight. It was a reception room in the most traditional sense, presented as it might have been when the big grey sandstone house was built and first occupied. Outside the sun shone on a garden which was equally conservative in its design, with rose-beds set around and in the centre of a carefully cut lawn which stretched out from the red stone-chip pathway in front of the house to the high privet hedge which maintained its privacy.

Skinner leaned forward in his chair. 'I'm sorry that we have to intrude, Mrs White, but there are matters which we have to discuss with you, so that the investigation into your husband's death can proceed.'

The widow nodded and sipped her tea. 'Please don't be so formal, Bob. It's Myrtle, remember. We have been introduced socially, after all.' She smiled gently, and he was touched by the realisation that she, the bereaved, was putting him at his ease.

She went on. 'Before you begin, can you answer two questions for me?' Skinner nodded. 'First, are you certain that Michael did not commit suicide?'

'Absolutely. For one thing, we haven't found the weapon.'

'I understand. My second question is, how quickly did he die? Jimmy told me how he was killed, but I need to know as many details as possible. I need to imagine that I was with him; it's a peace of mind thing, you see. Michael and I sometimes talked about death, and we both always assumed that when one of us went, the other would be there, to say farewell. Not goodbye: we're both Christians, you see. We believe in the concept of death as a gateway.'

Skinner looked into her eyes as he answered. 'I put that question to Sarah. She said that he would have become unconscious from his wound very quickly and died very shortly after that. But she believes that he was knocked out *before* he was killed, by a heavy blow to the head. The way she described it to me, he wouldn't have known a thing. You can regard his death as instantaneous.'

He waited, as she considered his answer. Eventually she nodded. 'Right. Now *your* questions.'

'Can I just take a step back? You asked about suicide. Did

you have any reason to think that Michael might have taken his own life?'

She shook her head vigorously. 'No, none at all. It's just that . . . As I said, we were very close. We've been married for almost thirty years. I couldn't imagine him having a worry so great that he'd conceal it from me, far less choose to die as an escape. That's been my great fear since yesterday. But now you've confirmed that it wasn't the case, and I'm relieved. Bizarre as it might seem to you, I can cope with the idea of murder more easily. It's strange, how the mind works.'

Skinner shook his head. 'No, not strange. You can't prepare the mind to cope with the sudden, unexpected loss of a loved one. When it happens, everyone reacts in a different way, but it all comes back to the same question.' Memories of the past came flooding back. 'I remember how I was when my first wife was killed. My great fear – no, more than that, my immediate assumption – was that the accident had been caused by a fault in the car that I should have seen and corrected. When sudden death happens, the survivor feels reflex guilt. That has to be dealt with, and put away.'

'And afterwards?' she asked. 'Tell me, how long does it take for the pain to stop?'

He looked into her eyes. 'My loss happened almost twenty years ago. Now I'm married again, to a woman I love as deeply as I can imagine, and I have a baby son. Yet still, there isn't a day goes by when I don't think of Myra. But the memories are warm, not painful. As I see it, each life is a book. It's a series of interconnecting chapters, and some will have different characters. You were in Michael's book, and he in yours. His was closed yesterday, much of yours still has to be written. As for the epilogue, well, that's a matter of faith.'

Myrtle White touched the policeman's arm. 'Thank you, Bob. I'll try to keep that concept in my head.' She smiled at him, then blinked and sipped her coffee.

'Tell me, do you think that the murderer was a thief?'

'His wallet and watch were stolen, but we're not making assumptions from that.

'You and Michael discussed everything, Myrtle, yes?'

'That was our way.'

'Did he mention any problems recently, any difficult deals, anyone with whom he might have been in dispute?'

'None that I can think of. After he sold the company, Michael did things purely for fun. If someone brought a development to him, he asked himself, "Do I like this person?" and, "Will I enjoy an association with this project?" It was only after that he'd look at the numbers involved. That's how it was with the golf club, more or less, although he admitted that he'd probably have done that even if the figures hadn't been so good.'

'Was there anyone, anyone at all whom he regarded as an opponent or an enemy?'

'No. Michael didn't have an enemy in the world.'

'I'm sorry Myrtle, but he had one. And my job is to find who that was.'

She looked at him, almost in a sly fashion. 'I don't think I want to know.'

'What d'you mean?'

'Well I can cope, the way things are just now. Michael's been murdered, I know, but it's surreal; I have no one to associate with it. If you catch the person who did it, I'll be forced to look at him. I'll be forced to hate him, and hatred is something I've never experienced. I'm not sure how I'd cope with that.'

'You will, though. You'll take comfort from the thought that he's paying for what he did.'

He glanced at the fine carved fireplace which dominated the White's high-ceilinged sitting room. A row of photographs in silver frames stood on the mantelpiece. He pointed towards two on the left, of a young man and young woman. 'Are those your children?'

'Yes. Sheila and David. Sheila and Gavin live in Edinburgh, in Dean Village, but David's working in Australia just now. He's in advertising. Gav phoned him last night. He's flying back on the first plane available.'

'What does Gavin do?'

'He's a surveyor. Lovely boy. He can be a bit wild, but he's devoted to Sheila, and he was wonderful yesterday.'

'Will Michael's death give you Inheritance Tax problems?'

She smiled at him again. 'I shouldn't think so. We have a very good tax planner. Most of the money is in trusts, from which we draw income. So do the children, and they each have capital of their own. The rest is what Michael called our "play money". It's a sort of private investment pool that he used to fund projects and to do daft personal things. For example, a couple of winters ago we were watching Test cricket from Australia on television. I just happened to say that I wished I was there, and two days later I was.

'Oh I'm sure there'll be some tax to pay, but it'll be manageable. Our accountant will make sure of that.'

Skinner grinned. 'Worth their weight in gold.'

'But would you want your daughter to marry one?' said Myrtle White, with a smile.

He winced. He shot a quick glance at Sir James Proud, then

looked back at the woman. 'My daughter's given up doing what I want, Myrtle.'

She smiled again. 'Don't be daft. They all go through that stage. If she's giving you problems, she'll come round.'

'Maybe, maybe not. Anyway, one more question. Did Michael ever mention someone called Mike Morton?'

Suddenly the smile faded from her face. 'Yes, he did. On a few occasions. He was supposed to be playing golf with him yesterday, wasn't he?'

'Yes, that's right. What else do you recall about him?'

'Well, Michael did say that he'd been difficult over the tournament. Hard to deal with. He mentioned a couple of times that he was having trouble with him, but I think that he had sorted it all out.

'I remember he said once that he'd met a few people like Morton in business, and that mostly they'd been shady. "Shady" was probably Michael's strongest term of disapproval.'

'Hmm,' Sir James Proud grunted. He still stood behind the woman, as if protecting her. 'He was a very generous man, your husband, in his view of his fellow beings. Many of us could learn from his example.' Skinner looked up at the Chief, and was astonished to see a moistness in his eyes. He sensed that it was time to go, before grief could force its way through the calmness of the room.

'Unless there's anything else you can recall that might help us, Myrtle, we'll be off. I'm sorry that we had to intrude at all.'

'Not at all, Bob. I welcome your presence, yours Jimmy, and yours too, Miss Rose.' She nodded to the Detective Inspector, who was seated at the other end of the long sofa. 'I was glad of the chance to be involved. I've never been good at sitting around. In fact, I had been thinking of phoning Lady Proud and inviting myself round for coffee.'

'You do that very thing, my dear,' said the big, bluff Chief Constable, his composure fully recovered in the relief of knowing that the interview was over.

'One thing, gentlemen,' said Myrtle White. 'When can I plan on having the funeral? I mean when will you release...'

Skinner interrupted quickly. 'Strictly speaking, that's for the Fiscal to say, but in the circumstances, I'd say the beginning of next week would be OK. Monday or Tuesday. I'll speak to Davie Pettigrew myself, and let him know that's your intention.'

'Thanks, Bob. That's good of you. There'll be a lot to arrange. I'd imagine that we might have quite a turn-out.' For the first time that morning, there was a catch in her voice, but almost instantly, her shoulders squared and she recovered herself. She stood up and the others followed suit.

Proud Jimmy led the way out to the hall, and to the front door, where Myrtle White reached up on her toes and kissed him on the cheek. She shook hands with Skinner and Rose.

'Thank you again for your help,' said the ACC. 'I'll keep you informed of any progress that we make.'

She shook her head as she opened the glass-panelled door. 'No, Bob. Don't do that. I really don't want to know. I can't allow myself to be taken over by thoughts of revenge or retribution. The punishment end of it, that's your business, and I'm happy to let you get on with it.

'Michael's dead, and as you say, that chapter of my book is over. I'll give him a damn good send-off and after that I want to get on with the rest of my life, without looking back in anger.' She waved a farewell as she closed the door behind them.

'Some woman,' muttered Sir James Proud, as the three police officers crunched their way down the red gravel path.

'Aye,' said Skinner. 'It sums up police work, what Myrtle said. Michael deserves retribution. And she's right: it's down to us to see he gets it.' He looked down at Rose, as he opened the garden gate. 'Those are the clients of our detecting profession, Maggie, the victims and their families, first and foremost. That's where our duty lies. We're their avenging angels.'

Ten

It was the silent hour when the rest of the force were at lunch. Skinner sat at his desk, checking the note of the interview with Myrtle White which Maggie Rose had dictated on their return to the Fettes Avenue headquarters building. The Detective Inspector sat facing him, like a schoolgirl awaiting an exam result.

He grinned at her. 'Ten out of ten, Maggie. Have two copies made, one for the Chief, and the other for Alison Higgins.' There was a knock on the door, which lay ajar. 'Yes,' Skinner called, and Ruth McConnell stepped into the room. 'All lips, legs and self-assurance,' was Andy Martin's classic description of the ACC's confident, capable secretary, but now she wore an air of uncertainty which Skinner had never seen before. He could tell that she had something to say, but she was hesitant, as if she was fearful of his reaction.

'Aye, aye, Ruthie,' he said. 'Who's rattled your cage, then?'

She tried to look puzzled by his banter, but failed, and gave up the attempt.

'It's Superintendent Martin, sir. He's on the phone.'

Skinner's eyebrows rose. He felt an involuntary tug in the pit of his stomach. 'I see.' He smiled at her, to put her at her ease. 'What does he want?'

'He said that it has to do with the Witches' Hill

investigation. I told him that you were with Inspector Rose, but he said he'd hang on.'

She looked at him, enquiring, but with the apprehension gone from her eyes. Skinner leaned back in his chair and stared out of the window. Five people in the world knew the truth of the explosion between the two men, and Martin's transfer had been presented as routine police business, but he knew full well that rumours of a rift were circulating and being accepted as fact.

He assessed his options for what seemed like an eternity to the two women as they watched him. He had made it clear that Alison Higgins was in charge of the Witches' Hill investigation. If he took the call it could be seen as undermining her authority, yet if he referred it to her it could be seen by Martin as a snub.

Eventually he swung back to face Ruth. 'OK, put him through.' The secretary left the room, and Maggie Rose, without being asked, stood up and followed her. Skinner thought that both were suppressing smiles.

A few seconds later the white phone on his desk buzzed, once. He picked it up. 'Mr Martin, sir,' said Ruth. There was a click. 'Andy, what can I do for you?' He held his breath, ready to read every inflection in Martin's voice.

The reply was cool and controlled. 'I'm sorry to disturb you, sir, but I thought you'd want to hear this. I had a call this morning from Kay Wilson, the editor of the *Scotsman*. She's had a very odd letter, and she thinks it might have some connection to the White murder. It's handwritten, and it was left on the counter of their front office. Their receptionists were both away from their desks, so they didn't see who left it.

'Legally, she can run it tomorrow, and she's going to, but

she's taken a copy and had the original delivered here. Want me to read it?'

Skinner considered his reply for a moment or two. 'Don't you take this the wrong way, Andy, but I don't. I've told Alison that this is her investigation. I've got myself involved in it once already today, so on this one I've got to give her her place. Whatever you've got there you should show to her. She's based at the club just now. Sarah and Jazz are out at the cottage in Gullane all this week, so I'll be calling in on Alison on my way home. She can show your letter to me then . . . if she chooses.'

'Very good, sir. I'll do that. I'm sorry to have bothered you.'

Skinner sighed. 'Andy . . . Andy, my friend, this stops now. I've been keeping clear of you to let you cool down, but the time has come. We've been mates for far too long. I admit it, I made an absolute arse of myself that morning. My mouth overrode my brain completely, and it all got out of control. I said and did some wild things, and I'm sorry for them.'

'So did Alex, Bob, but she isn't.'

'Hah, don't I know that! If it's any consolation, I'm in the doghouse too. Look, I don't know what happened between you two after I made my theatrical exit. But I guess that when I upset her, she took it out on you.'

'Something like that. I lost it a bit, too.'

'Yeah, well, as I said, I'm sorry, as sorry as I can be. It's all down to me.'

'No it isn't, not all of it. You were right about one thing. I should have spoken to you a lot earlier. At first, you weren't around, then when you were back and I was going to say something, I let Alex talk me out of it . . . even though I knew she was wrong. The trouble is, she's proud of being a nineties woman, but you and I, we're eighties men.'

There was an edge of relief to Skinner's laugh. 'Speak for yourself, boy. I'm pure seventies!'

And then the laugh turned into a sigh. 'Listen to me, pal. You and I are going to approach this thing in a manner appropriate to our ages and gender. In other words, we'll go somewhere discreet and we'll get rat-arsed. In the process we'll talk through you and Alex, and you can convince me that you're a proper suitor for my only daughter. That's if you're still brave enough or daft enough to want her. Agreed?'

'Aye, Bob, you're on. But one thing!'

'What's that?'

'Wherever we go, they'd better have a hell of a lot of beer!'

Eleven

Witches' Hill Golf and Country Club seemed to have exploded into life, after the unnatural quiet of the previous day.

The car park was almost full. As he stood at the entrance to the clubhouse, Skinner could see, through a thin copse of trees, scores of brightly branded vans drawn up around the tented village as exhibitors, caterers and brewers unloaded their goods. In the middle distance to his left, five golfers were on the practice range. He shaded his eyes from the sun which shone over his shoulder and watched them. Soon he identified among the quintet of contrasting styles, the classic, disciplined swing of Darren Atkinson, the more fluid, expressive style of Andres Cortes, and the three-quarter thrash of the squat Tiger Nakamura.

He was still there, smiling in envy as he watched the straight flight of the shots, when the clubhouse doors slid open. Mario McGuire emerged from the building, pulling on his sports jacket as he walked. He pulled up short when he saw Skinner. 'Evening, sir.'

The ACC laughed. It was just after 5 p.m. 'What d'ye mean evening, man? It's still afternoon in my book. Are you setting your own hours these days?'

'Aye, sir. Ten-hour shifts like always . . . not counting Sundays, of course.'

'Don't remind me. I've got some DIY to finish when I get home tonight. You'd better trot on too. Maggie made a point of telling me about those Festival Theatre Tickets. Seven o'clock start she said.'

McGuire nodded. 'Yes, and she bought the tickets, too! They're a wedding present. I've never seen *Turandot* before.'

'That's the one with that tune, isn't it? "No one sleeps while I'm singing" or something?'

''S right, boss. And tonight it's the man himself who's singing it. It'll bring the Italian out in me, I tell you. I'll have trouble stopping myself from joining in.'

'Christ, don't do that! I've heard you sing remember.' He moved towards the door. 'On your way then, Mario. Superintendent Higgins inside?'

'Yes sir. She's using the boardroom.'

Skinner entered the building, nodding to Laurence Bennett, the bookings manager, who sat behind his counter in the foyer. He took the door to the right then turned again, sharply, into the boardroom. Alison Higgins was seated at the end of the table closest to the door. She looked over her shoulder, then stood up, as he entered.

'Sit down, Ali, sit down. How're you doing? What're you doing?'

She glanced down at the papers strewn across the table. 'The usual routine, sir. Lots and lots of interviews. First interviews with Mr Bennett, old Williamson the steward, and Iris McKenna, Joe Bryan's assistant, and with other people who weren't here yesterday, but who knew Michael White. Second interviews with the people we spoke to yesterday, just to see if they recalled anything else that might be significant.'

'Anything?' Skinner asked, guessing the answer from Higgins' expression.

'Not a scrap, sir. All we've got is friction between Morton and White, which Morton didn't mention. But we know for sure that the man was never alone yesterday. Masur and Weekes finished their game first. They waited for Morton and Nakamura, then all four went into the clubhouse together. To add to that, Brian Mackie reported that his Florida people gave Morton a good write-up. I suppose it's understandable that if you have a private tiff with someone and that someone is murdered, you're not going to mention your disagreement.'

'Maybe so,' Skinner conceded.

'There is one thing, sir,' said Higgins. 'Andy Martin dropped by with something very odd. Have a look.' She reached for a paper on her desk.

'In a minute,' said Skinner. 'Come with me first. I had a thought this afternoon.' He swept from the room and she followed him, across the foyer, down the changing-room corridor, past PC Pye, who was guarding the door to the murder scene . . . and who returned Skinner's nod with a smart salute . . . and out on to the course.

He looked across the first tee. 'Our main theory, with no likely killer on the premises, is that somebody walked in, zapped the victim in his Jacuzzi, then walked out again without anyone seeing him. That, incidentally, does not rule out Morton. You know the old saying, "If a job's worth doing, it's worth getting a man to do it well."

'But if that happened, there's no way that the murderer just casually walked into the clubhouse and did the business. Unless this was a random thing, with someone prepared to kill for a few quid and a watch, he watched White and he waited.

White's Jacuzzi routine was well known. It was a fair certainty that he would take his ritual tub after the match.

'So let's assume that our killer is well planned. He knows about the Sunday bounce game. He watches them arrive. He sees that White, who is the only one who hasn't stayed overnight at Bracklands, is the only one who isn't changed and ready to play. He waits and from a safe distance he watches them tee off. Then he moves closer. He doesn't want to wait in the Jacuzzi for three hours. Too risky. So he hides somewhere else, somewhere close to the clubhouse. Somewhere that won't be in use.'

As he spoke he began to walk, down the teeing ground, to the brick-built, white-clad, starter's hut which was positioned on the left of the big square area of tight-mown grass. 'Like here, for example. The course isn't open for general play yet. There are only three pros here, and no more golf after they and the VIPs have gone out.'

He looked down at Higgins. 'You agree so far?'

'Yes sir.' Excitement gripped her voice.

'Right. Then suppose, once the three games are well in play, our man slips into the hut. He waits here until he sees the first game finish. It's White and Cortes. Our man picks his moment and slips inside, to wait behind the door of White's Jacuzzi and to drop him the moment he walks in.'

He led Higgins round to the door of the hut, which was out of sight of the clubhouse. It had only one lock, a Yale, and an L-shaped brass handle. He took the handkerchief from the breast pocket of his jacket, and very carefully, holding it by its tip, turned it downwards. The door swung open. 'Not even locked,' he muttered. 'Ali, from the look of it, the technicians haven't touched this place. I suggest that you get on to Edinburgh and get them back down here now. By 9 a.m. tomorrow, you'll need to have every last inch of it covered, and every fingerprint lifted. It's an official practice day for the pros tomorrow, and the public will be allowed in, so this thing will be in use.'

She looked up at him. 'I should have worked all that out sir, shouldn't I?'

He smiled. 'Don't think that, Superintendent. I've been at this game longer than you. Anyway, it's probably just another wild Skinner theory!

'Here. Use this to call in.' He handed her his mobile phone. 'When I'm running an investigation, Ali, I always try to get a grasp of the whole picture as early as I can. Sometimes, if the picture's a bit grey, I have to colour it in myself. I only learned to do that through experience . . . which is what I'm giving you on this enquiry.'

He waited as she made her call. 'Right, what about this paper of Andy's?'

Higgins led the way back through to the boardroom. She picked up the paper for which she had reached earlier, and handed it to Skinner. It was enclosed in a clear plastic slip.

It was a single piece of blue A5 writing paper. It bore that day's date, but no address. Its message was scrawled in black fountain ink. Skinner read aloud:

> *Dear Editor,*
> *'By the blade . . .' said Agnes.*
> *Thus it was.*

'What the hell's this?' he muttered.

'Local loonies, probably,' said Higgins. 'Or it may not be connected at all.'

Skinner shook his head. 'Funny. It rings a bell somewhere. Alison, have someone make me a copy of this, before you send it off to forensics. I want to give it some thought, and maybe the bell'll ring a little louder.'

Twelve

They crested the rise and looked westwards down the Forth estuary. The mild September evening was cloudless, and across the wide bay they could see Edinburgh and Leith bathed in sunshine. Further on, the two contrasting bridges stood out clearly, although they were around twenty miles distant.

'Beautiful, isn't it?' said Sarah. 'At times like this I wonder whether we were right to bother with the Edinburgh house at all.'

'Sure,' said Bob, laughing, 'then you go for a run one morning, maybe in a couple of months, or even days, and the weather's turned full circle, and the hailstones are whistling at you with a gale behind them. What d'you wonder then?'

They trudged along the dune path, Bob walking more slowly than usual, because of his burden, three-month-old Jazz, secured in the carry-frame which was strapped to his chest. The baby had been lively when they had left the cottage a quarter of an hour before, but the movement and the fresh air had soon taken effect. Now he was asleep, with Bob holding him steady and picking his steps carefully. Jazz was growing at an alarming rate. The dark birth hair had gone, to be replaced by blond, wispy strands which flicked down towards his forehead. His father smiled as he made a burbling sound in his sleep. 'Dreaming of his next feed already, the wee bugger!'

'Don't remind me,' said Sarah, with genuine feeling. 'That boy is going to be huge, I can tell it already!'

'Must be the Yank half. When're you going to try him with his first Big Mac?'

'Never! Our child will have a proper diet. Junk food will be banned! And you'll have to set him an example. Fruit, fibre, fish, some lean meat on occasion, but not to excess. Sarah's F-plan.'

'But I like Big Macs and Burger Kings . . . and I know what that "F" stands for!'

'Skinner! I don't do that . . . not out loud anyway.'

'Not awake, maybe, but in your sleep, Christ!'

'Bob!'

'See when you were pregnant? When you were asleep you could raise the quilt three inches off the bed! It's difficult to make double-glazed window units rattle, but honey, you managed it!'

Her cheeks were flushed from more than the exertion of the walk. 'That's not true!'

'Oh no? Well next time you get up the duff you can stay awake and listen!'

'Enough,' she shouted, suppressing her laugh, 'of the police station talk!'

'Shh!' He held a finger to his lips. 'You'll wake the bairn. But here, how did you know we talked about you in the nick?'

'Bob!!' She gasped, and then the laughter exploded from them both, only to be silenced by an extra loud burble from Jazz.

They left the dune path and turned to walk along the beach, heading eastwards back towards Gullane. The tide was going out, so they chose to take the firm wet sand. The evening was still as well as clear. 'Can you hear that throbbing noise?' Sarah asked.

Bob pointed out across the Forth, towards a distant tanker which was making its way up the estuary, empty and riding high in the water. 'See that? You're hearing its engines.'

'From this far away?'

'Sure. The sound carries for ever across the water.'

Eventually they headed away from the sea, back through the dunes and up the steep path which led towards the tourists' car park. Sarah noticed that Bob had fallen silent. 'Hey, are you both asleep?'

'What? Oh sorry, love, I was miles away. Thinking about something I brought home. It may relate to the investigation. Andy phoned me about it.'

'Andy! He called you?'

'Yes.'

He sensed her expectancy. 'Don't worry, it was OK. We're going to have a man-to-man session, sort things out.'

'That's great!' Then her tone changed. She sounded hurt. 'You might have said earlier. You make me feel left out.'

He grinned awkwardly. 'Sorry, love. But you went on so strong about taking Rover here for a walk that I didn't have a chance. Anyway, I wondered whether you had talked him into finding an excuse to call me when you saw him yesterday.'

'Not me. Not consciously anyway. You really were OK, the two of you?'

He nodded. 'Yes. I feel such a prat about the whole thing now.'

She punched his arm gently as they walked along the tarmac road. 'I'll let you into a secret. So does Andy.'

'Yeah,' said Bob, suddenly sombre. 'That just leaves Alex. I wonder how she feels?'

She took his hand. 'Time will tell, my love. Only, when it does, I think you'll both have to accept the answer . . . whatever it is. She may be your daughter, she may – or may not – be Andy's girl, but sure as hell, she's her own woman.'

Eventually they emerged from the narrow lane which led from the beach road to their cottage. Jazz was snickering and smiling in his sleep, as if he knew that his bathtime and evening feed were imminent. As soon as Bob stepped through the front door he woke, bright and alert. He beamed as his father undid his fastenings, and lifted him out of the carry-frame, to hand him over to Sarah.

'OK, young man, let's attend to your needs.'

While Sarah bathed and fed the cheerful child, Bob busied himself in the kitchen with drill, hammer and rawlplugs, fixing, securely at last, the shaky shelf which had been a talking point for years. Then he began to prepare their evening meal, slicing the vegetables and fresh white fish which were to be the ingredients of their stir-fry. As he worked, he heard a sound outside the back door; looking over his shoulder he saw a familiar visitor: a huge cat, with black coat, white chest and paw, and right ear torn by many territorial disputes. They had christened him Rag, although they knew from his sleek, healthy coat, and his red collar, with its green magnetic key attached, that somewhere he had another name, and another family.

Bob trimmed the skin from a piece of fish and put it on a plate with some scraps. He opened the door and laid it in front of the purring cat. 'There, fella. I'll bet you smelled that from the other side of the Green. That's your lot for tonight, though. Maybe there'll be fish at home as well.'

When he closed the door behind him Sarah was in the kitchen, at work with the wok.

They ate at the glass table in their conservatory, enjoying the last warmth of the evening sun, and washing down their stir-fry and noodles with a bottle of Frascati, complementary to the lemon grass which was an essential ingredient of the dish. Jazz was on the floor between them strapped, nappy-less, into a plastic chair, and gnawing happily on a teething ring. In the garden outside, the black-and-white cat watched them reproachfully through the glass. When they were finished, Bob cleared away the dishes and brought a steaming cafetière. While Sarah depressed the plunger, Bob left the room once more, returning with the plastic-enclosed letter to the editor of the *Scotsman*.

'This is Andy's note,' he said, handing it across the table. Sarah took it, and as she read, her forehead wrinkled and a puzzled look came into her eyes.

'Cranks,' she said, as Jazz began to signal his readiness for his last feed of the day. She handed the letter back across the table, then took the baby from his chair. Cradling him in her right arm, she pulled up her sweatshirt and presented him with the object of his earnest desire.

Bob looked again at the letter. 'You're probably right. It's just that there's something about it that won't go away.'

'*By the blade . . .*' said Sarah. 'Sounds sort of witchy, doesn't it?'

He stared out of the window at the red sunset sky. 'Wait a minute,' he said, but to himself. When he turned back to face her, the look on his face was one that she had seen before, a look of recollection, but mixed with something else, something which, in anyone else, she would have taken for apprehension. 'Back in a minute.'

When he emerged from the hall Sarah had carried Jazz into the living room. They were seated in a corner of the long sofa, the child still feeding, but cradled now in his mother's left arm. Bob sat down beside them. His expression had changed. It was wistful. Sarah glanced at the dusty folder which he carried and knew the reason at once.

The cover bore the title, hand-printed, 'East Lothian Project,' and the name, 'Myra Skinner, Primary VI, Longniddry Primary School.'

'Not long before Myra was killed,' he said, softly, 'the school researched a history of East Lothian. It was a project for the Queen's Silver Jubilee, I think. The teachers and kids all pitched in and each class did a different period. Myra's lot drew the sixteenth and seventeenth centuries. Eventually the whole thing was typed up and published, but these are Myra's notes and tapes. I found them in a cupboard after she died. I was going to give them to the school, but I never got round to it. They've been up in the attic for the last fifteen years.

'I remember one tape she played me at the time. It was a wee girl telling a family story, and it was something else. Let me see if I can find it.' He opened the folder. There were two tape cassettes inside in plastic boxes, labelled 'Children's Stories', in a firm hand.

Bob carried them across to the mini hi-fi unit which had replaced the equipment moved up to the Edinburgh house. He used his headphones, cutting off the sound from the speakers as, head bowed and hunched over the machine with his back to Sarah, he reviewed the tapes. After ten minutes, on the second tape, he found the section for which he had been listening. He straightened up and unplugged the headphones. 'This is it.'

He pressed the play button. There was a hiss for a second or two, then a woman's firm, clear voice filled the room. Her accent was as Sarah imagined Bob's might have been two decades earlier, before Edinburgh had begun to knock the hard edges from his Lanarkshire tones.

'OK, the red light's on, so we're recording. I'm in the staff-room, alone with Lisa Soutar, who's going to tell me a story for the Jubilee history project. Let me get this right, Lisa. You were told this story by your great-grandma?'

The child's voice was faint. 'Yes miss, by ma Nana Soutar.'

'Are you ready to begin?'

'Yes, miss.'

'Right, just step a wee bit closer and speak into the mike. On you go now.'

There was a pause, and then the child spoke again, her thin reedy voice much clearer than before.

'Well miss, in the olden days, there were these witches in Longniddry, and they worshipped the Devil, and did harm to people, and cast spells, and put a curse on the King's ship and he wis nearly drowned.' She paused for breath.

'Well one day, the minister and the laird, they rounded up a' the witches, ken. And they took them a' to Witchy Hill . . .'

'Do you know where that is?'

'Aye miss, it's up by Aberlady . . . they took them a' tae Witchy Hill and they tied them tae trees, and they piled wood a' around, ken. Well, the head witch was called Aggie. They were just goin' tae light the fires when Aggie said . . .'

The child's voice rose and changed. It became shrill and strangely menacing. Sarah, listening almost twenty years later, felt a shudder go through her.

"This is oor master's place, not yours. This is the Devil's kirk, not God's. What you are doing is des-ec-ra-shun!" It was as if the child's voice was no longer hers. It had risen to a shriek. *"You can burn my body but you will not dissolve my spirit. I will always be here. I curse you all and all others who desecrate this place. Here is your doom:*

> *by the blade,*
> *by water,*
> *by fire*
> *and by lightning*
> *shall the desecrators be destroyed."'*

A silence filled the living room, broken only by the background hiss of the tape. And then the adult spoke again, breathlessly.

'And what happened then?'

'Oh they lit the fires, miss, and a' the witches wis burned tae ashes!'

'And what happened to the desecrators?'

'A dinna ken, miss, ma nana never said.'

Bob stepped over and switched off the tape. Sarah saw that his face was pale. 'I take it that the other voice was . . .' He cut her off with a nod. 'Does it make you feel strange, hearing her speak again after all this time?'

He shook his head. 'Sarah, honey, I heard her voice every night in my head, for about ten years afterwards, whenever I settled down to sleep. But gradually it faded away. I loved her very much, but she's been gone for a long time. I can cope with it.

'But I must give those tapes to Alex. Would have done a long time ago, if I hadn't pushed them to the back of my mind.'

'Apart from the accent, Alex sounds just like her.'

'Yeah, and looks like her too. She's just past the age Myra was when we first met.'

'Her mother would be proud of Alex,' said Sarah.

His laugh had an ironic tone. 'Aye, even if she does have a law degree! Myra had very clear views about what should be done with lawyers. Her father was one. He left her mother with three kids and used the law to get out of paying decent support. Right now, Alex probably feels the same way about policemen.'

He paused. 'But enough of the recent past. What did you think of the kid?'

'Spine-chilling.'

'It fairly ties up with Andy's letter, doesn't it? I wonder what Miss Lisa Soutar's doing now. I think we'd better find out.

Meantime, let's see what the *Scotsman* does with that letter tomorrow; let's see what sort of a hornets' nest it stirs up.'

He sat down on the couch beside Sarah and Jazz, who was asleep once more. She put a hand on his thigh. 'It's a great story, but is it any more than an old wives' tale? Shouldn't you research it?'

He thought for a moment. 'You're right. I probably should. I think I'll put Maggie on to it. She's got an arts degree, and I know the very man who might help her too.'

'Who's that?'

'Henry. Henry Wills, at the University.'

'But he's the Registrar.'

'That doesn't stop him from having been a lecturer in Scots history! Yes, I'll brief Maggie tomorrow.'

She smiled. 'That's tomorrow, but for now you've got another task.'

'Whassat?'

'To take this guy from off my chest and get a nappy on his ass . . . without waking him up and having me start all over again!'

'And after that?' It was a loaded question.

She smiled. 'Yeah, OK. I'll let you watch *News At Ten*!'

Tuesday

Tuesday

Thirteen

'You're an early bird, Skinner. Trying to catch your people on the hop?'

The Marquis of Kinture sat stiffly upright in a green leather captain's chair, which had been positioned in the bay window of the boardroom to provide a clear view of the eighteenth green. The morning sun shone strongly into the room, glinting off the metal frame of the wheelchair which sat empty alongside the newly installed throne. He was dressed immaculately, in a tailored pale blue blazer and grey slacks with knife-edge creases. There was a badge on the blazer's breast pocket, a heraldic crest which Skinner guessed was the emblem of the new club. The Marquis seemed in high humour, and the policeman noted that on this occasion at least he had chosen to recognise him without preamble.

He returned the smile. 'I'd need to be up earlier than this, sir, to surprise my troops in a murder investigation.' He walked slowly down the room. 'No, I called in to make sure that our technicians had finished their work in the starter's hut.'

The twin crests of wiry grey hair above Kinture's temples rose with surprise, like wings on an ancient helmet. 'The hut? What the devil would they want there?'

'It's just something we needed to cover. It's possible that the man we're after hid in there until Michael had finished his round, so we've had our forensic people lifting fingerprints and other traces . . . fibres and fag-ends, that sort of thing.'

'And have they finished?'

Skinner nodded. 'Yes, the starter can have his hut back. We'll take his prints when he turns up, for elimination purposes. We're looking for matches between prints found in the hut and those which we've lifted from the Jacuzzi cubicle. If we're really lucky they'll tie up quickly with criminal records, and we'll have ourselves a suspect.'

'What'll you have to do if you're unlucky?' asked the Marquis.

'Then we'll have to put a name to every set of prints, in the hut and in the changing room and bathroom. That'll mean interviewing and fingerprinting builders, joiners, plumbers and painters, every bugger who worked on the clubhouse contract, just to rule them out. Eventually we should be left with just one unidentified set . . . if our man was in the hut, that is. It'll be a tedious job, but that's police work for you. Endless preoccupation with detail.'

Kinture used his upper body to swivel the chair towards the window. 'Know what you mean. When I was a youngster, I was a merchant banker. I used to dream of the day when my pa would snuff it, and I could escape from that refined form of boredom to run this place.'

Skinner looked at him in surprise.

'Shock you does it,' said Kinture, 'anticipating one's old man's demise? Fact is, I couldn't stand him when I was young. Felt he ignored me, except when he was making all my decisions for me. Where I'd work, whom I'd marry . . . my first marriage, that was.'

'You've been married twice?'

'Mmm. Susan came on the scene after my divorce. She and I met at a golf tournament, and we were happy as Larry until Pa finally snuffed it and I inherited the estate, and found out about the work and worries that go with it. No wonder the poor old bugger seemed remote. I was just getting to grips with everything when I had the accident. I inherited this thing as well . . .' he tapped the wheelchair, '. . . and became the cantankerous bastard I am today. Poor Sue, I really do give her a hard time sometimes, and do sod all to make amends . . .' His voice tailed off, and for a time, he stared out of the window in silence.

Then suddenly he swivelled the chair round once more, awkwardly, to face Skinner. 'But enough of this whingeing,' he said loudly.

'What d'you think of the new togs, then? This is my President's blazer. That's what I am, you know, as if I didn't have enough bloody titles. His Excellency the President of the Witches' Hill Golf and Country Club. Complete with uniform, just like you.'

'Rather yours than mine,' said Skinner with a grin.

'Mickey's idea, that we should have blazers,' said the Marquis. 'He would have been wearing his today, too. He decided we should pinch the idea from Augusta. The winner of the Murano Million will be presented with one of these, immediately after the tournament, and he'll be the first honorary member of the club.'

'Who chose the colour?' asked Skinner.

'Susan picked it. Quite nice, don't you think?'

'Sure. Very tasteful.'

'I know what you're thinking, Skinner. "Pretentious bastards!" And you're probably right. But it's just a bit of rich men's fun.'

The policeman laughed. 'Sir, I wouldn't think that badly of you. I think it's a nice idea, and I'm sure that this week's winner will wear it well.'

For an instant, the Marquis looked embarrassed by the compliment. 'Let's hope so.' He smiled hesitantly.

'Talking about winners, indirectly; I'm glad you dropped in, saved me a phone call. Look, the thing is, Mickey's death has left a hole in this week's field. I called Myrtle White last night, and asked her if she would nominate a substitute. She suggested you; said that Mickey had mentioned that he had enjoyed his game with you.

'So, how about it. Would you like to join our pro-am field?'

Skinner was taken completely by surprise. 'It'd be an honour. I have no unbreakable engagements this week, so I'd be very pleased. Thank you, sir, very much. I must call Myrtle, to thank her too.'

'Good, that's settled. I've got you a caddy too, if you'll have her. Susan was going to caddy for Mickey, and she's desperate to do the same for you.'

'Again, sir, that'll be an honour!'

'Fine, I'll tell her. What's your club, by the way?'

'I'm a member of Gullane, and of Pals, in Spain.'

'Damn fine courses. O'Malley said that he tried to make Witches' Hill reminiscent of Pals.'

'In that case, he succeeded. Those holes around the turn with the tight tree-lined fairways are bloody good likenesses.'

The Marquis looked wistful. 'Yes, aren't they. Oh, if only . . .' He slapped the wheelchair in frustration. 'What's your handicap?'

'Seven at Gullane. I've been five, but I've been putting like a gorilla for the last couple of years.'

'You'll be a bandit round Pals, off a Gullane seven handicap.'

Skinner grinned. 'That has been suggested!'

'Need to be on your game this week, though. You're in Darren's team.'

'Jesus! Then I'd better get some time in on the practice ground.'

'Hmm. And on the putting green, from what you say. Tell you what, let's check outside and see if Darren's about. Might as well introduce you, if there's a chance.'

The Marquis swivelled the captain's chair slightly, until it lay virtually parallel to the wheelchair, and reached under to operate a locking lever. He reached sideways and grasped both arms of the wheelchair. Automatically, Skinner stepped forward to help. 'No, no!' Kinture barked. 'Thank you, but I can manage.' With the tremendous upper-body strength of the paraplegic he raised himself up at an odd angle on his forearms, and swung himself across. 'Got to be able to do that y'see, otherwise I'd feel really helpless. Come on.'

He rolled out of the boardroom, with Skinner following behind, noticing for the first time that the doors of Witches' Hill were all slightly wider than normal. He wondered idly to himself whether he was in the world's first barrier-free golf clubhouse.

They made their way along the corridor leading to the course. Halfway along, the Marquis pushed open the door of the main changing room. 'Atkinson!' he bellowed.

'Not here,' came a muffled voice from inside. They made their way outside. A group of three men was gathered on the edge of the practice putting green, around a huge white golf-bag standing upright. The trio were in earnest conversation.

'Ah, there he is. Atkinson, hello there.' All three looked across, two in surprise. The third showed a trace of annoyance in his expression, but it vanished at once as he recognised the Marquis. He walked across towards them with a smile. 'Good morning, sir. Good to see you here. You've done a magnificent job with the course, by the looks of it.'

Skinner felt as if he was renewing an old acquaintance, since, like millions he knew Atkinson vicariously from countless press and TV stories, from the occasional visit to an Open Championship, and most recently from the satellite coverage of the US Open, which he had won by four shots.

The Marquis was pleased by the champion's compliment. 'Thanks, old chap. High praise, from you. Let's see how tough you find it, though.'

He looked up at Skinner. 'Darren, let me introduce your new team member. Assistant Chief Constable Skinner, our local crime-buster. A seven handicap.'

'Welcome to the team, Mr Skinner.'

'The name's Bob.'

The world's top golfer was just over six feet tall, perhaps an inch shorter than Skinner, but his huge hand seemed to swallow the policeman's as they shook. He had wide shoulders and blacksmith forearms, but the tight cut of his designer shirt emphasised the slimness of his waist, while comfortably cut trousers hid the thickness of his thighs. He had weather-bleached hair and the yellowish tan of a man who plied his trade in summer conditions all year round. Inevitably, his eyes were wrinkled from peering down a thousand sun-baked fair-ways. In his mid-thirties, Darren Atkinson looked supremely fit, and supremely confident, a human being at the height of his powers.

He eyed Skinner up and down, appraising him. 'Seven, eh. Any pro-am experience?'

'Never played one in my life. And I'm seven and climbing, I'm afraid.'

Atkinson smiled. 'Let's see if we can do something about that before Thursday morning. I'm having a team meeting on the practice range at six-thirty this evening. Then we're on the tee tomorrow at one-thirty for a public practice round. Can you make those times?'

'I'll make a point of it. Who are the other guys in the team?'

'There's one of the Murano guys – the son and heir, I think – and Norton Wales, the little singer chap. You'll be the leading amateur in that group. I've played with Norton at Wentworth. He said he was off twenty-two, but he was kidding himself.'

'What's the format?'

'Best-ball medal play. Amateurs get full handicap allowance.'

'With four of us, the rounds could be fairly long.'

Atkinson shook his head. 'Shouldn't be too bad. The high handicappers pick up if they're out of contention on any hole.' He laughed. 'Don't see old Norton having too many putts, unless he's improved a lot since last time.'

Skinner winced. 'You could see me having quite a few, way I've been putting lately!'

'Hah! That's why it's seven and climbing, is it? Well that's what you'll practice most for the next two days.' He looked over his shoulder. 'Must go, I'm on the tee. I'm taking some money off young Mr Urquhart this morning. I'll see you tonight then, Bob. And bring that putter!'

Fourteen

'Where's today's *Scotsman*, Maggie?' Skinner peered over the pile of correspondence on his desk.

'It's in Ruth's office, sir.' Without being asked she rose from her seat and left the room to fetch the newspaper.

'That's an odd story about the murder on the front page, sir,' she said, returning to hand the broadsheet across the desk. 'It's unusual for the *Scotsman* to give credence to an anonymous letter.'

He glanced at the front page. 'Yes, but look how they're reporting it.

' "*Police were studying a mysterious unsigned letter handed in to the* Scotsman *office yesterday, to establish whether it might be linked to Sunday's murder of Edinburgh millionaire Michael White, at the luxury Witches' Hill Golf Club, where the world's richest golf event begins on Thursday.*"

'It goes on to say that the phrase may have connotations in witchcraft, but that no one yesterday could pin it down. Based on that they leap to the conclusion that there may be a coven active in the area today.'

Rose looked at him, puzzled. 'All a bit tenuous, isn't it, sir?'

He grinned. 'So you might say, but it lets the editor put an "exclusive" tag on her story, and it's colourful enough to tempt every other newspaper in the land into following it up. And with the *Scotsman* holding the only copy of the letter in circulation, apart from the original, it's a real feather in their cap.'

The grin widened still further. 'Anyway, it isn't as tenuous as you think!'

The Inspector was intrigued. 'What d'you mean?'

Skinner reached behind him, into the pocket of his jacket, which was hung over the back of his chair, and took out a tape cassette, in its clear plastic box. 'Wait till you hear this,' he said. 'It's a copy of something that's been lying in my attic for nearly twenty years.' He explained the origins of the cassette, then reached into his briefcase, and took out the original of the *Scotsman* letter.

'I'd like to know more about this story. The child on this tape says that the story was told to her by her great-grand-mother. But where did she get it from? Is it commonplace? Is it documented at all? Is it just a local legend, or does it have any historical basis?

'You see, Mags, while it's probable that this letter is just the work of a crank,' he waved the single sheet in the air as he spoke, 'there is just an outside chance that it's a confession of murder.

'So here's your chance to do some real detective work. The *Scotsman* experts couldn't come up with anything, but they didn't have this tape. Let's see if you can do better. I want you to make an appointment at Edinburgh University to see Henry Wills, the Registrar. He's a good friend of ours, and a historian into the bargain. When he was teaching, his speciality was Scottish History. You play that tape to Henry, and see if it excites him.

'And once you've done that, perhaps you'd better check on the present whereabouts of the grown-up Lisa Soutar.'

Fifteen

Suddenly Skinner realised that everyone was looking at him. He disguised his discomfiture behind a cough, and gathered his concentration together once more. His hands, which had been miming the shape of his putting grip slapped down on to the table.

'Sorry, Constable. I didn't realise you had finished. That's all you have to say to the Board, is it?'

The square-shouldered young man, sitting bolt upright in the chair opposite him, nodded his close-cropped head. Skinner looked left along the table, then right. 'Any other points?' he asked his four companions.

'No?' He looked back at the Constable. 'In that case, thank you for your attendance, PC Harris. You will be advised in writing of the outcome.'

The young officer rose, replaced his uniform cap, and saluted smartly before turning on his heel and marching from the room.

Skinner had no time for the formality of the Interview Boards which were part of the process of determining fitness for promotion. For one thing, it obliged him to wear uniform which, secretly, he hated. For another, he would have opted for a more relaxed approach, to contribute towards more analytical discussion with the applicants. Ultimately, he would have preferred to rely on his own judgement of a police officer's capability to cope with higher rank. But the system was entrenched, with observers from the Police Board and Police Federation among those entitled to attend, and he knew that he would have to live with it, and its imperfections, at least until he was in a position to do something about it.

He glanced again at the two officers nearest to him, on either side. They were the voting members of the Board. One was a Superintendent, and the other a woman Chief Inspector. 'Have you completed your assessment forms?' he asked.

'Yes sir.' The answers came simultaneously.

'Right, the next applicant is WPC Polly Masters. She was a lateish entrant to the service, after working in marketing for a while. Now aged thirty-four, she's done very well in the written part of the process. I note that she served in Dalkeith for three years, until she was transferred six weeks ago to the Press Office. I have to confess that I haven't met her as yet, but Alan Royston sent me a private note commending her. For all that, her experience is weak without a stint in CID.'

He checked along the table. 'Everyone ready? Right, let's have her in.' He pressed the green button on the panel by his right hand. A few seconds later the door opened, and a small woman entered, immaculate in a Constable's uniform. She sat down on Skinner's nod, and took off her cap, revealing short, well-groomed dark hair. Huge brown eyes looked nervously, but smiling, along the five Board members, finally coming to rest on Skinner with a directness which, a few years before and out of uniform, might have caught his attention in more ways than one.

His uniform belt dug uncomfortably into his ribs, and cut

off the smile which was twitching at the corners of his mouth. 'Right, WPC Masters . . .'

Three hours and seven applicants later, Skinner, thoroughly irritable, hung up his uniform on a hook in the small changing room attached to his office. The face of the little WPC was still fresh in his mind. He found her annoying in a strange way, but could not work out why. She had passed her promotion examination with flying colours, but Skinner made a mental note to transfer her from the Press Office to CID, and out of headquarters, at the first opportunity.

He slipped on his jacket and glanced at his watch. It was three-fifteen; another hour of paperwork lay before him before he could beat an early retreat to prepare himself for his appointment on the practice ground with Darren Atkinson. He stepped out of the changing room to find Brian Mackie standing in his office. The Chief Inspector held several sheets of fax paper in his hand.

'Hi, Brian,' said Skinner. 'What's up?'

'A message from South Africa, boss. They want us to pass some dodgy news on to someone.' He waved the fax pages.

The ACC frowned. 'Oh? Who is it?'

'It's one of the golfers in the big tournament, sir. The young chap, Oliver M'tebe. Apparently someone's kidnapped his father. They don't know whether he's dead or alive.'

'What does the message tell you about the background? Is it a gangland thing, or what?'

Mackie shook his dome-like head. 'No, sir. That's the odd thing. The South African police say they don't understand it at all. M'tebe senior is a Presbyterian minister. He's very popular, does lots of work for poor black families, doesn't upset people by getting involved in politics, so apart from his son being famous he doesn't have a high profile at all. Just not the sort of chap to get into trouble.

'Yet, apparently he left home this morning for a meeting with some elders in his church. Didn't turn up, and he hasn't been seen since. His car was found forced off the road along the route. One eye-witness, a parishioner, claims that he saw the minister being bundled into a Land Rover by two men, both white. He said that he looked bewildered, as if he didn't know what was going on.'

'Sounds like a real mystery, doesn't it? I take it that the South Africans want us to ask the son whether he can suggest a motive for his father being snatched.'

'Mmm, that's right.'

Skinner raised an eyebrow. 'Could be that the kidnappers are after a ransom from the son? Any communication from them at all?' Mackie shook his head.

'OK. I'm heading out that way. Get me a copy of that message and I'll take care of it. Gives me an excuse.' He pointed at the pile of correspondence on his desk. 'I've seen enough of that stuff for now. On days like this I feel like a paper-pusher, not a copper!'

Sixteen

'It is a pleasure to meet you, Miss Rose. You are clearly on a path to glory!'

Henry Wills's small brown eyes twinkled as he shook the Detective Inspector's hand. She looked at him, curiously.

He explained. 'The first time I ever met Andrew Martin he had just left the post which you now occupy, as ADC to my friend Bob. He made the jump to Special Branch at an early age, and, of course, he's moved up the ladder since then. After Andy, Brian Mackie followed the same route. So obviously, one will have great expectations of you.'

Maggie looked at him, sceptically.

Wills raised his hands in mock horror. 'Detective Inspector, please don't think that I'm being patronising. I mean every word quite sincerely. I have all the time in the world for Andy and Brian. As for Bob Skinner, why I've known him since I've been in this post, and I know that he chooses his personal assistants with the greatest care.'

Rose smiled, at last. 'In that case, thank you for your kind words. I hope I can live up to them.'

'There's no doubt of that.'

Wills paused. 'Speaking of Andy, how is he? I mean personally, rather than professionally.'

'Fine, as far as I know,' Rose answered, non-committally.

'Good. It's just that I haven't heard from him since he came to see me, a couple of months ago, to give me back the keys to my place in Florida. Poor chap was terribly depressed. He didn't give me all the details, but it was clear that something had gone disastrously wrong between him and Alex.'

Maggie felt her stomach drop. Had Wills been looking at her he would have seen a sudden expression of uncontrolled astonishment sweep across her face, until she recovered herself.

'You know, when they came to ask if they could rent the place for a couple of weeks, I couldn't have been more pleased for them. I'd only met Alex once before, when she did that Festival thing last year, but she struck me as a very dynamic young lady – her father's daughter all right. For all that there must be at least ten years between them, she and Andrew seemed perfect together. They couldn't have been happier. Alex said they were going to surprise Bob with their news. She asked me to keep our arrangement to myself, for a while.'

'Twelve years,' said Rose, quietly.

'Pardon?'

'There's twelve years between them in age. Alex is twenty-one.'

'Is she? Well, no matter. They seemed as well suited, as my mother would have said, as Sarah and Bob. That's what made it such a shock when it went wrong. All that Andy said was that they had had a row, and that Alex had gone off on some sort of tour of Europe. But for it to have happened on the day they were due to leave, it must have been pretty catastrophic. No wonder the chap jumped at the chance of getting out of Edinburgh for a while. Bob must be pretty sad too.'

'You know Mr Skinner,' said Rose. 'He keeps things pretty tight.'

'*Yes*,' thought Henry Wills. '*And so do you. Bob has chosen well*.'

Aloud he said, 'Well anyway, let's just keep our fingers crossed. Now to the business of the day. Which of our radical foreign students is in trouble this time?'

Maggie smiled, more in relief at the change of subject, than at Wills's ironic question. 'None that I know of, sir. That's DCI Mackie's province. No, this is more of an academic matter. Mr Skinner thought you might be able to help us, since I gather it's your field.'

'Intriguing. Most people forget that I was a pure academic before I lost myself in this administrative jungle! So what is it?'

She put her briefcase on Wills's desk, which seemed huge in the small, dusty office, at the upper rear of the Old College Building. Taking care not to scratch the surface with the sharp metal studs on the base, she opened it and took out a folder of papers, and the tape cassette box.

'First of all,' she said, 'I take it that you've read about the murder of Michael White.'

He nodded vigorously. 'Yes. Damn shame. Quite a benefactor of this University, in a quiet way.'

'And have you read today's *Scotsman*?'

'No, not yet. I have a frightful confession, Miss Rose. I'm a *Guardian* man.'

'OK.' She took a copy of the newspaper from her folder and passed it across the desk. 'Read the front-page story, please.'

As Wills read his expression changed from puzzlement to intrigue. 'How strange,' he said, putting the paper down on the desk. Rose passed him a copy of the original scrawled letter. He studied it closely for more than a minute, his excitement growing visibly.

'It looks like a line from the old Witch's Curse.'

'What's that?'

'It's part of the East of Scotland folklore from the time of the persecution, around the sixteenth and seventeenth centuries. None of that stuff was ever properly documented, and not just because illiteracy was the order of the day. The people who led the witch-finding did it to divert people's attention away from the real evils of poverty, servitude, and the local laird having power of life and death over ordinary folk. The witch-burnings were no more than lynchings. They had little basis in law even in those days, so no one involved wanted to be tied too closely to them.

'Most of the stories survived only by word of mouth, until they were written down decades, sometimes centuries, after the event, invariably in garbled form.'

He paused. 'The Witch's Curse relates to the burning of one Agnes Tod, spelt with one "d", in East Lothian in the late sixteenth century. The Marquis of Kinture claims to own the site of the burning. I understand he's built his new golf course around it.

'As far as I know, the curse has only ever appeared once in written form, in a mid-nineteenth-century history of Haddingtonshire. It said that Agnes Tod, as the flames were lit, cursed all there with blade, water and fire, and that since then the hill on which she and her coven are said to have met, and where they were burned, has been a place of strange happenings.

'Not history at all really, that stuff, just legend and superstition.'

Maggie Rose produced a small Walkman-style cassette player from her jacket.

'In that case sir, listen to this tape. It was made in 1977. The teacher you'll hear is Mr Skinner's first wife. It's been stored in his loft ever since.'

Wills frowned, but took the player from her. She watched him as he put on the headphones, inserted the tape, and pushed the play button. She watched him as his eyes widened, and his mouth dropped open. She heard the indecipherable hiss of sound escaping from the earpieces, and she heard its sudden stop. Wills blinked and rewound it, then played it once more. Eventually he took off the headset.

'That is amazing,' he whispered. 'What was the child's name again?'

'Lisa Soutar.'

'Then she's a Teller.' Rose looked at him, puzzled.

'There are old legends,' he explained, 'which are handed down within families. They are passed on through the female line by word of mouth, skipping generations where necessary. The bearers are called "Tellers of Tales". If Lisa Soutar was told this story by her great-grandmother, then I think you'll find that in her family she was the first girl of the line for three generations.

'That story has never been set down in full before. It's so pure. Did you hear the child's voice? It's as if she was hypnotised by her great-grandmother, and the story implanted in her mind. Maybe she was! Maybe they can do that, these "Tellers of Tales".'

'Is it possible,' said Maggie, 'that the child could have built the story up herself? Could she have seen the earlier account?'

Wills shook his head. 'Not a chance. There's only one copy,

and it's in the National Library of Scotland, accessible only to academics.

'No, young Miss Lisa Soutar got this story straight from the horse's, or rather the old mare's mouth. D'you know what? If you dig into the parish records, you could, just possibly, trace the line of Tellers right back to the burning of Aggie Tod!'

Rose whistled, and shook her red locks. 'I may do just that! At least I know where to begin.'

'Well, here's another strange thing for you to ponder on,' said Wills. 'I remember that 1977 East Lothian history project. There were very few copies of the finished work. The schools involved kept one each, one went to the Queen, with a letter signed by all the children who took part, one went to the National Library, and one came to the University. I remember it; I read it. And I'm quite certain that tale didn't appear in it.

'Either Myra Skinner decided not to include it in the typed-up chapter which her class contributed to the book, or someone decided that it shouldn't be published!

'So there's yet another mystery for you, Inspector. Did someone want the Tale of Aggie Tod's curse to be suppressed?' He stood up. 'Now, Miss Rose, it's close on one. Can I tempt you to lunch?'

Maggie shook her head. 'That's very kind, but another time, perhaps. Right now, I must go back to school!'

Seventeen

There was a light knock at the door.

'Come in, Brian,' called Skinner. 'Is that photocopy ready?'

Mackie stepped into the room, slowly. 'Yes, boss, it is. But there's something else. You've got a visitor.'

Skinner frowned in exasperation. 'Can't you deal with it, Brian? I'll need to get moving if I'm to catch M'tebe.'

'Yes, but boss, I really thought you'd want to say hello. It's Mr Doherty of the FBI. He's waiting in Ruth's room.'

'Joe!' Skinner's face lit up. 'Christ, you should have brought him straight in. Joe's a VIP – Very Important Polisman!' He strode out of his office and round to Ruth McConnell's small room. 'Joe, my man! Too long a time. Welcome to Edinburgh!'

He beamed down at the slight figure of the American and shook his hand warmly. Doherty was around five feet nine inches tall, but the slimness of his build made him seem smaller. Caught between Skinner and his statuesque secretary he seemed almost tiny.

'Well, Bob,' he said, in a Midwestern drawl, 'you know damn well that this far north the cold gets into my poor bones any time after July, but there are some things that would tempt me out of doors. Like even a small chance of making life awkward for the guy you asked me about yesterday.'

'You've got something on him?'

126

'Goddamn yes!' Doherty's thin, lined, sallow face lit up with pride. He squared the shoulders of his Savile Row suit and stuck out his chin. 'If it's there, then the World's Finest Law Enforcement Agency'll find it.'

'Hah! Can't be too goddamn hot, if the World's Finest Law Enforcement Agency hasn't succeeded in locking him up for it.'

The smile left Doherty's face abruptly, and he winced. 'That's a sad story, Bob. Come and I'll tell you about it.'

'OK,' said Skinner, 'but let's think about this. You booked in anywhere?' He nodded at the overnight bag on the floor between them. Doherty shook his head. 'OK, you are now. My place.'

'Hey Bob, I can't let you do that.'

'Are you kidding? If my wife found that I'd let her fellow American put up in a hotel – even if he is a bloody spook – she'd kill me! Come on.' He led the way back through to his office, and telephoned Sarah. As she answered he could hear Jazz crying in the background. She sounded tired. 'Hello love,' he said. 'You OK?'

'Yeah, I'm fine. Motherhood gets to be a ball and chain from time to time, that's all.'

'In that case . . .' he hesitated '. . . here's something to lighten your life. D'you fancy having an American house guest this evening?'

'Of course, but who . . .'

'It's a guy named Joe. You'll like him. I'll bring him home now, then I'll have to go out for a while. I'm replacing poor Michael in the pro-am, and my team captain's called a practice session.'

Sarah, a keen golfer, perked up at once. 'Yes? That's terrific. Whose team you on?'

'Darren Atkinson's, that's all.'

'Darren? You're playing with him? My God, will Alex be sick when she hears! Darren is our hero. Can Jazz and I come as your cheerleaders?'

He laughed. 'Only if you can guarantee that the wee fella won't howl at the top of Darren's backswing! Look, Joe and I are heading off. We'll be with you soon.'

He replaced the phone and picked up his briefcase. Ruth and Doherty were standing just inside the door. 'Ruthie, I'll be in tomorrow morning by eight-thirty, until around midday, and I should be contactable after that. Thursday and Friday I'll keep in touch.'

Ruth's grin was slightly lopsided, Brian Mackie called it her 'Kim Basinger look'. 'Sir, as you said, you need to practise delegation. Enjoy yourself: you'll be fulfilling a million golfers' dreams.'

Skinner nodded, suddenly solemn. 'Sure. But I'll always be remembering that I've stepped into a dead man's golf shoes. Come on, Joe.'

He led the way downstairs and out of the building to where his white BMW was parked in its designated space. Doherty placed his overnight bag on the back seat and climbed in, holding a document case on his lap.

Rather than take the shortest route out of town, Skinner turned right as he exited from the headquarters building. 'Let's take a look at my old town, Joe.' The day was overcast but dry as he headed along towards Stockbridge, past Raeburn Place, where the recently re-erected rugby posts signified the coming of autumn, then climbed the hill towards the hogsback centre of the New Town. Turning into Charlotte Square he pointed along George Street towards St Andrew Square, a straight kilometre away. 'They call this part of town "The Dumbbell" because of its shape. Not so long ago, there were billions of pounds managed here. Insurance companies, banks and fund managers used to litter this area. Now most of them have moved out to new buildings, still in and around the city, but state-of-the-art, to let them count even more money. That's what we do now. We don't make *things* any more. We don't make steel, we don't dig coal, we don't build ships. We just count money, and serve teas to tourists. Oh sorry, I should have remembered. We make beer. We're very good at making beer.' He turned down Castle Street and left into Princes Street, resplendent in its Festival colours.

'I love this place, all year round, but there are times when I worry about where it's going. I mean look at this.' He waved his right hand in the air as he drove past the Royal Scottish Academy. 'All the flags, all the Festival handbills littering the street and fly-posted on empty shop windows: sometimes I think that Edinburgh's become just another bloody theme park, built around history and the Arts, rather than around cartoon characters.'

Doherty laughed at his friend's cynicism. 'OK, Bob, but so what? Theme parks make money; they give people work. Your city probably earns more foreign currency now than it did when it was building ships. And is there more crime now, or less?'

Skinner scowled sideways as he turned right, heading across the North Bridge and into the Old Town. 'Okay, our crime figures are down, but that's because of my people's good work.'

'Or because the nature of crime is changing,' Doherty interrupted. 'Remember the old saw that you can steal more with a fountain pen than with a gun? Well, you can steal even more with a computer, or with financial products where the company takes so much out in management fees that the poor suckers who buy them would be far better just putting their dough in the bank.'

Skinner shook his head. 'Not here you can't. Our money men are unimpeachable, and even if they weren't, this place is so much of a village that if anyone was up to naughties, word would get out soon enough.

'Ah, don't listen to me. I know that Edinburgh is one of the great cities in the world. It's just that I grew up in an industrial society, where men made tangible things. That's where my core values lie, in every way. The twenty-first-century version isn't a natural state of affairs for me. As I said to another friend yesterday, I'm Seventies Man – and I guess I always will be.'

Suddenly he laughed. 'In fact, if you asked my daughter, she'd tell you I'm set further back than that. She'd say that I'm in the same mould as the old bigot who lived in there!' He jerked his left thumb sideways. Doherty followed its direction and saw that they were cruising past the house of John Knox, Scotland's Reformation firebrand.

Skinner drove in silence for a while, down the narrowest part of the Royal Mile, towards the Palace of Holyroodhouse. He skirted the grey stone residence and cruised through Holyrood Park, round the crumbling Salisbury Crags and the Radical Road, past the reed-encircled Dunsapie Loch and out through Duddingston Village. As they picked up the eastward route once more, Skinner nodded down towards Doherty's document case.

'What's the big secret, then, Joe? What've you got on Morton that the Florida people don't know about?'

Doherty's drawl broadened. 'Why nothin' at all, pardner.

They know all about Morton. They just choose to ignore it. You figure out why.'

He unzipped the document case and took out a manilla folder. 'This here's a summary of the FBI file on Mike Morton, CEO of Sports Stars Corporation. First thing it tells us that his real name is Luigi Morticelli. Mike Morton came into existence at Yale Law School. I guess he figured that an Italian surname could hamper his career opportunities. That's one explanation. The other is that his father, Guiseppe Morticelli, is rumoured to be connected.'

'Rumoured,' said Skinner. 'Is that all?'

'Yeah. He's a very slippery customer. Officially, he owns a light engineering company, but once or twice his name's been mentioned by informants as being a man of influence . . . very great influence.

'Luigi graduated from High School in his own name but when he went to college it was as Mike Morton. He practised law for a while, with a corporate firm on Wall Street. They had great plans for him, but in his late twenties, he left and went to Florida to set up SSC. Within three years it was the top sports management company in the US. Within ten years it was the most influential promoter in world sports, and Mike Morton was the number one man.'

Skinner smiled. 'How'd it get so big so fast?'

'Good question. That's why we took an interest in him in the first place. SSC seemed to attract top-name clients from the off. Morton targeted baseball first. Within a year he had signed up virtually all the top names. In most cases he didn't have too much difficulty. He was promising the earth, and in those days damn few of these guys had representation. When he did run into problems, they always seemed to have lucky solutions. One guy wanted too much money: he was busted for drug-dealing. One of the top pitchers refused him point blank. He had an accident at home, involving his pitching hand and his waste disposal. After that one, baseball was sewn up and SSC moved on to other sports.

'When it came to golf Morton's tactic was to leave the big names alone, and to concentrate on buying up the young guys as they came out of college. He just threw money at them and pretty soon all of the new generation were SSC clients.

'That gave him his chance to develop into golf promotion. He had so many guys signed up that he could stage his own events. It got so that if you wanted to make real money in golf you had to go with Morton. Non-Americans began to find that too. If they wanted to play the big-money invitation events in the US, they had to give SSC American management rights. By the end of the seventies, Morton/Morticelli had international golf by the balls, you might say.'

Doherty grinned at Skinner as they swept on to the A1. 'Eventually SSC began to look for investments in sports-related enterprises all over the world. It had plenty of opportunities. Along the way, one or two people said "no". There was an automobile accident. Another guy came home to find his wife dead. After that, everybody just seemed to say "yes".'

'Except for Michael White and the Marquis of Kinture,' said Skinner, quietly.

'Yeah, interesting, isn't it? And it gets better. Because now, SSC isn't the only game in town any more.'

'You mean Greenfields? You got something on them too?'

'Sure have.' Doherty nodded, and took a second folder from his case. 'There was something of a power shift in world golf in the first half of the eighties. The Yanks stopped producing superstars, and the non-Americans sort of got their shit together. All of a sudden the US stopped winning the majors. At the same time, the Japanese started to pile serious money into Pacific and Australasian golf, and they had the sort of dough that could overcome even SSC's resources.

'Bill Masur and Greenfields rode in on that magic carpet. They began to sign up all the top Japanese, the way SSC had done ten years before with the American college kids. Pretty soon there were rival Pacific invitation events, to attract the top Southern Hemisphere players, and the Europeans.

'They made ground in boxing too. They set up a new organisation, with their own champions, and again, the Japanese money talked. SSC started to lose out on the biggest TV deals.'

'Interesting,' said Skinner. 'So how is it now?'

'There seems to be a sort of truce in operation. SSC still dominates American golf, and baseball, of course. Greenfields runs Australia and the Far East. Europe is neutral territory. Your event this week's a good example. The guys who own the course couldn't run it themselves, so they did the sensible thing. They hired SSC as promoters and managers, and they found the sponsor through Masur's Far East contacts.'

'What about Darren Atkinson's new organisation?'

'The big boys don't seem to mind it, for now. As long as he sticks to Europe, and doesn't try to muscle in on their territories, SSC and Greenfields will leave him alone, so my people reckon. They wondered if Masur might have been pissed when the young South African kid signed up with Atkinson, but so far there's no sign of it.'

'I wonder,' said Skinner. He told Doherty of the mysterious kidnapping of M'tebe senior.

'That's interesting. If there's anything behind that, Darren could be in line for some burned fingers.'

'Let's hope not. He seems like a good guy.' He paused, slowing as he approached the Meadowmill junction.

'There's one thing I don't understand about your scenario, Joe. If Mike Morton's a son of the Mob, how come Masur was able to muscle in on him?'

Doherty's grin was infectious. 'The Mafia ain't the only outfit, my friend. I take it you've heard of the Yakuza!'

'Jesus Christ, you mean they're Masur's insurance policy?'

'Yup.'

Skinner turned the car on to the North Berwick road and accelerated. 'You're telling me that I'm teeing up this week, in my own home county, alongside two bloody gangsters!'

'You might be taking an extreme view of the situation, my friend, but no one could really fault you for it. That's why I thought I'd better tell you about it in person.'

'You're confirming something else for me too, Joe; that one of them might have had Michael White killed!'

Eighteen

'Oh yes, I remember the Jubilee Project. I was in Aberlady Primary then, and my class was involved too. We did the farming section. I never taught with Myra Skinner, but I knew her.

'Later on, after I moved to Gullane Primary, I taught Alex. A very clever child, she was, with a father who doted on her. That was a one-parent family with absolutely no problems!'

'You should see them now,' thought Maggie Rose.

Anne McQueen, the head teacher of Longniddry Primary, was a formidably fit woman, dressed predominantly in serviceable black; mid to late forties, Rose guessed. Hers was a large school, with a non-teaching head; and so she had been available to meet the Inspector at short notice.

'What's all this about?' she asked. 'You said on the phone that you were looking for help: with what?'

'It's something that's cropped up as a line of investigation in one of our enquiries. I'd like you to listen to this tape. Myra Skinner made it as part of her research for the Jubilee Project.' She handed over the Walkman, with the cassette in place.

Mrs McQueen listened to the tape in an emotionless silence, but when it was over she looked as astonished as Henry Wills. 'That's a new one on me, and I've taught in this county for over twenty years. I've heard a few children spin stories in my time, but I've never heard a delivery like that. Nana Soutar must have been some character!'

'There's no chance that she could still be alive, is there?' asked Rose.

Mrs McQueen looked doubtful. 'A great-granny, twenty years on? Not much, I wouldn't have thought. Mind you, there are Soutars in Longniddry Primary today. One of them in Primary Seven, that's Edward, and his wee brother Gareth's in Primary Five. Their father, Davie, he was here too. He could well be a brother or cousin of the child – woman now – on that tape.'

'But the name Lisa Soutar, that means nothing to you today?'

'No. Nothing at all. She could be Lisa anything by now, of course, and that really widens the field. It was a popular girl's name in the sixties; still is for that matter.' Suddenly she stopped, and looked at the policewoman, appraisingly. 'OK, I've heard the tape. Now how can I help you?' She smiled. 'I don't imagine you're investigating the murder of poor old Aggie Tod, four hundred years on.'

Maggie Rose put the player, and the tape, back in her jacket pocket. 'No . . . at least I don't think I am. I understand,' she said, 'that the project was published as a very limited edition book, and that the schools each kept a copy.'

Anne McQueen nodded. 'Yes, that's right. Ours is kept right here in my office. Would you like to see it?'

'Yes please. Just to confirm something I was told earlier.'

'Hang on just a minute then.' The head teacher rose and opened a glass-fronted bookcase, from which she took a thick volume, expensively bound in red leather. The title *East*

Lothian, A Jubilee History was picked out in gold leaf on the cover. She placed it on her desk in front of Maggie Rose.

The book was still stiff. She could tell that it had been used very little. She found an index, and turned to the chapter headed 'Witchcraft and Superstitions' on page 78. Slowly, she read through it. There was a single brief mention of the burning of Agnes Tod and her coven, but she could find no mention of the doomed witch's curse. 'So,' she muttered to herself, 'Henry Wills was right.'

She made to close the volume, but as she did, her eye was caught by the title page.

She read aloud. '"A Chronicle of the County of Haddington, now East Lothian, compiled by the children of its schools, and edited by the Marquis of Kinture."'

'Is that the present Marquis?'

'No,' said Mrs McQueen. 'That would be his father, the old Marquis. He died about ten years ago. He was very good to the schools in the area, was old Lord Kinture. His son's very generous too, but things have changed since then. The parents like to do more for their children's schools today, and that old-fashioned patronage isn't needed so much.'

She picked up the red book. 'Right, I've heard the tape, and you've read the book. I also remember something I glanced over in the *Scotsman* earlier. That gives me a clearer idea of why you're here. So how else can I help?'

'You've helped plenty already, Mrs McQueen. But you couldn't give me an address for Mr Soutar, could you?'

'I could, but you won't need to go to his home. Davie's a police Sergeant. He's stationed at Dalkeith, as I remember, but I imagine that you can have him come to you!'

Nineteen

'I have to call in here on the way home, Joe. Come in with me, if you like. Who knows, you might catch a glimpse of your pal Morton.'

With some difficulty, he found a space in the car park in front of the Witches' Hill clubhouse. He stepped out of the BMW and gazed across to the practice ground, where five brightly dressed figures were ranged in a line, surrounded by coaches and caddies. They were too far off for him to make out faces, or even skin tone, but each swung his club in a way that was almost a personal signature. Between the languid action which could belong only to Cortes, and the bludgeoning style which Skinner knew to be Tiger Nakamura's trademark, there was a swing full of the grace, touch and suppleness of youth. 'A swing of beauty is a joy for ever,' he said.

'You're suddenly poetic, Bob,' said Doherty, closing the passenger door.

'Golf is poetry, my friend, and the boy I'm looking at will be its Laureate one day. Come on.' He led the way around the corner of the clubhouse and down the tarmac cart path at the left side of the first fairway. A single rope ran on their right, erected during the day to enclose spectators.

'Ever go to golf tournaments, Joe?'

'Gawd no!' said the lean American, vehemently. 'Grosvenor

Square is the wide open spaces as far as I'm concerned. I'm a city bird; I get dizzy in this much acreage.'

'Pity,' said Skinner. 'Golf is one of the few mass sports you can follow where you know that the crowds will be well-behaved. When either of the big Glasgow football teams come to play in Edinburgh, our officers, in strength, escort them from the railway stations and bus parks down to the ground, then back again when the game's over. You work in London, so you know what I mean.

'At this event we'll maintain a presence, as required, but we're here to assist, or to deter any thieves who might see this as easy pickings. We're not here to guarantee crowd behaviour.' He looked around. 'It's so peaceful that it's bizarre to think of being here on Sunday to investigate a murder.'

The practice area was set a little off the fairway. It was around 100 yards wide, and 350 long, with marker flags set in the ground at different distances, so that the players could test their accuracy with the different clubs in their bags. Skinner looked along the line of five, and confirmed his earlier guess, that Darren Atkinson was not among them. He recognised Ewan Urquhart, closest to him, and Deacon Weekes furthest away. Each had a swing which was carefully designed to allow as little room for error as possible, upright and without the suggestion of a loop in the hitting action. In the centre of the group stood a tall, slender black man; still, in fact, a youth. Oliver M'tebe seemed almost frail, and yet as Skinner and Doherty watched, they saw that he hit the ball prodigious distances. His swing was more full than the rest, with an almost exaggerated cocking of the wrists at the completion of the backswing which laid the club parallel with the ground, pointing in the exact direction of the eventual flight of the shot.

The downswing relied on perfect co-ordination rather than on force, the graphite head of the driver making a beautifully sweet sound as it struck, then carrying the hands on to a high finish. The ball, in its perfect flight, moved very slightly off the straight, from left to right. Skinner would have described the process as effortless, had he not known of the days, months, and years which had to be spent in practice and of the thousands of golf balls which had to be hit to achieve such perfection. 'I think I may give up this game,' he whispered to Doherty.

They watched for several minutes, not wanting to interrupt the practice session. Eventually, M'tebe's caddy placed another hundred-ball basket in front of his client, and handed him a mid-range iron. Changing his method only by shortening his stance, the young African began to pepper the 200-yard marker flag. Eventually the caddy wandered towards Skinner and Doherty.

'Just call in on your way home, gents?' he asked, in his bag-carrier's whisper. He smiled, proudly. 'Worth watching, in't he? I've caddied for all the big names in my time, for Chuck, for the Eagle, for Cortes over there, even for Darren when 'e was a youngster, but this lad . . . You mark my words, gents, this could turn out to be the best golfer ever. If we can get 'is short game about three-quarters as good as what you're watching now, there'll be no stopping 'im.'

The caddy gave his charge one more admiring smile, then lit a cigarette. He was around the same height as Doherty, but twice the width, with skin the colour of a walnut. It had been more than a day since his last shave, and everything about him was shabby, with two exceptions. He wore tan leather golf shoes which looked as if they might have been hand-made, and as he raised his cigarette to his lips, the sleeve of his sweater fell back, revealing a gold Rolex. 'Nice watch,' said Skinner.

The walnut face creased into a smile of pride. 'Yeah, in'it. Darren gave it me on Sunday. He had an 'ole in one on the last round, and that was the prize. We were playing with 'im. 'E's got a Rolex, so's Bravo . . . that's 'is caddy . . . and so's Oliver, so after the presentation, he gave it to me. "I'd feel a prat, wearing two watches," 'e said. Some bloke, is Darren.'

He fell silent, looking back at M'tebe with an appraising eye.

Skinner tapped him on the shoulder. 'Listen, don't make a fuss, but we're not just here to watch. We're police officers. We need to talk to Oliver, about something that's happened at home. When he's ready to take a break, could you ask him to join us.'

The caddy frowned, then glanced again at M'tebe. 'Should be ready to change clubs now. 'Old on.' He sauntered across to the golfer as he was setting up yet another ball and, putting a hand on his arm, muttered in his ear. The young African looked across in sudden alarm, handed his club to the caddy and walked over.

'What is this you have to tell me?' His voice was raised slightly. Tiger Nakamura paused at the top of his backswing and glared over his shoulder in annoyance.

'Let's move further away from the rest of them,' said Skinner. He introduced himself, and Doherty, describing the American simply as a colleague. Together they led the young man about thirty yards away from the practice range.

'Mr M'tebe, please be calm,' said the ACC, slowly and gently. 'I'm afraid that we have some unpleasant news for you.

It concerns your father. It appears that he was kidnapped this morning, in Durban. He was bundled into a vehicle by two men. That's all that the South African police know. There's been no communication since, no ransom demand from anyone, nothing at all.' He paused, to let his words sink in. 'We have been asked by the South African authorities to find out whether you know anything about your father's work that might help your police? He's a clergyman, a minister of the Church, yes?'

Oliver M'tebe was shocked speechless. His eyes were moist. He nodded his head.

'There's a history of political violence in your home city, I understand. Did your father involve himself in politics at all that you know of?'

With an obvious effort, the young golfer regained his composure. 'No. My father would never come down on the side of either faction. He sees his role as helping to bring the two sides together to solve problems, and he has often succeeded in doing that. He has never expressed a political view, not even to my mother or to my brothers or me.'

'Has he ever been threatened? Say by extremists on either side who might not want compromise?'

'Not that I know of. My father never becomes involved publicly.'

Skinner paused. 'In the old days, before the new government, did your father make enemies on either side?'

Young M'tebe shook his head. 'No sir. My father is a man of God. No one could be his enemy.' Without warning he began to sob. Skinner and Doherty watched him, helplessly for a minute or two, as he stood with a hand over his face, his shoulders shaking very slightly.

Eventually he wiped his eyes and straightened himself. 'I must go home, to help.'

'Why don't you phone first?' said Skinner, gently. 'Call your mother and ask her what you should do. Come back to the clubhouse with us. Maybe she'll tell you how you can help best.'

Twenty

'Are you normally on day shift, Sergeant?'

Davie Soutar nodded his large head. 'Yes, ma'am. Admin. might be a bore, but at least the hours are regular and there's less stress on the wife. She disna' have to sit at home worrying about armed robbers, or demented junkies, or anything like that.'

He hunched the shoulders of his white uniform shirt as he reflected for a few seconds. 'I always say that far too few polismen think about the effect that their job has on their wives. They go home and they expect everything to be just so, weans quiet, house neat and tidy, washing done, tea on the table. A lot of police marriages break down because of it.'

Maggie smiled, grimly. 'I'll bear that in mind, Davie. My fiancé's a Detective Sergeant. But I think that if I tried to persuade him to take a desk job, my marriage would break down before it started. Mario thinks that being shot in the line of duty makes you statistically bullet-proof.'

Soutar looked at her in surprise. 'You're engaged to big McGuire?' He laughed. 'I heard that the Big Eyetie had been tamed. Now I can see how! Mario and me shared a panda for a while when we were a bit younger. I mind one night we were checking shops in Dalry Road, and I got set upon by three casuals. I was getting a right doin', ken, till the boy Mario arrived. One of them threatened him wi' a knife; he went face first into a wall. The second one, oh my, but he just wrecked him. The third one put his hands up!'

His expression changed to one of concern. 'I heard he got quite badly hurt. Any after-effects?'

Maggie shook her head. 'None that I've been able to see. Physically he's fine, and there don't seem to be any psychological scars.

'Anyway, to business.' They were seated in a small interview room in the Lasswade station. The architecture of police buildings in the Edinburgh area is of inconsistent quality. At best, Lasswade drew mixed critical reviews.

'Aye,' said Soutar. 'A family matter, but nothing to do with my kids, you said. What is it then?'

Rose put the cassette player on the table. 'How long has your family lived in Longniddry, Davie?'

He smiled. 'Since God was a boy, they say.'

'Do you have a relative named Lisa Soutar? A cousin, sister, niece even?'

'Aye. I've got a sister called Lisa. She's a couple of years younger than me.'

'Right. I'd like you to listen to this tape for me.' She pushed the Walkman across the desk. The sergeant put on the headphones and pressed the play button. He listened with an expression of growing interest and surprise. By the end his mouth was hanging open slightly.

'That's amazin', Inspector. Can ah have a copy of that?'

'I'll need to ask Mr Skinner, but I'm sure it'll be all right. So, that was your sister?'

'Oh aye, that was oor Lisa OK. A heid full o' fairies, we used to say. She was a weird lassie right enough. She and ma nana were as thick as thieves. Nana hardly spoke to the rest of us. What age would Lisa be then, ah wonder?' He searched his memory. 'Let's see, if she was in Mrs Skinner's class, she'd have been ten or eleven.' A sudden thought struck him. 'Here, I mind that that Mrs Skinner was killed. Was she . . . ?'

'The boss's first wife?' Maggie finished his question and nodded. There were a few seconds of solemn silence.

'Now, about your nana,' said Rose, dragging Soutar back to the subject of their meeting. 'How old would she have been then?'

'Let's see. She died in 1982, and she was ninety-nine then, so she'd have been ninety-three or thereabouts.'

'What about Lisa, where's she now? Is she married?'

Sergeant Soutar nodded. 'Aye, she's married on tae a soldier called Roy Davies. He's in the Royal Engineers. They're stationed in Germany just now. Dinna like the man much. He's far too strict wi' Lisa, and wi' their wee lass.'

'How about your parents. Are they still . . . ?'

'Ma mother's dead, but ma father's still around.'

'Would he know anything of your family history?'

Soutar laughed. 'What, ma da'? He'll tell you who won the Cup in 1952, or what won the three-thirty at Carlisle last Thursday, but he knows bugger all about his own family. He thought ma nana was as daft as a brush, and so did his father before him. The auld witch, they used to call her. No, Inspector, if you want to know anything about the Soutar family history, you'll need tae ask oor Lisa. Nana Soutar passed it all on to her, and that's where it is tae this day, in her head.'

He handed the tape player back to Rose. 'Do you have a number where I can contact your sister?' she asked.

'Aye, sure.' He took a notebook from his pocket, scribbled

on it, tore out the page and passed it across the desk. 'That's her home number in Germany.

'There's one thing you havena' told me, though. What's a' this about?'

The inspector took from her bag a cutting from that morning's *Scotsman*, and handed it, without a word, to Davie Soutar. He read it in silence, astonishment returning to his broad features. 'What? D'you think our Lisa might have written that?'

Rose shook her head. 'Not if she's in Germany, no. But as far as I can gather, the story on that tape has never been written down in full. I need to find out whether it's been passed down through any other family, and right now, your sister seems to be the only lead I've got.'

'But so what? It's just a crank letter, isn't it?'

Maggie shrugged her shoulders. 'Maybe yes, maybe no. A lot of people believe in UFOs, and a lot believe in witches. And – leaving your sister out of this – just suppose some believe that they're witches themselves?'

Twenty-one

'If you don't mind me asking, Bob,' said Darren Atkinson, his voice betraying the faintest trace of his Midlands upbringing, 'where did you get those scars on your leg?'

Skinner glanced down at the small, round, blue scar at the front of his tanned right thigh, and at the big ragged rip towards the rear. 'I fell on to a spiked railing,' he lied.

Atkinson winced. 'Ow! It hurts even to think of something like that.'

They were in the main locker room for gentlemen at Witches' Hill, changing from their formal clothes into golfing kit. The golfer squared the shoulders of his blazer on its hanger and muttered, almost to himself. 'When I have my own club, it will have a sensible dress code. The gear that we're wearing now probably costs more, piece for piece, than the stuff we're hanging up, yet we can't wear it in the bar. That was the first thing that the Marquis told me when I arrived. I was astonished, and a bit annoyed too.' He grinned wryly. 'After all, I get paid a right few quid to wear this stuff.'

Skinner laughed. 'Yes, I know. And indirectly I'm one of the punters who pays you!' He pulled his sweater over his head, and tapped the manufacturer's logo on the sleeve. 'But to be fair to the Marquis,' he said, 'his dress code is the norm around here. The difference seems to be that Witches' Hill doesn't have a Dirty Bar, where you can go in your golfing gear. I suppose it shows the sort of clients they're looking to attract.'

'Yeah,' drawled Atkinson. 'In their dreams.'

'You don't think this place will succeed?'

'Not if they stick to the toffee-nosed approach. A lot of Americans and Japanese just don't understand it. It'll alienate them, and they'll tell their chums. If the course was good enough, it wouldn't matter, but frankly it isn't.'

Skinner was surprised. 'You don't think so?'

Atkinson shook his head. 'No, for us pros there's just that bit of severity missing. I'm afraid I don't rate O'Malley as highly as most people seem to, or as he rates himself for that matter. I'll be disappointed if I don't shoot well under two hundred and seventy this week, and I think one or two others might as well. I reckon that on a perfect day, I could break sixty out there. That's not bragging. I played it properly for the first time today, and I had a sixty-five. Young Urquhart had a sixty-seven. Scores like that send out the wrong message about a course.

'It's a bit of a Hollywood tart, is Witches' Hill. Looks beautiful, but when you get into it, the performance is disappointing!'

Skinner, tying his shoelaces, laughed. 'Are you speaking from experience?'

The golfer grinned. 'Sadly, no. I'm only good at one game.'

'You surprise me. My old dad used to say that there are two things which no man will ever own up to doing badly . . . and the other one is driving!'

'Hah! Well come on and I'll show you my speciality.' He led the way from the locker room and out towards the practice putting green. Skinner hefted his clubs on to his shoulder and followed. 'We're a bit early, so let's have a look at your putting stroke. Mind you,' he cautioned, 'like most pros, I'm no use as a putting coach. If I was I'd make more money than I do playing. It's the most difficult thing of all to teach.'

Skinner took from his bag his flat-headed Ram Zebra putter and two golf balls. He lined up on a flag twenty feet away and stroked smoothly through the ball. It finished four feet short. 'Bugger,' he muttered. 'Every time, I'm either short or past by that much.' He putted the second ball. It missed on the left and rolled at least a yard past the hole.

'Show me again,' said Atkinson. He crouched down as Skinner hit two more putts, with the same results. 'This one's easy,' he said, straightening. 'You're almost grounding the club-head, and so you're hitting underneath the ball, chipping it very slightly instead of putting. That's affecting both weight and line. Concentrate on keeping the head half an inch clear of the ground. That way you'll hit through the middle of the ball. Try it.'

Skinner tried a few practice strokes as Atkinson instructed, then hit two more practice putts. The first missed on the right and stopped six inches past, and the second rolled smoothly into the hole. Five minutes later, the policeman was beaming all over his face. 'Right,' said Atkinson. 'Now let's see if you can hit the bloody thing. I see Norton and Hideo Murano heading out to the range. Let's get after them.'

Skinner shouldered his bag once more, and the two headed off down the side of the first fairway.

'I heard about Oliver's dad,' said Atkinson. 'He told me you'd been to see him. That's a bloody awful thing, isn't it? The lad says he can't think of a single reason why anyone should want to harm him.'

'Did he call his mother?'

Atkinson nodded. 'Yes. She persuaded him to stay here. I'd have understood if he went home, but he's going to play. His mother said that was the best way for him to sustain his father.'

'You manage him, don't you?'

'Well, my company will do. Oliver was quite a catch. Masur made him an offer, but he approached me. He hasn't signed formally yet, but we've reached agreement, and we're acting for him.'

'How did Masur feel about that?'

'He grumbled, but not too hard. I don't think he's too interested in black African golfers. The white guys, Aussies and Japs are his main strengths, although he's making inroads into America. Morton hates that.'

He paused. 'Mind you, he'll hate it even more if the Tiger leaves SSC.'

Skinner looked at him in surprise. 'Is that likely?'

Atkinson nodded. 'His contract's almost up, and Masur's made him an offer. Greenfields has strong Japanese connections, and they feel that the Tiger should be with them. Morton's pulling out all the stops, since the Tiger's his star attraction in the Far East, but that's the way it'll go, I think.'

'That's interesting,' said Skinner. 'How do Morton and Masur get along generally?'

'They don't.'

'How do they feel about your company?'

'They're polite to me, but I've made it clear that I'm sticking to golf, and to European tour players.'

'Will it always be that way?'

'Shrewd question, Bob. No it won't, but I'm not going to let them in on that secret.' They were approaching the practice ground, and had almost caught up with their teammates, each of whom was pulling a caddy-car. Atkinson called out to them. 'OK, guys, let's get together. That's my caddy over there with the practice buckets.' He pointed towards a tall red-haired figure who stood with one hand on a huge golfbag, on which Atkinson's name was emblazoned. Beyond him, still swinging powerfully, was the colourfully clad figure of Tiger Nakamura. Skinner noticed that Bill Masur was watching him practise, a contented smile on his face.

As the four came together, Atkinson introduced Skinner to his playing companions. He was struck by the difference between Norton Wales in the flesh and on television. He knew that the singer was over fifty, but for the first time he realised that he looked every day of his age. Hard living had carved deep traces which were normally covered up by stage make-up. Alongside him, Hideo Murano, the thirty-year-old heir to the car-building fortune, looked almost cherubic. 'And this is Bravo,' said Atkinson, introducing his caddy. 'To answer the obvious question, his real name's Charlie, and I've no idea why he's called Bravo. Neither has he. Most of the older caddies go by nicknames, and Bravo's been around for longer than me.

'OK, let's grab a bucket of balls each, and let's see you swing. Murano-San, you first, please.'

The Japanese nodded, teed up a ball and hit it competently, to just short of the 200-yard marker. 'That's good,' said Atkinson. 'You keep that up and I won't need to do much for this team. Norton, you next.' The tubby singer set himself up and took a tremendous thrash at his ball, knocking it no more than sixty yards along the ground. Atkinson shook his head and smiled. 'Look, man, there's no need to be in such a rush. The bloody ball isn't going anywhere until you send it. Swing at half that speed and you'll play twice as well. Right, Bob, let's see you.'

Skinner had never felt so nervous on a golf course. But he steadied himself, thought only of the ball, concentrated on timing rather than power, and swung smoothly. The Titleist made a satisfying 'click' on the face of his graphite-headed driver, and soared away. It moved from right to left in flight, pitched just short of the 225-yard marker and ran on for another forty yards. Atkinson watched it until it came to rest, then turned towards him. 'You should be arrested for playing off seven,' he said with a grin. 'You've played this course before, haven't you?' Skinner nodded. 'What did you shoot?'

'Seventy-eight,' he said, adding quietly, 'with a ball in the water up the last.'

'See, I told you it wasn't testing enough! Right. You and Hideo concentrate on hitting targets. Bravo, you keep an eye on them. I'm going to do some serious work with Norton.' As Atkinson set about one of the greatest challenges of his career, Skinner and Murano followed instructions, aiming at different targets with different clubs, working their way through their bags from long irons to the pitching clubs. Skinner had almost emptied his practice bucket when his concentration was shattered.

'Hey asshole, get your butt out of here. The Tiger's still my man, and if he knows what's best for him he's going to stay that way.' Mike Morton's raised voice cut through the stillness of the practice ground. His shoulders were back and his jaw thrust out as he approached Bill Masur and squared up to him.

The Australian looked coolly down at him. 'Face up to it Mike,' he said calmly. 'You've been assuming too much for far too long. It's time you took a tumble. Tiger belongs with

Greenfields, and he knows it. Ain't nothing you SSC boys can do to change that.'

Without warning Morton shoved him violently in the chest. Masur took a pace back to steady himself, but stayed on his feet, still smiling. Skinner stepped across quickly. He put himself between the two and seized the American by the arms.

'Let's have less of the playground stuff, Morton.' The man struggled for a second or two, but the policeman's grip was unbreakable. Frustrated and still enraged, he glared hotly at Masur and hissed something in Italian.

'Not here, he won't,' said Skinner. 'Mr Morton, I don't imagine there's anything in your contract to stop Mr Masur watching the Tiger practise, so I think it's best if you leave. And by that I mean leave the club! Masur, you wait here for a while. Morton, I'll warn you once only. I don't care who or what you are. Behave yourself properly or I'll have you barred from here.

'Now. On your way!' He released the American from his grip, and pushed him, none too gently, towards the pathway, where a golf buggy was parked. For a second Morton stood his ground, until Skinner caught his eye. Finally, his teeth clenched in anger, he spun on his heel and stalked off. 'Masur,' said the policeman, 'you wait here till his buggy's well out of sight.' The Australian shrugged his shoulders and nodded, still smiling. Then Tiger Nakamura motioned to him, and he turned to watch the Japanese as he resumed his interminable practice.

Skinner took the few steps back to his practice bucket, where Darren Atkinson stood waiting. 'What did Morton say to him?' he asked.

'Well my Italian isn't that great, but I think that "Sleep with the fishes" just about covers it!'

Twenty-two

'Christ, Bob I wish I'd been there! From the sound of things, the mobster in Morton must still be pretty near the surface.'

'No doubt about that, Joseph. I've seen that look only a few times in my life. Right at that moment, Morton would have killed Masur, given the means and the opportunity.'

Doherty scratched his chin. 'It's as well he didn't have either then. The Yakuza would have taken a dim view of that. From what Atkinson told you, I'd guess that they've told Nakamura that he's going to sign with the home-boys.'

Skinner nodded. 'That's a fair guess. Morton may not take it lying down, though. Still, "Star Wars" between him and Masur and their backers isn't my worry, as long as it doesn't happen here. I've got another priority, and what I saw today of Mike Morton when he's crossed makes me even more interested in him in connection with the White murder.'

The two policemen and Sarah were sat round the small table in the conservatory, the remains of a meal before them. It was just after 10 p.m., and Jazz had been settled soundly in his cot for over an hour. They sat for another half-hour until Doherty, who had decided to extend his stay in Scotland to visit Special Branch heads around the country, pleaded tiredness and retired for the night.

'So how did you two Yanks get on while I was out?' Bob asked his wife, in their bedroom, as he watched her undress.

'Great. He's quite a character is Joe. He worked in New York for a while, so we had some common ground. That can be a problem for us. The US is such a big place that when a New Yorker meets a Midwesterner it can be like encountering someone from a whole different country.' She stepped out of her jeans and pants and turned, naked, to face him. He smiled at her, admiring the way in which her exercise regime had helped her recover a flat, if stretch-marked, abdomen so soon after childbirth. She misunderstood his expression and took a heavy breast in each hand. 'Yeah, they're still monsters, ain't they? But get ready to bid them farewell. Another couple of weeks and Jazz is on the bottle. Natural feeding and my new university job just won't mix.'

She slipped into bed, nestling beside him, her swollen breasts hot and heavy on his chest. 'So how about you, my love? Apart from breaking up a gang-fight, how did you do this evening?'

He smiled. 'Couldn't have been better. The world's greatest golfer cured my putting problem, and I met up with my titled caddy in the bar afterwards. I suspect that Darren's the real reason she's offered to pull my trolley.'

'As long as that's all she pulls,' said Sarah. She disappeared below the duvet. A few seconds later his eyes widened, and his mouth dropped open in an involuntary gasp.

Wednesday

Twenty-three

Gullane was easing itself into a wakeful state . . . or as close to that condition as it could manage . . . when Skinner slid his car into its main street, and headed, past the Old Smiddy on the left, for Edinburgh.

He drove slowly past the first tee of Number One course where a clutch of caddies stood waiting, hopefully, for their morning hires. He nodded in their direction. 'They're probably expecting a party of your countrymen, over for the tournament. We don't usually see so many of these fellas around so early on a weekday morning.'

Beside him Doherty shifted in his seat. 'When does the thing begin?'

'The main event begins tomorrow, but this is the official practice day, with the course and the tented village open to the paying public. Darren's taking us out for a round at one-thirty. He thought it would be a good idea to get the team used to the crowds. Can't say I'm looking forward to the chance of making a chump of myself in public!'

Doherty grinned. 'Come on, Bob, surely you've done that before!'

'Cheeky bastard! I suppose I have done a few times in the witness box, but doing it on a golf course'll be a first. You know what it's like when you have a raw suspect in for questioning, and he sits there wondering what it's going to be like, so nervous that you'd swear you can *hear* his arsehole pucker? Well that'll be me, facing my first shot this afternoon.'

Instead of sticking to his normal route along the coast, he took the exit at Luffness corner and up the mile-long straight, then following the road westward until it led past the entrance to Witches' Hill. He eased his foot on the throttle pedal, and glanced over towards the practice ground, where a solitary figure stood in the address position. 'That's the man, Joe,' he said to Doherty as a perfect swing sent a tiny white speck soaring through the air. 'That's Darren. Look at the time and it'll tell you why he's Number One. No one's perfect, but the more he practises, the closer he gets.'

He picked up speed again and headed towards Longniddry and, beyond, Edinburgh. They drove in silence for a while, watching the thickening traffic heading in the opposite direction, towards Witches' Hill, until Skinner spoke suddenly. 'I'm glad you're sticking around for a while, Joe. I know you want to freshen up your Special Branch contacts in the other forces, but before you do that, could you maybe do me – and Brian Mackie – a favour?'

Doherty blinked and looked across at him. 'Name it, my man and it's yours.'

Skinner eased the car up the rise which led out of Longniddry. 'I'd like to call on the resources of the World's Greatest Law Enforcement thingy once more.

'The more I think about the way Morton reacted to Masur yesterday, the more I fancy him to be involved with the White murder. Now I know that when Michael was killed he was in another room surrounded by witnesses, but if a job's worth doing . . .'

'. . . it's worth paying someone to do it well!' said Doherty, nodding, and picking up Skinner's favourite saying.

'Right. So what I'd like you to do is ask the Bureau to look again at SSC, but to look past Morton, or Morticelli, and to pull out everything they know about his associates in the company, and anywhere else for that matter. I'm sure that they'll all be law-school guys like Morton, or accountants, but I'd like them all checked out, just to find out whether anyone isn't what he seems. While you're doing that, I'm going to do some digging at the UK end.

'Is that OK?'

'Sure,' said Doherty. He glanced at his watch. The time was 8.03 a.m. 'I'll take great pleasure in waking the duty team from their beauty sleep. God knows, they've done it to me often enough!'

Twenty-four

Ruth McConnell was already at her desk when Skinner arrived in the Command Suite, having installed Doherty in Brian Mackie's Special Branch office.

She made to stand up but he waved her back into her chair. 'Good morning, sir,' she said brightly. 'How was your golf?'

'OK,' he grinned, beginning to flick through the morning's post, which lay, opened, in a pile on Ruth's side table. 'By my standards, anyway. But I'm playing for the next five days with a man who reckons he can break sixty . . . and I'm quite sure he can.'

'Better have some coffee to steady your nerves, then. Your filter machine should have brewed by now. I've laid out a plate of biscuits for your visitors.'

He looked up from his mail. 'Visitors.'

'Yes sir, Detective Superintendent Higgins asked if she could see you at nine, and Miss Rose wanted me to keep some of your time free for her.'

'That's fine. I'll see them both, but I don't want to do it in my office. Book a conference room for nine-thirty, and tell Miss Higgins that I want a full meeting. As well as Maggie Rose, she should have Brian Mackie there; oh yes, and McGuire and McIlhenney. I want you there too, to produce a record, and Alan Royston, since we might decide to issue an update report to the media.'

Ruth nodded. 'Very good, sir.'

'One other thing. Arrange for Joe Doherty, Brian Mackie and I to have coffee with the Chief after the briefing's over. Joe should pay a courtesy call while he's with us.'

He picked up his paperwork. 'Right, you do that, and I'll spend a happy hour with this lot. Keep everyone at bay until half-nine.'

Twenty-five

'Good morning, ladies and gentlemen. If I could have your attention.'

As Skinner spoke, Alison Higgins took her place alongside him at the head of the small conference table. Ruth McConnell sat a little apart with a shorthand notebook on her lap and a pencil in her right hand. Brian Mackie, Maggie Rose, the two Sergeants and Alan Royston were ranged around the table.

'I've called this meeting,' the ACC began, 'to summarise progress so far in our investigation of the murder of Michael White. Alison, bring us up to date please.'

Higgins glanced at him briefly, and began. 'The first thing that we have to say is that there are no obvious suspects within White's close circle. The man seems to have been universally popular among his acquaintances, and faithful to his wife . . . and she to him, beyond a doubt. So I think we can discount any thoughts of jealous lover involvement.

'I'll kick my briefing off with the two reports from the scientific people: the first on the changing room and Jacuzzi area, the second on the starter's hut, where we think that the murderer might have waited. The first location has yielded precious little. Both the changing room and the Jacuzzi cubicle are cleaned regularly, and the steward makes sure that they are spotless. So we lifted relatively few prints. Mario and Neil have been checking those that we did lift. Any other traces, hair, et cetera, we have identified as coming from White himself.

'The starter's hut, on the other hand, was a mess. The technicians lifted a whole raft of fingerprints, and again Mario and Neil have been at work identifying and eliminating their owners. The only other things that were found were dust and grass cuttings, and two cigarette ends. They're being checked out.'

She paused and looked around the table. 'All the interviews which were carried out on Sunday have been transcribed out and analysed. Everyone to whom we've spoken can account for his movements, and everyone has been accounted for by others in the course of their statements.

'So to sum up, as far as witness statements are concerned, the investigation has made zero progress. Mario, Neil, what do you have to report on your follow-up of the fingerprints?'

McGuire glanced at McIlhenney, and picked up a sheet of paper. 'Believe it or not, ma'am,' he began, 'we've matched the lot. There isn't a single wild print left, either from the murder scene or from the starter's hut. The Jacuzzi area was easy; it had been cleaned on Saturday. The only prints there were those of White himself, Williamson the steward, and Mrs Shaw the cleaner. As you said there were a lot in the starter's hut, but they all traced back to the starter, the professional and his assistants and to painters and builders.

'As far as the fag-ends are concerned, the scientists had a look at them for spit samples for DNA traces, but they found none. The only thing they found was the remnant of a brand name, showing on one of them, so they've sent it back to the manufacturers to see if they can tell us anything about it.'

'Like who bought it, for example?'

McGuire returned the Superintendent's smile. 'Hardly, ma'am, but they might be able to give us a list of local stockists.'

Higgins nodded. 'OK, all of that is good work. It doesn't take us any nearer catching our man, but it takes a lot of people out of the frame.' She turned to Skinner. 'Sir, is there anything you'd like to say at this stage?'

The ACC stood up. 'Thank you, Alison.

'As you will know, I've been involved in one or two interviews, principally with the Marquis and Lady Kinture, and Mrs White. From these and from my own knowledge of the dead man, I can confirm everything that Superintendent Higgins said about him when she began this briefing. Popular, friendly, and very well respected. A good, sound, family man. Not an enemy in the world . . . or so it seemed.

'But there's one more thing about Michael White. He always got his way. When he had a problem, he never made a fuss, he never made a threat, he just solved it.

'It seems that in the lead-up to this week's golf tournament, he had a problem with Mr Mike Morton of SSC . . . you remember, do you, he was there on Sunday. Mr Morton wanted to change the competitors at the event, and as the organiser he might have been able to do that. Except that Mr White went to the principal sponsor, and the problem was solved. Now that was the second occasion on which White had crossed Morton. The first was when he and the Marquis refused to let him buy into Witches' Hill.' He paused and looked around the table. 'You all with me so far?' Five heads nodded.

'Right; well this is where it gets interesting. Our friends in the FBI have come up with some family background on

Mike Morton. He is the son of a man rumoured to be connected with organised crime. His business face is outwardly respectable, except for the fact that as he was on his way up the ladder, a few people seem to have fallen off. I saw the other side of Morton for myself last night. There's an undercurrent of dispute in the world of international golf management at the moment, and it led to an altercation between Morton and Bill Masur, who was also at Witches' Hill on Sunday. On the basis of that, I'd say that the FBI are right. The guy *is* capable.'

He paused again. 'Now we all know that Morton couldn't have murdered White himself. He's accounted for at the time the deed was being done. But that doesn't mean that he knows nothing about it. I've asked Joe Doherty, who's here this morning . . . you can't miss him, Brian, he's the strange wee guy in your office . . . to go back to the Bureau and run a check on all the senior people in his business and on other "known associates". When he comes up with something, you might want to take it further, Alison.' He sat down again on his straight-backed chair.

'Thank you, sir.' Higgins glanced at Mackie. 'Brian, since Mr Doherty's on your network, so to speak, perhaps you could follow up any information he brings us. See if you can establish the whereabouts of all of Morton's close associates. Most important of all, see if there are some whose movements can't be accounted for. But do it quietly. The Morton connection may be a tenuous line of enquiry, but it's the only one we have at the moment, so let's not alert him if we can avoid it.'

Maggie Rose coughed. 'Excuse me, Superintendent, but there is another line of enquiry.'

Higgins looked around, surprised for a second, before her face cleared. 'Ah yes, the *Scotsman* letter, and the tape. Mr Skinner said you were looking into them. How have you got on so far?'

'I've covered a lot of ground, at least,' said Rose, 'and had a few surprises. One interesting thing is that the story on the tape has never been published, other than in fragmented form over a hundred years ago. It wasn't selected for inclusion in the Jubilee Project that the schools were working on, and no other member of the Soutar family knows anything of it.

'The great-grandmother who's mentioned on the tape seems to have been, as Mr Wills at the University described it, some sort of keeper of family legends, and she seems, according to Lisa Soutar's brother, Davie, who's one of ours . . .' she glanced at McGuire, who smiled '. . . to have passed the lot on to the girl.'

Higgins interrupted, with more than a hint of impatience. 'Where's the relevance in all that? Where does it take us?'

Rose bridled, visibly. 'It doesn't take us anywhere yet, because my enquiries can't go any further until I talk to Lisa Soutar, and according to her brother she's married and living in Germany. I went back out to Longniddry last night and spoke to a couple of local historians that Sergeant Soutar mentioned. Neither of them had ever heard the story of the Witch's Curse. I also spoke to a couple of people who were in Lisa's class. They had no recollection of the story.

'If you'd like me to sum up the direction in which I'm heading, it's that we have a family in possession of a secret story about a curse on anyone who desecrates the Witches' Hill, that a potential desecrator is killed in exactly the way described in the story, and that public attention has been drawn to the fact by the *Scotsman*'s anonymous letter. As I see it, we *have* to take an interest in whoever wrote that note.

'I know it sounds like a load of old cobblers, and that the Morton connection is probably a hell of a lot more likely to show a result, but this is a legitimate line of enquiry and we *must . . .*' she slapped the table as she emphasised the word '. . . see it to its conclusion. If Lisa Soutar's in Germany, and couldn't have written that letter, we have to find out who did, if only to confirm that that person *is* a harmless nutter and to eliminate them from our enquiries.' She leaned back, her cheeks reddening slightly. 'I'm sorry to be so blunt, ma'am, but that's how I see it.'

Higgins shook her head. 'No, Maggie, you're dead right. If we didn't follow things up just because they sounded a bit daft, half our investigations would never succeed.' She looked round at Skinner. 'What d'you think the next step should be, sir?'

The ACC shrugged his shoulders. 'Don't see we've got much choice. Maggie, you'd better go to Germany to interview the woman. I'll approve the cost. There's something else we should be doing too. Let's make some enquiries locally. Far-fetched it might be, but Alison, I want you to ask Andy Martin to set all of his people to asking around, to see whether there might actually be a latter-day coven in East Lothian.' He caught McGuire's sceptical glance. 'Come on, Mario. Just because *you* don't believe in it, it doesn't mean to say it can't happen. You go and see your old neighbour Davie Soutar. Maybe there's more than one oddbod in his family.'

Twenty-six

'How's Alison Higgins shaping up, Bob?' The Chief leaned back in his chair as Skinner finished his account of progress in the White investigation.

The ACC glanced at his watch; five minutes remained before the ever punctual Brian Mackie would arrive with Joe Doherty. The ACC knew that Proud Jimmy was not given to asking idle questions, and so he thought carefully before he answered. 'She's far from the finished article, but overall I'd say she's doing all right. I like people to exercise authority when they're given it. She's still a bit hesitant in that respect, but I'm working on that.

'She gets on well with her junior officers, although she took a wee pop at Maggie at our briefing this morning.'

'Brave woman!' said the Chief.

'Maybe, but she learned from it. She had to apologise to her in front of the troops. I'll bet you she never puts herself in that position again. She's a quick learner, and she's capable of going higher.'

'You mean she could become a chief officer?'

'Yes, I'd say she has that potential. Whether she fulfils it, well, that's up to her. I'd say, though, that once she's gathered enough experience of high-level CID work, she'll be happiest, and most effective as a commander, in uniform.'

'Like me, you mean,' said Sir James with a twinkle in his eye. Suddenly he scratched his chin, as if something had popped back into his mind. 'Talking about area commanders, Charlie Radcliffe called me this morning. He's making a fine recovery from his operation, and he expects to be fit to return in two months at the latest.

'So that means . . .'

'. . . that I'm getting back my best detective officer,' said Skinner, emphatically.

The Chief looked at him in pleased surprise. 'I was going to say that we'd have to find something for Charlie in this building.'

'No, thank you very much. Charlie's a great field commander; Andy Martin's a great detective. We both know where each of them belongs.'

'So you and Andy are on speaking terms again! Well, thank Christ for that. How about Alex? Has she been in touch?'

Skinner shook his head. 'No, only with Sarah. I think Andy and I'll have to conduct separate peace negotiations with our Alexis. Ach, if I had just gone straight home that morning!'

Proud Jimmy touched his sleeve. 'Water under the bridge, son. You two eedjits have taken the first step. The next ones'll happen by themselves, believe me.'

Skinner's reply was cut off by the buzz of the intercom on the Chief's desk. He pressed a button. 'Yes, Gerry.'

'DCI Mackie and Mr Doherty are here, sir,' said the Chief's new civilian secretary.

'Bang on time. Send them in, and bring in the coffee, please.'

A few seconds later, the door opened, Brian Mackie holding it ajar and ushering Joe Doherty into the room. The

Chief Constable, all silver braid in his full uniform, advanced on him, hand outstretched. 'Joe! Good to see you. The lads were right, I'd have been huffed if you'd been here and not said hello.'

The four settled themselves into low leather chairs around the coffee table as the secretary set down a tray laden with cups, biscuits and two steaming cafetières, with plungers depressed. 'Thanks, Gerry,' said the Chief. 'We'll pour, once these settle.' The young man nodded and left the room.

Proud turned back to Doherty. 'So, Joe, you're "helping us with our enquiries", are you?' he asked, with a smile.

'So it seems, Sir James. I find an excuse to escape from London, and here I am stuck behind another desk!'

'Still it's in a good cause. My colleagues across the water are very excited even by the outside chance that we might be able to pin something on Morton, suppose if it is on your turf.'

'They really think he's a bad 'un, do they?'

The sallow-faced American nodded. 'They're certain of it, Chief. They've just never been able to get close enough to hang anything on him.'

Skinner leaned across the table as Brian Mackie poured the coffee. 'Do your people think they'll be able to help us any further?'

'Sure they will. We have a whole section on Morton's organisation. I've got guys researching it right now. One thing they told me right away. SSC doesn't run a branch office in Europe or anywhere else. Morton likes to keep everyone close. But they do go to every major golf event where their men are playing, and there were three or four in the field at last week's European tournament.'

'Do you expect a report today?'

'Shit, yes, Bob! I've fixed a meeting with the new Special Branch in Glasgow for 4 p.m. this afternoon. By that time I expect to have wrapped this thing up and taken the Chief to lunch, and you too Brian . . . if you're allowed to eat at the same table as your boss!'

Sir James smiled. 'I think we could allow a dispensation, Joe, but I'll have to decline, I'm afraid. I'm lunching with the Chair of the Joint Police Board today, and since she's a new girl, I don't know her well enough to be sure that a short-notice cancellation wouldn't upset her. Don't let that hold you and Brian back though.'

'One thing might,' said Skinner. 'I've got another task for you, Brian, apart from checking out any SSC names that Joe can give us. I want you to call South Africa and ask them how they're doing in their investigation into M'tebe's father's abduction. Give them a nudge as well. Tell them that young M'tebe was made an offer by Greenfields, Bill Masur's group, but that he turned them down. He's going to sign instead with Darren Atkinson's company.'

He glanced at Proud. 'Darren told me that yesterday, Chief. He seems to think that Masur is OK about it, but maybe he's being naive. From what I saw of the way he handled Morton, Masur isn't a guy to be put off easily. And if he's connected in the way Joe says, he may think he can persuade young M'tebe to think again about signing with Darren.'

He stood up. 'So you throw that pebble of knowledge in the South Africans' pond, Brian. Then enjoy your lunch. You might introduce Joe to the Waterside in Haddington, especially if the FBI's paying. As for me, I'm off to uphold the honour of this constabulary on the golf course.'

Twenty-seven

Skinner pulled his car to a halt and looked out across the wide expanse towards the unladen supertanker, its stern pointing towards him. He had turned the corner at the very moment when the tide in Aberlady Bay had reached full ebb.

The sand flats stretched away for more than a mile. From road level, the distant, calm sea showed only as a sun-speckled silver ribbon, tied across the bay's mouth, and the tanker, riding high as it waited for its summons to take on cargo from the oil terminal, looked for all the world as if it was grounded.

In a county of quiet spectacle, it was one of Skinner's favourite sights. Always, when he encountered it, driving from the narrow village which had given its name to the bay, he stopped for a time to look and reflect. He remembered the first time that the mirage had ever caught his eye, the vanished sea with the ship cruising across the shimmering sand.

Seventeen years before, summoned to the scene of a road accident, a fatal road accident, he had seen it and had stopped, to gather his thoughts and perhaps to wish away what he knew was waiting for him a little further on. And the thought had come to him that if this natural phenomenon had been in its full display around an hour earlier, then perhaps Myra would have stopped to look also, and perhaps she would not have been travelling so fast when eventually she had come to Luffness Corner, and perhaps . . .

The thought crept back as it always did. He shook his head to throw aside impossible comparisons. He was still disturbed by the rediscovery of Myra's tape, and by the thoughts which it had stirred from their banishment to the deepest recesses of his mind. If his car had a time switch to take him back those seventeen years, to save Myra's life but to wipe out all else, would he press it?

He squeezed his eyes shut and took his wallet from his jacket. Flipping it open, he opened his eyes at the same time, and looked intently at the photo of Sarah and Jazz behind its Perspex panel. As he did the clenched muscles of his face relaxed into a smile. Replacing the wallet in his pocket, he slipped the car back into gear and drove on, into the present.

He had reached the outskirts of Gullane and the brown brick facility which his golf club had provided for its visitors, when the carphone rang. He pushed the receive button and Joe Doherty's voice filled the car. The background noise indicated that he was on the road also.

'My guys have come good, Bob. They've sent over a full list of the executive Vice-Presidents in SSC. As we thought, they're mostly lawyers, real Ivy-Leaguers in their early thirties. They're organised within the company on a divisional basis, each one concentrating on a different sport, or global sector. For example, there are three V-Ps looking after golf, each with his own group of clients.

'But there's one of them who doesn't have any special interest. He reports straight to Mike Morton, and from what we've been able to figure out, all the other guys seem to defer to him. He's older than the rest, about Morton's age, in fact, and he ain't no law school guy. His name is Richard Andrews, at least it is now. If you trace him far enough back, you'll find that when he was given exemption from military service on compassionate grounds, his name was Rocco Andrade. If you look a little further you'll find that his request for exemption was countersigned by old man Morticelli. Dig even deeper and you'll find that young Andrade's mamma's given name was Angela Morticelli, and that she was the old man's sister.'

'Tasty,' said Skinner, turning off Gullane Main Street. 'What sort is Mr Andrews?'

'He's a big, mean mother. A few years back, SSC had trouble with one of its fighters, a good champion with more smarts than were good for him. He wasn't happy with his end of the money for an up-coming fight, so he said he wouldn't sign. Andrews went to see him, and the guy signed on the dotted line. By the time the fight took place, SSC had the opponent under contract too. The champ took a swig from his water bottle after the first round, and was kayoed in the second. He never fought again.'

Skinner drew the car to a halt outside the cottage. 'How do they describe Mr Andrews inside the organisation? He must have some sort of title.'

Doherty laughed. 'Sure he has, and you'll like it. Morton calls him Vice-President in charge of special negotiations.'

'You're right, I like it. Do we know where he was last weekend?'

'Yup. Our informant inside SSC tells us that Andrews and one of the golf V-Ps, Bert Holliman, were in the UK for the PGA tournament last week. Holliman flew back on Sunday evening, but so far Andrews hasn't shown up back at the ranch.'

'Fascinating. I wonder where he was on Sunday? Listen, where are you just now? Is Brian with you?'

'Yeah, he's driving. We're heading out of town towards Haddington. We got a table booked at this Waterside place, then Brian's taking me to the station for the Glasgow train.'

'OK, don't bolt lunch, or break any speed limits, but tell Brian that as soon as he's done that, he should check out Mr Andrews. He should find out which hotel had him as a guest last week, and when he booked out. Tell him to try the car hire companies too.

'If this man can't account for himself on Sunday, I may want to have some "special negotiations" with him myself.'

Twenty-eight

'Honest to God, Skinner, look at you. Forty-five years old and nervous as a kitten. Where's the man I married? What happened to the father of this child?' She stood in the doorway, leaning against the jamb.

Jazz was curled in the crook of her arm, smiling. Approaching four months old, he held his head upright. His experiments with sound were growing more inventive by the day, and now he babbled out a string of sounds, as if mimicking his mother.

Bob threw him a mock glare. 'You can wind your neck in for a start, boy. One piss-taker in this family's quite enough.

'And you madam, should be enough of a golfer to understand what it's like to be about to tee off with Darren Atkinson with people watching. Knocking a few balls down the practice range is one thing, but this is public play, on a nice day, with hundreds, maybe thousands of people in the gallery.

'This isn't going to be like teeing off in the Friday evening bounce game in front of Craig, or Bobby, or Ken or Eric.' He slipped on his blazer, over a fresh white shirt.

She laughed. 'Well, just imagine that's who is watching you. Look, what's the worst that could happen?'

He pondered her question. 'I suppose the worst case would be if Norton Wales out-drove me. Mind you, I'd back Jazz to knock it further than Norton!' He took his son and raised him up high towards the ceiling, tickling him with his thumbs. The baby grinned and chortled.

'Careful, Bob, he's just had a feed.'

'You wouldn't barf on your dad, would you, son? Any more than your sister did in her time.' All the same, he handed Jazz carefully back to his mother, smiling.

'You know, my love, you've never looked more beautiful than you do now standing there, son on hip, all eyes, lips and suntan. Christ, if I wasn't going to golf.'

She grinned back at him. 'Yeah, too bad. I'll tell you something, copper, just between the three of us. I'm happier now than I've ever been in my life, happier in fact than I've ever imagined being. Going back to work'll be a lot tougher than I'd thought.'

'Then don't,' he said at once. 'Tell the University you've had second thoughts about the job. A lot of women need to work to sustain a lifestyle. You don't. We own all our properties, and I've got extra income from my legacy investments. And, you're right, we don't *need* both this house and the Edinburgh place. We want Jazz to go to school here anyway, don't we?

'So tell the University "Sorry, I made a mistake." Stay at home and enjoy being a full-time mother, for a few years at least!'

His sudden vehemence astonished her. 'Hey honey, is this pre-match tension or something? What brought all this on?'

He shrugged his shoulders. 'I don't know. I suppose I've been going along with the University thing because I know that a Chair at your age is an honour, but most of all because I thought it was what you really wanted.

'Now, if you say it isn't, then there's no question. Let it go, and stay here with Jazz. Nothing would make *me* happier.'

She took his hand and looked him in the eye. 'Slow down, big Bob, and listen to what I said. Going back to work *is* going to be tougher than I thought, especially in the first few months, but it's still what I want to do. I'm your wife and Jazz's mother, but I'm more than that. I'm me as well.

'It was me you fell in love with, not Jazz's mom. You're right, I *don't* have to go back to work. But it's part of being me, and if I throw it away, a big part of me will go with it. I'll change, I'll become someone else, someone different from the woman you fell in love with. OK, you might love her too, but maybe not as much . . . or maybe not at all. I ain't going to take that chance.

'Mellow motherhood may have its hooks in me for now, but they'd loosen sooner than you think.'

He stared at her, with a strange, almost pleading expression that she had never seen before. 'OK I hear that, but surely a year wouldn't hurt. Defer the job till next session. Do that at least for me, and for him!'

She smiled gently. 'Darling, it's for both of you that I'm going back to work.

'The decision's made, I've given my word, and the students are enrolling. Now, put all this out of your mind. Get down to Witches' Hill and knock that first tee-shot way past Norton Wales!'

Twenty-nine

'Does the name Richard Andrews mean anything to you, Darren?' Skinner asked as he finished tying the laces of his brown golf shoes.

Atkinson looked at him in surprise. 'Mr Nice? Oh yes, I know him well enough.'

'Why d'you call him that?'

'That's what everyone calls him. You might say that he's the unacceptable face of Mike Morton . . . if you can handle that as a concept! He's been around Morton for as long as I've known him, and if you thought that Mike behaved like a shit with Masur yesterday, you should see Andrews in action. I've heard him talk to world-class golfers like I wouldn't talk to a dog. And the amazing thing is that they take it. I mean, these guys are effectively his employers, his and Morton's, yet they're told where to play, where to live, what deals to sign. They just surrender themselves to SSC, completely.'

'Did SSC ever try to recruit you?'

The golfer nodded. 'Sure, just over ten years ago, just before I won my first tournament on the US tour, I had a call from Morton. He made me an offer, said that if I signed with him, I'd get access to invitation events that would be closed to me otherwise, that I'd make a guaranteed million dollars a year in endorsements.

'I told him I was earning that much already, and that I didn't have a problem filling my schedule. Next day I had a visit from Mr Nice, in my hotel room. He said to me that if I didn't sign with SSC then maybe I would start to have schedule problems. I said to him that I was very happy with the way that my brother Rick was managing my affairs, and that I wasn't about to change things.

'Then Mr Nice said . . . and I'll never forget the way he said it . . . "Yeah, but anyone can have an accident. Suppose something was to happen to your brother?" He came straight out with it.' Atkinson pulled on his sweater, and headed towards the changing-room door.

'So how did you react?' said Skinner, following.

'I told him that if Rick as much as caught a cold I'd go straight to the FBI. Then I threw him out.'

'Was there any follow-up?'

Atkinson opened the door at the end of the corridor and stepped out into the daylight. He shook his head. 'Not from them. It got me steamed up though. I went out and won the tournament that week. Paul Wyman was SSC's top dog then, and I beat him in a play-off. A few weeks later I won my first Masters, and all of a sudden I was big news, and even bigger box-office. Whether they liked it or not, SSC needed me at their events. So Morton and I reached an agreement, that I'd give their tournaments preference and they'd pay me appearance money.'

Skinner glanced at him, as they strolled towards the first tee. 'And he didn't give you trouble when you set up your own company? No more visits from Mr Nice?'

'No. I told Mike from the start that I was mainly interested in guys who base themselves on the European tour. He said that he didn't have a problem with that.

'How come you're asking about Andrews all of a sudden, Bob?'

The policeman shrugged his shoulders. 'Oh, the name was mentioned, that's all. And I'm just a nosey bastard by nature.'

Atkinson grinned. 'Yeah, and I'm the next Pope!'

Norton Wales and Hideo Murano were waiting on the tee as they approached. Bravo stood, with two wizened, weather-beaten caddies and their heavy burdens, beside a tall signboard bearing the legend, 'The Murano Million. Hole No 1. 465 yards.' Skinner wandered across and looked at the champion's bag. 'You play Shark's Fin clubs, Darren?'

'Yes, they're the best. I'm paid well to use them, but that's secondary for me. I've known pros who've changed clubs just for the money they've been offered to make the switch, and who've lost their game as a result. You want to be the best, you have to use the clubs that are best for you.'

'D'you carry a standard set?'

'No. I have three wedges, one for fairway play, a sand-iron and a thin-soled job for short play around the greens. I find that I can do without a nine-iron. Actually, in any given round I tend not to use any more than ten out of the fourteen. If I could be sure in advance which ones they were going to be, I could take some weight off Bravo's shoulders!'

He clapped his hands. 'OK guys,' he called. 'Ready for action?' He looked around. 'Where's your caddy, Bob?'

'Lady Kinture? She said she was going to change her shoes, that's all.' He looked round. 'Here she comes now.'

The others followed his gaze and saw the immaculate figure of Susan Kinture sweeping elegantly towards them. She was dressed in a peach-coloured trouser suit, with a white shirt and golf shoes, and was pulling a wide-wheeled caddy-car, on which Skinner's clubs were loaded. 'Hello, chaps,' she called as she approached. 'Ready for action?' She smiled warmly enough at Skinner, Wales and Murano, but when she looked at Darren Atkinson, the light of hero worship seemed to shine in her eyes. 'Hello, Lady Kinture,' the golfer said, formally, and with the briefest and most courtly of bows. Skinner thought that he saw the faintest flash of disappointment cross her face.

A grandstand had been set up behind the tee, looking down the first fairway. It was filled by around three hundred seated spectators. Skinner tried to banish all thoughts of the gallery from his mind.

'Right chaps, we'll play this as a medal round, but just for interest, let's make a match of it. Norton and I'll take on you guys. Let's give Norton and Hideo a shot at each hole. Bob, there are ten par fours. I'll give you a shot at each of them. OK?' The three nodded agreement. 'Right, Hideo,' said Atkinson, 'you're up first.' The Japanese stepped forward and asked his caddy for a number three wood. He wasted no time, teeing his ball up and clipping it carefully and sensibly down the middle of the fairway.

'May I have my driver, please, Susan?' said Skinner. The tall blonde looked at his clubs, found the longest in the bag, pulled off its woollen head cover, and handed it to him. He teed his ball and stepped back, looking down the fairway. The hole was a slight dogleg easing right around the slope of the Witches' Hill towards the green which was, according to the sign, a good drive and a long second shot distant. There was a wide bunker on the left, two hundred yards away; the reason, Skinner guessed, why his Japanese partner had played deliberately short. He gave the club a swish to loosen his shoulders, then lined up his drive. 'No chances here, boy,' he muttered to himself. 'You've got one of your shots at this hole, and you'll need to make use of them all.' He addressed the ball and swung, slowly and smoothly. There was a gasp from the gallery as the ball headed straight for the sand-trap, then an exhalation of relief as it carried easily over the hazard, took a hard high bounce and careered for another thirty yards down the left-hand side of the fairway. Behind him, there was a smattering of applause. Skinner stepped back to stand beside Murano.

Norton Wales stepped up to the mark, clowning and waving to the gallery. Atkinson spoke to his caddy, who handed his client a five-iron. The singer took the club with a nod to his team captain, who mouthed the words, 'Swing slow.' Wales followed the instructions and was rewarded with a satisfactorily straight shot, shorter than Murano's or Skinner's, but like theirs safely in the playing area.

Darren Atkinson took the tee to a round of sustained applause from the gallery in the stands, and from the crowds lining the fairway on the left, swelled in number by his appearance on the course. He acknowledged them with a smile and a wave, then turned to begin his day's work. As he flexed the golden shaft of his metal-headed driver, rehearsing his swing section by section, Skinner was aware that this was no longer the amiable coach of the previous evening. This was a warrior readying himself for battle, not against another man but against the course itself, against its challenge to his supremacy, to his mastery of his craft. He looked down the fairway, selecting the point to which he would strike his first blow, and Skinner recognised in his eyes an expression which, in his earlier years as a karate player, he had seen often in the eyes of opponents out to attack his black belt status. He had been able, invariably to face them down, and now, he sensed, Atkinson's challenger was in for a pounding.

The US Open champion teed up and addressed the ball. The crowd, with traditional Scottish courtesy and discipline, was totally silent. Across on the Truth Loch, a goose cried out, but Atkinson's concentration was unbroken. Without seeming to exert overpowering physical force, he smashed the ball away into the distance, its left-to-right flight following the curve of the dogleg. Its first bounce was beyond Skinner's drive, satisfactory by his standards, and it ran on and on, so far into the distance that it was almost out of sight. The gallery's cheers, which had begun almost at the moment the ball left the club-head, echoed around the teeing ground. Atkinson grinned and, waving to the crowd in the stand to follow, led his team off down the fairway.

'See what I mean about the course, Bob?' he said as he and Skinner walked, side by side towards Norton Wales's drive, around 160 yards from the tee. 'It doesn't have sharp enough teeth for a championship venue. The hill isn't really in play, and that bunker isn't a hazard at all for a pro, or for you, for that matter. There's nothing to stop me using all my length off the tee, and with a short iron for my second shot, it's a birdie there for the taking.'

'Shall I tell Hector to do something about it?' asked Susan Kinture, earnestly. Atkinson looked over his shoulder in surprise.

'I'm sorry, Lady Kinture. That was very rude of me. You and the Marquis are my hosts this week, and here I am criticising your course.' He paused as Norton Wales duffed his second shot, impossibly, into the bunker. 'Don't take it to heart, though. Witches' Hill is in the finest condition I've ever seen in a brand-new course, and your visitors will enjoy it as it stands. It's quite natural for adjustments to be made to a new venue as it matures.'

Susan Kinture's eyes shone like those of a schoolgirl. 'Could you suggest any? If you could, Darren, it would be wonderful.'

Atkinson smiled at her, as Hideo Murano hit his second shot, a conservative three-wood, which he tugged into light rough, eighty yards short and left of the green. 'I probably could make one or two suggestions, but I'm not sure that the Marquis would welcome them. It's his course, and he has his own architect. He and O'Malley may well have long-term development plans.' He took her hand for a second, as Norton Wales picked up, after his third unsuccessful attempt to extricate himself from the sand-trap. 'Tell you what, I'll give it some thought on the way round, and perhaps you and I could have a chat about it over a nightcap tonight, after the dinner.'

'That would be great!'

'Right, it's a date. Now I must concentrate on my game. I could have a battle on my hands with these two guys.' They had reached Skinner's ball. 'Right Bob. Show us your stuff.' The kidney-shaped green, two hundred yards away, was guarded front left by a bunker, and a second lay to its rear on the right. The big policeman looked at the lie of his ball, thought for a moment, then took a three-iron from his bag. 'Slow,' he said, aloud and fired in a high shot which bounced on the front edge of the green, bit hard, and trickled to a stop just short of the right-hand bunker.

'Bugger,' said Atkinson, forgetful of Lady Kinture's presence. 'That's you there for nett one, counting your shot.'

Bravo was waiting by his ball when they reached it, sixty

yards beyond Skinner's drive. 'Eight-iron, please, Brav.' He approached the shot as carefully and as methodically as he had prepared his tee-shot, seeming to ease, rather than force, the ball towards the green. It pitched six feet past the hole, but spun back sharply to stop inches away. The gallery, now numbered in thousands, roared its applause behind the rope barrier.

Hideo Murano took two shots to free himself from the rough, then hit his fifth into the bunker behind the green. He signalled that his caddy should retrieve his ball, and stood beside Norton Wales on the edge of the green as Skinner surveyed a putt which was all of thirty feet long. 'What d'you think, caddy?' he asked Susan Kinture.

Obviously pleased to be asked, she stood beside him and looked down the line. 'It looks as if it'll come in from the right, about two inches. But it's slightly downhill, so be careful not to hit it too far past.' He nodded and lined up the putt. Remembering Darren Atkinson's advice, he kept the Zebra's head clear of the grass and stroked the ball delicately. For a moment, he thought that it would fall into the hole, but at the last moment it ran out of pace and stopped on the lip. Unable to suppress a smile, he tapped in for a four, nett three, leaving Atkinson to confirm the half with his tiny putt.

'Well played, partner,' said Hideo Murano, with his first grin of the day, as they walked towards the second tee.

'Enjoy it,' said Skinner. 'I think that's as good as it's going to get.'

It was a measure of Atkinson's class that he did not lose a single hole on the way round, even though Skinner managed to use five of his ten shots to secure nett birdies. His golf was awesome, and the match ended on the sixteenth green when he rolled in his eighth birdie putt to put his team three up on Skinner and Murano. Norton Wales looked crestfallen as the four shook hands. 'Worse than a bad night at Batley, that was,' he muttered.

'Don't worry,' said his captain. 'Suppose you pick up just two or three birdies with your shots in the competition proper, you'll have done your bit for the team. No one's expecting you to break par. This might not be the toughest course for us pros, but it's a bloody good test for high handicappers.'

They played on to complete the round. With the clubhouse in sight, and the gallery swelled still further, Skinner and Atkinson chatted as they walked together down the eighteenth fairway, alongside the Truth Loch with its raucous geese and its newly reinstalled ducking stool.

'What made you decide to set up your company, Darren?' the policeman asked.

The golfer shrugged his shoulders. 'I felt that a good management company dedicated to golfers was one thing that the European Tour lacked. Then when I thought about it, I realised that Rick and I *had* in effect, a good management company devoted entirely to my interests. So we decided to expand its operations, and to put it at the service of others.'

'Do you plan to ease yourself out of playing one day, and into the company?'

Atkinson shook his head vigorously. 'Rick runs the company. That's what he's good at. I'm good at golf. At the moment, I'm the best golfer in the world. Some say I'm the best there's ever been. I can't agree with them, not yet. But I think I can be, and that's what drives me on. Every time I tee up, I want to win. Sometimes I *expect* to win, and when I'm in that sort of form I usually do. If you're a betting man, put some dough on me to lift the Million this week. I'm a racing certainty. Then back me to take at least two more majors next year. I've got thirteen in the bag so far. My dream is twenty.'

They stopped by Skinner's drive. He asked Susan Kinture for a three-iron and hit a low shot to the fringe of the green. As Wales and Murano played what seemed like a separate game along the edge of the left-hand rough, Skinner, Atkinson and their caddies strolled on towards the champion's ball, its position the result of a long, beautifully flighted shot which had made the Truth Loch seem pointless as a hazard. 'You said something yesterday about having your own course. When are you going to fit that in? In your lunch-break?'

Atkinson laughed. 'I'm always looking for development opportunities. One day I'll find the right one. There must be plenty of people out there who would love to have the World Number One involved in their project.'

As the gallery filled the surrounding stands, he selected a five-iron and smacked a beautiful shot into the heart of the green, fifteen feet left of the flag. Again the crowd cheered, but Atkinson was less impressed by his work. He slammed the club back into the bag in annoyance. 'Poor,' he said to Skinner. 'From this range I should finish no worse than ten feet away.'

The policeman laughed. 'Back here in the world of the mortals, I'll settle for two putts for a par!'

As they approached the green, he held back, leaving Darren Atkinson to walk alone up the slope, to receive the acclaim of his public. The champion marked his ball then signalled the crowd into silence as Murano, then Wales finished their rounds.

Susan Kinture handed Skinner his putter, drawing murmurs from the crowd as she helped him line up his forty-foot putt. Out on the course, the gallery had been more distant, but now in the amphitheatre of the eighteenth, he fought to control the churning of his stomach. Thinking of nothing but the ball, he managed a smooth stroke and ran his approach a mere foot past the hole. Smiling with relief, he walked up, amid applause, and topped in for his par. His blonde caddy, who was holding the flag, stepped up to give him a brief hug as he stood up after picking his ball out of the hole. 'Super golf,' she whispered. 'Michael would have been so pleased to see it.'

The line of Atkinson's birdie putt ran across a sharp slope, and down into a small flat area where the hole was cut. Watching him judge the borrow, Skinner realised that it was probably the most difficult shot of the afternoon, yet when the ball swung sharply down the slope and rolled unwaveringly into the hole he was not surprised in the slightest degree.

He applauded with the rest, as he walked up the green to shake the champion's hand. 'Wonderful round, Darren. I think I'll go and put those bets on now.'

Atkinson smiled. 'Let's just hope I haven't used up my ration of birdies before the tournament begins!' With Susan Kinture between them, they walked across the green, towards the clubhouse entrance, where Arthur Highfield stood waiting, with Andres Cortes, Ewan Urquhart, and a rugged man Skinner recognised as Sandro Gregory, the Australian.

'Well,' said Gregory, with more than a trace of irony. 'How was it? Have the rest of us got a chance at the money?'

Atkinson looked at him evenly. 'Sure,' he said. 'All you have to do is go round in fewer shots than me.'

'What did you shoot, Darren?' asked Urquhart.

'Oh, just one or two birdies,' he replied vaguely.

'Yes,' said Skinner, quietly. 'Nine, to be exact. That last putt was for a sixty-three.'

Andres Cortes shook his head and muttered something obscene in Spanish.

'That's physically impossible, Andres!' said Arthur Highfield. He rubbed his hands together. 'Gentlemen, you will remember this evening's dinner.' The four golfers nodded. 'It was really you I wanted to see, Mr Skinner. The PGA is hosting a pre-tournament dinner in the clubhouse dining room. Seven-thirty for eight p.m., lounge suits. I should have mentioned it before. You will be able to come, won't you?'

'I'd be delighted. I'd better head home right now though, to break the news to my wife … gently.'

'Bring Sarah,' said Susan Kinture at once, 'otherwise I'll be the only lady present.'

'She'd love to come, but we have a four-month-old social handicap, with an established routine. And we'd never find a baby-sitter at this notice.'

Susan Kinture folded her arms across her chest. 'No excuses, officer. We have a wonderful girl on our staff at Bracklands. She'll sit for you. Off you go home and help Sarah to get herself prepared. Otherwise I'll tell her she was invited, but you said "no" on her behalf.'

Bob smiled. 'I give up. But you phone Sarah anyway, and tell her all about your wonder girl. I'll head off home, meantime.'

'Time for a quick team shandy first,' Atkinson interposed, and led his playing companions to the changing room. Hideo Murano and Norton Wales, each sweating heavily from their exertions, decided to shower, but Atkinson and Skinner simply washed and changed into blazers, slacks and shirts.

In the bar, they found a window table, to which Williamson, the elderly steward, brought their drinks. 'That was a lifetime of golfing experience in one afternoon, Darren,' said Skinner, sipping his Coke. 'I'll be the club bore for months. But tell me, isn't it disconcerting for you to be playing with the likes of us?'

Atkinson smiled. 'When I play, Bob, I don't even notice you're there. I don't see anything but the ball or the course. I don't hear the crowd, not even in the States.'

'That's dedication for you. Is your brother like you?'

'Rick? Yes, I suppose he is, in his own way.'

'Is he around this week?'

'No, he doesn't come to all the tournaments. We have field people who look after our clients' interests, just like SSC and Greenfields.'

Skinner nodded, thoughtfully, and took another sip of his drink. 'Speaking of them, did you see Richard Andrews at the tournament last week, by any chance?'

'Mr Nice? Oh yes. You always know when he's about, he's such a loud-mouthed bugger.'

'Was he there every day?'

Atkinson considered the question for a moment. 'Come to think of it, he was there on Thursday, Friday and Saturday, with his gopher, a bloke called Hollywood, or something . . . Holliman, that's his name. But on Sunday, the gopher was around on his own. I didn't see Mr Nice at all.'

The golfer looked at the policeman, curiously. 'How come you're so interested in him anyway? You don't think . . .'

Skinner shook his head. 'Of course not. Tell you what; try to forget I asked about him, OK? But if you see him around this week, give me a whisper. Remember that. Not a shout. A very discreet whisper.'

Thirty

'Honey, you are wonderful! Imagine swinging an invite to the tournament dinner for me too! And finding us a baby-sitter, into the bargain! Ooh, come here!'

She pulled him to her, ran her fingers through his hair and kissed him; a long squashy kiss of sheer delight.

Bob frowned, to keep his confusion from her. 'So Susan Kinture called you,' he said, in what he hoped was a knowing tone.

Sarah squeezed him again. 'Yup. She told me about Highfield inviting you to the dinner, and you saying that given the short notice you'd only come if you could bring your wife, and then about you asking her if she could fix us up with a short-notice baby-sitter.'

He smiled, relaxing. 'She's quite a woman, that Susan. You're happy about the sitter?'

'Oh yes, Susan told me all about her. She's working as a maid at Bracklands during the summer, living in. With all the house guests at the dinner tonight, she's surplus to requirements. I said you'd pay her thirty pounds.'

His jaw dropped. 'That's a bloody good hourly rate. Did you say we'd lay on a taxi too?'

'Of course I did. But she's got her own car.'

'Thank Christ for that!' he whispered, through clenched

teeth. Then aloud, 'OK, it's six o'clock now, we'd better get cracking.'

Together they bathed the rumbustious Jazz, sticking to their vow that bathtime should be a joint exercise whenever possible. The baby seemed to fill more of the plastic basin with every day. 'It's soon going to be easier to get in the bath ourselves and take him with us,' said Bob.

'I have done before now, on the odd occasion you've been away.' She grinned. 'I think it might be a bit tight for three, though.' She lifted the child from the tub, still kicking and wriggling, and wrapped him in a towel. 'I'll take him to the nursery to dry him off and package him up. Meantime, you can get into the shower.'

'Yes, ma'am.' Bob gave a mock salute and wandered into their bedroom unbuttoning his shirt. He enjoyed a long, leisurely shower in the en-suite bathroom, easing his tightening muscles in the pulsing of the strong jets, and kneading the Paul Mitchell shampoo through his thick, greying mane.

A momentary dip in the air temperature told him that the cubicle door had been opened, even though his eyes were squeezed shut. Then Sarah's body moulded itself against his, and they opened with a start. She reached up and drew his mouth to hers. She kissed him, in earnest this time, not in fun, and he felt her salty tongue in his mouth, flicking, probing. Her fingers wound through his wet chest hair then down, down, until he felt himself throbbing as she held him, there in the pulsing water of the shower. He lifted her up, effortlessly, with his massive strength, bracing her back against the shower's tiled wall, and entered her unerringly. She gasped and shuddered, gripping his hips with the inside of her strong thighs and binding her legs together behind him. He moved inside her barely at all, clenching muscles rather than thrusting, but it was enough to send her into a writhing frenzy. Her hair whipped against his face as she shook her head from side to side, crying out aloud. And at last he felt the tremors of impending orgasm; in his legs at first, then rushing up through his entire body as he pushed himself as deep inside her as he would go, drawing one last hoarse shout of pleasure from her, in unison with his own.

They stood there in that position as they recovered, kissing and nuzzling, breathing heavily together, wearing the secret smiles of total intimacy. Eventually he raised her from him, then lowered her carefully, supporting her until he was sure that she would not slip on the cubicle floor. He kissed her once more, then took a foaming sponge and began to rub her body, as she smoothed soap over him. When they were finished he twisted the wheel of the shower control, stopping the flow, and held the door open as she stepped out. She turned and looked up at him, something in her eyes, one of those perfectly timed punchlines, waiting to come out. 'And I only came in to tell you that Brian Mackie phoned earlier!' she said. He laughed out loud and threw a big, pink bath towel over her. 'Just as well I had water in my ears, then, and couldn't hear you!'

They dried off together, filling the small bathroom, and went back together naked into the bedroom. They began to dress, then Bob paused and touched her gently on the shoulder. 'Hey, honey.' It was almost a whisper.

She looked round, her eyes still soft from her climax. 'What?'

'I'm sorry I was so daft earlier on. About going back to work. You're not a plant to be kept in a greenhouse, or a nanny in a nursery.'

She reached up and touched his cheek, gently. 'It's OK. I understand. Maybe even better than you do.'

'How d'you mean?'

She looked at him, hesitating for a second. 'Well, I think it's that tape. It's hearing Myra's voice again, after all these years. It's stirred up all sorts of things in your mind. Most of all, it's reminded you that Myra was a working mother, and that she was coming home from school when she was killed. And something in you, way below the surface is saying, "Don't take that chance, that lightning *could* strike twice."'

'But it won't, honey, it won't.'

He looked at her with complete and utter love. He opened his mouth, but could find no words. Instead he simply drew her to him and kissed her. After a few seconds, she put her hands on his chest, and drew back, smiling. 'Enough, Skinner! We got places to go, people to meet.' He nodded and picked up a clean shirt.

'Oh, by the way,' she said. 'I really meant it when I said that Brian had called. It was around five. He asked if you could get in touch, when you've a minute.'

He pulled the shirt over his head and reached for his tie. 'OK. I'll get it over with now, while you're feeding Number One through there. I can hear him calling for supper.' He sat on the bed, picked up the telephone and dialled Mackie's mobile number.

'Hi Brian. ACC here. You called earlier.'

'Yes sir, thanks for getting back. I thought you'd want to hear this. There are two developments. First, we've discovered that Richard Andrews checked out of his hotel at last week's tournament on the Saturday ... the day before it finished. We're looking all over the Edinburgh area to see if he's checked in somewhere else, but so far there's nothing.'

'Mmm,' said Skinner. 'From what Darren Atkinson told me, I'd guessed the first part of that. As for the rest, if he came up here to bump off Michael White, in revenge for crossing his boss, he isn't the sort of guy who'd leave a calling card. What's the second thing?'

'That's from South Africa, sir,' said Mackie. 'I passed on your suggestion to Durban. They rang back late this afternoon. They'd done a hotel check earlier, and had come up with the names of two Australian guys who signed in on Monday, the day before M'tebe's old man was lifted, and checked out yesterday morning. The South Africans checked the register details with Oz, and they match two guys who are regular caddies on the Australian golf circuit, often for players who are clients of Greenfields.'

Skinner whistled. 'Well, did you ever! What a swell party this could be tonight! Give me those names, quick. I might bounce them off friend Masur, just to see if I can crack that smug Aussie smile of his!'

Thirty-one

The clubhouse dining room was situated directly above the bar and boardroom. Its panoramic view stretched out over the ninth and eighteenth greens, and beyond, across the rest of the undulating course, across the Truth Loch and across Witches' Hill itself, as it cast its great evening shadow across the land.

Places were set for thirty-six, but there was still ample floor space for the guests of the Professional Golfers' Association to mingle. Sarah and Skinner were welcomed formally by Andres Cortes, the PGA Chairman, and by Arthur Highfield.

As they took drinks from the tray offered by a striped-waistcoated waiter, Darren Atkinson, called across. 'Bob, over here!' The golfer was standing with a group which included Norton Wales and Hideo Murano, and five others, among whom Skinner recognised Ewan Urquhart and Deacon Weekes, the US Masters Champion. He took Sarah's arm and led her across.

'Hi, Captain, you sound in good form. Got over that rotten second shot at the eighteenth?'

Atkinson laughed. 'Yes, the putt helped me to forget!'

'Darren, Norton, Hideo, this is my wife, Sarah.' Atkinson shook Sarah's hand, Hideo Murano bowed and smiled, and Norton Wales gave her a twinkling wave. The golfer was about to complete the introductions when Susan Kinture flowed into the room.

'My dear,' she called out, advancing on the group, 'so glad you could come.' She gathered Sarah in one arm and Atkinson in the other, her primrose trouser suit in contrast to, but not clashing with, Sarah's square-shouldered black dress . . . only slightly tighter around the hips and bust after the birth of Jazz . . . or with the golfer's pale blue tuxedo. 'I've fiddled the table plan, my dear. Darren's got me on one side and you on the other. Now come on and let's circulate.' She swept them away towards another group.

As they moved off, the Marquis of Kinture rolled up in his wheelchair. 'Evening all,' he barked. He glowered at Atkinson. 'Hear you took the piss out of my golf course this afternoon!'

The golfer smiled softly. 'Perfect conditions, Hector, just perfect.'

The Marquis glowered again. 'If you even whisper "I told you so", I shall arise from this chariot and smite you!'

'I wouldn't do that old chap . . . whatever I was thinking.' There was an air of tension between the two which puzzled Skinner, but before he could dwell on it Deacon Weekes moved alongside him, introducing himself. 'I hear you're the top cop in these parts,' said the Masters winner.

'Second top, in fact.'

'That'll do for me, sir. Has your being here got anything to do with that thing on Sunday?'

'Indirectly. I'm taking Michael White's place in Darren's team.'

'Ah,' said Weekes. 'Were you out with him this afternoon?' Skinner nodded.

'How was he?'

'In two words? Bloody awesome!'

'I heard he shot sixty-three.'

'You heard the truth. Nine birdies. It was like playing with God.' He paused. 'How about you, did you play a full round today?'

'Yeah, three of us played together,' said Weekes. 'I got it round in sixty-seven. So did Ewan. We were both pretty pleased with that, till we heard what Mr Merciless had done. The poor kid Oliver, though, he was really off. That thing with his pop has really shaken him up.'

'Mmm,' said Skinner. 'You didn't play with your teams, then?'

'Nah! That's Darren's scene. Nothing left to chance. It'll be like Christmas in Georgia for me, if I win the Million. But Darren won't be happy unless he wins the team prize as well. What's your handicap, Bob?'

'Seven.'

'Better be sure you play to it! How many shots did he give you today?'

'Ten. I thought he was being generous, till I found I'd shot a gross seventy-five and hadn't won a hole.'

Weekes shook his head. 'Tell you something. If he'd given you eleven shots, he'd have shot sixty-two and you still wouldn't have won a hole. Darren hates to lose to people he thinks he should beat . . . and he thinks he should beat everybody. When he finished second in the US PGA, I knew the rest of us were in for a lean time through to the end of the season.'

'Even you pros rate him that highly?'

'Hate to say it, but yeah, we do. The kid Oliver might have the talent to give him a game, but he doesn't have the steel. It isn't just golf with Darren. Sure he wants to win first prize every time he tees off, and he hates it when he doesn't, but he thinks that way in everything he does. He doesn't only want to be Number One in golf, he wants to be Number One in the game of life!'

Skinner looked across the room. Atkinson stood in a circle with Susan Kinture, who was still holding his arm, Sarah, Mike Morton, a solemn Oliver M'tebe, Frankie Holloway, the actress and another man whom he did not recognise. The golfer, on the eve of a million-pound event, was as relaxed as anyone he had ever seen.

'He's got no nerves, has he?' he said to Weekes.

'You guessed it. I was in a play-off with him once, at Augusta. I was so nervous and so hot I was hyper-goddamn-ventilating. I'll swear his heart-rate was about fifty! What a guy.'

'Dinner is served, ladies and gentlemen,' the head waiter called from the doorway. Skinner and Weekes strolled across to check their places on the table plan. Atkinson was indeed between Sarah and Susan Kinture, but Bob was seated at his wife's right hand. The Marquis was across the room, between Highfield and Cortes.

They took their places and Skinner found himself opposite Oliver M'tebe, who sat between Bill Masur and Hideo Murano, who was alongside Tiger Nakamura, and the golfer's unofficial interpreter for the evening.

The starters were served, a spoon rapped on the central table, and Andres Cortes rose to recite a brief grace in Spanish. The wine waiters circulated with Chablis and Strathmore, and the meal began. The sight and smell of the cockaleekie soup made Skinner realise suddenly how hungry he was. He set to without a word, even to Sarah.

In the lull as the waiters served the fish, he glanced across to M'tebe and caught the young man's eye. 'Have you been in contact with South Africa today?'

He nodded. 'Yes sir, but there is no good news. My father is still missing.'

'I know, and it's a pity, but at least there's been no more bad news. I asked one of my people to check with the South African police. They're doing everything they can, Oliver. They say that they're convinced, like you, that it's not political. It may be a kidnapping for ransom, in which case there may be no contact at all for a few days.

'The police do have one small lead. They've found that two men stayed overnight in the hotel nearest your father's home, and checked out just before the kidnap.' He paused. 'The names in the register are John Mallett and Steve May, and the addresses are Sydney, New South Wales.' He kept his voice casual, and glanced at Masur as he spoke. There was the briefest flicker of an eyebrow, in instantly suppressed surprise, but otherwise the Australian's expression was unchanged. 'The Australian police have been asked if the names mean anything to them. I know it's pretty tenuous . . . I mean for all we know these guys could be Jehovah's Witnesses . . . but at least it gives you something to hang on to.

'How about you, Mr Masur?' he said suddenly. 'Do those names mean anything?'

The Australian shrugged his shoulders, impassively. 'There's Malletts and Mays all over bloody Sydney, mate.'

He tapped the young South African on the arm. 'Don't you worry, Olly son. It'll be OK. You win the Million for your old man.' M'tebe smiled weakly.

Dinner continued in a welter of small talk, about the day's rounds, or recent golf tournaments, or the newest endorsement and sponsorship deals. Eventually, with coffee and liqueurs on the table, Andres Cortes rose again. 'I should like to say some words about this competition. I am pleased that we are all here to open this fine new course, and naturally, I am pleased also that we are here to play for so much money.

'But I am very sad about the terrible thing that happen on Sunday, and that Mr White will not be with us tomorrow. Whoever wins this week, we should all think of him.' He sat down in silence.

'True indeed,' said Masur, across the table. He stood up. 'Still, even in sadness life and golf go on, and I have a happier announcement to make. Today, Tiger Nakamura's contract with SSC expired. Tomorrow he signs a contract appointing Greenfields as his global manager, in all of his golf and business dealings. The times they are a-changing, my friends.' He sat down.

There was dead silence across the room. It was broken, almost bizarrely, by the trilling of a mobile telephone. Around the table a dozen hands reached automatically into pockets, but it was Darren Atkinson who produced the intrusive instrument. He switched it off, apologetically.

As the buzz of conversation resumed, Skinner looked across the room towards Morton. His face seemed bright red, and suffused with rage. 'Tell me, Masur,' said the ACC, 'when you went to Charm School, why did you skip the diplomacy classes?'

The Australian followed the direction of the policeman's gaze and laughed. 'Don't waste your sympathy on that guy, Skinner. He's had it coming. Tomorrow will be a great day. It will mean that we've got a million-pound field without a single SSC player in it.' He drained his brandy.

Skinner shook his head in disgust, but his retort was cut off by Sarah's tug on his sleeve. 'Bob, over there. It's our taxi-driver. I'd say he's just in time.'

Thursday

Thirty-two

For once they were not awakened by the early morning phone call. Jazz had put in an unscheduled appearance and lay with them in their bed, refreshed and chortling between his drowsy parents.

'So, did you enjoy last night, aside from Masur's gloating wee speech?' asked Bob, sipping from a mug of restorative coffee, his naked shoulders cool against the pine headboard.

'Yeah. You know how much I like meeting new people. And it was a minor triumph to get into that black dress again, after having this fella.'

'Tell you something, I enjoyed watching the heads turn when you walked into the room.' She smiled and rubbed a leg against his.

'What did you think of my golf partner?'

'Special. He's got quite an aura about him. There were two guys in that room last night who stood out from the crowd, and I had one of you on either side of me at the dinner table. I'll tell *you* something. Susan Kinture's got the hots for Darren!'

Bob laughed. 'I am only a dumb copper, my darling, but even *I* had figured that one out! D'you think she's really in the market, though?'

Sarah propped herself up on an elbow. The duvet slipped down her side, and Jazz seemed to eye her left breast, hungrily, as it swung closer to his face. 'She probably is. She's a fine healthy woman, is Sue, and it's questionable whether Hector, with his disability, is capable of meeting her needs.

'But leaving her appetites aside, d'you think Darren would be interested . . . or available? Is he married?'

'No. He's a legendary golf bachelor. He told me he's had opportunities, but he's always put golf first. Probably right, too. D'you have any idea of the time these guys spend practising?'

She smiled. 'In that case, you better not let this week make you too keen on golf.'

Jazz looked up in surprise when the telephone rang. 'Bugger!' Bob snapped, and picked it up, pulling himself upright. He glanced at the bedside alarm clock. It showed 6.21 a.m. 'Skinner!'

'Sorry, Boss. It's Andy. We've had another death at Witches' Hill.'

'Oh, for fu . . .' He stopped himself short. 'Suspicious?'

'Depends what you read into a bloke being tied to the imitation seventeenth-century ducking stool and dropped into the Truth Loch!'

'Jesus Christ!'

'The club pro found him. He went out at five-thirty to position the flags and cut the holes for today's play. He did the eighteenth first, and was on his way back down the fairway when he saw that the stool was in the water.' He paused. 'You remember how it's usually held clear by a rope.

'He thought that the rope had slipped, and went over to replace it, but when he tried to haul the stool out of the water, it was a ton weight. But the device has a sort of pivoting lever, and he was strong enough to haul it up and swing it on to the bank. As soon as it was clear of the water, even in the grey light before dawn, he saw that there was a stiff in it. He belted back to the clubhouse and phoned Haddington. They called me. I've got men on the way there, I've called Ali Higgins, and I'm en route myself. Now I need a doctor.'

'Could the pro identify the body?'

'Well the light was dodgy and he looked a bit grotesque, but he said that he thought it was Masur, the Australian.'

'Oh shit! That's all I need, a bloody gang war!'

He glanced across at Sarah. She was looking at him with a mixture of puzzlement and concern. Even Jazz seemed to be curious as he looked up at him.

'OK, you've got your doctor. She'll be there inside fifteen minutes. We're not quite at the stage of taking the baby to crime scenes with us, so I'll be down as soon as Sarah's finished and back here.

'See you later!'

Thirty-three

The air still felt damp with the morning dew as Sarah pulled her car into the park in front of the clubhouse, from which she had emerged with her husband less than eight hours before.

The sleek black dress which she had worn to the PGA dinner had been replaced by a waxed cotton jacket, a heavy grey sweatshirt and her oldest, beachcombing denims, tucked into a pair of blue wellington boots, tied at the top. She parked her Frontera Sport alongside a shiny silver Mondeo with new registration plates, and was surprised when Andy Martin climbed out.

'This is a bit conservative for you, isn't it?' she said, pointing to the car. 'I thought you were a sports hatch man.'

Martin shrugged his shoulders. He was in plain clothes, looking relaxed and, in his leather jacket, much more like the man she knew. 'After I smashed up the last one, I thought I should have something more in keeping with my age and status.' He grinned, and his mischievous look was back. 'Don't be fooled, though, Sarah. It might look like a dumpling, but it's a twenty-four-valve!'

She made to climb out of the Vauxhall but he motioned her to stay where she was. 'Your car's better equipped for where we're going.' He climbed into the passenger seat and directed her around the clubhouse, past the eighteenth green and out on to the buggy track, heading towards the lightening sky in the east. Three hundred yards beyond the green they came to a point at which the rope barrier was untied. Sarah, following Martin's sign, turned the Frontera to the left, and headed through the thick rough and out across the fairway. As she crested a slight rise she could see, for the first time, the banks of the Truth Loch.

As she looked down the slope, the long thick pole of the ducking stool stood out on its tall central pillar, angled, stark and black against the smooth waters of the loch. One end was high in the air, and a thick rope dangled from it, the other rested in the thick grass of the bank, with a black shape around it. A little apart from the scene a police Range Rover was parked, its blue lights flashing. The angle at which it stood, side on to the loch, showed how steeply the bank sloped.

She took the Frontera as close as she dared, and stopped, pulling on the handbrake and leaving it in gear. She grabbed her bag from the back seat. Martin followed. He wore brown Panama Jack boots, and his slacks were tucked into thick grey socks.

Two uniformed officers stood guarding the body. One, a middle-aged Sergeant, nodded to Martin; the other, much younger and a Constable, saluted smartly. Sarah recognised him as the officer who had been on duty at the clubhouse entrance on the Sunday before. She smiled at him, and pointed to the object on the ground. 'Were you afraid someone might steal him?' she asked PC Pye. He looked back at her, bemused.

'With all that's happened here this week,' said Martin, 'you never know!' He turned to the Sergeant. 'Switch off the lights on the Rover, Boyd. There are farms quite nearby, over the rise, and it's still dark enough for the flashes to be seen a way off. We don't want to advertise this before we have to.' The veteran grunted and clambered off up the slope.

Sarah, suddenly grim-faced, stepped down the last few yards of the embankment. The stool had been landed only feet from the edge of the Truth Loch, and the ground around it was almost swamplike. She squatted down beside the body, unclipping the catches of her bag.

The clothes were dark and sodden, the face was swollen and grey in death and the thinning brown hair was plastered over the forehead. She leaned closer and saw, on the cheeks and nose, a series of small, irregular puncture wounds. She lifted up the head in both hands and looked into the face. For a second her professional detachment faltered, and she gave a small shudder.

'Yes, Andy, this is William Masur. I sat opposite this man at the dinner table last night, and now at . . .' she glanced at her watch '. . . six-forty-nine a.m., I can certify that he is very dead.'

'I suppose that must mean that he wasn't a witch, then,' said Martin, with the macabre humour which policemen sometimes need to make their job bearable.

The body was lashed to the low-backed chair of the ducking stool by a thick blue nylon rope. 'I can't give you cause of death until the pathologist opens him up and looks for water in the lungs. As to the time, going by the general condition of the body, I'd say he'd been in there for between five and seven hours.' She let go of the head, which fell forward with a squelch on to the chest.

Martin knelt down beside her. 'What are those marks on the face, d'you think?'

'One or two fish have been taking an early breakfast, I'd guess.'

She put her hands back to the temples of the dead Masur, probing gently with her fingers, working her way gently round to the back of the head. 'There's an irregularity there. It's not as pronounced as in the case of White, but I'd guess that when they do the autopsy they'll find a skull fracture.

'My supposition is that the method is much the same as with Michael White. Someone cracked him on the head, knocked him unconscious, then finished him off. Only in this case the victim was drowned. I could be wrong. There may be other wounds that I can't find, and we can't untie him until the photographers are finished. But I don't see any rips in his blazer or his shirt, or anything else that would take us to another conclusion.'

Martin shook his head. 'You sure you couldn't work out a suicide theory for us on this one, Sarah? It'd make life a hell of a sight easier. One murder's bad enough, but two, on a site where we're expecting about sixty thousand people over the next four days!'

'Given enough time, Andy, I could work out a suicide theory for Abraham Lincoln. But I don't think anyone would buy it, any more than they'd buy this one. Sorry, but my conclusion is that the man who killed White has notched up another.'

They stood up together and clambered back up the bank to drier ground, where Sergeant Boyd and PC Pye maintained their solemn guard. Suddenly the silence was broken by the sound of two motor vehicles approaching beyond the rise. The four looked back up the hill until they swung into sight. 'Good,' said Martin. 'That's the scene of crime team, and that looks like Higgins and McIlhenney too. The sooner they all get to work, the better.'

Sarah nodded. 'I don't think that there's much more for me to do here, Andy. I'll write up a note for the record this morning, and fax it in. I'll speak to Alison, then I'll be off. Do you want to go back to your car?'

'Not just now thanks. I'll stay here for a while.' But then his mobile telephone warbled its own dawn chorus.

Thirty-four

Skinner shambled across the kitchen and perched on a stool.

He caught his reflection in the glass door and smiled. His hair was tousled, there was a grey stubble around his jawline and his yellow towelling dressing-gown was knotted roughly around his waist. 'If the boys could see you now,' he muttered.

Jazz wriggled excitedly in his high feeding chair as he smelled the warm milky rusks. 'You realise,' said Bob solemnly, 'that this is far too bloody early for you to be having breakfast. You do understand that, do you?' He dug the baby's horn spoon into the grey mixture and held out a mouthful, just out of his reach. 'You do appreciate that no allowances will be made when you're yelling for more before lunchtime? That your mother will just ignore you till she's good and ready?'

Jazz bounced up and down against the straps of his chair, laughing and slapping its tray. 'Well, as long as you understand that.' He fed the baby the first spoonful, which he swallowed voraciously. 'Better than sex as far as you're concerned, isn't it, wee man?' he said, inserting the second mouthful in answer to an affirmative shout by his son. Their bizarre conversation continued until the bowl was empty, and until Jazz had been convinced of the fact.

Breakfast over, Bob unstrapped him, and carried him, draped across his shoulder through to the living room, where they sat together on the smaller of the two couches. 'You just be quiet for a while, pal,' he said, picking up the telephone directory, and looking up the number of the Marquis of Kinture.

The telephone at Bracklands was answered by a bright voice which Skinner recognised as that of the girl who had sat for them during the PGA dinner. 'Kylie, you're up early! It's Mr Skinner here. Look, I need to speak to Mr Highfield, urgently. If he's still asleep, can you waken him, and ask him to telephone me at once. If he has a mobile, tell him I said to use that.' He gave her his number. 'But listen, don't make a fuss about it, and try not to disturb anyone else. Is that OK?'

'Sure, Mr Skinner,' the girl drawled. 'I'll do that right away.'

He replaced the receiver and looked down at the contented Jazz. 'That was your girlfriend from last night, pal. You took a right shine to her, and don't tell me otherwise. I saw the way you were looking at her when we got home last night. You and your sister, you're two of a kind!'

When the phone rang a minute later he was ready and picked it up at once. 'Skinner.'

The voice at the other end sounded both curious and anxious. 'Mr Skinner, what is it? Have they found Oliver's father? Is that it?'

'Not as far as I know. No, this is much closer to home. When was the last time you saw Bill Masur?'

'Last night, at the clubhouse.'

'Not at the house?'

'No. I came back on the bus with the boys. Masur said something about enjoying the night air. Why?'

Skinner took a deep breath. 'Because Jimmy Robertson, the pro, fished him out of the Truth Loch about an hour ago.'

'What! Had he fallen in? Was he drunk? Had he decided to go swimming?'

'No, Mr Highfield. Maybe you don't understand me. He was dead.'

'Oh my God!' Skinner thought that the man was whispering, until he realised that he had taken the phone from his mouth. When Highfield spoke again, his voice was tremulous. 'What happened?'

'All I know so far is that he was found in the loch, beside the eighteenth fairway.' He decided not to go into detail. 'My people are there now, and so's my wife. She's a police surgeon. I'll head down there myself, as soon as she gets back here.'

'What do you want me to do about the tournament?'

'That's what I wanted to discuss. When does the first team play off?'

'We're scheduled to start at nine-thirty a.m., gates open at eight forty-five.'

'OK. My first instinct was to seal the site, and call the thing off. If I thought that the public would be at risk, that's exactly what I would do. But these murders are very specific, and I have to assume that they're connected in some way. Instinct tells me that the best chance I have of catching the killer is to let the thing go on, and keep everyone here.

'I could simply call off today's play, but with thousands of people heading for the course, and some of them probably underway already, I don't want to do that if I can avoid it. My technical people will be there by now. They'll do what they have to do there as quickly as possible, and we'll move the body as soon as the photographers are finished. I'd like to keep the immediate area sealed off until we've given it a thorough sweep. Once we've done that I'll feel able to reopen the course.

Can you postpone the start until ten-fifteen and keep the punters out till nine-thirty?'

'Anything you ask, Mr Skinner, we'll do. We've got a commercial firm handling the admissions. I'll call them and let them know.'

'No, leave that for the moment. I want you to keep this to yourself for now. I'll be along at Bracklands by eight o'clock. That'll give you time to alert your people at the course. Meantime, I'd rather no one else knew about this till I get there.'

'Of course,' said Highfield. 'I shall stay in my room. I can hardly cope with this, you know. Good God, you saw Masur last night, so full of himself. Why on earth would he want to do something like this?'

Skinner smiled grimly. 'See you later, then.'

He ended the call, then dialled Andy Martin's mobile number, which he still knew by heart.

'Andy, 's'me. Where are you?'

'Down by the loch with Sarah. She's just finished. She says that it's Masur all right. She thinks that he was cracked on the head, then dunked in the pond. He's been in there long enough for the fishes to have had a few nibbles.'

A shiver of sudden excitement ran through Skinner as he remembered Mike Morton's Italian imprecation, a day and a half earlier.

'The crime scene people are here, plus Alison and Neil.'

'Good. I'll be down as soon as Sarah gets back. How many uniforms have you got with you?'

'Boyd and young Pye are here, and there are three more up at the clubhouse.'

'OK. Use as many people as you can to do a fast sweep of

the area around the stool, looking for anything at all. Hankies, footprints, blunt instruments . . . oh yes, and fag-ends. You never can tell.'

He paused. 'Once that's under way, I want you to head up to Bracklands. See the Marquis and tell him – and him alone – what's happened. And take McIlhenney with you. I don't want anyone leaving there for the moment. I'll join you there as soon as I can.

'With a wee bit of luck, when the house guests come down to breakfast you and I'll be there to give them all a nasty surprise . . . except that for one of them, I don't think it'll be a surprise at all!'

Thirty-five

His wellies were less trendy than his wife's. They were the old-fashioned, wide-topped, black sort, and they had lain in the dark recesses of successive car boots for over ten years. The dried mud of countless crime scenes packed the ridges of their soles, and another layer was being added as Skinner crouched to look into the grey, mottled, dead face of Bill Masur.

The body still sat in the chair, crumpled and shapeless. The right eye was slightly open. There was no sparkle there, no light, no life. The weight of the head was pressing the jaw into the chest, and the fleshy bottom lip stuck out grotesquely.

'Old Japanese proverb,' said Skinner, softly, conversationally. ' "He who play in heavy traffic sometimes get run over." I don't think your Yakuza pals are going to know what to make of this at all. I just hope that if they decide to do some getting even, they do it well away from here.'

He pushed himself to his feet. With a squelch, he backed away, then climbed up the slope to where Alison Higgins and Mario McGuire were standing on firmer ground.

'A right nasty bastard, was Mr Masur,' he said. 'I thought he might have had something coming to him. Didn't think it'd arrive so fast, though. Have the photographers finished?'

'Yes, sir,' said Higgins, 'and the technicians say they can't do any more here either. They've taken samples from the rope that ties this thing down. Now they're looking for footprints around the bollard to which it's attached. They think they've found the exact point where Masur was loaded into the chair.

'D'you see how it was done?' She took several steps past the pillar of the stool, which rose from the ground beside the steepest point of the bank to an area where the flatter ground widened out. She grabbed the rope which hung from the end of the long wooden boom which carried the chair. It was at least ten feet above her head. 'When there's nothing in the stool this can be moved about, no bother, and can be swung over there.' She pointed to an area behind Skinner and McGuire where a square had been sectioned off with Day-Glo tape. 'That's where it happened, sir. There's an indentation in the ground that seems to match the base of the chair, and we assume that it was made when Masur was tied into it.' She took a few steps to her right, to where a small, mushroom-shaped metal bollard was fixed securely into the ground. It was roped off also. 'Once the chair was loaded, it was raised up, swung round and dropped in over there. You can tell how deep the chair went by looking at the water mark on the boom. There's mud on it, and on Masur's legs, so it must have been sitting right on the bottom.'

Skinner walked across towards the Superintendent, his eye following her pointing arm to the surface of the loch. 'Could one man have done it all, I wonder?' He strode across to the end of the boom and took hold of the rope with both hands. Winding it around his wrists for added purchase, he tugged downwards.

On the other end of the boom, the chair and Masur's dead weight rose, dripping, into the air, with surprising ease. 'No problem. The length of the lever makes it relatively simple, if you've got the basic strength to get the bugger off the deck.' Holding the body aloft, he stepped to his left, to the very edge of the bank, and lowered it, gently, on to flatter, drier ground, just beside the sectioned area. He unwound the rope from his wrists, and brushed the hemp strands from the sleeves of his jacket, then walked back, ducklike in his flapping wellingtons, to rejoin Higgins and McGuire.

'You can have the body removed now. PDQ in fact, just in case there are any long-range cameras on the scene already. Make sure the ambulance doesn't go out past the clubhouse, but along the buggy track and out through the Bracklands Estate road.

'Complete the sweep of the ground as fast as you can, then tape off the spot where the body was landed, and clear everyone out of here; by nine-thirty if you can manage it.'

McGuire looked at Skinner in surprise. 'Is the tournament going ahead, boss?'

'I don't see why it shouldn't, unless I have to arrest all the players! The body'll be out of the way, and the public can't contaminate the site. Deacon Weekes's team will be one short, but I'm sure he'll manage.

'OK, you two attend to all that stuff. I'm off to join Andy for a working breakfast at Bracklands!'

Thirty-six

Bracklands was a truly great house, a palace of yellow stone. It stood in the centre of a vast oval paddock, enclosed by a surround of high trees, planted over the centuries to shield its masters' eyes from the privations of their tenants, and to hide from theirs, in turn, the splendour which their toil helped to sustain.

'So what's new?' Skinner said aloud, as he steered Sarah's Frontera through the break in the trees and up the long drive which led to the Kintures' ancestral seat. 'The tenant farmers still pay him rent, and the Webbs, the Watts and the Hays still cut his grass, and mend his fences and fix his burst pipes. The difference is that now he has an international share portfolio, and that through it he'll own parts of companies whose wealth is founded on subsistence level wages in Third World countries.'

Yet even as the thought spoke itself, he pondered on his own inherited comfort, his investment and his pension provision. 'The really big difference, though, is that today, so does a guy like you!'

A silver car stood on the red gravel concourse which lay between Bracklands and its lawn. Two men leaned against it and from afar, he recognised them. He drew the Frontera up parallel to the new Mondeo, a few yards away, and stepped out.

He took the few paces to close the space between himself and Andy Martin, both literal and symbolic, with a smile spreading across his face and his hand stretched out in greeting. Martin pushed himself off the Mondeo's rounded side and came to meet him halfway.

Normally, Skinner would have avoided such an obvious punch as it looped towards him. Instead he stood his ground, motionless, as the fist smacked into his chin. He rocked back on his heels, but stayed on his feet . . . and the smile never left his face. Neil McIlhenney started forward in confusion, until Martin, breathing slightly heavily, grasped the still-outstretched hand, and shook it.

Skinner nodded slightly, and the smile became a grin of delight. Martin looked at him and laughed. It was as if the fist had punched through the last barrier between them. They stood there, neither finding a word to say, just two old friends reunited after a long separation.

Eventually, Skinner released his handshake, and turned towards McIlhenney. 'So there you are, Neil. Now you know about the family quarrel, and now you know it's over. You're family too, you and Brian, and Maggie and McGuire. The whole team's back together again, so the bad people can look out.'

He slapped his hands together. 'Right, gentlemen. What have we got inside?'

'I did as you asked, boss,' said Martin. 'I told the Marquis, but no one else. He says that they're serving breakfast in the dining room from seven-forty-five this morning, and that all the house guests should be up by then.'

Skinner glanced at his watch. The time was 7.46 a.m. 'Come on then,' he said, 'let's see if anyone *doesn't* choke on his corn flakes when we give them the news.'

224

The three strode towards the vast house and up the wide stone steps which led to its doorway. Light shone through the morning gloom from several of the upper windows and all along the ground floor to the right of the entrance. Martin pointed in that direction. 'The Marquis's suite is along at the far end. It's been wheelchair-adapted. That's where I saw him. I don't know where Lady Kinture sleeps, but that was certainly not a woman's bedroom. Plenty of *Paco Rabanne*, but no *Rive Gauche*.'

The simple plastic bell-push was something of an anticlimax, but the echoing sound of its chime was impressive. The door was answered after a minute by a small middle-aged man in a dark suit. 'Hello again, Mr Burton,' said Martin to the butler. 'We are expected back. This is Assistant Chief Constable Skinner.'

'Yes, sir. The Marquis told me to show you to the dining room, and to serve you with breakfast. Please follow me.' He ushered them into the house, and into a wide entrance hall. It was floored in yellowish marble and a stairway of the same stone, its crimson carpet held in place by heavy brass runners, seemed to flow upwards out of its centre. Ancestral portraits lined its walls, and tall double mahogany doors led off in several directions. The policemen followed Mr Burton through the first doorway on the right, and down a corridor. Twenty paces on, he stopped and opened another set of double doors, then stood aside to allow the three policemen to enter the dining room.

Twelve people sat around the long dining table. 'Morning Skinner,' boomed the Marquis from his place at its head. 'So glad you and your chums could join us for breakfast.' The ACC saw a gleam in his eye; he was enjoying the grim game.

At his shout, ten heads swivelled round in surprise to stare at the trio framed in the doorway. Arthur Highfield looked tense and nervous.

The butler showed Skinner to a chair at the end of the table directly opposite Kinture, seating Martin on his right, McIlhenney on his left. Around them three maids bustled, serving breakfast to the party. 'Thank you, sir,' said Skinner, taking his place. 'Let's see, is everyone here?' He looked around the table, from left to right and from place to place. 'Mr Gregory. Nakamura-San. Mr Weekes. Mr Wyman. Mr Morton. Mr Highfield. Lord Kinture. Lady Kinture. Mr Atkinson. Mr M'tebe. Mr Urquhart. Señor Cortes. Yes, that seems to be everyone.' A maid placed a huge platter before him, piled high with scrambled eggs, bacon, sausage, black pudding and mushrooms. Kylie, his baby-sitter of the previous evening, filled his cup with thick black coffee.

'What about Mr Masur?' said Susan Kinture, a puzzle-line creasing her forehead.

'I hadn't forgotten him, Sue. He's been detained elsewhere. We've just left him in fact.' He stared down the table towards the Marquis, who was biting his lip with some vigour.

Darren Atkinson leaned forward and looked along. 'What's that, Bob? Detained? Are you saying that Masur killed Michael White?'

Skinner shrugged his shoulders. 'Whether he did or not, Darren, makes no odds now. I didn't say that *we'd* detained Mr Masur. No, he's been kept from his breakfast on account of being dead.'

Susan Kinture gave a small shriek. 'You're kidding,' said Atkinson. Highfield went even whiter. Gregory, Weekes, Wyman, M'tebe, Urquhart and Cortes all stared at him in blank astonishment. Tiger Nakamura looked simply bewildered. Skinner could not see Mike Morton at all. He had shrunk back into his seat.

'Sorry, Darren. I wish I *was* kidding. I don't like looking at bodies at any time of the day, but just before breakfast is absolutely my least favourite time.'

'But he can't be dead,' said Atkinson. 'I mean, we all saw him just a few hours ago.'

'Believe me, my friend, if my wife says he's dead, then don't look forward to him buying you your next drink. And my wife isn't in any doubt.'

'What happened? Did he have a heart attack walking back?'

He snorted. 'It was a bloody weird one if he did. Look, I don't want to go into the details just now. What I need to know is where everyone in this room was at the time he died. That means between leaving the clubhouse and around two a.m.'

He glanced at McIlhenney, but the Sergeant had anticipated his request and had produced a notebook and pen.

'Let's begin at the clubhouse. After Sarah and I left in our taxi, what happened, and how did the party disperse? Lord Kinture, perhaps you could tell us?'

The Marquis nodded, and pulled himself a little closer to the table. 'Let me think.' He scratched his eagle's-wing temple and gathered his thoughts. 'OK, the Murano party first. They're all based at North Berwick Marine. We couldn't put them all up here. They're hosting the celebrities too, all the politicians, singers and stuff. They went back to the hotel by bus, not long after you left. The others, the local people, all drifted off around then too.' He waved a languid hand at his table companions. 'That just left this lot.

'We all had another drink, while we waited for the estate bus and for my chauffeur with my battle-wagon. While we were doing that, Morton here and Masur had a shouting match.'

Skinner leaned to his right, forcing Morton to look back up the table towards him.

'To be fair to Morton,' said the Marquis, 'Masur was rubbing his nose in it over the Tiger business. Man was bloody rude, being the sort of Aussie that gives Aussies a bad name.' He nodded down the table. 'Savin' your presence, Sandro.'

'That's all right,' said the golfer. 'I was downright ashamed of him. In fact, I told him that if he didn't shut it he'd be losing a client while he was gaining one.'

'Anyway,' the Marquis continued, 'the bus and the Range Rover arrived just then. I didn't want Morton and Masur to be going at it on the bus, so I insisted that Morton travel back to Bracklands with me. We loaded up and we left.'

Skinner nodded, caught with a mouthful of breakfast. 'OK,' he said at last. 'How did everyone else get back, and what happened to Masur? Mr Highfield?'

The PGA man jumped as Skinner addressed him, but gathered himself together quickly. 'It was all quite simple really. The rest of us were climbing aboard the bus, when Masur said that he fancied some fresh air. He said that he'd probably had too many sherbets, and that the walk back to Bracklands across the course would do him good. He set off, and the rest of us got on the bus.'

'Immediately?'

Highfield thought for a moment. 'Couple of the chaps went off to the gents, but after that yes.'

'Very good. So we've established how everyone headed back to the house. Now, what did you all do when you got here? Lord Kinture?'

The Marquis waved his coffee cup at a maid. 'Can't speak for everyone of course, but Arthur here, Ewan and Andres had a nightcap with me in my study. The Tiger was with us too, watching some Japanese channel on satellite TV. I suppose that we packed it in around . . . what was it boys, quarter to one?' Urquhart and Cortes gave brief nods of agreement.

'Right, that's five accounted for. How about the rest of you?'

Sandro Gregory raised a hand. 'Oliver, Paul, the Deacon and me, we all were in the billiard room for a couple of hours. The snooker match of the decade: US versus the Rest of the World. We called it a tie eventually around one-thirty, and split to our rooms.'

Skinner looked down the table. 'Darren?'

Atkinson leaned forward. 'Lady Kinture and I sat for a while in the drawing room. You remember, don't you; we said we'd have a chat about the course after the dinner.' The Marquis looked round sharply. 'I suppose we must have talked until just after midnight.'

'OK, that gives us one group in the study, one in the billiard room and you two in the drawing room. After that you all went straight to bed, yes?' An assortment of assenting grunts came from around the table.

'And how about you, Mr Morton?' he asked, heavily. 'What did you do when you got back to Bracklands, after your argument with the late Masur?'

Fourteen people stared at the American in silence. Morton fidgeted in his chair. He stuck out his chin aggressively, and glared around the table. 'I went straight to my room, OK? I was still pissed by Masur's little speech at the dinner, and by the Tiger running out on SSC. I didn't want to see either of the bastards, so as soon as the Range Rover got back here, I said goodnight and hit the sack.'

'Can you confirm that, Lord Kinture?'

'Afraid not, Skinner old boy. The car drops me at my ramp at the rear of the house. Sue and I got out there. Morton was still in the back seat last time I saw him, waiting for the chauffeur to drive him round to the front door. It's quite a long walk, y'see.'

'Yes, I see,' said Skinner. He looked at Martin. 'Superintendent, any thoughts?'

The blond policeman straightened up in his chair. His striking green eyes gazed steadily across the table, at the red-faced American. 'With everyone else accounted for, and in company, only one scenario can't be discounted; that Mr Morton, having had two recent run-ins with Masur and having suffered a painful business loss to him, watched the estate bus return, thinking that he would be on board, and that he could renew the earlier confrontation. When he saw that the man hadn't returned with the rest, he guessed that he would be walking back across the course, and headed out into the night to confront him.'

'Hey, wait a minute!' Morton sat bolt upright in his chair, redder than ever, with the beginnings of panic in his eyes. 'This is a stitch-up!'

Skinner looked at him evenly. 'Relax, Mr Morton. As the Superintendent says, that's only a scenario. You have to face it. You *have* had violent disputes with Masur, in public. He *has* damaged your business. Alongside that, the fact is that from the moment you got out of the Range Rover there's no one to vouch for your movements.

'We're not saying positively that's what happened, and if we were it'd be up to us to prove it. So don't get excited, unless you have something to be excited about.'

He paused and glanced back down the table. 'Lord Kinture, this is a bit awkward. There is something that I should do, to progress our investigation. Now the last thing I want to do is to go to the Sheriff in Haddington and ask him for a warrant to search Bracklands. It would be a great help if you would allow me to look around informally.'

'For my part, Skinner, I have no objection. Only thing is, I do have an obligation to my guests.'

'Of course. But I know exactly what I'm looking for, and I'd be happy to have any search witnessed by those whose rooms we go into. I'm sorry about this, but it is necessary, and I really don't want to do it the hard way. Any objections?' There was something in his expression which made the question rhetorical.

'Good. In that case, since you're the man with the whereabouts problem, Mr Morton, we'll start with your room. If you'll come with the Superintendent and me...' He rose from the table, and Andy Martin followed his lead. On impulse, he looked back down the table. 'Susan, just to give Mr Morton added comfort, perhaps you'd like to come along as an independent witness.'

'Yes, if it'll help.' She left her seat, resplendent in the bright sweater and slacks which Skinner guessed were to be the day's caddying uniform and walked round the table to join them. He held the door open for her, then for Morton.

The American's suite was front-facing, directly over the main entrance. 'I have to say, you couldn't have had a better view of the bus when it got back, Mr Morton,' said Skinner, idly.

'Let's keep this simple, shall we, sir? Show us the clothes you wore last night, please, and all the shoes you have with you.'

The American hesitated, and the look of panic intensified. Skinner nodded towards the room's tall wardrobe, catching his reflection in its central mirror. 'In there, I think. Andy.' Martin stepped up and opened the right-hand door. A dozen hangers were occupied by a variety of suits, slacks and jackets. Eventually, Morton walked across, reluctantly, and removed the one bearing the blazer and slacks which the ACC recognised as his dress of a few hours before. 'Susan?'

Lady Kinture took the hanger and held it up. She peered at the clothes, then felt their fabric with her left hand. 'They're damp.' She looked even more closely at the slacks. 'And I think that's mud, just there.'

'Now the shoes, please,' said Skinner.

Morton's panic had been replaced by a look of resignation. He delved into the wardrobe and produced a pair of black leather moccasins, which he handed again to Susan Kinture. Their uppers were dull and lustreless. She turned them over and saw black mud wedged into the angle between sole and heel.

Skinner hid his surprise. 'This doesn't look too good, Mr Morton. At this point I have to give you a formal caution that you do not have to answer our questions, but that anything you do say will be noted, and could be used against you. Now, on that basis, would you like to tell us now how this happened, or would you rather go to a police office and be interviewed formally?'

The American sat down hard on the bed. 'No, I'll tell you right now. It's dead simple, but like you said, there ain't no witnesses.

'I did come straight up here when I got out of the car. And yes, I did look out and see the bus get back, and I saw that Masur wasn't on it. I was still as hot as a stove, and if he had been there, I was ready to go down and take a swing at him, or challenge him to pistols at dawn, anything to wipe that grin off his face.

'Your scenario is correct, Superintendent, but only up to a point. I did think about going out and catching the sonofabitch in the dark. But eventually I gave up the idea. I was steamed, though, so I decided to take a walk in the gardens to cool off. I'd been humiliated at that dinner, and I didn't want to see anyone else last night, so I went out down the back stairs.

'That's where my clothes got damp, in the garden, and that's where I must have picked up the mud, although I didn't realise till now that it was there. One of the gardeners must have left a sprinkler on. I didn't see it, so I walked right into it. I just stood there, laughing like a dummy, and thinking, "What the hell else can go wrong tonight?" Then I found out. The moon went behind a cloud. All of a sudden it was black as the Devil's waistcoat, and I walked right into a flower-bed. That was enough. I gave up, came back into the house, and went to bed.'

He looked up at the two policemen. 'And that is the truth. Happy as I am that that asshole Masur is dead, I swear to God I did not kill him.' Skinner stared at him hard, until the man dropped his gaze.

'I'll need a formal statement to that effect, Mr Morton. You're a lawyer, you can draft it yourself and sign it. However, I have to take these clothes, and your shoes, for forensic examination. I'm not going to detain you, for the moment at least, but I should warn you that you'll be under constant

233

police scrutiny, at least until we get the results of the lab tests. Understand?'

Morton nodded, his face no longer florid, but pale. Skinner picked up the blazer and slacks on their hanger, and Martin took the shoes, carefully.

They made to leave, until Skinner turned in the doorway. 'By the way Morton, where's Rocco Andrade?'

The American looked up with a start, and shook, visibly. 'Richard! You mean Richard Andrews. He ain't been Rocco since we were kids.

'I don't know where Richard is. He told me he was checking out from the tournament early last week, 'cause he had personal business to attend to. I don't know where he is or what he's doin'.'

Skinner stared at him. 'Come on! He's your right-hand man. You're kidding us!'

Morton shook his head, solemnly. 'No sir, I ain't. No one ever asks Richard where he's going, or what he's doing. No one at all!'

Thirty-seven

'I know you said I wasn't to, but I've been worrying ever since you called me, Miss Rose. If you've come a' the way to Germany to see me, it must be serious. It's got nothing to do with poor Davie, has it?'

The Inspector smiled and shook her head. 'No, not at all. Sergeant Soutar's fine. I saw him the day before yesterday in fact.'

Lisa Davies, née Soutar, was as far removed as it was possible to be from the adult that Maggie Rose had imagined. On the flight to Hanover, and on the drive to her overnight hotel, she had formed a mind picture of a fey, folksy lady, bejewelled, in long skirts and open-toed sandals, holding court amid the scent of joss-sticks. The reality was a small, nervous person, with dull sunken eyes, and streaks of grey in her hair which made her look well past her thirtieth birthday, even though she was still a year or so short of that milestone. Her child, who squatted in the middle of the floor playing with a doll, was scrubbed shiny and neatly dressed, but the mother, still in slippers and housecoat at 9.45 a.m., had the air of a woman who, long since, had given up caring about herself. As Maggie looked at her, and around the severe, soulless living room, she recalled Davie Soutar's vehement dislike of his brother-in-law and wondered about life with Corporal Davies.

'Sit down, please,' said Lisa. 'I'll make us a cup. D'you take sugar?' Rose shook her head as she sat on the mock-leather couch; her hostess disappeared into the kitchen, directly off the living room, to return a few minutes later carrying a tray, with two steaming white mugs and a plate of cream biscuits. She handed the policewoman a mug, and sat down opposite her.

'So what's it about, then?' she said, trying to be matter-of-fact.

Maggie smiled again. 'You might say it's a voice from the past. I'd like you to listen to this.'

She produced the tape cassette from her handbag, and reached across the back of the couch to an expensive music centre, positioned in the centre of a cheap sideboard. She dropped the tape into one of its two drives and pressed the play button.

As Lisa Davies listened to the recording from her child-hood, an incredible thing happened. She became Lisa Soutar once more. A smile of wonder grew on her lips, her dull eyes brightened, and colour came to her pale face. 'Oh my God,' she whispered, as it ended. Suddenly tears welled up and spilled down her face.

'D'ye ken, I'd almost forgotten. But not quite, not quite. Oh aye, I remember telling that story in the class, and I remember poor Mrs Skinner. She was a smashin' teacher, and she was married to a great-lookin' young fella. I remember once he came to the school, wi' their wee girl, to collect her. Ma pal and I were just going out the gate. Mrs Skinner waved tae us and he smiled. We just stood there and stared at him!' She laughed, suddenly, a strange wistful sound like small bells tinkling. 'My first love, he was. I used to wonder what happened to him, after she was killed.'

'He survived. He's my boss now. Their wee girl, she's twenty-one.'

Lisa wiped her eyes with the back of her hand. 'My, but that tape gave me a turn. Can I keep it?'

'Course you can. It's a copy. The boss would want me to leave it with you.'

She smiled once more. 'See the trouble I got into over that!'

'What d'you mean?'

'Well I got back from school that day, and I told my nana all about the history project, and how I had told our story. My God, but she went mental. I never saw her like that before. My dad always said she was a witch, and right then I thought she was goin' to turn me into a fly and squash me!

'She said that the story of the curse was ours, the Soutars' alone, and shouldn't be told to strangers, only to family, or to the Queen if she came to ask about it.'

'She said that? What did she mean, d'you think?'

'That's part of the story, but I don't know what it means. The only people allowed to hear the curse are the sovereign and Lord Kinture. I didn't think she meant it when she told me that at first. I was just ten, and I thought, "What's the point of a story if you canna tell it to everyone?" But she meant it all right. She hit me wi' her stick to prove it! That story's ours and ours alone.'

'Did Mrs Skinner ever tell you why it didn't appear in the book?'

'No, she never did. But I remember ma nana saying she'd have to speak to the Marquis about it. The whole Jubilee Project was his idea. He paid for the books to be printed.'

Rose delved into her handbag once again, and produced a folded A4 photocopy of the *Scotsman* story. 'Lisa,' she asked, 'have you heard of a new golf course being built just outside Aberlady? It's called Witches' Hill.'

'Aye, they were talking about it at Easter-time, when we were home last. When I heard the name it gave me a turn.'

'OK. Well, on Sunday one of the developers of the course was murdered, in his bath, in the changing room. His throat was cut. Next day, this was handed in to the *Scotsman* newspaper, addressed to the editor.' She handed over the cutting.

The woman-child read it in silence, and her face grew grim. 'That's awful. Who'd have written that?'

'That's what I was hoping you could tell me,' said Rose. 'Did anyone else in your family know the story?'

'No, no one at all. That's not the way it works.'

'Did you ever tell it to anyone else, a school pal for example?'

'After the row ma nana gave me ah never even spoke it out loud, in case someone would hear me.'

'What did you mean when you said "That's not the way it works"?'

Lisa sat forward on her chair and pulled her knees up to her chin. 'Ah don't know if I should tell you even that.'

Rose looked at her earnestly. 'Lisa, it's important. I promise you that no one will ever know more than they need.'

Eventually the woman loosened her grip of her knees. She nodded. 'All right. I trust you.' She sat back in her chair and took a deep breath. 'Remember I said that it was our family's story?'

Maggie nodded.

'Well it was even closer than that. Even within the family, very few of us knew about the curse. It was passed on through the women, but only through those women who were blood kin. There were no females in the blood line between ma nana and me. She passed the tale on to me when I was nine. She said I was far too young, really, but that she was so old that she couldna' take the chance of waiting any longer. So she told me the curse and the story of it, and made me swear to tell my daughter in turn, or my granddaughter, or if it came to it, my great-granddaughter, like she was doing.' She nodded towards the child on the floor. 'I'll tell wee Cherry there, in good time, when she's old enough. She'll think I'm daft, no doubt, clinging on to a four-hundred-year-old family tradition, but apart from her, it's all I've got.

'Do you understand that?' There was a sad, plaintive tone in her voice. 'The story of the curse is the only thing I've ever had that makes me feel I'm worth anything. Now I see a bit of it in a paper, it's like a part of me's been cut off and put on public show.'

'Maybe it's the best thing that could happen,' said Rose, 'if it makes you value yourself again. You're worth a hell of a lot more than the story, you know.'

'You should tell that to my fine husband. Useful for cooking and the other, he says to me, but not very good at either.'

The Inspector looked at her sadly, appalled that a man could voice such a thought. She forced herself back to business.

'Through all this time, Lisa, was the story handed down simply by word of mouth?'

'Aye.'

'And it's not written down anywhere.'

The woman hesitated, as if weighing a heavy question in her mind. Suddenly she jumped to her feet. 'Hold on.' She rushed from the room. Rose heard her footsteps on the stair-case, then a noise, as if something heavy was being dragged across the floor above. A few seconds later she descended the stairs, slowly and steadily, and reappeared in the living room, carrying a massive black-bound book. She placed it carefully on the laminated table.

'This is where it began,' she said softly, 'and this is where the line is kept.'

Maggie looked at the book's leather binding. It bore no title. 'It's the old family Bible,' said Lisa Soutar. 'It's earlier than the King James version, so it must be very rare. God himself alone knows where it came from. My nana gave it to me, with the curse. Her grandmother gave it to her, and so on and so on. Look here.'

Gently, she opened the book, holding the cover carefully, lest she break the spine. Maggie leaned past her. She gasped in amazement, her mouth dropping open, as she saw, written in the fly-leaf, thin and spidery but still legible, the story of Aggie Tod's curse, virtually word for word as Lisa had recited it on the tape. There was a scrawled signature at its end.

She peered at it and read aloud. '"Matilda Tod, sister. A witness in the year of Our Lord 1598." Good God!'

Lisa smiled. 'Now look at this.' She set the book on its face and opened the back cover. There on the back leaf, in many hands, some thin, some strong, some clear, some barely legible, and in many shades of ink, a family tree grew.

'See how it goes. Here am I, Lisa Soutar, born 1967.' Her finger traced down the page. 'Go back and here's Rosemary Baird . . . that was my nana's maiden name . . . born 1883, the last in the female line before me. Back again, and there's her grandmother, Lorna Grieve, born 1815. Her mother, Mary

Brown, born 1787, and hers, Anne Ross, born 1760. Then back two more generations to Mary Aitken, born 1689. We're getting close to the beginning now. Mary's grandmother, Frances Tullis was born in 1623. Her mother, there,' she pointed to the foot of the tree, 'was Elizabeth Carr. It doesn't say when she was born, but she was given the tale, and the Bible, by Matilda Tod. That's where the tale began, and where it came into my family's keeping.

'You'll see from that that our menfolk havena' been very good at siring women, but that those they have produced have tended to live for a long time . . . long enough for the female line to have passed on the tale, and its beginnings, through almost four hundred years.'

She closed the book. 'All these women were the Tellers of the Tale. We've kept it, secret but still alive, and guarded the Bible where it's written down, for all that time. Ever since Matilda Tod, Aggie's sister, wrote down the curse in 1598.'

Rose, normally phlegmatic and practical, was awestruck. 'Lisa,' she whispered. 'Do you have any idea of the value of all this? The historical value of the story, and the potential worth of that Bible?'

The woman smiled, grimly. 'Aye, of course I have. But it's worth more to me to keep the secret. My nana thrashed that into me. There are bits of the story that aren't written down; the bit about revealing the curse only to a Kinture or to the King or Queen, and most of all, the bit about what Aggie Tod's Master will do to any Teller who betrays the tale.

'After that article in the paper, I feel like putting an advert saying "To whom it may concern: honest, it wisnae me!" in tomorrow's *Scotsman!*'

'Do you know who Elizabeth Carr was?'

'Only that she was my blood relative, and the second witness, the second bearer of the tale. I'm the ninth. But I don't know why Matilda Tod chose her, and us, to keep the curse, and the secret.'

She paused. 'Come into the kitchen, and I'll make us some more tea.' Maggie followed her into a small room which was as poorly furnished as the other. Lisa refilled the stainless steel kettle and switched it on. 'How does all that help you, Miss Rose?'

'Call me Maggie, please. To be honest, I haven't a clue. We've got a body, and we've got an anonymous letter which claims that Aggie Tod's curse is being fulfilled. There was a hint of the existence of the curse over a hundred years ago, but it's been forgotten by everyone bar a few historians. So, given what you've told me and since you didn't do it yourself, I'm all the more anxious to know who wrote that *Scotsman* letter.

'The idea of a connection may be far-fetched. But then so is the idea that a story can be kept alive in secret by the women of a single family for four hundred years. It gets more confusing by the minute, but more fascinating too.

'Lisa, is it all right if I copy out that family tree, and take some photos of it and the Bible? We'll keep the secret for as long as we can, but I'd like to do some research into the origins of the story, and there's a man who can help me. I know that he'll be as amazed as me at the idea of the Devil riding out on a golf course in East Lothian.'

Thirty-eight

'Miss Higgins, why didn't you cancel the tournament because of this incident?'

The questioner held a microphone across the table in the mobile police office, which had been parked on the edge of the tented village. The limited space was packed tight with journalists and cameramen. Alison Higgins sat, flanked by Andy Martin and Alan Royston, at a narrow table against the wall closest to the single entrance door.

'I'll answer that, if I may,' said Martin. 'That decision was taken only after all the circumstances had been considered. The body was removed by eight o'clock, and the scientific team were finished their work by nine-thirty, so our work here is complete for the minute. The only practical reason for cancellation would have been public safety, and we're satisfied that there's no general risk. Postponement of the start for twenty-four hours was an option, but it was decided that since thousands of people would be on their way here already, it would be fairer all round to let play begin as soon as possible.'

'Who took the decision?' asked the journalist with the microphone.

'I'm the area commander here,' said Martin, brusquely.

John Hunter laughed, hoarsely. 'We know, that, Andy. I

think the boy here's just a wee bit shy of asking if Big Bob didn't relish missing a day's golf!'

'I'll treat that as a joke, you old scoundrel. The ACC's on leave this week, and for those of you who don't know, he's playing in the pro-am in Mr Michael White's place, at the request of Michael White's widow. As for what Mr Skinner did or did not fancy, *I* didn't fancy turning five thousand motorists away from the gate.

'I believe that the PGA intend to stop play at one o'clock, when everyone's out on the course, for two minutes' silence, in memory of Mr White, and now of Mr Masur.'

'Have you established a link between the two deaths, Superintendent?' asked a young Sunday newspaper reporter, in a light Irish brogue.

'That's one for Miss Higgins,' said Martin.

Alison Higgins leaned forward with a brief nod of thanks. 'The answer is no. We are pursuing specific lines of enquiry in each case, but as yet they don't converge.'

'Are you considering a connection with the kidnapping of Oliver M'tebe's father?'

'That's a separate investigation, being carried out by the South African police. So far they haven't established any connection with events here. And I can tell you that there has been no contact made by the kidnappers with Oliver or his management.'

'What about the letter to the *Scotsman*? Given the letter's allusion to witchcraft are you looking into the possibility that there might be a coven active today in East Lothian?' asked Julian Finney, of Scottish Television, a little bulldog of a man.

The Superintendent paused for a moment, considering her reply. When she did speak, she looked straight into the television cameras. 'Frankly we're following up every line of enquiry, however bizarre it might seem.'

'Your statement says that Mr Masur's body was found in the Truth Loch early this morning,' Finney went on. 'Can you give us any more detail than that?'

'No.'

'Nothing on his injuries? May we take it that drowning was the cause of death?'

'That will be determined by the post-mortem, and will be part of our report to the Procurator Fiscal.'

'Were any extra security measures put in place following Mr White's murder?'

'There's been a police presence here throughout the day since Sunday, and private security in the exhibition area at night.'

'But individuals haven't been given police protection?'

'No, but no one's been refused it either.'

'Will there be extra security after this second death?'

'Come on, Julian,' said Martin. 'That's a Command decision, not one for CID. We'll protect everyone here to the best of our ability and resources. But we've no idea who or what we're protecting them against.'

'You don't see a terrorist connection?'

'No, and neither do you, so stop trying to drum up an angle. Terrorists do it for the publicity. There's been none of that, other than the *Scotsman* letter, and whatever that was, it sure as hell was *not* a terrorist communiqué.

'What we're investigating here are two unexplained, violent deaths, with no possibility of suicide in either case. An alleged murder mystery, to give you a non-prejudicial, legally correct headline.'

Thirty-nine

Skinner was striding towards the first tee when the stocky figure of Julian Finney fell into step beside him.

'Yes Julian, what can I do for you?'

'I know that officially you're on holiday, but I wondered if you could give me a quick interview.'

'Officially and unofficially, son. No chance. Didn't Royston fix you up with Andy and Alison?'

'Yes, but Bob, I no more believe that you're not involved in this investigation than I believe your scratch score will beat Darren Atkinson.'

Skinner smiled. 'Thanks for your confidence! Look, there's nothing I can say to you that won't have been said already, and I can't step in over the heads of the officers in charge. You know that so let's cut the crap, I'm on the tee in five minutes. What do you really want?'

Finney looked diffidently at his feet. 'Oh, it's just that I heard a whisper that there had been a big argument between Masur and Mike Morton on the practice ground the other day, and that you were there. Is Mike Morton one of the lines of enquiry that Superintendent Higgins was talking about?'

Skinner stopped in his tracks, a few yards from the tee. 'Julian, I've never lied to you, and I'm not going to start now. Yes, there was an argument between Morton and Masur the other night. In fact there was another disagreement between them last night, at the PGA dinner.

'I'm not going to comment at all on our investigation. All I'll say to you – strictly off the record – is that if someone goes out and commits murder immediately after having a heated public argument with the victim, then he has to be either crazy or dumb. I know that Morton isn't dumb. Time will tell whether he's crazy.

'Now, go to the press office for any further information. I've got some golf to play, and I *don't* need distractions.'

Finney smiled. 'Thanks Bob.' He made to leave, then hesitated. 'Might as well hang around and watch you tee off.'

Skinner growled and stepped up on to the tee beside his team. He glanced around, tasting the tension which hung in the air. The crowds were much thicker than on practice day, the television cameramen were on their rostrums and in their fairway buggies, and already there were numbers on the leaderboard.

Skinner peered at the board closest to the tee. Andres Cortes was the early leader, three under par after eight holes, a shot ahead of Deacon Weekes. The others were all level par, with the exception of Oliver M'tebe, who was two over after ten.

Darren Atkinson stood beside Bravo on the tee, arms folded across his chest, staring heavy-browed down the first fairway. The muscles at the base of his jaw were clenched tight, and he seemed to Skinner to be standing an inch or two taller.

'This is it, Bob,' he said softly. 'This is where the hard men come out to play. This isn't a matter of money, there's honour involved. No one but me is going to walk off with Murano's million quid, because only the best has the right.

'As far as the team competition is concerned, remember that the best ball, mine included, on any hole registers the score. I'd be grateful if you'd look after Wales and the Jap. Make sure they pick up once they've had half a dozen whacks at any hole. I'll be concentrating so hard I won't even notice them.

'You're on seven shots against the course today, with your handicap. If you can pick up a nett birdie with each of them, you'll have done your part for the team. Your other eleven holes don't matter.'

Skinner smiled, but there was a hard edge to his expression also. 'You don't know me very well, yet, Darren. All eighteen matter to me. Game on, pal.'

The green-blazered announcer stepped forward, microphone in hand. 'Finally, ladies and gentlemen, we have team eight. Mr Norton Wales; Mr Hideo Murano; Mr Bob Skinner.' He paused, allowing modest applause after each introduction. 'And finally, the world's Number One golfer, the reigning US Open Champion, the King of the Majors, Mr Darren Atkinson.' The stands erupted in applause which faded only when Atkinson stepped up to the tee. It renewed itself as he crushed a three hundred and ten-yard drive down the centre of the fairway.

Skinner steered his tee shot well clear of the cross-bunker, keeping the ball as low as possible for accuracy, and gaining ground through a favourable bounce. Murano and Wales followed him, hitting conservative iron shots on to a fairway which seemed, thanks to the thick crowd on the left, to be much narrower than twenty-four hours earlier. Wales's shot was still in the air as Atkinson strode from the tee. The battle for the Murano Million had been joined in earnest.

As Skinner and Sue Kinture walked side by side down the first fairway, the policeman noticed that his noble caddy was more animated than ever. 'Did Darren give you any ideas on course improvements last night then, Susan?'

She laughed. 'Oh yes, he gave me lots of ideas.' She paused, looking across at the golfer as Norton Wales fluffed his third shot and picked up. 'He says that what he'd like to do is tweak Witches' Hill until it's tough enough for him to find it difficult. Then, he said he'd like to have a tournament here every year, just to sort out the men from the boys.'

They had reached Skinner's drive. Adrenaline had sent the ball ten yards further than in the practice round. He selected a four-iron and fired in a high shot aimed on the right-hand bunker, but drawing into the centre of the green. A buzz rang along the gallery behind him, followed by an intensely satisfying round of applause. 'Oh good shot, Bob,' cried Susan Kinture. Norton Wales, who had joined them, slapped him on the shoulder in encouragement. The team captain acknowledged him with a wink and a brief wave and strode after his shot.

When they paused, as arranged, on the third tee for the two minutes' silence, Atkinson was one under par, having taken par at the first hole and birdied the par-four second. With Skinner's nett three at the first the team stood two under.

As they walked together down the par-five seventh following two good tee shots, Atkinson was three under, and ahead on the professionals' leader board. The team was five under par, thanks to a second nett birdie from Skinner at the fifth. Atkinson had settled into a groove of brilliant golf and was more relaxed than he had been at the start of the round.

'I've been thinking, Bob,' he said. 'This course has a lot of potential, if someone other than O'Malley could get to grips with it. I said as much to Sue last night. So I've got an idea. I don't imagine that poor old White's widow really wants to be left with forty-five per cent of a golf course. I think I'll offer to take her share off her hands. I don't think I'll find a better investment opportunity. Certainly not in Europe.'

They stopped at Skinner's drive, which had carried just over 260 yards, leaving as much again and more to the guarded green. 'Three-wood, please, Sue.' She seemed not to hear him at first as she looked, smiling, at Atkinson. As awareness dawned, she jumped, taken by surprise. 'Sorry Bob. Miles away. A three-iron?'

'No, three-wood. I'm not playing that safe.'

He cracked a long straight approach shot, which finished in the centre of the fairway thirty yards short of the green. They walked on, the gallery to the right of the hole keeping pace with them.

'I like your idea, Darren,' said Skinner, as they approached the leader's drive. 'But there's just one problem. Maybe Sue didn't know about it. The company holds a substantial insurance policy on Michael White's life, to cover that situation. So Myrtle isn't looking for a buyer. The Keyman arrangement means that she has one already. If you want to buy into Witches' Hill you'll need to talk to Hector Kinture.'

Atkinson frowned, as he asked Bravo for his three-wood. He lined up more quickly than usual, and smashed into the ball. It soared away towards the green, but hooked left in flight and plunged into a thick copse of trees.

Bravo stood, head bowed against his white bib. 'Sorry boss. Should have given you a two-iron.'

Atkinson shook his head. 'No, Brav, it was me. Club was

right, shot was crap. It was a concentration lapse, that's all.'

The ball was unplayable, and the drop-out, with a one-shot penalty, still left a difficult approach. Despite a valiant effort, a fifteen-foot putt caught the lip of the hole and swung past, leaving the tournament leader to tap in for a six, and a dropped shot.

'Sorry lads,' said Atkinson to Wales and Murano.

'That's all right, skipper' said Skinner, mischievously, rolling in a six-foot putt. 'Mine was for a birdie. I told you that all eighteen holes matter to me. To the team too, it seems!'

Forty

'Mr Wills? Hello, it's Maggie Rose here: Mr Skinner's personal assistant. I'd like your help on something, but I'm calling from Schiphol Airport, and I haven't much time.'

'Yes, Miss Rose. What on earth are you doing in Holland?'

'I'm travelling back from Germany. I've been to see Lisa Soutar.'

Rose could almost hear Wills sit bolt upright in his chair. 'Oh yes! And was your trip worthwhile?'

'By God, but it was! You should see what she's got. I'll tell you all about it, but not over the phone. The important thing is that I've traced the Witches' Curse, right back to the source. It was written down in 1598, by Matilda Tod, who seems to have been Aggie's sister. She passed it on at some point to one Elizabeth Carr, and that's how it came into Lisa's family.

'What I don't know is who Elizabeth Carr was, and why Matilda Tod should have handed on the tale with its condition and its warning to her. I wonder if you'd be prepared to help me find out? Could you research the contemporary records of the Parish of Longniddry, or whatever it was called then, to see if you can find any trace of an Elizabeth Carr? All that I can tell you about her is that she married a man called Tullis, and gave birth to a daughter named Frances in 1623.' She stopped, and a tone in her ear signalled the passage of another minute.

'Well, would you do that for me? It'd save time, and I'd persuade the boss to authorise a fee.'

Wills laughed. 'I'd be happy to help. And you can forget the fee. I smell a doctorate in this!'

'Oh no,' said Rose, emphatically. 'The story of the curse has to be kept secret, at least until Lisa says otherwise. The women of her family have guarded it for four hundred years. If it's published without Lisa's agreement it'll be a breach of trust . . . and more besides.

'I mentioned a condition and a warning. The condition is that only a Kinture, or the sovereign of the day may hear the tale. The warning is that anybody who betrays the secret will have to answer to the Devil himself! *My* warning is that Mr Skinner would take the view that all this, bizarre or not, is evidence in a murder investigation.'

'In that case,' said Wills, 'I will respect Lisa's wishes. I might not be too bothered about Beelzebub, but I wouldn't want to fall foul of Bob Skinner!'

Forty-one

Skinner rolled in a two-foot putt for a four on the eighteenth, completing a round of 74. The crowd in the grandstands and around the green applauded politely, unaware that they were watching a man who had just played the best golf of his life.

They fell silent as Darren Atkinson stalked his putt, a tricky 20-foot downhiller with no margin for error if the ball was not to run five or six feet past on the fast green, its surface spiked by the shoes of over thirty golfers and their caddies. But his stroke, when it came, was smooth and the Titleist rolled straight as an arrow. The crowd's shout rose as it travelled, and reached a crescendo as it dropped into the hole for a three, and a round of 64.

Skinner, with Wales and Murano at his heels, stepped across to shake his captain's hand. 'Well played, partner,' he said. 'That was even better than yesterday.'

'You don't know how much better,' said Atkinson. 'When you're playing for this sort of dough, the fairways, and greens, even the hole itself, are helluva narrow. The hole seems barely more than the width of the ball. Look at some of the other scores.'

Skinner peered up at the board behind the stand to the left of the green. Atkinson was four shots clear of Andres Cortes, who was alone in second place, with Ewan Urquhart and

Deacon Weekes a further shot back. Oliver M'tebe had recovered to level par, but Tiger Nakamura had crashed to 75.

'The team must be well placed too, Bob. You chipped in with five birdies on top of my eight under, then there was Norton's crazy two at that short hole. I make it we're fourteen under in total. We're on a roll, boys.' Arms around the shoulders of Skinner and Wales, he led them towards the Recorder's tent to register their cards. 'Too bad I let you down with that six.'

'You didn't, pal,' said Skinner, with undisguised triumph. 'I covered your tail on that one, remember!'

Atkinson laughed aloud. 'I told you you were a bandit off seven. A gross seventy-four for Christ's sake. D'you realise you shot one better than the Tiger? Come on, I'll buy you all a drink to celebrate. Let's hand our cards in, talk to the press, then go change.'

They stopped at the entrance to the tent, totalled and signed their scorecards. Skinner handed his to Atkinson. 'If you'll register that for me, I'll join you guys in the bar. I want to call in on my people, and I'd rather do that *before* I have a drink.' He glanced towards the clubhouse and saw Sarah, seated beside Arthur Highfield, through the window of the first-floor dining room, which was in use as a competitors' hospitality suite. 'Tell my wife where I am if you get there before me, will you?'

Skirting the clubhouse, and waving to Sarah as he passed, he jogged round to the tented village, and to the mobile police office. He jumped up the three steps and thrust the door open. Inside, Alison Higgins and Andy Martin – looking as uncomfortable as ever in his Superintendent's uniform – were seated at the table which they had used earlier for their press conference. They were watching television, and looked round in surprise as Skinner entered.

'What the hell's this?' he barked, in mock anger. 'There's a murder investigation on here.'

Higgins took him seriously, and looked flustered. She switched off the TV. 'We've gone as far as we can go on the enquiry, sir. We've got Morton more or less under open arrest, we've got all the other players and celebrities under very discreet police guard, and we've interviewed everyone relevant. There have been a couple of developments, though sir.'

'OK Ali, calm down and tell me what they are. No, let me guess one of them. There's been another letter to the *Scotsman*.'

The detective looked up sharply. 'Not quite, sir. This one was shoved through the letterbox of the *Herald* office in York Place. They called us and faxed a copy down here.' She picked up a sheet of curling A4 paper, sliced from a fax roll, and handed it to him.

Skinner looked at it and frowned. 'I was afraid this would happen. Typed this time,' he muttered. 'Wonder why that should be?'

He read aloud, '"*Dear Editor, By water . . . so goes another.*"

'Brief and to the point. Right, I want the original, not a fax. I want publication stopped too. The *Herald* might not like it, but enough's enough. I let the first one go because I thought it was a crank, to see if we could smoke him out. But now, with a second murder I'm beginning to get a chilly feeling. Do we know when this was received?'

'Mario's been to the *Herald* to check that out, sir. It was found in the hallway at York Place around ten, behind the door, but it had been there since the receptionist got in at nine. It was in a dirty envelope, with footprints all over, and the girl thought it was rubbish that the cleaner had missed. A delivery rider picked it up eventually and handed it to her. She tore it open, saw the 'Dear Editor', and stuck it, as usual, in the newsdesk in-tray. They get lots of punter stuff handed in like that. It didn't come to the top till twelve-thirty. The *Herald* contacted us just before one. The editor called me, personally.'

'When did you hold your press conference?'

'We began at nine-forty-five, and finished about ten past ten.'

'And no details of the death were reported before then?'

'No, sir. The first report of a second incident at Witches' Hill was on Radio Forth at nine o'clock, and that said only that the start of play had been delayed by a police operation on the course. No one said anything about a death, before we issued our statement at the press conference.'

'Therefore...' he paused '...whoever dropped that note off at the *Herald*, knew about the murder, and the detail of it, before it was made public. Apart from us, Jimmy Robertson, the club pro, who's been in shock since he found the body, and the ambulance drivers – who are all tight-lipped – only twelve people at Bracklands knew about this. They have all been under police guard since Masur's death, so none of them could have slipped up to Edinburgh to stick this through the *Herald*'s door.'

'Could one of them have been playing silly buggers, sir, phoning an accomplice in town?'

'Nice thought, but no way. Andy, Neil and I were with the house party until around quarter to nine. The envelope was through the *Herald* letterbox by nine. I'd say that possibility is ruled out.

'That just leaves the killer in a position to drop that note, or have it dropped. We were entitled to be sceptical about the first letter. The second makes it deadly serious. Do we know how Maggie got on in Germany with the Soutar girl?'

'She called in from Amsterdam Airport, sir. She's coming here to report at eight-thirty tomorrow morning.'

'Good, I want to hear what she's got to say.'

He paused. 'Right, what else do we have? Post-mortem results, forensics on Morton's kit?'

'On the P-M results, yes, sir. Sarah was right as usual. Blow to the head, then death by drowning. The lungs were full of water. There's nothing from the lab about Morton yet though. That could take a couple of days. They're having to take mud samples from the garden, from the banks of the loch, and from the fairway to see if they're different. They've found grass traces on the trousers, and they're having to take samples of that as well.'

'Bugger!' snapped Skinner, impatiently.

'Yes, boss, but here's some good news. The manufacturers of those cigarettes called. They're sending up a full report, but what they're saying is that the stub we sent down is special. The company is about to launch a new brand of luxury fag, and last week they handed out some samples . . . last Saturday morning in fact, at the European Golf Tour event in England. They won't be on sale anywhere for another month, and they've never been distributed anywhere else. So whoever smoked that cigarette in the starter's hut brought it all the way from last week's golf event, and he was there on Saturday.'

Skinner beamed with pleasure. 'Ali,' he said, 'you may have

made an unusual day even more memorable. Keep the pressure on our colleagues to find Richard Andrews, and let me know when they do. Now I must go. There's someone I have to see.'

He paused at the door, jerking a thumb towards the television set. 'What were you watching, by the way?'

Martin smiled. 'I had the TV people give us a monitor and a live feed in here. This event's going out worldwide. You were very impressive, boss. But what I want to know is, who taught you to putt like that?'

'Only the best, my boy. And now I must go and talk to him.'

He jogged back to the clubhouse, and changed, after the briefest of showers, into his formal wear. Sarah and Jazz were the centre of attention when he reached the dining room. The baby was holding a golf glove, twisting it in his strong little hands. Skinner gave Sarah a quick kiss, as Darren Atkinson handed him a pint of McEwan's 80 Shilling ale. 'Cheers, skipper, I need this.' The policeman took a generous mouthful of beer, savouring its smoothness. 'Whose is the glove, Jazz?' he said.

The baby looked up at him, and gurgled.

'I thought I'd try to interest him in the game early,' said Atkinson.

'That's nice of you. I'll see that it's preserved. He can hand it on to his firstborn. The way you played today you could still be Number One then.'

'Keep your eye on me. I haven't peaked yet. You wait till Sunday.'

'Hector Kinture's going to hate you if you do any worse damage to his course!'

Atkinson smiled and shrugged. 'He should have got himself

a decent bloody architect then, shouldn't he, instead of the Wild Colonial Boy.'

Skinner glanced across at the Marquis, but he gave no sign of having heard. He stepped to one side, and motioned Atkinson to follow. 'Darren,' he said, quietly. 'Remember that bloke Andrews, the one I didn't ask you about the other day?'

The golfer nodded. 'Mr Nice, yeah.'

'Can you remember if he's a smoker?'

Atkinson looked at him blankly. 'Eh? Let me think. Yes, of course he is. I remember the first time I met him he was a chain-smoker. He's cut it down a lot since then, but, yes, he still smokes. How come you're concerned about his health, I wonder?'

'Like before,' said Skinner, 'don't wonder too hard. You just concentrate on the golf. Leave the detecting to me.'

Forty-two

'He really is a nice guy, that Darren, isn't he?'

'You're just chuffed because he made a fuss of your wean,' Skinner grunted.

'Don't be silly. He's charming, and you know it.'

'He's God's own golfer, I know that much. I've played two rounds with him now. In all that time he's hit one bad shot, and when he did that it just made him sharpen up even more. Apparently today was his fourteenth successive round under seventy.'

'You didn't do too badly yourself today, honey.'

'That was the effect that playing with him had on me. Hideo and Norton reacted the other way. I was sorry for them.'

He put his arm around her as they sat on the bench, watching a group of children as they attacked the apparatus of the Goose Green playground. Jazz was dozing in his cradle, strapped to his father's chest.

'Tell you one thing, babe. You're right about Sue. She is smitten with the man. You should have seen the way she looked at him this afternoon. I hope she doesn't do anything daft.'

'I shouldn't think she will. She likes being Lady of the Manor.'

'Aye, but in golf, Darren's bigger-time nobility than a mere Marquis. He's King of the World.' He squeezed her arm. 'Come on, let's go home. It's getting near supper time for Bonzo here . . . and I'm bloody starving too.'

They left their bench and walked back up the sloping village green towards their cottage.

'What was the autopsy finding on Masur?' Sarah asked, facing him as she stepped backwards up a grassy ridge. 'You said we'd talk about it later.'

'Banged on the head, then drowned. Just like you thought.'

She nodded, with a look of professional satisfaction. 'I've been thinking some more too,' she said. 'About how it was done.'

'What d'you mean?'

'Try to picture it. There's Bill Masur walking back to Bracklands, across the golf course. He's full of the joys of victory. He's rubbed his arch enemy's nose in the dirt, in public. He's had a few drinks, but he isn't drunk. It's a pleasant moonlit night and he's as wide awake as he's ever been in his life.'

They had reached the cottage. Bob stepped aside as she opened the door with her Yale key. 'OK,' he said, 'so?'

'Well, for openers, it would not be easy to sneak up on this man. There are no trees around there. The fairway's wide open. No place to lie in wait.'

Skinner lifted Jazz from his cradle, handed him to Sarah, then headed off to prepare the baby's bath. 'Who says he was there?' he said, over his shoulder as she followed him. 'Couldn't he have been walking along the cart track close to the trees?'

'What happens to the buggies at night?'

'They're all locked up.'

'Did your people find any tyre marks on the fairway?'

'No.'

'Did they find any marks as if someone had been dragged across the fairway?'

'No.'

'OK, Masur was a big, heavy guy. He could have been slugged on the path and carried across to the stool, but it would have taken more than one person to do that. A reasonable conclusion, yes?'

'Yes,' he said, hesitantly, as he filled the bath.

'Were there lots of footprints around the stool's mooring point, or around the place where Masur was loaded and tied to it?'

'No.'

'OK. Now lets go back to where he's walking along enjoying the moonlight. He's walking towards Bracklands, remember. So what happens?'

'Someone softshoe's up behind him and banjoes him, yes?'

'I doubt it. He'd have to be very quiet about it. It was a still night as well as a bright one. And the angle of the head injury was wrong.'

'What d'you mean?'

She smiled, and Skinner could sense her triumph to come. 'Well if it happened like that, even if the guy had come up behind him like Marcel Marceau, he'd have been hit a downwards blow to the top of the head. He wasn't. He was knocked out by a sideways blow to the base of the skull.' She peeled off Jazz's ripe disposable nappy and wiped him clean, then lowered him carefully into the bath, trying in vain to keep clear of the splashes from his kicking legs.

'I think,' she said, soaping the chortling child, 'and I'd stand in the witness box and say this, that someone walked right up to Masur . . . someone he knew. Someone with whom he was relaxed, and off-guard.

'This person walks right up to him, coming, not necessarily from Bracklands, but from the *direction* of Bracklands, and says something like, "Hi Bill, you out for a stroll too?" They strike up a conversation. They walk side by side in the moonlight. The newcomer falls just a pace or two behind. Masur doesn't suspect a thing . . . until the man whips out a cosh, or some such, and drops him where he stands.

'He's chosen his moment, so he doesn't have to carry him far to the stool. Or maybe he means to finish him off with the club, then sees the stool in the moonlight and indulges a sense of the theatrical.' She squeezed a sponge over Jazz's round tummy, triggering a new round of squeals.

'That's my story, copper, and I'm sticking to it.'

Skinner leaned against a wall and looked at her thoughtfully. 'He couldn't just have been overcome by a couple of guys?'

'Come on Bob, you don't believe that a mean sonofabitch like him could have been tackled straight on, even by two guys, without a battle. The head knock was the only injury, remember. This man would have got a few licks off himself. He'd have had scraped knuckles, and facial bruising. But the only marks on him were caused by the fishes.'

He sighed. 'Yes, you're right, as bloody usual. I'll buy it. It doesn't make things easy, though. The only guy in the house party who isn't accounted for is Morton, and the way those two went at it, I hardly see him – or his fixer Richard Andrews – walking up in the moonlight and saying, "Hiya Bill, how's it goin'?" So if Masur did meet someone in the middle of the eighteenth fairway, I have no tiny idea of who it was . . . unless one of Aggie Tod's witches flew in on a broomstick and zapped him!'

Friday

Forty-three

'So what's she like now, Myra's magic child? What did she turn into?' There was a strange sadness in his tone.

Maggie Rose put down her notes, her account of her German interview completed. She looked at Skinner, through the eyes of someone who knew him well, and saw, written on his face, the depth of the old memories which the rediscovery of his dead wife's tape had stirred in him.

'She's grown into a kind of pathetic wee woman, sir. She's married to a man who obviously treats her like a skivvy, but that's not all. She's borne down by possession of that bloody curse. It took me a while to realise what it is about her. She's possibly the loneliest person I've ever met.'

'Why's that, Mags? She's got her kid, hasn't she? And she must have friends around her, living in married quarters. Are you telling me she's homesick for Longniddry!'

Rose smiled and shook her head. 'No, sir. It's not that. It's Aggie Tod's curse. I've told you how Nana Soutar reacted when she found out that Lisa had made that tape for Myra. Possession of the tale sets you apart from others. It makes you unique. It's been handed on in that family for four hundred years. I mean, just look at that tree. It's fantastic.' She pointed to the piece of paper on the table, in the mobile police office.

'The thing has built up its own tradition within that string of descendants, and gathered its own power. They've had four centuries of believing that if they betray the witch secret they've been entrusted with, then the Devil will show up to sort them out. They've had four centuries of submission to the tale, of its being beaten into them when necessary. Within their own family, these women have been set apart, seen as different, somehow.'

Rose picked up the paper and looked at it again. 'D'you know what keeps Lisa going, through the drabness of her life, and what makes her tolerate that bloody husband of hers?' Her anger boiled over. 'Honest to God, in that whole house there was nothing to show that Lisa is *cared* about!'

Skinner reached out and touched her hand. 'Maggie,' he said kindly. 'I know that sometimes it's hard not to get steamed up over people's problems. But that's the job. We're police officers, not marriage counsellors or social workers. You mustn't allow yourself to be deflected from the task by sympathy for others. Have compassion, but professionally, you've got to stick to what's relevant. You know that.'

'Yes sir, I do. And this is relevant. I *do* have a point to make. Lisa is driven on by one thing. She's living for the day when wee Cherry is old enough to be told the story, and to take her place in the line of the Tellers. Then it won't be just her alone. There'll be two of them to share the secret, two strange women a bit different from the rest.

'Yet Lisa's still marked by her nana's warning, and until I came along, with the tape and the press cutting, there's no way that she'd have breathed the story of Aggie's curse to another living soul. I'm certain of this. Whoever sent those notes to the *Scotsman* and the *Herald* didn't hear the story from Lisa Davies.'

Alison Higgins stood up and refilled her mug with coffee from a Thermos jug on the table. 'If that's the case, what other possibilities are there? Didn't Henry Wills say that there was a nineteenth-century reference to the story?'

'Yes, he did. I'm seeing him later today. I'm going to follow that up with him. I've asked him to help me find out who Elizabeth Carr is too.'

'Come on, Inspector,' said Higgins. 'You heard what the ACC said about keeping to the point. Is that strictly relevant?'

'I don't know, ma'am, but I can't say that it isn't, and neither can you. It's bizarre and it's a bloody nuisance, but the Aggie Tod story is linked into two murder enquiries. If we run it completely to earth, we may find out who else knew of the curse. If we do, we may have found our killer.'

'Touché,' said Higgins.

'There's something else I want to do, that might not be so relevant, but it is connected to the story.'

'What's that?' asked Skinner.

'I want to find out as much as I can about Lisa's Bible, sir. It's an extraordinary thing for an ordinary person to have.'

'If you can call Lisa Soutar ordinary!' said Higgins.

'Granted. But even at that . . . I mean we're talking about a Bible which pre-dates the King James edition. And apart from its age, it's a remarkable work. The cover is rich beaten leather. It's been well cared for by all its keepers, and inside there are some beautiful illustrations. I persuaded Lisa to let me take some photographs of it. I'm going to find an expert, to see if it can be identified, and to get an idea of how much it's worth.

'She'd never given a thought to its value. Now that she has, she's decided to keep it in a bank deposit box. Her husband doesn't know it exists, but she reckons that if he ever found it he might take it and sell it.'

She looked up at Higgins, still standing coffee mug in hand. 'I don't know,' said the Superintendent. 'I'm more interested in finding out who else could have written those notes to the press.'

'Aye, Ali,' said Skinner, 'but this investigation is already so weird that we can't rule out anything. Maybe, just maybe, researching the Bible will help us to answer that very question.

'OK Mags, you get on with all that, and report back to Miss Higgins on each part of the investigation.'

'Very good, sir.' She got up from the table, put her notes back in her briefcase and left the office.

Skinner and Higgins were alone. The ACC picked up the Thermos jug. Guessing by its weight that it still held coffee, he twisted its screw cap and poured himself a refill.

'You're doing a good job on this investigation, Alison,' he said. 'No one's going to fault you for lack of achievement.'

'Thank you very much, sir.'

'But there is one thing. It's an essential skill of command. It's a bit like football; no, let's say sailing, since that's your sport. You can either be the sort of captain who issues every order, and who sees the crew simply as implements of her will, or you can be the type who keeps a steady hand on the tiller and lets her crew get on with their different tasks, backing their judgement all the time . . . even if on occasion they're wrong.

'I don't succeed all the time, but I try to be the second sort of skipper. If I have a crew member who's idle or slipshod, then he'll walk the plank, but I always respect those who do their best. If someone comes to me and proposes an initiative, then

I give them the same trust I expect them to place in me, and I let them run with it.'

'And that's what I should have done with Maggie?'

'Yes, as second nature. It may be that at the end of the day, all she'll achieve is a free valuation of her family Bible for Lisa Davies. But that's not her objective. She wants to find out all she can about that book, and about how it might have come into the hands of a burned witch's sister, because that's what her training and her instinct tell her she *should* do.

'You're in command of good detective officers, Ali. And their second greatest asset, after their attention to detail, is their instinct. Never suppress it, or countermand it . . . unless *your* instinct tells you different!'

Higgins nodded. 'Thank you, sir, I appreciate the advice. I'm grateful to you.'

'Don't be, Superintendent.' He waved his right hand vaguely around him, circling the room. 'To finish my sailing analogy, I'm Admiral of the CID fleet and it's my job to see that we all make a safe landfall! One other thing. How's that coven hunt doing? Have we had word of local witches?'

Higgins smiled. 'As a matter of fact, sir, we just did. One of the PCs in the Haddington station was told by his daughter that there's some sort of group in her school. The kid said that it's older girls and boys, and that they meet every Friday in an old quarry behind the town.'

'Oh aye? To do what?'

'Maybe we'll find out tonight. Andy Martin's taking some people to the quarry tonight, to see if there's anything in it.'

'Could be interesting. Meantime, I've got some golf to play!'

Forty-four

East Lothian is one of the driest counties in Scotland, but when it rains in summer it does so in full measure.

A brief visit to the practice ground had convinced Skinner that while the opening day of the tournament had been the finest of his life on a golf course, the second round would be an ordeal to be endured. Like most good links golfers, he was accustomed to windy conditions, but he detested heavy, still days with rain pouring from leaden skies.

He had begun his practice wearing his favourite waxed cotton hat, made by Christy and guaranteed waterproof, only to find that it lived up to its warranty so well that as he stood over the ball, rainwater flooded off its brim like a water-fall, obscuring his vision. Laughing helplessly at the ludicrous picture which he offered to the three foolhardy spectators who stood, huddled under umbrellas, around the practice area, and to the television camera on its rostrum behind him, he zipped his Gore-Tex jacket as high as it would go and retired, stopping in at the professional's shop on the way back to the clubhouse to buy a brimless rain hat and a new non-slip glove.

Now he stood in the changing area corridor, studying the full list of scores from the opening day. At 14 under the Darren Atkinson team had a six-shot lead. Of the twenty-four amateurs in the field, fifteen had handed in completed cards having played out every hole. Skinner saw with satisfaction that in the handicap section his nett 67 put him two shots clear of a Japanese player, off 12, named Hirosaki, while in the scratch calculation, his 74 was one clear of Everard Balliol, an American three-handicapper, and a member of Team Nakamura. He checked its line-up and saw that Mike Morton was among their number, but that he had posted an incomplete card, littered with wasted shots and conceded holes. 'Must have something on his mind,' he muttered to himself with a grim smile.

He stepped out of the clubhouse into the pouring rain, and squelched across to the first tee. Even in the morning gloom, Sue Kinture shone out like a beacon. She wore a Day-Glo hat and cape and carried a huge umbrella bearing the Witches' Hill name and crest. A tall young man stood beside her wearing weatherproofs and carrying a second umbrella.

'Hello Bob,' she called as he approached. 'This is Joe, from the estate. I thought we could use an extra umbrella-carrier today. Hope it's not against the rules.'

Beside her, Darren Atkinson laughed. 'No Susan, that's OK. No more than fourteen clubs, but as many Witches' Hill umbrellas as you like – especially when there's a chance to flash the logo at a few million television viewers!' She looked at him with a faint smile, but the downpour seemed to have drenched some of her sparkle.

'Ready for battle then, team?' called Atkinson. 'We're off first today, so the rest of the field will be shooting at us. In these conditions, the idea is just to get round. Forget all about yesterday and the day before. This is a different golf course today, and you'll need to take a fresh look at every shot.

Whatever your caddies tell you to do, take their word for it and do it.'

He put a hand on Norton Wales's shoulder. 'Today is made for you, friend. So far everyone's been expecting you to be a showbiz clown . . .'

'And I haven't let them down! Given them some bloody laughs so far,' said the singer, emphatically.

'So what? Today they'll be saying, "My God, but he's game to be playing in that." They'll cheer every decent shot you play and go "Shame" if you duff one. How about you, Hideo, you OK?'

The heir to the automobile fortune laughed softly. 'You think it doesn't rain on Japanese golf courses? This is nothing for me.' He pointed up at his umbrella, on which the name 'MURANO' was emblazoned in huge blue lettering. 'And I can do my advertising too!'

'Bugger this,' said Skinner. 'I should have brought one with a black-and-white check band around it!'

The announcer introduced the team through a PA system which crackled in the rain, and Atkinson stepped up to the tee. He chose a three-wood, rather than the driver which he had used on the earlier rounds. Teeing up his ball, he stood back under his umbrella, which Bravo held aloft until the last possible moment, before booming out a long, high shot which faded in flight along the line of the dogleg. It carried around 260 yards before pitching and pulling up short.

'Remember, Bob,' he said, stepping back amid the applause. 'Give it height off the tee. If you use your driver, tee it high, or the rain will force the ball down. You won't get much run either. Today we're playing target golf.'

Skinner nodded. Normally he detested umbrellas on the

golf course, but on this occasion he was glad of Joe, the estate worker, shielding him from the rain as he surveyed his shot. He took out his driver and set the ball as high as he could on the tee, concentrating as hard as he could on keeping his head down and swinging smoothly. The click of the club-face sounded almost damp, and he had trouble in picking the ball up in its flight, but eventually he saw it, soaring high and pitching around 230 yards away, to the right of the fairway, and stopping dead. His sigh of relief was so loud that the television effects microphones picked it up, even above the applause.

He looked over his shoulder and saw Mike Morton, in the gallery less than twenty feet away, glaring towards him from under an umbrella, with a dark, sullen look on his face.

He waved to him as Hideo Murano stepped up to the tee. 'Enjoy your round when it's your turn, Mike,' he called, with a soft smile. 'But watch where you put your feet. It's helluva muddy out here!'

Forty-five

'To think, Inspector Rose, that this was once part of a department store.' He paused, awkwardly. 'But pardon me, you'll barely be old enough to remember those days.'

Maggie laughed. 'Oh no, Mr Wills. My mother used to drag me around Patrick Thomson's every Saturday morning. Usually she didn't buy anything, but it was part of her ritual. Nowadays, your behavioural psychologists would call it mother/daughter bonding. I just remember girning all the time, because I wanted to be playing with my pals, not looking at school shoes, new lampshades and God knows all what.' She looked nostalgically around Carlyle's Coffee Shop on the North Bridge, where Henry Wills had suggested they should meet. 'I guess this would have been the cosmetics section. Another regular stopping-off point.'

She smiled. 'Rituals don't change, you know. Only their locations. She still drags me out on the odd Saturday morning … except now we go to the Gyle Centre, together with half the folk in South-east Scotland!'

A fresh-faced young waiter appeared at their table, order pad in hand. 'Hello there,' said Wills. 'You're a student, aren't you? Law Faculty, yes?'

'That's right, sir.'

'I thought so. May we have a pot of coffee for two, and

something self-indulgent for me, an eclair, I think? Miss Rose?'

The Inspector shook her head. 'I wouldn't dare. My wedding dress will be tight enough as it is. That's something else I'm doing for my mother on a Saturday morning. Personally I'd rather get married in uniform!'

The young waiter left a copy of their order on their table and disappeared towards the kitchen. 'You've got a good memory for faces, Mr Wills. You have thousands of students in the University.'

The Registrar smiled at the compliment, and heavy laugh lines creased his eyes. 'I always have had. Every so often I'll see a face I think I recognise, and it'll come to me a day or two later that it was someone I taught twenty years ago. My trouble is that I'm not so good at putting names to the faces.'

He paused. 'Now, talk of names brings us to Elizabeth Carr. What can we find out about her? Why don't you begin by telling me about your meeting with the former Lisa Soutar.'

Step by step Rose took him through her visit to Germany, and through Lisa's story. From her briefcase, she produced her copied version of the family tree and handed it to him. He read it eagerly. 'Fascinating,' he said, when he had finished. 'Parentage is traced back through the line, until Elizabeth Carr. We are given no clue as to who she is, or why Matilda Tod chose to entrust her story to her.

'And what of Matilda Tod herself! The sister and last witness of a doomed woman accused of witchcraft, and rightly accused according to the words of the curse as it is written down. What an amazing occurrence: to stand history on its head! Our understanding of the witch hunt is one of superstitious persecution of simple, innocent women. Yet here we have Agnes Tod, with the firewood piled around her, declaring, "Yes

I'm a witch, and you who are crossing me will suffer for it."
And here's something else. This self-proclaimed witch has a
sister who is literate, an uncommon attribute in those days,
when country people were no better than serfs.

'Oh yes, Miss Rose, we must find out all we can about
Elizabeth Carr, but Agnes and Matilda Tod are even more
important. Who were they? What of their lineage? Who are
their descendants, and who else might hold the knowledge
behind these letters to the press?

'Is there someone else guarding the Devil's altar of Witches'
Hill, and are they prepared to kill for it? Doesn't it set your
detective's blood tingling?'

Wills's excitement had infected Maggie Rose, in spite of
herself. As the young waiter delivered their coffee-pot and
cups, she realised that she was gripping the table-edge so
tightly that her fingers had gone white.

'Realistically,' she said, 'can we find out anything about any
of them? After all, we're talking about people who lived four
hundred years ago.'

'I won't know that until I start to look.'

'Where will you begin?'

Wills poured coffee for each of them. 'I'll begin and
probably end at the General Register Office. Registration as we
know it today began about a hundred and fifty years ago.
Before that records were kept in parishes, fairly informally, and
those old records that still exist are stored now in the GRO.
Some of them are even computerised . . . courtesy of the
Mormon Church, believe it or not, but that's another story.

'I know the staff in New Register House fairly well, so I'll
have ready access. It all depends on whether they have records
from Longniddry covering the period in which we're

interested. If that is the case, then Lisa's family tree will get us off to a flying start. Elizabeth Carr gave birth in 1623. We can trace back to find her marriage to Tullis and see what that tells us.'

Maggie shook a few grains of salt into her coffee and stirred it. 'If the records are there, how far back will they go?'

'Far enough, if we're lucky. Many parishes had informal recording going back to the sixteenth century. If that's true of Longniddry, we'll be able to go in search of the Tod sisters, to see what sort of people they were.'

'What d' you mean?'

'Later birth records show the father's occupation. In those days it depended on the whim of the local minister. If we find the Tods' birth records, let's hope that theirs was a stickler for detail.'

'But how will it help us, to know what their father's work was?'

Henry Wills raised his eyebrows. 'Inspector Rose, even today we categorise people by occupation. In those days such things were absolute. The fact that Mr Tod produced even one literate daughter sets his family apart from the mass of artisans of the time.'

Rose sipped her coffee, savouring the sharpened taste. 'When can we get started?'

'You want to come?'

'Of course. This is detective work, after all.'

'Very well. I have some things to do at the University, but I should be clear by around two o'clock. Let's meet in the Café Royal bar, at around two-fifteen. I always welcome an excuse to look at those tile pictures.'

Rose nodded. 'That suits me. My photographs of Lisa's

Bible should be ready by then. I'll let you see them. After that I'll have to find an expert.'

'No difficulty about that. The National Library of Scotland is where you should go. They're book historians, after all.' He paused, leaning his head back slightly, as if he were giving a new idea an airing in his mind. 'You know, that's another thing. That volume was in the hands of Matilda Tod. She gave it to Elizabeth Carr. Yet the family tree begins with Tullis and Carr. Something odd about that, too.'

He smiled. 'Now, any other medieval mysteries to be solved before we go?'

Maggie Rose looked at him, with an expression which was as close to coyness as she could manage. 'Well, it's not quite medieval, but I did wonder if you could shed some light on the nineteenth-century reference to the curse which you mentioned the other day.'

Wills's smile widened into a beam, and the look in his eyes reached close to smugness. 'I've anticipated that one, Inspector.

'When I thought about it I realised that the story was virtually received wisdom among Scots historians, and that I myself was no longer sure of its foundation. So I did some digging.

'It comes from a history of Haddingtonshire – that's what East Lothian was then – written by one John Smeaton and published in 1843 . . . except that isn't quite true. Actually it comes from a review in the *Scotsman* of that work. The author must have been wounded when it appeared, because it was an extremely poor review. It said that the book was badly researched and badly written and described it as "a ragbag of gossip and old wives' tales". It made a particularly disparaging reference to what it described as a fairy tale of a bizarre witch's curse, calling down vengeance by blade, fire and water.'

Suddenly his beam by-passed smugness and attained triumph in a single stride. 'But do you know, Inspector, that is all that it said.'

Rose looked at him, intrigued. 'So?'

'Don't you see? It made no mention of Agnes. Now, think back to the note to the *Scotsman*. Remember its wording.'

Comprehension dawned on her face. '*"By the blade, said Agnes."* Of course. But what about the book itself, couldn't the writer of the note have a copy?'

'That's remotely possible, but it doesn't counter my argument. I have checked with all the Scottish university history faculties. None of us has a copy. But I did find one. Smeaton was an advocate, and he presented a copy of his work to the Advocates' Library. It was passed on to the National Library when it was set up in the early part of this century. I've seen it. It makes a very vague reference to the Witches' Hill burning, and paraphrases the curse more or less as the *Scotsman* described it, but nowhere does it mention Agnes Tod, or her sister Matilda.'

'John Smeaton; do we know anything else about him?'

'Oh yes,' said Wills. 'His life is well documented. He was a cousin of the then Marquis of Kinture. An undistinguished man, who saw no success at the Bar, and who died in a riding accident, a few months after he published his *magnum opus* on Haddingtonshire.'

He paused. 'While I was at it, I checked the records of the trial and burning of Agnes Tod's coven. It was a very summary affair. Statements were made before the Earl of Kinture, he found guilt and pronounced sentence. There were three defendants in all, Agnes Tod, Christian Dunn and Mary Lewis.'

'But could the Earl do that? Didn't it have to go to a proper court?'

'In those days, my dear, the Earl of Kinture *was* a proper court! He had what was known as "power of pit and gallows" over his people. That meant that he could imprison wrongdoers, or execute them as he thought fit. Awful as it may seem today, the burning of Agnes Tod and her friends was quite legal.'

'But what was their crime?' asked Rose, real anger in her voice.

Wills's smile of triumph had gone. 'They were accused, believe it or not, of trying to kill King James VI by raising a storm against his ship, in Aberlady Bay, as he sailed down the Firth of Forth towards Leith.'

'What!'

'That's right. And what's more, if you take Agnes Tod's curse, written down by her sister, at face value, they were guilty!'

Forty-six

The rain hammered down as if the plug had been pulled from the Truth Loch and the heavens were trying to keep up the water level.

Skinner stood on the tee of the 230-yard par-three twelfth, not far from the clubhouse, and looked in astonishment as Darren Atkinson hit an immaculate three-iron, cutting upwards through the rain and feathering down on to the green, no more than six feet from the hole. The US Open Champion was one under par for his round, thanks to a birdie at the par-five seventh. Skinner himself was scrambling to play to his seven handicap, while Norton Wales and Hideo Murano were splashing their way around the course as best they could, every shot being applauded sympathetically, by a crowd which was smaller than on the opening day, but which still ran into the thousands.

'Shot, skipper,' said the policeman in admiration, as the gallery gasped its approval. He emerged from under Joe's protective cover to hit a five-wood, high and wide of the green. Shaking his head, he retreated beneath the umbrella, as Murano stepped up to play. As he watched the Japanese ready himself, a hand tugged his sleeve. He looked down to see a small boy, clad in waterproofs from top to toe, proffering a squeezable plastic bottle of the official soft drink supplier's newest isotonic product. He put a hand on the child's shoulder, stilling him until Murano had played, then took the drink with a smile and a soft 'Thank you', imagining his own son, seven or eight years on.

A few seconds later the child returned, and handed a drink to Bravo. Then a moment later he stepped up for a third time, holding out a drink, and an autograph book, to Darren Atkinson. The golfer took the bottle from him solemnly, unzipped his golfbag and slipped it into the big container pocket. He reached out his hand to Bravo. 'Gimme yours too mate,' he said, 'we'll be on the move in a second.' The caddy handed over his drink. Atkinson stowed it in the bag, then squatted down to sign the autograph book. 'No school today?' he asked. The boy flushed and looked guilty. It struck Skinner that even during competition, when he was at his most intense, Atkinson had never turned away an autograph-seeker.

Norton Wales hooked his drive into deep grass to the left of the fairway. 'I think I'll leave it there, Darren,' he called, loudly enough for the spectators to hear. 'It might meet one just like it in that jungle and live happily ever after!'

They hustled down the fairway. Having underhit his drive, Skinner's second shot was too strong, but a good long putt from the back of the green secured him a four, one better than Murano's score. He stood at the side of the green, pressed alongside Sue Kinture and Joe, as Atkinson lined up his birdie attempt. He glanced at his caddy. She seemed in another world. 'Is the weather getting you down, Susan?'

'What? Oh, no. Sorry, Bob, I was miles away. Thinking about our cocktail party at Bracklands tonight. You and Sarah will come, won't you?'

'Of course, we're both looking forward to it. We've got a

local baby-sitter this time. Sarah's joined a mother's circle. It's a sort of co-operative, operating on a knock-for-knock basis. No one gets paid money. They all have wee plastic rings and each one's worth an hour.'

'Sounds very WRI!' she whispered.

They were interrupted by the bellow of the crowd as Atkinson's putt rolled unerringly into the hole for a two. As it fell into the cup, the ball made a small splash. Skinner looked up at the sky as they walked across to the thirteenth hole. 'I don't know if the course can absorb much more water,' he said as they reached the tee. 'Mind you the sky's getting a bit lighter.'

Atkinson delved into his bag as they reached the tee. When he stood up he held the two isotonic drinks, and a plastic bag containing golf ball wrappings and damp hand towels. He threw the bag into a dustbin, and handed one of the drinks to Bravo, opening the other himself, and taking a long draught.

'As long as it doesn't get too light, mate. I remember one time I played in the Open, not very far from here, in the worst July weather I've ever seen in Britain. It was the second round and I went out early. A howling gale, hail, freezing cold rain, you name it, God chucked it down that morning. I shot a seventy-one in that, and I still count it as maybe the finest round I've ever played. The next best that morning was a seventy-seven.

'Then, as soon as I stepped off the last green the wind dropped, the rain stopped and the skies cleared. Sandro Gregory was standing on the first tee waiting to play off. He gave me a big smile, the bastard, then went out and shot sixty-four. On the Sunday, he beat me for the championship by one shot. I've never forgiven God for that one!'

He stepped on to the tee and crunched a booming three-wood up the fairway of the par-five hole, leaving the ball placed perfectly for his second shot to the green. Skinner followed him, hitting a conservative two-iron which left him well behind the champion, but safe. The rain was easing slightly by the time he reached his ball. From where his drive had finished, the green was nowhere near in range. He asked Susan Kinture for his three-wood.

He was almost at the top of his back-swing, but was able to check the shot when he heard the crash of clubs and the surprised cry of the crowd. He turned to see Bravo, Atkinson's caddy, lying on the ground. His legs were kicking and convulsing, and he clutched himself in pain. Atkinson stood over him looking aghast. Skinner rushed over to the fallen caddy. His eyes were rolling wildly, and his mouth was working.

'Darren, does he have any medical condition that you know of?'

The golfer shook his head. 'Not one that he's ever mentioned. It looks like he's having a fit, doesn't it?' He knelt beside Skinner, concern mingling with shock. 'Hold on Brav, old son. We'll get help.'

Skinner looked around towards the crowd. 'I need a doctor,' he called. In swift response a short man in a long raincoat ducked under the rope barrier and bustled across the fairway. He turned to Sue Kinture. 'Susan, in my bag you'll find a telephone.' She unzipped the side pocket of his golfbag and, finding his flip-phone, brought it across. He switched it on, dialled in the unlocking code, impatiently, then pushed a short-coded number.

'Andy, this is Bob. Where are you?'

'I'm in the command centre, boss. The television's on so I know what the problem is. There's an ambulance on the way.'

'Could you see what happened, exactly?'

'Yes, the camera was on him at the time. He put down the bag then he just crumpled up. What is it?'

'Don't know.' He looked at the little doctor, who had joined them and was bent peering into Bravo's unfocused, panicking eyes. 'Doctor?' he asked, kneeling beside him.

'Could be an epileptic attack, or some other sort of cerebral incident, even stroke or haemorrhage. We'll need to get him out of here, quick.'

'It's all right,' said Skinner. 'The paramedics are on their way.'

He spoke into the telephone again. 'Andy, tell Highfield to suspend play for the moment.' He turned to Atkinson. 'Darren, do you want to call it off?' Suddenly he felt his sleeve being gripped, tightly, as he crouched. He looked down. Bravo was staring at him, his eyes still wild and his brow knitted tightly. 'No!' he whispered insistently. 'Don't, boss. Be OK! Drink. Tasted funny.'

Skinner looked across the grass. The plastic soft drink bottle lay beside the fallen clubs. 'Doctor,' he said, 'could this be poisoning?'

'It could,' said the little balding man, 'though I'm no expert. Equally, a cerebral incident could affect the sense of taste.'

'Still, just in case.'

The ambulance swung on to the fairway as Skinner stood up, telephone still in hand. 'Andy, where are Neil and Mario?'

'McIlhenney's watching Morton. McGuire's about on the course, just keeping his eyes open.'

'Right, find McGuire and get him here on the double. And

get the nearest uniform over here to collect a drinks bottle from me. I want it off to the lab for testing pretty damn quick. But even before you do that, there's something else. Do it very quietly, but very quickly. I want you to shut down every one of the drinks dispensing points around the course, and make sure that all of the stock stays where it is.'

'Yes, boss. I'll attend to all of that. Meantime you just hang on there.'

'Got nowhere else to go, Andy.'

Skinner ended the call, and, as the paramedics prepared to lift Bravo on to a metal-framed stretcher, walked across to Atkinson's fallen clubs. Carefully, with his gloved left hand, he picked up the bottle. He looked around, and saw PC Pye running towards him, his uniform raincoat flapping.

'Well done, son, you got here fast.' He held out the bottle. 'Right, I want you to take this to Superintendent Martin at the command centre. Touch it as little as you can, and hold it inside your coat so it doesn't get any wetter than it is already.' PC Pye took the container from him, gingerly. 'Right, Constable, on your way.' The young man turned and bustled away, with his left shoulder hunched oddly as his coat shielded the bottle.

Skinner took the few steps back across to the ambulance, as Bravo was being loaded inside. Atkinson walked beside the stretcher, his face lined with concern, squeezing his friend's hand. 'Sure you don't want me to come, Brav?' he asked quietly.

'No . . . bloody . . . way,' hissed the caddy, with as much vehemence as he could muster. The paramedics lifted the stretcher into the ambulance, and the little doctor climbed in behind them.

'Where'll you go, Doc?' called Skinner. 'Haddington?'

'That'll be our first stop, yes,' said the little man from inside the ambulance, as its driver jumped out.

'Good. I guess he'll have his stomach pumped as soon as you get there. When that happens, don't let them throw anything away!' The doctor's face was screwed up with distaste as he closed the door.

As the ambulance headed back up the fairway towards the clubhouse Skinner turned to Atkinson. 'Do you feel OK, Darren?'

'Shocked, but otherwise, yes. Why?'

'You had one of those drinks, hadn't you?' Atkinson nodded.

'I finished it back on the tee, and threw the empty in the bin. But you had one too, hadn't you?'

''Sright, and I feel OK. But I was given mine separately. Remember what happened. The wee chap gave Bravo a drink, then gave you one. But you put them both in the bag.'

'What are you saying?'

Skinner looked at him, seriously. 'If Bravo's drink checks out OK, I'm not saying anything, but if anyone is handing out spiked isotonics, then you're a far likelier target than him! If that drink was dodgy, then I'd guess it was meant for you, but that they were mixed up in the bag.

'Christ, we could be looking for the world's smallest poisoner.'

'You won't have to look far, then.' Atkinson pointed over the policeman's shoulder to the crowd, twenty yards away. 'He's over there.'

Skinner looked round in surprise, but his eye was caught by the figure of Mario McGuire, broader than ever in his waterproofs.

'Sergeant, good to see you. I've got a job for you.'

'What's that, sir?'

'This is Darren Atkinson. He's got five and a half holes to play, and he needs a caddy. There's just a chance that he might also need protection. Welcome to big-time golf, Mario.'

Skinner looked at Atkinson. 'OK?' The golfer nodded solemnly. 'Good. You two get to know each other. Before we get started again, I'm off for a quick word with the master criminal over there!'

Forty-seven

'Edinburgh is full of absolute enchantments, that its people take for granted,' said Henry Wills. 'Look at those tile pictures. Works of art, unique, and yet hardly anyone who comes in here gives them a second glance.'

Maggie Rose gazed around her. The Café Royal bar was busy, packed with men and women in business clothes lingering over the last lunch-hour of the week. They stood in groups, deep in conversation, not one looking up to admire the magnificent likenesses, picked out in hand-painted tiles, James Watt and Michael Faraday among them, as each advanced human knowledge in his unique way.

'I suppose,' she said, 'that we should be grateful that they're still there, and that this place has been preserved.'

'True. Our City Fathers have allowed far too many old pubs to be gutted and turned into unspeakable resorts for the young. Much of the town's history was made in its public houses. They were important meeting places, yet apart from this one, the Abbotsford, and one or two others, they've all been swept away.'

He took a generous mouthful of his Guinness. 'When I was a young man, there were around three dozen fine old pubs along Rose Street. Now there are perhaps a dozen, and most of them are *not* . . .' he leaned heavily on the word '. . . to my taste!'

'Nor mine,' said Rose, grinning. 'We, I mean the police, like the old places too. They never give us any trouble. Our weekend call-outs in the city centre usually come from the places with the strobe lights and foreign beer at three quid a bottle.' Awkwardly, she took a bite of her mutton pie. It was hot and juicy, and she savoured its sharp peppery taste and the feel of the firm, doughy pastry in her mouth. 'I love this. When we have a Saturday off, Mario and I sometimes treat ourselves to the Roseburn Bar and a pie-and-a-pint lunch. We can relax there, knowing that we're not going to run into someone that we've nicked a month or so earlier.'

Henry Wills laughed in his delight. 'You're a woman after my own heart, Margaret. Young Mario doesn't know how lucky he is.'

'Oh yes he does! I've made damn sure of that!'

Wills spluttered into his Guinness. Suddenly his eye was caught by the door as it swung open. A stocky, balding, whey-faced figure shouldered his way into the bar and looked around. As he caught sight of the University Registrar, he broke into a smile. He waved across the bar, and eased his way through the press. Wills waved to a barman and pointed to the Guinness pump.

'Hello, Henry,' said the newcomer, in a North of England accent blunted, Maggie guessed, by years of exposure to Scottish tones. Wills shook his hand.

'Inspector Rose, this is Jim Glossop, an old friend. He's something terribly important in the General Register Office, and, in return for a pint of the Liffey Water, he's going to help us with our search . . . I hope.'

Glossop shrugged his shoulders. He and the patrician Wills made an odd couple. 'As much as I can, Henry. I have been able to find out one thing. We do 'ave parish registers covering Longniddry, back almost to the start of the sixteenth century. The only thing is that the oldest volumes are in use today. We've got some researchers in from America. You can go back as far as 1601, though. Cheers.' He took the black Guinness from Wills and drank, savouring the creamy head. 'Nice pint, that.'

'1601, eh,' said Wills. 'That might well be far enough back for our purposes.'

'What's this all about anyhow?' asked Glossop, between swallows.

'It's just a piece of historical research that I've been asked to do,' said Rose, non-committally. 'Mr Wills is being good enough to help.'

'Ah! Secret, is it? We'd better get on wi' it then.' He drained his glass and motioned them to follow.

The doorway of New Register House was no more than a few yards from the Café Royal. Glossop led them into the anonymous grey building, past a security guard who saluted clumsily, trying at the same time, but failing, to hide a cigarette. They made their way along a series of corridors, until they came to a grey-painted wooden door with a plastic notice, screwed on at eye level, which declared it to be a study. Glossop unlocked it with a key, and held it open for them to enter.

In the centre of the room stood a library table, with two chairs on either side. Five volumes, bound in beige leather, lay upon its angled top. 'Those are what you're after,' said Glossop. 'Enjoy yourselves. When you're finished, or if you want owt else, just give me a call on that phone by the window. Dial two, seven, zero; that's me.' He dropped the latch of the Yale and closed the door solidly behind him.

'Well,' said Wills. 'Let's see what we've got.' He leaned over and looked at the spine of one of the books. 'Sixteen sixty-one to sixteen eighty. Twenty years, five volumes; Jim's left us the whole of seventeenth-century Longniddry, or *Lang*-niddry, as it was called then. The name is believed to be derived from a primitive form of Welsh, as spoken by the Gododdin, a nomadic tribe which inhabited East Lothian in Roman times. The Romans called them the Votadini.'

He checked the spine of another volume. 'This is 1621 to 1640. Let's see what we can find here.' He took a pair of round gold-framed spectacles from his breast pocket and put them on, pinching them tight against the bridge of his nose. '1623, the family tree said.' He cleared space on the table, and, carefully, opened the heavy book near the beginning, standing over it to read more easily. The pages were stiff and yellow with age, and their thick paper creaked as they were turned. 'What have we here?' Wills muttered. 'March 22, 1621. A marriage record, signed by William Friel, the Minister and by the witnesses, between one Robert Glen, labourer, son of Mathew Glen, labourer, and Mary Glen, and Susan Watt, chamber-maid, daughter of Hugh Watt, carpenter, and Susan Watt the elder. How interesting; the witnesses are both named Glen, and they both signed with a mark. No Watts there at all. I wonder if this alliance caused a family rift. The daughter of a skilled man marrying a labourer might have been considered in those days to have chosen beneath her.'

Maggie Rose snorted. 'You could say the same about me, marrying a Sergeant!'

'Ah, yes, Inspector, but your chosen one has the prospect of advancement. In those days, your birth dictated what you would become. Self-made men usually ended up on the gibbet.'

He delved once again into the book, peering sometimes to decipher the crude script. 'The records are simply in order. Marriages, births and burials are listed in the order they occurred.' He turned the pages. Suddenly, he stopped. 'Ahh, how sad,' he sighed. 'This is a burial record. November 6, 1621, Susan, wife of Robert Glen, died November 3, and her son, Mathew, born November 3, baptised November 4, died November 4.' Maggie looked down at the yellow page with its black writing. In the awkward silence, she felt a catch at her throat. 'Sometimes it's best not to look too closely,' said Wills. 'These people must have had a great stoicism, to live in times when such tragedies were commonplace.'

He continued to turn the pages, tracing down their columns as he went. At last he straightened up. 'Yes! July 2, 1622. A marriage record between Archibald Tullis, estate clerk, son of William Tullis, estate clerk, and Rosina Tullis, deceased, and Elizabeth Carr . . .' His voice tailed off and he looked, bright-eyed at Rose. 'How very strange! There is nothing about Elizabeth Carr. No occupation, no parentage: nothing at all to give a clue to her background or her birth.'

He looked down at the page again. 'The witnesses: ah yes, here they are, two and both literate. William Tullis, and...' he gasped: '...Matilda Tod! The witch's sister. We meet her again twenty-four years on. A witness twice: first to a pagan burning, and now to a Christian marriage. Astounding.'

He closed the book. Rose looked at him. 'Don't we want to go on, to trace the birth of Elizabeth's daughter?'

Wills shook his head, impatiently. 'No, no. We know about her already, from the family tree. That, and the existence of Matilda Tod are authenticated by what we have found here today. We must go back in time, not forward, to find the origins of Elizabeth Carr. Back beyond her too, if need be.'

'But if there's no record of Elizabeth's parentage at the time of her marriage, will there be a record of her birth?'

'Unless she came from furth of Longniddry – and, Inspector, in those days Scots people were not mobile – my guess is that there will.

'This woman was married in the kirk. That means she was baptised, and if that is the case, somewhere there *will* be a record.' He stepped round the table to the volume containing the oldest registers, and opened it at its first page.

He scanned the pages swiftly but carefully, tracing a finger down each page, pausing occasionally to peer through his spectacles at a piece of difficult script. On and on he went, starting occasionally, only to shake his head in frustration a few seconds later.

Eventually, he closed the book. 'I've gone all the way through to the year 1611. There are several Carberrys, and a few Clares, but not a single Carr. That is worrying, but I'm not giving up yet. If she's there, Elizabeth must have been born before 1601.'

'I suppose that means we'll have to wait until Monday.'

'Oh no, Margaret, my blood is up. There are few things less stoppable than a historian on the trail of a scent. Only one thing for it. I must bribe Jim Glossop with sufficient Guinness to persuade him to let me in here tomorrow morning!'

Forty-eight

Andy Martin was waiting as Darren Atkinson's bedraggled quartet made their way off the eighteenth green. He wandered across as Skinner paused, with Susan Kinture, beside the grandstand, totalling up his card.

The rain had eased from torrential to merely heavy. 'How's Bravo?' Skinner asked at once.

'He'll be OK. Doctor Collins, the chap who treated him on the course, phoned from Roodlands Hospital. They've got him stabilised, and they've ruled out any cerebral problems. They've pumped his stomach, and the contents are on the way to our lab at Howdenhall for analysis, along with that bottle.

'Doctor Collins wouldn't commit himself, but he said that he once treated someone for atropine poisoning. He reckoned that the caddy's symptoms were very similar.'

'Atropine?'

'Yes, our old friend. Deadly nightshade extract.'

'Shit!' said Skinner. 'That figures. I spoke to the wee boy who handed out the drinks back on the twelfth tee. He said that a "great, big, tall man" gave them to him, one by one, and said that he could hand them over. Thinking it over, it occurred to me that they don't have people doling out the drinks. There are containers on the fifth, twelfth and fifteenth tees and that's it. You want a drink, you help yourself.'

'The kid couldn't have been fantasising?'

'No. His dad was right there. He confirmed it. He said that the bloke handed over three bottles one after the other. The first one, he said to give to Norton Wales, but the wee chap made a mistake and gave it to me. The second he said to give to Bravo, and the third he said to give to Darren.'

Martin looked at him, concerned. 'So the thought is that this man was trying to fix Darren but that the bottles got mixed up.'

'That's right. In Darren's golfbag.'

'Could he describe the man?'

Skinner shook his head. 'Not beyond saying that he was at least six feet tall, broad-shouldered and wore glasses. The guy was completely encased in waterproofs. All that the father remembered was that he was standing beside the drinks cooler, and that he was a smoker. He stubbed out a cigarette on the ground before he gave the wee chap the first drink.'

'What about his accent?'

'He couldn't pin it. Nondescript, he said.'

'Sod it,' said Martin, exasperated. 'Not much to go on.'

'No, but let's keep flying kites. I know it's the longest of long shots, but get some people across to the tenth tee, once the crowds have gone, to pick up every fag-end they can find close to that drinks cooler. You never know your luck.'

'OK.'

'Who's handling the press on Bravo's condition?' Skinner asked.

'We haven't had any enquiries yet. If we do, they'll go to Royston in the usual way.'

'No. Let's not do that. Have Alan refer everything to the

hospital, and tell him to make sure that its press officer says that he was treated for a gastric complaint and that he's progressing. I don't want to stir up any more media excitement.'

He put a hand on Martin's shoulder. 'Do one other thing for me, Andy. Have Brian Mackie contact Joe Doherty. Ask him if he can come up with a physical description of Richard Andrews.'

The Superintendent smiled. 'Yes. We know already that he's a smoker. It'd be nice if it turns out that he's six feet tall, broad-shouldered and wears glasses.'

'Wouldn't it just. And you know me, Andy son. If there's one thing I hate in a criminal investigation it's "nice" solutions.'

He paused. 'Look, if anyone wants me, I'll be up at Fettes this afternoon … in the dry! I'll record my score, have a bite of lunch with the team and then I'll be off.'

'OK boss. How d'you score after all that?'

'Gross seventy-nine, nett seventy-two. I'm bloody chuffed, given the weather. Darren was phenomenal again. He got it round in sixty-eight.' He nodded up towards the leader board beside the green. 'Look at the rest. Only young M'tebe's under par. Even Cortes is struggling. Right, see you later.'

He strode off towards the Recorder's tent, where Susan Kinture waited, in her Day-Glo cape and sou'wester, with a sodden Mario McGuire at her side. As he reached them, Atkinson stepped out of the tent. 'Well done, skipper,' said Skinner. 'Good news for you. Brav's going to be all right.'

'Thank Christ for that. Now I can concentrate on winning us some money.'

'What're you going to do with the million?'

'Pay bloody tax on it!' said Atkinson, regretfully. 'Never mind me, what are you going to do with the scratch amateur prize? It's a car, you know, and you're well on the way to winning it.'

The policeman laughed. 'Two rounds is a long time in golf!'

He nodded in McGuire's direction. 'How did you find your replacement caddy?'

'Fine. He's got the gift. Knows when not to offer advice, which is every time that I don't ask him for it!'

'How d'you feel about having him for another couple of days?'

Atkinson looked at him, grasping his meaning at once. 'If you think it'd be a good idea, and he's willing, that's fine by me. A pro caddy would need time to get to know my game anyway.'

'How about it, Mario? Are you willing?'

'Haud me back, boss,' said the Sergeant, grinning.

'Fine,' said Atkinson. 'Come on and I'll show you where my clubs live when they're off duty. See you for lunch, Bob.' The two set off towards the clubhouse, leaving Skinner with Lady Kinture.

He looked at her with a hesitant smile. 'Listen Susan, you're a great caddy . . .'

'But . . .' she interrupted.

'Yes. "But", indeed. That thing with Bravo's got me worried. It looks like an attempt to nobble Darren. McGuire isn't a caddy, he's a bodyguard, and Darren knows it. It's only a precaution, and I don't expect any more trouble, but if it did I'd feel happier if you were nowhere near it.

'So. Would you mind?'

She shook her handsome head. She had the gift of making a bright orange rain hat look like a high fashion garment. 'Not a bit, my dear. You've been very good, indulging me as you have, letting me be so close to my idol.

'But the gilt has worn off a bit after two days. I've actually been feeling guilty about neglecting old Hector. This is his big week, after all, and he deserves my support. So don't you worry, Bob; I'm more than ready to step aside.'

'Thanks, Susan. I'm really sorry, you know. Detective Sergeant McIlhenney isn't going to be nearly as much fun as you.'

Forty-nine

The National Library of Scotland always made Maggie Rose think of Lenin's Tomb. The windowless stone face which it presented to the thoroughfare of King George IV Bridge she found profoundly depressing, and she had often pitied the civil servants who spent their working lives confined behind it.

The reality, as she entered it for the first time, was less bleak than she had imagined, once she had made her way through the gloomy entrance and into the main reception area, high sided and surrounded with galleried bookshelves.

She introduced herself to a young receptionist. 'I have an appointment with Stephen Knox.'

The man who appeared behind the desk a few minutes later was a stereotypical bookperson. He wore a baggy grey tweed jacket over a check shirt with a frayed collar, and the end of the black belt which secured his crumpled trousers swung loosely from the buckle. He had a long nose and a pinched face, with hair which stood out from his head in a manner which reminded Maggie of a recently departed Cabinet Minister. Stephen Knox, she thought, was possibly the dustiest human she had ever seen, not so much in need of a wash as of a good vacuuming.

But then he smiled, a bright brilliant smile, and all his shortcomings disappeared. 'Hello, Inspector. You have made my year. I have always wished I could have a visit from the police.

'I have lots of callers in here, researchers, students and others and they are uniformly boring. I can't imagine what you want, but I am sure it will be a welcome break from the norm. Follow me, please.'

He led her out of the hall and into a small windowless meeting room, with a desk and two hard grey chairs. 'I'm sorry I can't offer you anything. The coffee here is an embarrassment.

'Before we begin let me tell you something about me. They call me a librarian here, but curator would be a better title. When you called my boss he thought from what you said that I'd be the man to help. So, satisfy my curiosity by letting me satisfy yours.'

She smiled at the odd expression and produced a large envelope from her briefcase. 'It's about a Bible, Mr Knox. A very special Bible, I think. It's at least four hundred years old.' From the envelope she shook a handful of colour prints, blown up to A4 size, shook them loose and passed them across the desk. 'I took these photos yesterday. They show the cover, the title page and four of the pages. I hope they're clear enough.'

Knox took them from her, and looked through them, one by one. The first was of the cover. When he saw it, he gave a small start. The second was of the title page, and as he looked at it his eyes widened. He gulped, making his Adam's apple jump. Slowly and carefully, and silently, he studied each of the remaining exposures. When he had finished, he placed all six on the table and looked up at Rose. He tried to speak, but then his eyes filled and tears spilled, uncontrollably, down his face. She waited, astonished, for him to recover.

Eventually, after almost two minutes, he dried his eyes with a grey handkerchief which had once been white. 'Once in a lifetime,' he whispered, 'and only for a privileged few. When I said that your visit was a refreshing change, Inspector, I had no idea . . .

'The Bible in these photographs is more than just special. It's of great historic interest, and undoubtedly priceless. Where is it? Who owns it? Has it been stolen, or recovered from theft?'

'Neither of these,' said Rose. 'It's in good hands, the hands of a family which has held it, in absolute secrecy, since around the year 1600. I'm trying to establish how it came into their possession.'

Knox looked at her. 'What sort of a family are we talking about?'

'Ordinary, you'd call them.'

'Oh no, I would not. Whoever these people are, they are very special indeed.'

'Hold on to your seat, Inspector. Unless this is an elaborate and brilliant forgery, this is a King James Bible.' Maggie opened her mouth to interrupt, but he silenced her with another brilliant smile. 'No, not the James you're thinking about. His great-grandfather King James IV was a very careful man. His were times of violence and betrayal, and so he had very few close friends. Those he had, he trusted, literally with his life, and to them he was in turn very loyal. In fact, James had two great companions, the Earls of Gordon and Kinture. Court records show that, in 1540, James commissioned from the great French craftsman, DeLarge, a favourite of his wife, Mary of Guise, three illuminated Bibles, in Latin of course, bound in the finest leather. Each of the three were numbered, and were given as gifts by the King, just before he died in 1542.

'The first went to the Queen herself, and on to Mary, her daughter, who became Queen of Scots, and ended on the block in Fotheringay. She took it with her to France, when she married the Dauphin. It remained there after Mary's repatriation to Scotland, but was destroyed during the French Revolution. The second was given to the Earl of Gordon. It remained in his family for three hundred years, until it was given to the Duke of Grange in settlement of a debt. Around fifteen years ago, it was stolen from his castle in the Borders, and has never been recovered.

'The third and last of the DeLarge bibles was given by James to the Earl of Kinture. It is recorded that in 1598 it was destroyed in a fire at the Earl's mansion in East Lothian. But the record was wrong. This is it, the last of the three.'

'How do you know?'

'Simple. James signed them. The Gordon Bible was photographed, and we have copies here. I could fetch them to check, but I don't need to. They're printed on my memory.'

He picked up one of the prints. 'Look here. At the top of the title page.' He held the photograph up for Rose to see. '*Kinture, amicus*. Kinture, my friend. *Jacobus Rex*. James, the King. That's his autograph. He signed each one.

'My dear Inspector. Whoever has this Bible is guarding a national treasure of the highest order. In value terms, I'd say a million.'

Rose looked at him in astonishment. She shook her head. 'Mr Knox,' she said. 'You don't know the half of it!'

Fifty

'So where is it now? Has Lisa got it to a bank yet?'

'Yes, thank the Lord. I just called her again. She took it to the local Deutsche Bank this morning and lodged it safely with them.'

Skinner leaned back in his leather chair and gazed at the ceiling. 'A million-pound relic, kept for four hundred years by a succession of daft or gullible women. Jesus, but the world's a funny place.'

He looked across the desk at Rose. 'You're always thorough, Mags, but this time you've excelled yourself. Do you reckon that's it finished now?'

'Oh no, sir. Henry's going back to the GRO tomorrow. He's determined to keep on digging. We still need to know who Elizabeth Carr was, and whether Matilda Tod has connections with anyone else, and might have passed the same story on to another family.

'Remember the words on the first note, "*So said Agnes.*" That identifies the writer as someone who knew the curse, and they didn't hear it from Lisa.'

'That's right,' Skinner mused. 'The first note.'

He swung himself back to the present. 'OK Inspector. A great day's work. You've unearthed a missing masterpiece, and from the sound of it you've made friend Knox's career in the process. Now, away home to your man.'

'Thank you, sir.' Rose nodded and stood up.

'Incidentally,' said the ACC. 'Your man's had a rare day, as well. He wound up caddying for Darren Atkinson. He'll tell you all about it, but he did it so well that Darren wants him tomorrow and Sunday as well.' Maggie looked at him, bewildered. 'I've got a new caddy too: big McIlhenney. That leaves me short of someone to keep an eye on Mike Morton. D'you fancy a couple of days at the golf?'

'I've an appointment with Mario's parish priest tomorrow, sir.' The redheaded Inspector smiled slowly. 'So if you'd make that an order, I'd be delighted!'

'So done. See you there at nine. Have a good evening.'

The door had barely closed behind her when the telephone rang. 'Call for you sir,' said Ruth. 'From a Mr Salter, calling from London. He says he's a solicitor and that it's very important.'

'OK, let's find out whether it is. Put him through.'

There was a tiny click on the line. 'Mr Skinner?' The voice was deep and brusque.

'Yes, what can I do for you?'

'You can listen carefully. My name is Jacob Salter, of Rusk and Dean, Solicitors, of London and Edinburgh. I do not normally become involved with criminal work, but on this occasion I have been retained to represent the interests of Mr Michael Morton, whom I think you know.'

'Mr Morton is known to me, yes.'

'I am calling to advise you that there must be no further interviews with my client without my knowledge or presence. I consider that your behaviour yesterday, including your search and your removal of items of clothing, was improper, bordering on the illegal. I demand to know the purpose of the tests which you are carrying out, and to be kept informed of the outcome. I have given your secretary my office and home phone numbers.'

Skinner controlled himself with an effort. 'Mr Salter, some advice; watch your tongue and your tone when you speak to me, and don't ever presume to lecture me on the Criminal Justice Scotland Act or on the rights of the individual. My search yesterday was carried out, informally, with the full approval of the Marquis of Kinture, the owner of the premises, *and*, for the record, with your client's best interests in mind.

'The purpose of our tests is to rule out or confirm the possibility of your client's presence at the scene of the murder of a man with whom he had had two arguments, both heated, one of them physical. He denies being involved, and was quite willing to co-operate with us.

'That's all I have to say, except for this. This evening I will be at a cocktail party to which your client has been invited. If you don't want me to speak to him again other than in your presence, then you'd better get yourself an invite damn quick, or tell him to stay out of my bloody way!

'Frankly, from all that I've seen and learned about him, and from what I've heard from you, it might be better for you if you took the second of those options!' He slammed the phone down in its cradle.

He glanced at his watch and saw that it was almost 6 p.m. Slipping on his blazer, which he had hung over the back of his chair, he stepped out of his office and across to his secretary's small room. 'Ruthie, if that so-and-so ever calls again, pass him on to Roy Old or Alison Higgins. I want nowt to do with him if it can be avoided.

'Right, I'm off to a party. See you Monday.'

He was halfway to the door at the end of the corridor when Ruth called after him.

'Hold on, sir. There's something else. Mr Mackie wants to speak to you. There's been word from South Africa.'

Skinner groaned. 'OK, flower. I'll look in to see him on my way out. Sounds ominous. Having to break the bad news to young M'tebe will be just what I need to round off my day!'

Fifty-one

The Grand Ballroom of Bracklands lived up to its name. It was dominated by two magnificent glass chandeliers, hung from a gilded ceiling over a shining oak floor.

Skinner and Sarah were greeted formally in the doorway by Lord and Lady Kinture. Standing directly behind them was an elderly lady. She was tall and grey, with severely permed hair, and she wore a long evening dress. Her expression was on the glacial side of frosty.

The Marquis sat stiffly in his wheelchair, in a green tartan dinner jacket. Beside him, Susan was resplendent in a peacock-blue cocktail dress which drew an admiring whistle from Sarah as she shook hands. 'Sue, that's beautiful.'

'Why, thank you. I have this wonderful little designer. I'll give you her name. Not that you need her, that cream colour shows off the tan a treat. And what about your old man. I know we said formal, Bob, but I didn't think you'd take us that seriously.'

She looked at Skinner, their eyes almost level. He stood tall, the light from the chandeliers sparkling off the heavy silver braid of his dress uniform. 'Every so often,' he said, 'I like to remind people, and myself most of all, that I'm a policeman. Besides, I knew Jimmy was coming and he rarely wears anything else.'

'Tonight's the exception, then. He's over there with Lady Proud.' She chuckled softly, like a bell. 'You can't miss him. He's the one in the kilt!'

'That's great. Now I really do feel like a lemon!'

Susan turned to the elderly woman. 'Bob, Sarah, I'd like you to meet my mother-in-law, the Dowager Lady Kinture. Mother, this is Assistant Chief Constable Skinner and his wife.'

The matron's expression unfroze very slightly. 'How do you do?' she said, extending a hand to Skinner, and contriving to ignore Sarah. Bob guessed that she must approve of policemen, but of little else.

'Hector insisted that Mother join us tonight. She lives in a house on the estate now, but every so often she comes up to Bracklands, for an event.' Lady Kinture the elder frowned at her daughter-in-law down her long patrician nose.

'This week must be exciting for you, ma'am,' said Skinner, making an effort.

Her face iced over once more. 'Exciting is not the word I would use, young man,' she said, in a voice like the edge of a fine blade, then turned towards the next arrivals.

Bob led Sarah into the ballroom, into the heart of the throng of guests. 'Cheerful soul, isn't she?' he whispered. 'Hector must really have looked forward to going away to boarding school. I liked the "Young Man" bit though.'

He accepted two glasses of red wine from a liveried attendant. Handing one to his wife, he took a sip, nodding with approval as he recognised a Rioja, from a particularly good year. 'Mmm, nice. They must have known we were coming.

'Sarah love, why don't you go across and talk to Jimmy and Chrissie, and Mrs White? I'm going to seek out young Oliver. I'll be with you as soon as I've broken the news.'

'OK.' She reached up on tiptoes and kissed him softly on the cheek. He looked at her in surprise. 'What was that for?'

'I should need an excuse? See you later.'

Skinner looked around the long room. He spotted Atkinson a little way off, with Wales, Murano and Arnie Harding, the retired baseball player turned film star. Tiger Nakamura, bizarre in a gold tuxedo, stood beyond them, ogling Frankie Holloway, and nodding sagely, although he did not understand a single word that Toby Bethune MP, the Sports Minister, was saying. At last he spotted the slim figure of Oliver M'tebe standing alone, looking up at a portrait of a Kinture ancestor hung over the empty fireplace. Casually, he strolled over to join him. 'Hello young man. That was a fine seventy you shot today, all things considered.'

The slim African smiled politely. 'Thank you. All the way around I thought of my father. It helped.'

'That's good. Oliver, I've got some news for you on that front. We had a message this evening, from Durban. Your father has been found. He's safe.'

The young golfer's smile spread so wide that Skinner thought it would light up the room. Skinner took him by the arm. 'Come through here.' He led him into an ante-room.

'How was he released?' said M'tebe, as soon as the door closed behind them.

'We don't know. He stumbled into the road on the outskirts of the city, just a few hours ago. He was hit by a car . . .' The golfer's smile vanished instantly and was replaced by a look of panic. 'Hold your horses, he's OK. It was only a glancing blow but he was taken to hospital. He was dazed and confused, and it wasn't until he was recognised by a nurse at the hospital that anyone knew who he was.

'The doctor who treated him said that he was sure he'd been drugged, probably with a very heavy sedative. They've given him some more, to put him to sleep overnight. In the morning, once he's rested, the police will talk to him, to find out what happened.

'Your mother is at the hospital now, but the message as far as you're concerned is to stop worrying. When you tee off tomorrow, the chances are your dad will be sat up in bed, watching you on telly! That should knock two or three shots off your score.

'Now, this is a damn fine party. I suggest you get on out there and enjoy it!'

He held the door open for the young man, whose smile had returned, and followed him back into the ballroom. Darren Atkinson saw them return. 'Good news?' he called across. Skinner nodded and gave him a thumbs-up sign. 'Marvellous. Come on over here, Oliver, and get outside some of this wine!'

Skinner looked around the room once more until he caught sight of Sarah, listening intently to Susan Kinture. He started towards them, until the faintest shake of his wife's head caused him to pull up short. Puzzled, he seized another glass of Rioja from a nearby tray and headed in the direction of Sir James Proud, who stood, with his back to him, resplendent in his Highland dress, his head nodding in conversation. Lady Proud saw Skinner approach and touched her husband on the sleeve. He turned, revealing the third member of their group.

'Ah Bob,' he cried. 'Come and join us. Have you had a chance to meet Mr Mike Morton?'

Saturday

Fifty-two

Skinner shortened his stride as he slogged his way up the sheer, narrow path from the beach car park to the top of Gullane Hill. The rain had stopped but the rough grass was still sodden, and the ground still muddy, from the downpour of the day before.

It was still well short of 8 a.m., but already there was a clamminess in the air which made him thankful that he had chosen to leave his tracksuit in the wardrobe, and to run in teeshirt and shorts. Occasionally as he ground his way up the slope a bird would flutter out from the undergrowth, and once a young rabbit darted out across his path, forcing him to check his stride.

At last, chest heaving, he crested the hill and jogged out on to the golf course. He would have paused to enjoy the view from the seventh tee, but it was veiled by morning mist, and so instead he stretched his legs and loped easily down the middle of the fairway, allowing his breathing to return to normal after the effort of the steep climb.

Skinner enjoyed his morning runs around the three golf courses which were laid out on the grassy Gullane hill. They allowed him to plan the day ahead, and to think through the challenges and decisions which awaited him. But now as he skirted the seventh green and headed out across the links towards the lower slopes he felt his brow knit.

His week had become almost dreamlike. He felt himself uncomfortably out of control, being pulled along by events and reacting to them, rather than anticipating developments. He knew that he had been right to delegate command of the investigation of the two murders, and the apparent attack on Atkinson, but removed from the heart of the action, he felt isolated and slightly frustrated. He picked up his pace, punishing himself as he tried to piece the jigsaw together, to weigh the bizarre lead to the Witch's Curse alongside Mike Morton's twin grudges against Michael White, his very public hatred of Bill Masur, and even his potential antipathy to Darren Atkinson as a business threat. Morton was in the picture for all three crimes, and even, potentially for the kidnapping of the father of M'tebe, a client of Darren's company.

'But is Atkinson a threat to SSC?' he asked himself aloud as he ran. 'Of course he is,' his mind answered. 'He's completely devoted to being number one in everything he does, on and off the course. He's already conquered America in one respect, and it isn't in his nature not to want to wrap up the management side there as well. And if his businessman brother's anything like him in attitude, you have to bet on them doing it.

'That pitches them against SSC and Morton, and every-thing we know about him tells us that's a dangerous situation.

'But what about that bloody curse? A death by the blade. Another by water! How the goddamn would Morton or his minder Andrews know about that?'

He stumbled briefly in a rabbit scrape. 'Shit!' he cried out. 'Who'd be an effing copper!' He shook his head to clear the distracting thoughts, and looked around him as he ran through the misty morning, down on to the far reaches of Gullane's number two course. As if to remind him that he had reached the fringe of the nature reserve, a pair of late-breeding curlews swooped down towards him, their long beaks menacing, and their drawn-out cries warning him away from their nest. They swooped again, closer this time, almost within pecking distance. He looked ahead, and saw a line of four chicks, almost large enough for flight, waddling in single file across the path. He veered away, heading up the hill once more, back towards the village, with the cries of the watchful parents growing fainter behind him, only to rise in intensity once more as two deer broke from their camouflage against a clump of dark bushes, and raced across the course in the direction from which he had come.

He laughed to himself at the power of the place to lighten his mood, then set himself for the last punishing section of his run, back up and over the hill once more, at speed this time, along the roadside, into the village and across Goose Green to his cottage.

Sarah was seated in the kitchen, in a pale blue robe, giving suck to her son, as Bob sprawled through the back door, steaming, streaming with sweat and holding his pulse to check his recovery rate.

'Woah, hoss,' she cried. 'Stay away from me.'

He stripped off his running gear and stepped straight into the shower beside the kitchen, which he had installed when Alex was a child so that the sand from the beach could be washed off before being trailed into the house. Setting the valve to cool, he twisted the lever, arching his back and bunching his muscles as the powerful jet hit him.

As he soaped himself he heard Sarah call from the kitchen. 'Can't hear you,' he bellowed back. 'I'll be out in a minute.' It took longer than that for him to cool out completely, but eventually he stepped back out of the small shower compartment, drying himself with a fluffy white towel.

She looked at him as he stood framed in the doorway, tall, lean and powerful, his golden tan emphasised by the white patches around his hips and around his wrist, where his watch was normally worn. 'Well, did that help?'

He grinned at her. 'The older you get, the harder you have to work to stay in shape. You wait till you get to my age.'

It was her turn to laugh. 'I can wait. I can wait. I find it hard enough being a thirty-something as it is. But that wasn't what I meant. I meant did you get your head together? All night you were tossing like a ship on the stormy ocean.'

'Was I? Sorry. Ach, it's just this whole week, and everything that's happened. It's bizarre. I feel as if we're missing something. I get frustrated when an inquiry isn't going as fast as I'd like it, and it's worse on this one, where I've made a point of putting someone else in command.

'But it's OK, I've got myself sorted out now. Whenever I need a lesson in letting things take their course, a run through God's own country out there always does the trick.' He towelled his wet hair vigorously. 'By the way, what were you trying to say when I was in the shower?'

'Oh yes, Brian Mackie telephoned. He had a call from South Africa.'

Skinner's eyebrows rose. 'Already?'

'Yeah, he said they called him at seven-thirty. They've got more news on Oliver's father's disappearance.'

'That was quick. Did they say how he is?'

'He's fine, from the sound of things. He woke up early this morning wanting to talk. Brian would like you to give him a call.'

'Sure, soon as I'm dressed.' She followed him from the kitchen, through the house to their bedroom, with Jazz, who had finished his first feed of the day, sprawled contented across her shoulder. Skinner dropped his towel into the laundry basket and stepped into their shower room. Standing naked before his shaving mirror, he wet his chin with hot water from the basin tap and rubbed gel, liberally, into his tough stubble. As he drew the razor in its first long sweep down the side of his face, a memory from the previous evening resurfaced suddenly in his mind. He called over his shoulder.

'Hey, remember last night when you and Sue were deep in conversation and you waved me away? What was all that about?'

Sarah stepped into the shower room to stand alongside him. 'That . . .' she began, strangely hesitant. 'You might say that it was women's talk. Sue had something on her mind, and she's short of girlfriends to confide in.'

'What's her problem, then? Physical or emotional?'

'The latter.'

'Ah! Is Hector that tough to live with?'

'No, he's very kind to her, under all that crustiness.'

'But he can't attend to her physical needs, yes?'

'OK, so he can't, but that's got nothing to do with it, either.'

'Oh yes?'

She stamped her foot lightly in mock exasperation. 'Damn you Skinner! You're going to go on and on, aren't you! Look,

323

I'll tell you, but not a word or any sort of a hint to Sue . . . or anyone else, that you know about it.'

As he shaved, she recounted Sue Kinture's story. By the time the last of the gel was cleared from Bob's face, his smile had gone with it.

Fifty-three

He had just driven away from the cottage when he remembered that he had not called Mackie. He switched on his carphone and dialled the Headquarters number, knowing, even though it was Saturday, and not yet 9 a.m., that he would find the early-rising, workaholic detective at his desk.

'Mackie.' Skinner smiled at the cautious tone, and imagined his lugubrious colleague's brow wrinkling at such an early weekend call.

'Mornin', Brian.' He tilted his head up towards the hands-free microphone clipped to the car's sun visor. ''S OK, there's no new crisis. I'm just returning your call. Sarah said that there had been word from South Africa.'

'Morning boss.' His voice boomed around the car. 'Yes, that's right. I asked them to keep us informed, in case it ties into our investigation. The Durban people called me early doors. Old man M'tebe woke up bright and breezy, and wondering where the hell he was.

'He's pretty vague about most of what happened to him. It seems that his abductors stuck him full of dope as soon as they picked him up.'

'Was he able to describe them?'

'Yes, he said they were Maggie Thatcher and Ronald Reagan!'

'What!'

'They wore rubber joke shop masks when they snatched him, and every time they showed themselves to him. He heard their voices, though, and he's pretty certain they were Australians. After they kidnapped him off the street, they gave him a shot and took him to an abandoned two-room shack on the outskirts of the city.'

'Did they tell him why he had been taken?'

'No, boss. He said that he doesn't remember them speaking to him directly at all. He was pretty well out of it by the time they got him to the shack, and they kept giving him shots all the time he was there.'

'So how did he get away? Did they let him go?'

'No, sir. He said that one time they must have given him less juice than they intended, or forgotten to top him up, because he came round from it. But he played it crafty. When they came in to check him, he pretended still to be semi-conscious. They gave him some more, then went back into the other room. Once they had gone, he was able to climb out of a window and get clear of the place, before the stuff took effect. When he walked in front of that car he was legless again from the dope.'

'What were they giving him?'

'Just a strong sedative, according to the hospital; the sort of stuff you can buy over the counter in some countries.'

'And they didn't say anything to him? Nothing at all?'

'They didn't say anything *to* him, boss, but he did hear something interesting. Before they gave him that last shot, when they thought he was still out of it, they were talking to each other, and Maggie Thatcher said to Reagan that maybe they shouldn't give him any more. He said, according to

M'tebe, "RA only said to keep the fellow out of circulation for a few days, not to kill him." The police asked him if he was certain of the name they used, and he said he was. He said that to him all Aussies speak slowly, so he could make out every word they said.'

'And they spoke of someone called RA?'

'That's right boss. As in . . .'

Skinner finished for him. 'As in Richard Andrews! Brian, we've got to find this character!'

Fifty-four

T he weekend crowds were pouring into Witches' Hill as PC Pye, on duty at the main vehicle entrance, saluted Skinner through to the reserved area. The morning mist had lifted but the clouds still hung low and heavy over the course, and as he climbed out of his car the policeman felt unseasonal humidity growing in the air.

He took a holdall containing his golfing clothing from the back seat and carried it into the changing room, in which he had been assigned a locker. Squeezing the bag into the confined space beside his clubs, he locked the cabinet and strolled back out into the corridor, stopping at the scoreboard to check the team totals. As he had expected, the Atkinson squad's 19-under-par total gave them a commanding lead of nine shots over their nearest challengers, but he was surprised to see that his 79 had left him three shots clear in the scratch amateur competition, the American Balliol having slumped in the rain to an 81. In the handicap competition he had gained a further shot on his Japanese pursuer.

Smiling with satisfaction he made his way on to the course. Spectators were gathered around the first tee, where the members of Team Nakamura, at the tail of the field at the halfway mark, were preparing themselves for play. Skinner looked around until he caught sight of Maggie Rose, in jacket, jeans, and green wellingtons, leaning against the metal barrier which fenced off the teeing area, just where the players had gathered. He eased his way over and stood beside her. 'Hi, Mags,' he said in greeting. 'You're dressed for the occasion.'

She grimaced. 'Don't know that I am, sir. This jacket feels sticky already, and we haven't even started!'

'Give it to me, if you want, and I'll take it back to the van.'

'Would you?' She peeled off the heavy tweed jacket and handed it to him, replacing her small brown leather bag over her shoulder on its sling.

'You know which one you're observing, do you?'

'Oh yes, it's the cheerful one!' Mike Morton stood at the back of the group of golfers and caddies, head bowed and shoulders hunched, staring morosely at the ground.

Suddenly Tiger Nakamura looked up. Spotting Skinner, he reached across, smiling, to offer a handshake. Between them stood a taciturn, leather-faced man, whom the policeman recognised from the PGA dinner and from the cocktail party. He guessed that he was in his mid-forties, around his own age, but his weather-burned skin made it hard to be certain. He stood beside a caddy and a massive white golfbag, which bore the name 'Everard Balliol, Fort Worth'.

Shaking hands with the Tiger, he nodded to the man. 'Hello, Mr Balliol. I'm Bob Skinner. Good luck today!'

The man looked back at him, unsmiling, with a stare of such intensity that it was startling. 'I know who you are,' he said quietly. 'Life has nothing to do with luck, mister. It's about doing it right, or doing it wrong.'

Skinner recovered his composure in a second. 'In that case,' he replied, evenly, 'I hope you do fewer things wrong than you did yesterday. Me, I'll just ride *my* luck, as usual.' With a final wave to the Tiger, and a brief farewell to Maggie Rose he turned and walked away, his assistant's tweed jacket slung over his shoulder.

He made his way around the front of the clubhouse, and round to the mobile police headquarters. As he expected Alison Higgins was there before him. She was seated at the table reading a sheaf of papers. Martin, as uncomfortable as ever in uniform, and Neil McIlhenney stood at the other end of the big van, nursing mugs of coffee.

Skinner nodded to them and took a seat across the table from Higgins. 'Mornin', Ali. What have you got there?'

She glanced up, surprised, from her reading, noticing him for the first time. 'Oh, sorry sir. I didn't hear you come in.' She waved the papers which she had been reading. 'This just arrived. It's the lab report on Morton's clothing.'

She passed it across the table. Skinner took it from her and read it through, line by line, his expression darkening by the minute.

When he had finished he looked up and across at Higgins once more. 'Sod it! This means that I'm going to have to make a call I didn't want to make. I could delegate it to you, but I don't think that would be fair.' He took out his diary and checked a number, then picked up the telephone on the table and dialled a number, beginning '0181'.

'Yes?' The voice on the other end of the line was deep and brusque.

'Mr Salter? It's ACC Skinner here. I've just seen our lab report on the samples which were taken from your client's shoes and clothing.'

'And?' said Salter, aggressively.

'Well, it runs to several pages, but I won't bore you with it all. It confirms that the mud on Morton's shoes was impregnated with fertiliser. We took mud samples from the gardens at Bracklands and from the scene of Masur's murder. Both were laced with fertiliser, but they were completely different types. The mud on Morton's shoes came from the gardens. The grass from the hem of his trousers showed traces of the same compound. That would seem to confirm his story of going for a walk outside. There is nothing on his clothing that puts him at the murder scene.'

There was a long silence at the other end of the line. 'Skinner, I told you yesterday that I took the greatest exception to your conduct. Now, on behalf of my client, I demand a written apology, not from you but from your Chief Constable.'

Martin, watching from across the room, saw the ACC's shoulders stiffen. McIlhenney followed his gaze. A silence fell across the room.

Skinner's tone was even and icy. 'Salter,' he said, 'I told *you* yesterday that you were pushing your luck. Now get this. Neither my Chief Constable nor I apologise to suspects, and that's what your client remains, whatever that lab report says. His right-hand man, Richard Andrews, was unaccounted for at the time of each of the two murders, and he still is. Until we can eliminate *him* as a suspect, then your client – who I remind you, has been crossed in business by both victims – is still very much in our thoughts, and under our observation.

'You can tell him that when you speak to him. Morton denies involvement in either murder. He insists, too, that he doesn't have a clue where cousin Richard is. The best advice you can give him is to find out . . . damn quick! Good morning.'

He replaced the phone and glanced up at Higgins. 'Thank

Christ we don't have to deal with that character every day of
the week. Our criminal lawyers may be a pain in the bum at
times, but at least they remember their manners.'

He looked across at Martin. 'Andy, boy. How did your witch
hunt get on last night?'

A slow smile spread across the younger man's face. 'I've
been bursting for you to ask. We caught some. Videoed them
too, with an infra-red camera.'

Skinner was taken aback. 'What the hell . . .'

'It was kids right enough, four boys and seven girls. We were
well hidden and they never saw us. They lit a fire, then they all
stripped off and started dancing round it, chanting mumbo
jumbo.

'But then an older couple arrived, man and a woman. They
burst into the circle, wearing masks … and that was all. They
did some more dancing, then the woman picked out one of the
boys, and the man one of the girls. We put a stop to it at that
point, before any naughties happened. Just as well; the girl
who'd been picked turned out to be only fifteen.'

'Bloody hell!' said Skinner. 'Who were the couple?'

'A pair of nutters named Golspie, from just outside Dunbar.
He's a teacher. Some of the kids are his pupils. He filled their
minds full of nonsense about communing with the Devil. Sure
enough, some of the gullible ones took it seriously and started
scuddy dancing round the fire in the quarry. Then Golspie and
his equally kinky missus included themselves in, and the thing
turned into a weekly orgy.'

'How long has this been going on?'

'All through the summer.'

'Is it an isolated group? There aren't cells anywhere else, are
there?'

'Not in East Lothian, but the two of them moved up here from Derbyshire. The guy confessed that they had a similar operation there.'

'Evil bastards. What are you going to charge them with?'

Martin shrugged his shoulders. 'I'm going to leave that to the Fiscal. They haven't admitted to having sex with the kids on other occasions, and we stopped them short of that last night. Chances are, all we can get them for is indecent exposure. But if we charge them with that, the local Fiscal might feel the need to prosecute the youngsters as well.'

Skinner shook his head. 'No. I'll talk to his boss if that happens. You charge that pair with everything you can think of. Flashing, wearing false-faces out of season, the lot. We can convict on that with your evidence alone, and keep the youngsters out of it. If the whole story comes out Haddington will be crawling with tabloid reporters, and we don't want that.'

'I'll have to tell the parents though.'

'Sure, and send a report to the Education Department at once. If the mums and dads can be sure that the man's taught his last class, I doubt if any of them will cause a public row.'

The ACC paused. 'Did you question the Golspies about the *Scotsman* letter?'

'Of course. They denied any knowledge, and I don't think they were lying. They're not interested in witchcraft, just nooky.'

Skinner smiled and stood up from the table. 'Quite a night you've had, Andy. Make sure that you keep the video locked up tight. I don't want any copies turning up in CID offices.'

He looked across to McIlhenney. 'I'll be on the practice ground at twelve, caddy. Until then, well it's Saturday, so I'm off to do some shopping.'

Fifty-five

The exhibition tent was smaller than Skinner recalled from his last visit to an Open Championship, but nonetheless, an impressive number of clothing and equipment manufacturers and dealers had been gathered together by the SSC team who had organised the event.

The policeman wandered from stand to stand, testing the balance and weight of the high-tech clubs on show, continuing his impossible quest to find the ideal putter, and judging the effectiveness of the rainproof garments which make year-round golf possible in Scotland. Eventually, just after 11.30 a.m., he settled on a pullover-style garment which proclaimed itself 'Made in Scotland' and 'Guaranteed Weatherproof'.

He had just paid for his purchase and stepped off the manufacturer's stand when he was hailed from the other side of the tent. 'Bob, hello!' He turned to see Henry Wills making his way through the crowd.

'Henry. What are you doing here? I thought that you were detecting this morning in New Register House.'

'Yes, I was. I made an early start, and I was completely successful.' Henry Wills, in a grey three-piece business suit, looked completely out of place among the garish colours which were normal dress in the big tent. 'I was looking for Miss Rose, but since you're here, I'll tell you all about it.'

Skinner put up a hand to stop him. 'No, don't do that. I need all my concentration for golf, and anyway, Maggie's been making the running on this. If you've got good news for her it's only right that she hears it first.'

Wills looked only slightly crestfallen. 'Can you tell me where she is?'

The ACC glanced at his watch. 'Probably well into the back nine by now. She's walking round with the Nakamura team.'

'Back nine? Nakamura? I'm terribly sorry, Bob, but all this is virgin territory to me. I know nothing about golf, I've never been to one of these events in my life before, and the only player I could name is Young Tom Morris, because I saw his grave once in St Andrews Cathedral and read his sad story. You couldn't just tell me a *place* where I might find Maggie?'

Skinner laughed. 'See you city folk! OK Henry, the best thing you can do is to go and sit in the big stand beside the eighteenth green. That's the one to the right, looking from the clubhouse. If you find a place there, then in around an hour she'll be . . .'

'Reginald!' Wills's start and his sudden shout, took Skinner completely by surprise. He turned to follow his friend's gaze, but saw no answering reaction from anyone in the milling crowd. The only familiar figures were Sandro Gregory and Darren Atkinson, twenty yards away and deep in conversation as they stepped down from the Shark's Fin golf equipment stand, to disappear among the throng.

'Bob, how rude of me to interrupt you,' said Wills. 'I'm terribly sorry; it's just that for a second I was certain that I saw an old student of mine across there. I must have been wrong though, he didn't react at all. It has been around fifteen years since I taught the chap. But I was so certain; it was just an instinctive thing. That's why I shouted; I couldn't help myself.'

Skinner smiled. 'There can't be too many Reginalds around, my friend. If it had been the right bloke, he would surely have reacted.'

Wills nodded. 'I suppose so. But come to think of it . . .' he raised a finger in an almost theatrical gesture '. . . I recall now that he hated the name. It would annoy him terribly whenever I used it.'

'So, should you have called "Reg", or "Reggie"?'

'No, that wouldn't do either. He went by one of these awful modern pop-star corruptions, but it quite escapes me. I refused to use it, any more than I would have allowed anyone to call me "Hank", or the like.

'Anyway, back to Miss Rose. Be in the stand in around an hour, you say?'

'Yes. Wait for the first match coming in and look among the gallery. You should find her there.'

Wills looked perplexed once more. 'I'm sorry Bob, but which gallery is this? Is it beside the stand?'

Skinner shook his head. 'Tell you what, Henry. You just stand high up on the grandstand gangway wearing that suit. That way Maggie'll find *you*!'

Fifty-six

The third-day matches were going out in leader-board order, at half-hour intervals, and so it was 1 p.m. when Darren Atkinson led his team on to the first tee, before a gallery which had swelled into the thousands.

The day was as hot and humid as the morning had threatened, gasping for want of a breeze. As Skinner looked down the first fairway, he saw wisps of steam rising from the trees on Witches' Hill, and from the patches of thick, rough grass around its base. He was wearing his lightest slacks and a short-sleeved shirt, but already he could feel sweat trickling down his spine.

Atkinson grinned at him. 'Couldn't ask for better conditions than this, Bob. The course will still play two shots longer than on Thursday, but for us pros, there'll be no excuses today.' He glanced across at the nearest scoreboard. Skinner followed his gaze and saw that M'tebe had moved from four under to seven under par after six holes, cutting his captain's lead to five shots. 'Oliver seems to be the main threat. That's what I'd expected. Too bad he had that upset over the first couple of days.'

'You're not worried, are you?' asked Skinner.

'No. My game's in good nick, and the boy's too far back. Still he should be second. A tasty percentage for DRA Golf Management. My dear brother will be pleased with us both.

All I have to do now is to play the golf. Of course the same goes for you, with the amateur prizes to shoot for.'

Skinner marvelled that Atkinson could be so relaxed, after the events of the week, and under the pressure of playing for a million pounds. His thoughts were interrupted by the announcer, who introduced Norton Wales. He eased himself backwards as the singer took his applause and prepared to drive, and found himself standing between two familiar figures, McGuire, in a white caddy's bib, and McIlhenney. 'Had a good look around the crowd, lads?'

'Yes, sir,' McGuire muttered. 'I don't see any cause for concern.'

'Neither did Bravo, or Masur, or White,' said Skinner. 'Just remember, the pair of you, the real reason why you're out here. Keep your eyes peeled and your wits about you. If you see anything or anyone out of the ordinary, then give me a shout … as long as I'm not at the top of my back-swing at the time.'

Fifty-seven

As Skinner had forecast in jest, Rose spotted Henry Wills, a man apart from the rest in his sombre suit, before he picked out her red hair among the pack who had followed the first match home to the eighteenth green.

But eventually his searching eyes found hers. He waved and she nodded, signalling him to be quiet as Tiger Nakamura prepared what he hoped would be the final shot of a frustrating day. Oblivious to the golf, Wills made his way down from the stand and through the spectators, apologising as he went to those he disturbed. He reached her just as Nakamura holed out for his last bogey in a 76, tossed his putter towards his caddy and led his team from the green.

'Afternoon, Mr Wills,' she said. 'You're looking pleased with yourself.'

'Good afternoon to you, Miss Rose,' he replied, unfailingly courteous. 'I hope that your day has been as productive as mine.'

She laughed. 'Our days are a mixture of hard slog and achievement. So far, this has been a slogging day, watching a guy play bad golf and looking for another guy who might just show up in the crowd to make contact with him. This is day three now, and still he hasn't.'

She turned to a tall young man standing behind her. 'Kevin, you're on your own from here for a bit. Andrews would have been stopped by our people if he'd tried to get into the clubhouse, so once Morton gets in there he's isolated. Keep him in your sight all the way up to the door. Wait for him to come out then follow him. Ken Rodgers will be on duty at the main entrance by now, so you two can team up. The chances are that Morton will go straight back to Bracklands, but wherever he heads for, I want him in your sight all the time. Once he does get back to the house, you can stand down. We've got Detective Constables more or less in residence there, and we'll have others at the Marine tonight for the dinner that Murano are hosting.'

She looked across the green. Morton stood beside his caddy, checking his scorecard. 'OK, on you go. I have to speak to Mr Wills. Just remember, we know all about Morton, but Andrews is the man we really need to find. You've got the photos. If he does show up, make sure you spot him.'

She turned once more and took the older man by the arm. 'Come and let's find the caterers. Coffee's on me, then you can tell me what's put the smile on your face and the smug look in your eyes!'

As is usually the case with on-course refreshments at golf tournaments, the coffee which she and Wills were served in the catering marquee was expensive. Sucking her teeth at the meagre change which she received from her five-pound note, she carried the plastic mugs in their holders across to a table near the entrance which Wills had commandeered. The University Registrar looked like a fish out of water, down to the smooth leather soles of his shiny black shoes, but the satisfied smile had never left his face from the moment that he had joined the Inspector at the side of the green.

Maggie Rose sipped her expensive coffee. 'OK, Henry. Out with it. What's made your day?'

The smile widened, and the man seemed to swell almost to bursting point.

'I know who Elizabeth Carr was . . . and a lot more besides!' he blurted out, breathlessly.

'That's great. Those are the headlines, now what's the full story?'

Wills drank most of his coffee in a single gulp, making Rose wince inwardly.

'Well, remember where we left it yesterday, with the marriage of the mysterious Elizabeth?

'Today I was able to look at the Longniddry parish records for the sixteenth century. It didn't take me long. It was an odd entry, different from the rest. It said that in September 1596, a newborn female child was brought to the parish by its mother alone. Nothing unusual about that. People died young in those days, and widowed births were not the tragedy they are now.

'Except that this was no widowed birth. The child was baptised Elizabeth, and was given the family name of her father. The baptism was witnessed by two women.

'The father was named as James Carr, Baron of Haddington. That was the courtesy title borne by the son and heir of the Earl of Kinture.' Wills shot Rose the same look that she was used to seeing on Mario McGuire's face whenever Lazio scored a goal on *Football Italia*. 'Oh, I should have known, Margaret. Carr was, as it is today, the family name of the Earls of Kinture. No one else in the parish would have borne it. In 1596, the only males in the Kinture line were William Carr, the Earl, and James Carr, born 1577, Baron of Haddington.

'The mother of the child?' he said, smiling theatrically and pausing for sheer effect. 'The mother was Agnes Tod! And I can assure you, Margaret, my dear policelady, that there is no record of a marriage between the two proud parents.'

The cup of premium-priced coffee, halfway to her lips, slipped in Maggie Rose's fingers, and all but fell from her grasp. Wills laughed aloud.

'Wonderful, isn't it? Margaret, my dear, you may marry your Sergeant and live happily ever after, but you and I will always be entwined in another union, that of unearthing a piece of undiscovered, and quite spectacular history. An illegitimate child, born to a future Earl, by a woman whom he was to burn at the stake. Not only born by the woman, but brought forward for Christian baptism by her, and by the two women who attended the birth.

'And they were . . .' He stopped as he realised that she was no longer listening to him.

'That explains the Kinture Bible being given to Elizabeth by her aunt, Matilda.'

Her eyes flashed with excitement as she told Wills of her visit to Knox at the National Library, and of her own discovery of the Bible's provenance. It was Henry Wills's turn to look astonished.

'But I'm sorry, Henry. I interrupted you. You said there was more.'

'Yes, lots.' Piece by piece he recounted the remainder of his remarkable exploration of East Lothian's murky past.

'What do you make of that?' he asked, as he finished.

'I don't know,' said Rose. 'But I do know that we should tell the whole story to the boss, as soon as we can. I think that you and I go back out to that stand, and watch some more golf, while we wait for him to finish.'

Fifty-eight

Skinner whistled as Wills finished his story. 'That's very impressive, my friend. I wish all of my detective officers were as thorough as you.

'So Agnes Tod and her sister Matilda were the daughters of the factor of the Kinture Estate: not, I'd have thought, people who would be described nowadays as working-class.'

'No, indeed. Their father, Walter Tod, ran the Earl's estate on a day-to-day basis, collected rents, hired and fired staff, and all that. That would make him a very important man, and a man to be feared as well. They'd have been brought up in an estate house, probably quite a grand one. We know from the Bible that Matilda was literate, and now, from the parish records, that Agnes was too.'

'What do we know of their father?'

'Only that he was an elder of the Church and that he died in 1591.'

'And Matilda, what of her?'

'Her death is recorded in 1637 and the entry is witnessed by Elizabeth Carr. She never married. I'd surmise that Matilda brought up her sister's child.'

'And the witnesses to the birth?'

'One was described in the entry as a midwife, and the other as a maid.'

Skinner leaned back in the empty grandstand and gazed at his friend and his assistant in undisguised admiration. 'You two should set up in business. A detective and a historian, researching into the past.

'Henry, how do you feel about some more research? This is already the weirdest investigation I've ever known, but now that I've begun, I'm going to follow it as far as I can. I'd like to hear everything you can tell me about the so-called crimes that led Agnes Tod to her death.

'I want to know what the Burning of Witches' Hill was all about.'

Wills puffed up with pride. 'I should be delighted to assist. I will go back to Edinburgh now to begin my research. I'll work non-stop and call you as soon as possible.'

He stood up, hot and sticky in his suit, yet as dignified as always, and started off down the grandstand's stairway. At the foot he stopped, suddenly, and looked back at Skinner and Rose as they descended behind him.

'Oh, one other thing, Bob. Do you remember in the tent, this morning? That man I was so sure I recognised? Well, I think I've seen him again.'

Fifty-nine

Skinner's mind was spinning with a host of new possibilities as he washed away the sweat and grime of the sultry day and changed into blazer, grey slacks, white shirt and tie.

On his way through to the bar, he paused to look at the updated scoreboard. Darren Atkinson's dismissal of Witches' Hill as a test for top-class golfers seemed not to stand up to measurement against the performances of the other competitors. Only he and M'tebe had broken 70 on the third day, with the World Number One's flawless 66 only a shot less than the young South African, his only realistic challenger among his seven professional opponents. The rest of the field, with Ewan Urquhart at its head, was averaging around or just under par. On the amateur scoreboard, Skinner's third-round 77 had strengthened his position as leader of the scratch section, with Everard Balliol shooting 78, but in the handicap section he had been overhauled by Hirosaki, the Japanese, whose nett 67 had earned him a tie for the lead.

He made his way through to the bar, and found Atkinson, Wales and Murano, his teammates, grouped together in the midst of the throng. Their lead in the team competition seemed unassailable, and as they stood in their tight circle, bantering cries flew at Murano, from his Japanese companions, and at the little singer from some of the other celebrities in the room.

As Skinner reached the trio, Atkinson handed him a pint of beer shandy. He gulped at it thirstily, realising for the first time how demanding the day's conditions had been.

'OK skipper,' said Norton Wales beside him. 'Tell us how it's going to be tomorrow.'

Atkinson looked at him, unsmiling, deadly serious. 'Tomorrow? Eighteen holes to go. The last round, and that's where your man comes into his own. In way over sixty per cent of my tournaments I shoot my lowest score in the last round. That's why I'm Number One. That's not an ego statement, it's just a fact. In professional golf, you can play good golf on the Thursday, better on the Friday, and great on the Saturday. But if you can't do it on the Sunday, then you can't be the man.

'I am still, by a long way, the best Sunday player in world golf. Young Oliver, and Ewan, they're both coming up, and Andres does something spectacular every so often, but on Sunday afternoon, I'm your man. That's what it's all about. Hell, that's what life is all about.' He looked around his three teammates. 'Whether you play golf, or sing, or make cars, or catch crooks and killers, it's about being Number One, and to do that you have to be the best Sunday player in your own field.

'You guys all are great Sunday players in your own right, so you know what I'm talking about. You all know how hard you have to work to be the best, what you have to do, and how ruthless you have to be.'

Suddenly he grinned and the sparkle came back to his eyes. 'So what that all means is that if it's decent weather tomorrow and you're betting men, you should go see the bookies and ask them for odds on me shooting sixty-three or better. They'll probably say three-to-one, four-to-one, something like that, and if they do, bite their hands off. Statistically, the odds should be six-to-four on.

'You know, my brother makes all his beer money betting on me on Sundays!'

'Don't the bookies see him coming a mile off?' asked Skinner.

Atkinson grinned again, and shook his head. 'No chance! DRA Management is quite a big organisation now. He has people to do that sort of thing for him!'

Skinner's retort was choked off short by the insistent tug on his sleeve. He looked around, surprised by the interruption, to find the hot angry eyes of Mike Morton glaring up at him. 'A word, mister,' he said softly.

The policeman gazed down, coolly, at the newcomer for a few seconds, then nodded towards the only quiet corner of the room. They had hardly detached themselves from the crowd, before Morton turned on him.

'OK fella. I've just taken a call from my lawyer, Salter. He told me you heard this morning that those samples you took put me in the clear. I don't suppose you could have told me direct, no? Yet still I've got your people following me around, watching everything I do. Suppose I take a piss there's one of your people watching me. I tell you, guy, get your tanks off my fucking lawn, or there *will* be trouble.'

Skinner shrugged his shoulders. 'If you've got a problem with our procedure in informing you of the results of the tests, take it up with Salter. That was the way he wanted it.

'As for my "tanks", they stay where they are for as long as I decide. Our tests of those samples prove to me that you didn't kill Masur yourself. We know already that you couldn't personally have killed Michael White, or kidnapped Oliver M'tebe's father, or tried to poison Atkinson. But that doesn't put you in the clear, or under Scots law make you not guilty of murder.

'We know that you were stuffed twice by White, over investing in Witches' Hill and over the field. We know that Masur was doing you over in business. We know that you tried to gain control over Darren Atkinson, and that now you see him building up a stable of his own, with young M'tebe as one of his stars.'

Morton stuck out his chin. 'So what? White was a small-timer, an amateur. Masur was a crook. A thousand people could have wanted him dead. And as for Darren fucking Atkinson and his doppelgänger brother . . . Nothing. Skinner, you've got nothing, so get your people off my back!'

Skinner smiled, a soft gentle apologetic smile. 'Oh but we know other things too, Morton, like the name you were born with, and like the business that the rest of your family is in. I know all about you, friend. I know who Richard Andrews is, and I can guess what his job involves. What I don't know is where he is.

'As things are so far, when I draw up a realistic list of people who might have committed these crimes, then the only name on it is your cousin Rocco . . . and he works for you.'

And in an instant Skinner changed. The amiable mask fell away, and Morton met for the first time the man who lay behind it, as he leaned close to him, and took his tie in his right hand. He looked into his eyes, with an expression seen by very few people, all of them in the deepest trouble of their lives. As the American looked back at him, the last of his bluster left him. He tried to look away, but Skinner's thumb dug under his chin, forcing him to keep eye contact with his cold, implacable, frightening stare. Behind them, the buzz of conversation continued unabated, the others in the room ignorant of their confrontation.

Skinner could smell the rank sweat rising from the man. When he spoke again it was almost a whisper, but his tone was as cold as the look in his eyes. 'Back there, Morton, I thought I heard a threat. Maybe I was wrong. But here's one of mine. You have around twenty-four hours of liberty left, unless you can produce cousin Rocco, and prove to me between you that he had nothing to do with these crimes.

'This is my home patch, and someone's been leaving dead people all around. I don't like that. In fact I hate it wherever it happens, and however hard I try to delegate responsibility for its investigation, sooner or later I always end up getting involved. Everyone's got a professional weakness. Yours is lack of co-ordination between your brain and your mouth. Mine is that whenever I see crime, especially violent crime, a little piece of me is outraged for the victims, takes it personally, and gets involved. When that happens, like it has right now, then the bad people can look out.

'Now I'll surprise you. I don't really think you did these things. I look into your eyes and I know that you haven't the bottle to kill, or order it done. Yet I've been wrong about people before, and the facts before me tell me that any jury would say I am this time. So my twenty-four-hour warning still stands. I'll take my people off surveillance, for now. But if by this time tomorrow you haven't put my mind at rest over cousin Rocco, you'll be arrested and charged.'

He released the quivering American's tie. 'Now you can go

and enjoy the rest of your day. I won't be at the Murano dinner tonight; I've got other things to do. But that doesn't mean I won't be thinking about you.

'Remember, give me Rocco Andrade Andrews within twenty-four hours or you'll find yourself in a clubhouse that's a hell of a lot less comfortable than this one!'

Sixty

Sarah leaned across the dining table and tilted her wine glass first to her left, and then to her right, towards the two men who sat on either side of her.

'You don't know, you two guys, how much I've wanted us to be sat around this table, the way we are now. You don't know either, how hard it's been for me to hold myself back from taking the two of you and banging your heads together.'

She sipped her Barolo. 'But I knew that if I let you work it out in your own way, and in your own time, it would all come OK in the end.'

Andy Martin leaned back in his chair and smiled. Jazz was sleeping on his shoulder, drooling quietly on to his denim shirt. 'You know, don't you,' he said, 'that alongside my mum, you two are the best friends I have in the whole damn world. I wanted to put it right too, but the pride in me held me back . . . that and the fact that I didn't know how to go about it, or whether Bob wouldn't tear the front out of another shirt if I tried!'

He stroked the sleeping baby's back, absent-mindedly, as he glanced to his left, to the fourth, unoccupied side of the rectangular table. 'I was going to say that I couldn't be happier, but of course, that wouldn't be quite true. Not for any of us, I suppose.'

'Well, my friend,' said Bob, 'that's something else that has to be left to work itself out in its own time.'

'And it will,' said Sarah. 'The question is, how do you feel about Alex now, after the explosion, and now that you've seen the other side to her? When she comes back, how will you want it to be?'

Andy eased Jazz off his shoulder and into the crook of his arm. 'Like it was, of course. I love her. There was a time, all of a sudden a few months ago, when I realised that I had stopped thinking of her as a kid, as an honorary niece, and when I realised that she was all I'd ever wanted in a woman; bright, beautiful, clever, exciting and mature.' He chuckled, softly and sadly. 'Only maybe not quite as mature as I thought!

'Looking at her in that new, different way, it was like I was meeting her for the first time. And it was the same for Alex. We were scared at first. We both said, "Wait a minute, what is this?" But then we both said, "Why not? Why shouldn't it be?" The trouble is we should have said the same thing to you two, rather than letting Bob find out the way he did.'

Sarah put her hand on his. 'Andy, we weren't there for you. We were wrapped up in ourselves and in our new baby. Maybe if you had said something, we wouldn't have been in the frame of mind to listen, and we'd have given you the wrong answer.'

'So what's the right answer, Sarah?'

'As far as I'm concerned, whether you're asking me as Alex's stepmother or as your friend, it's that it's for you and she to run your own lives, and that neither Bob nor I have the right to interfere in them, even if we choose. If you ask me what I *hope* for, I hope that you two can work it out, because – apart from us – I've never known two people who were as right for each other.'

She drained her glass, and put it down on the table. 'But enough. Give me back my baby, and go and do your male bonding thing. To the pub, both of you. Just don't wake this fella by rolling in drunk!'

'Don't worry, love,' said Bob. 'I've got a big day tomorrow. I couldn't let my captain down by turning up on the tee with a bad head.' He rose from the table and beckoned Andy to follow. 'Come on, son. Let's see what the nightlife's like in Gullane these days.'

They made their way together past the three cars parked on the grass in front of the cottage, along the twisting path to the road then down the sloping Goose Green towards the village's main street. As they walked, Bob described his golf, fulsomely, and that of Atkinson. 'The man plays the game like God. In fact, when he stands up on that tee he thinks he is God, with complete power over the ball. When I'm up there with the guy, in front of the crowd, every so often I have to pinch myself mentally, to reassure me that it's real. But every so often I'll remember what got me there in the first place, and what Ali and you and the troops are investigating while I'm out there doing my best for Michael. This has been the most bizarre week of my life, and I've a feeling that there's more weirdness to happen yet.'

'Aye,' said Martin. 'It would be nice if we could wrap things up tomorrow by finding Andrews and having our scientists help us complete a nice tight case against him and Morton.'

'Only if they're guilty, son, only then.'

'Come on, let's see how the beer is in the Golf.'

The clock on the wall above the bakery showed, accurately for once, that it was just short of 10 p.m., as Skinner led Martin along to the old Golf Inn Hotel, set slightly back from the rest of the buildings on the Main Street. The public bar was at its busiest as they entered. Skinner looked around and saw several familiar faces, some friends of long standing. 'Hi, Tony, John.' He returned the greetings of two of them as he and Andy wedged themselves into a space at the end of the small bar, their backs to the door. They studied the list of the evening's guest ales on tap, but decided to stick to the heavy beer for which the village pub was renowned.

As they took their first mouthfuls, Andy dug Bob gently in the ribs. 'Hey, I'm sorry for taking that swing at you the other day. I don't know what came over me. All of a sudden your chin was there, and I just couldn't stop myself. Afterwards, well, it was just OK again, but I'll never know what made me do it.'

'Cathartic, Sarah would say,' muttered Bob, quietly. 'It was something you needed to do, something I needed you to do, I think, for everything to be squared away between us. You were well entitled. That morning I behaved like an absolute collar and front, as a little English chum of mine would say. I've never acted like that in my life before, without judgement or reason.'

'Oh no? What about that time with that guy, when Alex was in danger?'

Bob stood silent for a few seconds. 'No,' he said, eventually. 'Not even then.'

'Yes, but maybe you thought that she was in danger again. You had just finished a stressful investigation and taken a real hammering in the process. I've thought about it too. I reckon that you had a sort of post-traumatic reaction, and that all sorts of irrational things went through your mind.'

'Snap! That's what Sarah thinks, too. I guess I'll just have to buy it as a theory. Best if I do. Once or twice, when I've had to face up to the bad guys, something's come out in me, a side of me that scares me shitless. It's not just what I'm able to do, it's how I feel immediately afterwards, right in here.' He tapped his temple, lightly. 'Sort of satisfied, fulfilled. It's primitive and barely controllable, and if it ever came out in a crisis within the family . . .

'Just for a second I thought that was happening that morning.'

'Balls, Bob. That's balls. I've seen you in action, remember. And I've never once seen you do anything I wouldn't have done myself. As for your reaction, that's the survival syndrome. If you're in a situation where your very life is at stake, and you come through it, your first thought's bound to be one of triumph. Remember that time when we had the gunfight, and big McGuire was shot? When we'd downed the guy, I remember standing over his body, and thinking, "You won't do that again, you bastard!" without a trace of remorse, though I'd just put four bullets into him.

'All that, it's part of the job. All of us who do it have that beast inside of us, but what marks us out from the other people is that there's no way we'd ever take it home.'

Bob looked at his friend. 'You know, Andy, we should have had this conversation a long time ago. In all seriousness, next week I'm going to look at our counselling provision for all of our armed response officers. God knows what could be lurking in their heads.'

He finished his pint and signalled for two more. 'Anyway, whatever the cause, I offer you a most sincere apology for buggering up your life. And for the record, if you are daft enough to want, still, to develop a relationship with my firstborn daughter, then you have my blessing, for as usual, now that I've thought about it, I agree with Sarah. You two are a pretty good match!'

He reached across to pay for their beer and to accept the brim-full glasses from Wilf, the barman. As he passed the first to Andy he was jostled by the man next to him, and had to react quickly to avoid spillage.

'Hey, steady on,' he said to the intruder, turning. 'Oh it's you, Hughie.' He recognised a member of the multitudinous Webb family, and saw immediately that he was in his normal Saturday evening condition.

'H'lo Mister Skinner,' the young man slurred. 'Sorry 'bout that.'

'That's OK son, just go careful, eh.' He took his own pint from Wilf, carefully. 'You're on the greens at Witches' Hill now, aren't you?'

'Aye, that's right,' said Hughie, swaying. 'Ah seen you playin' wi big Darren this week did ah no?'

Bob smiled. 'That's right. Want me to get you his autograph?'

The greenkeeper Webb, lurched slightly. ''S a'right. Ah've got it. Got it at the weekend.'

'That was a good trick. Darren was playing in England at the weekend.'

''S funny. Ah wis sure it wis.' He plunged a hand into his pocket and produced a grubby Witches' Hill scorecard, which he thrust proudly towards the two policemen. 'Here it is.'

Bob glanced at the scrawled signature. 'Very good, Hughie, but it must have been Monday.'

'Aye. S'pose so. See yis.' He lurched off towards a group of his many brothers and cousins.

Bob resumed his stance against the bar, shaking his head. 'See that Hughie, his whole life is about cutting grass and getting so pissed every Saturday night that when he goes to the bog he has to take a pal to remind him where his dick is!

'That's the other side of village life, you know. Sure, it's nice living out here, but what makes it is the fact that you get out of it every day, to go to work, that it's the backdrop to your life not the be all and end all. Being here full time can be a very narrow existence. All right for some, but not for me.'

He took a mouthful of beer, licking his lips and standing silent for a few seconds.

Eventually he turned back to his rediscovered friend. 'Anyway enough of that. I was pleased to hear about Charlie Radcliffe's recovery. I guess you are too.'

'Too right. The sooner I get out of that blue serge suit the better it'll be.'

Bob nodded. 'That's in hand, don't worry. I want you back in Drugs and Vice as soon as possible. Roy Old's got one and a half eyes on retirement, and the job's too important for that attitude.' He leaned his head closer to Andy, and lowered his voice. 'Between you and me, this is the game plan. You do another year there, and get the drugs and the saunas well sorted out. Roy takes his pension about then, and you become Head of CID. Ali Higgins moves sideways to your job for some specialist experience, and . . .'

Simultaneously, Bob and Andy each felt a long sinewy arm slip around their waists. A head forced its way between theirs, a head topped with fold upon fold of dark, bouncing curls.

'Will you guys please stop talking shop and buy a girl a beer?' said Alex, quietly.

Sunday

Sixty-one

'It was the strangest thing. We were in Madrid, yesterday. We had done our set-up for last night's gig. The roadies were still tuning things up, setting the lights and so on, but the rest of us, the band and the backing singers, we were all finished.

'Square Peg are really big in Spain just now, so sightseeing was out of the question. Even on a Friday afternoon we'd have been mobbed. So we went back to the hotel, and sat around in one of the suites watching television. Usually it'd have been MTV. But yesterday, one of the boys wanted to watch the golf, so he switched on Eurosport. I was sat there watching, and all of a sudden there was a shot of the eighteenth green, and there you were, Pops, playing. I couldn't believe it.

'And then the shot widened out and in the background, I saw Andy, in a uniform, no less.

'My mouth just dropped open, and I felt my eyes stand out like doorknobs. I started gabbling. I must have looked weird, because soon everyone was staring at me, standing there pointing at the television. Eventually I was able to say "That's my dad. And that's my man." And then I burst into tears.

'All of a sudden it came home to me. What was I doing there? Making myself miserable, cutting myself off from all the people I love. And what had I done to you, Andy, with all those terrible, cruel, stupid, selfish, spoilt-childish things I said. I admitted to myself what I had really known all along, that you had been right all the time, and that it was my insistence on us doing things *my* way that had caused all the trouble. In that moment, I guess I finished my growing up.

'I got up from the couch, dried my tears, and said, "Sorry boys, but after tonight's gig, I have to go home." They were great about it. Gerry the manager paid me all the money I was due, and even bought me a plane ticket. Last night's concert was terrific, as well. We were never better, I was never better.

'But when I woke up this morning, all of a sudden I was scared. I didn't know what to expect when I got back, whether you'd kill the fatted calf, Pops, or just kill me. And as for you, Andy,' she nuzzled her head into his shoulder as they sat together on the living room couch, 'I was terrified that you'd send me packing. I thought about phoning, but I just couldn't dial the number.

'When I got to Gullane, and found that you were here too, I couldn't believe it. I was so scared I almost went back to Glasgow, but Sarah said she'd skin me if I didn't go straight out and track the pair of you down. The rest, as we know, is history.'

The clock on the wall said 12.30 a.m. The three, father, daughter and her lover, had sat in a corner of the Golf Inn bar in a virtual silence which came from absolute relief, until, just after midnight, arm in arm once more, they had wound their way home.

Bob beamed at his daughter as she kissed his friend. 'One thing's for sure, kid. Now you've got your voice back, you sure as hell don't talk any less for being all grown up!' He hugged Sarah to him, the balance of his world restored, then stood up, raising her to her feet with him. 'Come on, wife, I've got a big day tomorrow, and I think these two have got some more talking to do, on their own.'

The door was closing behind them when the telephone rang. Alex picked it up quickly. 'Hello.'

The man on the other end of the line sounded tense and anxious. 'Is that ACC Skinner's house, miss?'

'Yes . . .'

'Is Superintendent Martin there by any chance? Only he left this as his contact number. It's Inspector Davis from Haddington.'

'Hold on a sec. Andy, it's for you.'

Martin took the phone from her, frowning. 'Yes,' he barked.

'Hello sir, Inspector Davis at Haddington. Sorry to have to bother you, but there's more trouble at the Witches' Hill Golf Club. The Marquis had to call out the Fire Brigade. When he got back in tonight from his dinner in the Marine he saw a blaze on top of the Witches' Hill itself. One of the trees was on fire.'

'Fair enough, Bert. But you could have waited till morning to tell me that.'

'Oh, it's not that, sir. It's what the firemen found when they got there.'

Watching from the doorway, Skinner felt his stomach drop, as he saw Martin's frown deepen. 'Yes. OK. Yes, we'll be there.' He replaced the phone and looked across, ashen-faced, towards the doorway.

'Sarah, can you get your bag and drive us down to the club? First by the blade, then by water. Now it's by fire!'

Sixty-two

There were no trees on the very crest of the Witches' Hill. Instead there was a small earthen circle, like a monk's tonsure.

The area was lit by arc-lamps, powered by the generators of the fire tenders which were still parked at the foot of the hill. Skinner, Sarah and Martin climbed towards the light, until eventually they picked their way through to the open ground.

The beams of the lamps were concentrated on a single tree, or rather, on the blackened remains of what had once been a tree . . . and on the blackened remains of something else.

Skinner stepped closer to the still-smoking charcoal, approaching from the side to avoid casting a shadow. When he saw what was there he groaned with revulsion. 'Oh God!' he sighed. 'What an idiot I am!'

The lower half of the body was burned to ashes. It was as if it had been consumed piece by piece, sinking into the brushwood circle which had been piled around the tree, and whose grey traces remained. But the shape of the torso and head were sufficiently intact to show that something human had burned here, burned at the stake, burned as Agnes Tod and her two companions had burned together on the same spot, almost four hundred years before. The clothing was a black mass, sodden from the work of the firefighters, who had done their best, with limited equipment. The arms were pulled behind the body. Skinner looked behind the tree-trunk and saw that the wrists had been secured by steel handcuffs.

The skull was black too. The hair and most of the flesh had burned away, but the residual whites of the eyes still reflected the arc-lamp beams, and the teeth, protruding in a grotesque grin, shone in their light. Something black stuck out between them. Fighting nausea, Skinner bent closer to the remains, and looked more closely. He took hold of the object carefully, and tugged gently. Its colour changed abruptly as the bulk of a scorched white handkerchief emerged from the mouth.

'What sort of sick bastard would do this?' whispered Andy Martin, as he looked down at the scene, struggling to control the heaving of his stomach.

'Not sick, Andy,' said Skinner just as softly. 'Cruel, yes; sadistic, too and imaginative with it. But very determined and working to a plan, with clear objectives, rational and in control of every single action.'

'You know who did this?' said Martin, astonished.

'If this poor sod was who I think he was, then yes, I know.'

'And who do you think it is?'

Skinner did not reply. Instead, he looked behind him. 'Would you tell me what you can, please, Doctor.'

Shuddering in her Barbour jacket, Sarah stepped up. She swung her torch, slowly, around the remains for added light, then crouched down beside the truncated body, looking closely at what had been its face. Skinner and Martin heard her mutter softly to herself; they both knew that it was her way of keeping her mind on the job, and to stop it from dwelling on the human reality of her subject.

Eventually she stood up. 'I can't tell you much. You'll need a dental specialist to give you the definitive version. But this man . . . for it was male, the testes are charred, but still there . . .' Andy Martin groaned '. . . had some very expensive bridgework done, and he had it done in America.'

'Was he conscious when the fire was lit, d'you think?' asked Skinner.

'He was certainly standing up, at first, and probably straining against the flames. Do you see the way the tree has burned? The bark and the wood are marginally less consumed up here, where the body would be pressed at first, before it sank to the squatting position in which it finished up.'

They heard rustling footsteps behind them, and a sudden choking. Skinner looked behind him and saw Alison Higgins on the edge of the circle, doubled over and retching as she saw what awaited her.

'I wonder how he got up here?' said Skinner, aloud, but almost to himself.

'He must have come up to meet someone,' Martin answered. 'It would be bloody difficult even for two people to carry or drag a body up through the trees, and there's no way you'd get a vehicle up.'

'That's right. So our barbecued pal here has a message from someone saying "Meet me late at night, on top of Witches' Hill." And he goes. So like Masur, this man was killed by someone he knew, or knew of, and had no reason to fear.'

Suddenly Skinner smashed his right fist into his left palm, so violently that Sarah and Martin jumped. 'Oh, you stupid bastard! What have you done?' he snarled.

'What d'you mean, boss?' asked Martin.

'I took the watchers off Mike Morton. I gave him twenty-four hours to himself, to turn up Richard Andrews.'

'Either that *thing* there is Andrews . . . and with him dead there's no case against Morton . . . or, as I fear very much, this is Morton himself!' He called across the clearing. 'Alison, will you raise Joe Doherty and have dental records for Mike Morton and Richard Andrews faxed over here, right away. Get the technicians to work, fast. I want pictures taken, the mess cleaned up, and the area taped off, all before daybreak. I want no announcement made for now. In fact, if necessary, have a twenty-four-hour news blackout slapped on this affair.

'Sarah, you can go home to Alex and the baby. Andy, you and I are off to Bracklands, to find out whether Mike Morton is safely tucked up in bed, or burnt to a cinder on top of Witches' Hill!'

'Won't you cancel today's round?' asked Higgins.

'No, goddamnit! If we call time now we may never solve the thing. This whole game has to be played out to a finish, to the eighteenth green on Sunday afternoon.'

'I have a feeling that this investigation might even go to a play-off!'

Sixty-three

They guessed that the night bell must have rung in Mr Burton's bedroom, when the little butler appeared in the doorway, a minute or two after Skinner had pushed its button.

He wore an immaculate black silk dressing-gown tied, creaseless, over white pyjamas buttoned up to the neck. Even roused from bed at 1.50 a.m., his hair was neatly parted and combed. 'Yes?' he began, imperiously, then stood stiffly to attention as he recognised the two policemen outside the tall front door of Bracklands.

'Gentlemen? What may I do for you at this hour?' He moved aside, allowing them entrance to the great domed entrance hall.

'We'd be grateful,' said Skinner, 'if you could take us directly to Mr Morton's room.'

Mr Burton nodded. 'Certainly sir, but first shall I awaken the Marquis, or Lady Kinture?'

Skinner shook his head. 'No. I don't want anyone alerted at this stage. We have to check on something, that's all.'

For a few seconds, Mr Burton wrestled with the etiquette of the situation, until eventually, he nodded. 'Very well. If you believe there is no need to awaken them. Please follow me.' He led the way up the marble staircase which led to the upper floor, and towards the corridor to the right. He moved silently on black leather slippers until he reached the door of Morton's room. He knocked softly, then waited. After perhaps twenty seconds, he knocked again, slightly louder. Still there was no answer. He put his hand on the doorknob, and looked up at Skinner for approval. 'Go ahead,' said the policeman, quietly. Mr Burton turned the handle, and, without looking into the room, opened the door and stood aside for the two visitors.

The bedroom was empty. The curtains were pulled shut, and a bedside lamp was switched on. The bedspread was ruffled slightly as if someone had been sitting on it, beside the telephone, but otherwise the bed was undisturbed.

'Come in, please, Mr Burton,' said Skinner to the butler, who still stood in the corridor. The immaculate little man obeyed, closing the door behind him.

'When did you see Mr Morton last?'

Mr Burton put his hand to his chin and knitted his brows. 'At about two minutes past ten, sir, when he went out.'

'But wasn't he at the Murano dinner in North Berwick with the rest of them?'

'No sir. He informed Lord Kinture earlier in the evening that he had decided not to go.'

'Do you have any idea why?'

'No, sir. I do not believe he gave a reason. However he did have a telephone call, just before seven.'

'Who took the call?'

'I did, sir. The caller, a gentleman, asked for Mr Morton by name, but would not give his. He said merely that it was a business call. I put the call through to Mr Morton's room.'

'Can you describe the caller's voice?'

'Not really, sir. It was a bad line, unusual in these days. It was a deep voice, but I could not determine the accent with any degree of certainty.'

'British, American?'

'I could not say even that, sir.'

'Fair enough,' said Skinner. 'When Morton went out, what was he wearing?'

Mr Burton thought for a moment. 'A sports jacket, sir, grey slacks . . .' The butler paused and his mouth curled with distaste, '. . . and golf shoes. I remember hearing their sound as he crossed the hall.'

'He didn't say where he was going?'

'No, sir.'

'Did you hear him come back in?'

'No sir, I did not, but I was watching television in my room from that time on until Lord Kinture summoned me, upon the party's return from North Berwick, to say that he could see a fire on the course, and asked me to call the head greenkeeper, and the Brigade.'

Skinner nodded. 'After that, what happened?'

'Nothing, sir. Lord Kinture said that the fire seemed to be isolated. Probably vandals, he thought. He was annoyed, but he refused to allow it to spoil his evening. He said that he intended to set an example to the rest by retiring for the night in spite of it, and he suggested that his guests did the same.

'To my knowledge sir, everyone did.'

'And after that, could Mr Morton have come in?'

'No, sir, not without my knowing of it. At that point I locked up for the night.'

'OK.' Skinner glanced around the room. There was a notepad by the phone on the bedside table, with a faint scrawl on the top sheet. He picked it up looked at it and handed it to

Martin. The Superintendent squinted at it through his green-tinted lenses, and read aloud. 'Witches' Hill. Ten-thirty.'

'That tears it, Andy.'

He turned back to the butler. 'Thank you, Mr Burton. We'll go for now, but I'll be back in the morning to see Lord Kinture. In the meantime I'd like you to keep our visit entirely to yourself.'

Mr Burton looked puzzled, but nodded. 'If that is your wish, sir.' He led them from the room, and back downstairs to the front door.

As he held it open for the two policemen to leave, he coughed quietly. 'Sir, if I may. Should Mr Morton return, do you wish me to call you?'

Skinner grunted, grimly. 'I don't think that'll happen, Mr B. Cinders won't be back from this ball!'

Sixty-four

Alex was on the couch, where she had been when they had left. She was wearing cordless headphones, but the CD readout showed that the disc to which she had been listening had played itself out. Her dark curls had fallen across her face, and she was asleep.

Andy, still self-conscious in Bob's presence, leaned across and kissed her gently on the forehead. Her eyes opened wide and she jerked upright with a look of confusion, as she regained her mental bearings, and as the day's events flooded back.

She took Andy's outstretched hands and he drew her to her feet. Then he took off the headphones, about which she had forgotten, completely. Bob smiled. 'Look, you two, I'm off to bed. I need to catch what sleep I can, and you'll have things to, er, talk about, on your own.' He reached out and touched his daughter's hair. 'I've missed you, lass. And believe me, now that the shock's worn off, I really am pleased for the two of you.'

She looked back at him and her eyes moistened. 'Thanks, Pops.'

As he turned to leave, she had a sudden recollection. 'Oh, I almost forgot. While you were out, dear old Henry called; Henry Wills. He said he was sorry about the hour, but that he'd just finished his research and he thought you'd like to hear at once. He left a message.' She picked up a notepad, and read from it.

'He said that he rechecked the accounts of the witches' trial. He said that they confirmed that the only crime of which they were accused was of raising the storm off Aberlady. He said too that in 1597, James Carr married Louise Meynel, the daughter of the Count of Bordeaux, and a Catholic. James succeeded to the Earldom of Kinture in January 1598. The storm was in September that year, as King James was sailing back to Leith from Arbroath, and the trial and burning were in October. He said that one of the ships escorting the King was sunk in the storm, and that he was landed in Port Seton and taken by coach to Edinburgh Castle. He said I should tell you that specifically. Edinburgh Castle, not Holyrood Palace.'

Skinner's eyebrows rose. 'Edinburgh Castle indeed. I think I see what he's getting at.' He grinned. 'I think I'm going to enjoy my next visit to Bracklands.

'Night, you two.' He closed the door behind him and left Andy and Alex alone, for the first time in three months. He drew her to him. She was tall and her head rested easily on his shoulder. 'Andy, I'm so sorry,' she whispered.

'Hush.' He stopped her mouth with a long slow kiss, which lingered, on and on. Their bodies moved hungrily against each other chest to chest, groin to groin. When they resurfaced, gasping, he looked into her eyes. 'Have the last three months been anything like as bad for you as they were for me, d'you think?'

'I don't *think*. I *know* they have.'

'And in all that time, have you ever said to yourself, once even, "God, that was a lucky escape!"?'

She smiled and shook her head.

'And as we stand here now, are you thinking, as I am now, "Oh, how I want this person to be with me, more than I've ever wanted anything in my life"?'

'Oh boy, I surely am.'

'Then we've won. We've been tested – not by Bob, but by circumstances, and by ourselves – and we've survived. We've had our crisis and we've come through it stronger than we've ever been, as individuals and as a couple.'

He laughed softly, and she caught the hoppy scent of beer on his breath. 'Know what I've got back in my flat? A ticket for a crossing on the Channel Tunnel. For next Tuesday, the day after tomorrow. When you left I cancelled my leave. The other day I told Proud Jimmy I was taking three weeks. Come Wednesday, I'd have been heading down the Autoroute, in search of Square bloody Peg. And in search of you.'

She beamed at him, and kissed him again, hard and with delight. 'In that case, let's use it. Let's you and I get in that bufty car of yours and go away, like we were going to do before I made a bottom of myself! Pops'll give us the keys to the villa in L'Escala, and we can spend those three weeks lying in the sun, and walking in the rain, and whatever . . . especially whatever. Deal?'

'Deal. Don't even bother to unpack.'

'You don't have any work that'll suddenly stop you, do you?'

He smiled and shook his head. 'That's the one good thing about that bloody uniform. It lets you plan your life with certainty. I've got a feeling too that by the time we leave, Superintendent Higgins's first big investigation is going to be sorted, one way or another. With just a wee bit of help from your old man!'

Alex laughed. 'Poor woman! Delegation's my dad's real weak point, isn't it?'

'Come on, he tries! But thank heaven you're right, because this one's beyond even Alison, good copper that she is. I'm standing on the sidelines, but I can see Bob's mind at work. God, I can almost hear it! Over the next twelve hours or so there are going to be one or two explosions, I reckon.'

'Could be one a lot sooner than that,' Alex murmured, pressing herself against him, even harder than before. They kissed again, and emerged gasping once more. This time an awkward silence hung between them, until Andy broke it. 'How would you feel about, waiting . . . till we get away?'

'Very, very itchy!' She grinned. 'But I know what you mean. If we set about each other now, we'd wake the dead.'

'Maybe not them, love, but the household at least. And I don't know if Bob's ready for that!'

Sixty-five

Bracklands was a bustle of activity as Skinner and Martin entered the great hall, for the second time that morning, just after 8.30 a.m. On this occasion, Mr Burton was dressed in his customary dark suit as he held the door open.

'Good morning gentlemen,' he said. 'You wish to see Lord Kinture, I take it.'

'That's right,' said Skinner, 'but we'd like to see him alone, away from the guests.'

'Very well. In that case, please follow me to the library.' He led the way out of the hall, through a door to the left, which opened into a high, wide chamber which seemed to extend to half the length of the great house. 'This is the music room, gentlemen. The library is beyond it.' Their footsteps echoed as they walked across the polished wooden floor. Skinner had counted off eighty paces before they reached the double doors towards which they strode.

The library was more modest in its scale, but was still an impressive room, with high-tiered shelves, lined with leather volumes, and with windows on three sides, offering views to the front, right and rear of Bracklands. 'If you wait here, gentlemen, I shall advise Lord Kinture.'

He withdrew, leaving the double doors slightly ajar. More than five minutes later they swung open, and Hector, Marquis of Kinture, wheeled himself into the chamber, the plumes of white hair flying back like wings from his temples, and an irascible gleam in his eye.

'What's all this, Skinner? Big day today, y' know. Haven't got time for nonsense, so this better be important.'

Skinner leaned against the mahogany desk which was positioned in front of the central window, and looked down at the nobleman. Something in his eye made Lord Kinture's attitude change, slightly but subtly. In an instant his belligerence disappeared.

'Oh, it's important all right, My Lord. We've come to talk to you about six murders, an attempted murder, piracy, high treason; you name it, we've come up against it in this investigation. Before I'm finished I might even throw in wasting police time, but we'll see about that later.' He pushed himself off the desk and walked across to the window which looked out on to the gardens at the rear of the house. He glanced back over his shoulder. 'Have all your guests turned out for breakfast this morning?'

Kinture looked puzzled. 'All but Morton, he didn't come down. But he's a funny bugger, and rather *persona non grata* around here just now, so I left him to get on with it.'

'Mmm,' said Skinner turning once more to face the wheelchair. 'Except he isn't getting on with anything any more. He's dead.' Kinture reeled back from his words.

'Dead!'

'Remember that fire you reported last night. The one you assumed that vandals had lit? That was him. Someone lured Morton to a meeting last night, on top of Witches' Hill, overpowered him, handcuffed him to a tree, piled wood around him, and set it on fire. The poor bastard was immolated. We identified him from dental records half an hour ago. Another burning, a fourth murder on that old hill, four centuries after the first three.'

Kinture sagged in his chair, as white as a sheet.

'The thing that surprises me was your notion that the fire was a simple piece of vandalism. Especially after that bloody stupid note to the *Scotsman* last Monday morning. Didn't you realise what it had started, when Masur was murdered? But then you didn't know that there was a second note, did you? We kept that quiet, just as we're keeping Morton's death quiet until this bloody event of yours is over.

'That half-arsed note gave someone a great idea. "By the blade, said Agnes", indeed! It gave someone with an imagination a great idea to keep the police completely off balance, while some scores were settled.

'Did you send that note, Hector? Wasn't this event giving your new club enough world-wide publicity? Did you decide to use Michael White's murder to your own advantage by building a little mystique around it? That was all it was, wasn't it? A wheeze to bring in a few extra bookings from the ghouls, the cranks and the curious. I'll bet it's worked too. I'll bet the bookings have been flooding in to young Mr Bennett ever since Monday.

'Haven't they!' The sharp anger in his voice startled even Martin.

'Who delivered the note for you? Susan?'

'No!' said Kinture vehemently. 'You're wrong, Skinner. I didn't send the letter. My mother did.'

Skinner was rarely taken completely by surprise. 'Your mother!'

'Yes. I knew at once that she had done it, and she admitted it.'

'But why?'

'Ma is a traditionalist. She wants everything to be as it always was. She hated the concept of Witches' Hill from the outset, the idea of people sporting themselves on the family estate. When I told her about poor Mickey's murder, she actually smiled. Burton delivered the note for her.'

'Mr Burton, eh,' said Skinner. 'That's loyalty for you, running the risk of getting himself charged with bearing false witness, wasting our time, and anything else that I might decide to throw at him, and at the old Dowager for that matter.'

'The only thing is, they'd probably get off. You see, they didn't waste our time. The letter set us off on what turned out to be a completely different investigation into another series of crimes, just as heinous as anything we've seen here this week.

'I won't bore you with how we did it, but we uncovered the whole story of the Witch's Curse; we found Lisa Soutar, who carries it today; we found the King's Bible which your ancestor gave to Matilda Tod in 1598, as her reward for her complicity in the murder of her awkward sister.'

Kinture sat, head still bowed, but Martin stared at Skinner in complete astonishment. 'Yes, Andy. It's a hell of a story, but Henry Wills and Maggie Rose have taken us to the truth of it after all this time.

'You see, four centuries ago, to this very year, James Carr, an ancestor of the noble lord here, and heir to what was then an earldom, exercised a slightly premature *droit de seigneur* upon the body of one Agnes Tod, a well-brought-up, educated young woman who was the daughter of Walter Tod, his father's factor. I expect that the young lady was flattered. Perhaps she even had ambitions of becoming a countess.

'What she did become was an unmarried mother, of a girl

child. No offer of marriage seems to have been forthcoming from the Honourable, or rather the dishonourable James. So Agnes, not with its father, but with the two women who had attended the birth, Christian Dunn and Mary Lewis, a midwife and a maid, took her child to the minister in Longniddry, and had her baptised, in her father's name, and entered into the parish records. In other words, she had her legitimised and made into a person, a Carr, and if not a threat, at least a public embarrassment.

'Maybe Agnes still had hopes, but if she had, they were dashed. The very next year, James Carr married a French woman of birth as noble as his own, and a Catholic to boot. Imagine, a Catholic in the heart of reforming Scotland. Imagine too, here is James, with a new wife, and yet with a spurned mistress and her child, bearing his name, the two of them living in his own village on his own estate.

'But the story goes on, and grows even darker. A few months after the marriage the old Earl dies, and James succeeds to the title.

'And later that same year, 1598, a very strange thing happens. King James VI, five years away from the Union of the Crowns, a religious reformer who is in line to succeed Elizabeth as Defender of the Faith, is sailing down the Forth towards Leith when, just off Aberlady Bay, a great storm springs up. One of his escort ships is sunk, and the King is landed down the coast at Port Seton. From there, he's loaded into a coach and taken not to his palace, Holyroodhouse, but to Edinburgh Castle, up on its rock, and impregnable even then, taken to the King's Citadel, to which he retreated when he was under threat.

'Because you see, what I believe had really happened was

this. You might not think it now, as you look across those sand-flats at low tide, as some of us who live here like to do, but in those times, before the bay was silted up, Aberlady was a port; the port of the Earl of Kinture. And on that day, as the royal fleet sailed past, in bad weather, the Earl, with his new Catholic wife, and his new alliance by marriage with France, sent his men to sea, to attack James Stuart, the future King of England, where he was at his most vulnerable, and to kill him. They almost succeeded, but in the confusion, the King's ship escaped, and he fled for his life, back not to his unprotected palace, where his own father once murdered his mother's favourite, *but to the safety of his citadel.* Not to have a party to celebrate his lucky escape, *but to defend himself against any renewed insurrection.*' Skinner punched the air with a finger to emphasise his words.

Kinture sat unmoving, head bowed, in his wheelchair as the policeman continued. 'So there was the Earl, right in the noble shit. The King was a slow thinker, and he might not have known for certain where his attackers came from, but eventually he'd work it out.

'But, on the other hand, the last thing that James wanted at that time, with old Elizabeth on her last legs, was for the English kingmakers to see any sign of weakness in Scotland, or in his position.

'That, Lord Kinture, was when James Carr, the King's namesake and your murderous ancestor, had his brainwave. He summoned the local clergy and announced that the King's ship had been attacked by diabolical forces, and that a storm had been raised against his life by the power of witchcraft.

'And he denounced as the head of the coven Agnes Tod, and with her, Christian Dunn and Mary Lewis, the witnesses to his daughter's birth. So these women, these good women, who had wee Elizabeth baptised in Christ, were taken. Agnes, with her fatherless child, was already a figure of scorn, so there was no outcry by the people. The women were put to the torture. They confessed, of course. They'd have confessed to anything to stop the inquisitor's boot from crushing their feet. And James, the local judge, jury and executioner, sentenced them to a witches' death on an old hill on his land which had been a centre of local superstition since time immemorial. They were dragged up there, tied to trees, strangled and burned. With a single, brutal act, the Earl of Kinture had rid himself of a problem, and built himself a barrier against the possible vengeance of the King.

'But there was one other thing to be done. Agnes had a sister, Matilda. The Earl secured her compliance, by fear perhaps, but no doubt by bribery too. Matilda was given Elizabeth, to bring up. And she was given something else. The Bible, gifted to the Earl's grandfather by the King's grandfather, his friend. Finally, just in case the King was not mollified by Kinture's resolute defence of the royal person, he and Matilda invented the Witches' Curse. They wrote it in that fine Bible, and Matilda passed its secret on to Elizabeth as the truth, with the strange injunction that it should be revealed only to Kinture, the man who made it up, or to the King, the man it was invented to fool.

'Elizabeth did as she was told by her aunt and the story passed into legend, to dominate the lives of the women of her line through generations, until twenty years ago, when the latest of them told her story to a tape recorder.'

Skinner leaned back against the desk. 'You know,' he said, 'Darren Atkinson thinks that detecting is like golf, about keeping your nerve and concentration when things get tough. It can be, but it's a team game too, and I've got some very good players. Good enough to uncover the crimes of your ancestor, four centuries ago, and – who knows – to set history right.

'They've put together the story of the Kinture treason and of the murder of Agnes Tod which covered it up. Most of it can be proved categorically, the rest would stand up beyond reasonable doubt in a modern court of justice, if there were any point to it.'

Kinture looked up, with tears staining his white face. 'I can prove the rest for you,' he croaked.

'In 1977 a mad old woman came along from Longniddry, in a taxi, to see my pa. She was rambling; she went on that the curse had been betrayed; that it had been told to a common outsider. The old crone believed that she was a witch. She said that she would call down her powers against the outsider, but that Pa must do everything in *his* power to keep the secret.

'Eventually Pa realised that the old woman was in deadly earnest. Mad or not, she believed everything she was saying. He mollified her and delivered her back home. Then he searched our family records, and he found a deathbed document, written and sealed by James Carr himself, confessing to the events you have just described, with the curse written down in full.

'Pa told Ma and me the story. The three of us decided that some things are best left undisturbed. So the old lady's secret was kept, and James Carr's confession was hidden once more. I still have it, though.' He wheeled himself over to the mahogany desk, and opened a drawer. He reached inside and pulled a lever. Slowly, a leather panel in the centre of the desktop swung up to reveal a secret compartment. Kinture took out a thick, folded document, yellow with age and with a broken red seal, and handed it to Skinner. 'Here, take the damn thing. Do with it what you think best.'

The policeman looked at the Marquis, long and hard. Twice, Martin thought that he wanted to speak, but found the words caught in his throat. But finally, he reached out his hand and took the paper. 'Thank you,' he said. 'I know exactly what I'm going to do with it. There's a man at Edinburgh University who deserves some glory, and a young woman in Germany who deserves to be relieved of a burden.' He paused. 'One thing, though. Don't go trying to reclaim the Kinture Bible. The Soutar line have earned the right to it.'

He looked across at Martin. 'So, Andy, that's one of our two investigations at an end. The trouble is, it seems to have absolutely bugger all to do with the other one. James Carr's been dead for over three hundred and fifty years, but in the here and now there's another murderer about on his land, and he has to be caught too, before he's one day older!

'And in that, My Lord, from having been a bloody nuisance up till now, you have a chance to help! So has Arthur Highfield, if he's here. Could you ask him to join us, please? There are a few things he may be able to tell me.'

Kinture picked up a phone from the desk, pressed a button and did as Skinner asked.

'Good,' said the policeman. 'Now, while we're waiting for him, I want to ask you about something odd that you said to me last Sunday. I thought it was a throwaway line at the time, but it may be one of the last pieces of a bloody difficult jigsaw!'

Sixty-six

'This is the oddest breakfast I've ever had, I think,' said Bob. He, Sarah, Alex and Andy, sat round the conservatory table, just after nine-forty-five, surveying the detritus of boiled eggs, beef tomatoes, baguettes, and coffee. Beside them Jazz slurped happily, as his sister introduced him to the taste of another new baby-food.

'For the last twelve hours, my life's been turning somersaults. I've never known a week quite like this, for twists and turns, damn few of them expected. But I can see the picture now. I know who I'm after, although whether I'll be able to catch my quarry is something else.'

He stared at the ceiling. Sarah and Alex looked at him. This was a mood new to both of them. It was Andy who broke the silence. 'Bob. What the Marquis said back there, about the old woman calling down her powers and everything. I mean, that's all balls, and you mustn't let yourself dwell on it.'

Bob looked at him and smiled. 'Don't worry, Andy. I won't do that. Hector Kinture was right about one thing. Some things *are* best left undisturbed, and that one will be.'

He looked at the ceiling once more, focusing on a dark patch on the paintwork. 'All the same, faith is a dangerous thing. And old Nana Soutar had plenty of that; four centuries of it, in fact. She believed beyond all reason in the legend of

Agnes Tod. The whole world's built on faith, you know, Andy. It's held together by good faith, and it can be broken by bad. People with the sort of faith that Nana Soutar had, people like that can move mountains.

'One thing that I know for certain is that I don't know everything. And I'll tell you; I don't want to! So don't worry, my friend; I won't brood on what the daft old lady said. I'll let it lie, for my sake and for everyone else's.'

Alex wiped Jazz's mouth with a soft cloth. 'What the hell are you two going on about?' Sarah asked.

'I'll tell you later, and I'll let Andy tell Alex. Meantime . . .'

Once more, he was interrupted by the ringing of the telephone. 'What now, I wonder?' He picked up the remote handset which lay on the table, near to hand, extended the aerial and pressed the 'Talk' button.

'Skinner,' he said, his voice unusually tetchy.

'Hello, sir. It's Brian Mackie. I'm coming out to Witches' Hill, but right now I'm still in the office. There's been some news from England.'

'Oh aye? What's that?'

'Richard Andrews has been found.'

Skinner sat upright in his chair. 'Andrews! Where?'

'He's turned up in Farnham, in Surrey, sir. In a private clinic.

'When we started looking for him, we circulated the number of his hired car to every force in the country, with a request to locate at all costs. Last night, a Detective Constable on the Surrey force was visiting his mother in the Farnham clinic, when he spotted it in the car park.

'He went in and he checked the clinic's records. Andrews has been a patient there since last Saturday. He's due to leave today. The Surrey CID have him under observation, but they're taking no action till they hear from us.'

'Did they ask who made the booking?'

'Sure, it was made for him by his doctor in the States, two weeks ago, on an emergency basis. He turned up on schedule, last Saturday evening. He was checked over on Sunday, had his surgical procedure last Monday, and he's been recuperating ever since. He's never been out of his room, he's made no phone calls and he's received none. He's read no newspapers, just listened to music all week. Non-stop Pavarotti.'

Skinner, phone in hand, glanced across the table at Martin. 'So why the secrecy? Why didn't he tell anyone where he was going, not even Morton, his cousin as well as his boss? Do we know?'

He was surprised by Mackie's uncharacteristic laugh. 'I think I can guess, sir. The Farnham clinic is internationally respected, apparently. It specialises in the treatment of complaints of a delicate, personal nature.

'Apparently Andrews was the unhappy owner of one of the finest collections of haemorrhoids they've ever seen. Piles of them, you might say. Like a bunch of grapes, the Matron described them.

'I can understand a guy with a major dose of the Farmers being a bit shy about them, boss. They wouldn't do anything for his hard-man image, would they?'

Skinner laughed. 'No, I don't suppose they would. Still, it's nice to know that the Almighty bestows his bounty where it's most deserved.'

'What do you want the people in Surrey to do about him, sir? Pick him up?'

'No, Brian. There's no reason for that. All they've got to do is break the news to him that he's minus one cousin. Put that in hand, will you?'

He paused, in thought, for a few moments, and a dark gleam came into his eye. 'Eliminating Andrews completes the jigsaw, Brian. The picture's clear now.

'Listen, don't come out here yet. I want some enquiries made very fast in a couple of places. And I need a favour from my colleagues in the security services, in the communications section.

'Here's what you do.'

Sixty-seven

The weather had moved from overcast to oppressive as Skinner climbed the steps to the mobile office. He felt the humidity hanging in the air, and the mounting heat even in mid-morning. The conditions were alien to the Scottish climate, particularly in September, and they added to the feeling of unreality which gripped him.

Alison Higgins, Maggie Rose, Mario McGuire and Neil McIlhenney were waiting inside as he stepped through the door, with Andy Martin, in plain clothes, on his heels. To the Inspector and the two Sergeants, their arrival together rang of a reunion, but none voiced their thoughts.

Skinner looked around his grim-faced colleagues.

'Well people, it's been quite a week, hasn't it? Just when we were hoping it was over, we've lost another. But that's it, I promise you. It stops today.'

He turned towards Higgins, kindly. 'Superintendent, you've done a bloody good job. But it's been an impossible one. I believe I know the whole story, now. I still have to put it to the test, but I'm certain of it. There's no need for watchers on the course any more. Richard Andrews was found this morning, and he's out of the picture. I know who we're after, and how we'll find him.

'Alison, I only came upon the truth through an incredible

piece of luck, but once that happened, the whole thing came together, as clear as crystal. There was no step you didn't take, nothing you could have done that would have brought us to it any sooner. Knowing it's one thing though. Proving it will be something else again. Still, we'll see what the day brings. There are a couple of traps I can set. One of them's already in place.'

He looked across at McGuire. 'The other one, that's a back-stop, and for it, Mario, I need you to make a purchase for me. This is what it is.' As he gave the Sergeant-turned-caddy his instructions, even Andy Martin looked puzzled.

Sixty-eight

'Tell you what, Maggie,' said Skinner, as he and his assistant stepped down from the mobile office. 'Before I go off to practise, I think I might take my captain's advice and see what odds the bookies are giving on his score today.

'I know you're not much of a gambler – neither am I . . . with money at any rate – but if they're long enough, they might be too good to miss. Fancy it?'

The red-haired Inspector grinned up at him. 'OK, sir, if you're for it, so am I. I'll follow your lead.'

'Right then, let's find the bookmaker's tent.'

They turned towards the heart of the small tented village, past the big exhibition pavilion, into which Mario McGuire was disappearing, and headed past the champagne tent and the almost legendary bar which is reserved at major tournaments for golf club stewards, down towards a marquee which flew the colours of a leading gaming house.

'You're really certain you know who we're after, boss, aren't you? I assume you think all three murders are connected.'

He nodded. 'Absolutely. Everything's connected, apart from the Witch's Curse, of course. You, incidentally, are in line for a commendation for your work on that, and Henry Wills will have a letter of thanks from the Chief Constable, and, whether he likes it or not, a consultancy fee. You've worked it out, by now, haven't you?'

She looked at him, hesitant. 'Well I've worked out that James Carr framed Agnes and the other two women because they were an embarrassment to him, and he wanted them out of the way.'

'Good. I've got a document back in Gullane which will take you the rest of the way. I'll show it to you after this lot's over. In the office tomorrow, maybe.'

'I can't wait.' They walked in silence for a few paces, until Rose looked up at him again. 'Sir, I know I'm being presumptuous, but I've got to say this. I'm glad that things seem to be all right again between you and Mr Martin.'

Skinner smiled. 'There's nothing presumptuous about caring for friends, Maggie. I'm just as glad about what you and Big McGuire will be doing next weekend.'

'That's good,' she gulped. 'In that case, as well as coming to the wedding, I wonder if you'd give me away. My dad's dead, as you know, and I've got no brothers or uncles, and there's no one I'd rather . . . Or is that really too presumptuous?'

He stopped in his stride and looked at her, straight-faced. 'Maggie, giving you away would be an honour . . .' he broke into a grin '. . . provided I get you back after the honeymoon.'

The grin became more quizzical. 'You never know, it might be a dress rehearsal.'

Before she could ask him what he meant, she was interrupted by a cry from down the walkway, beyond the bookmaker's tent. 'Miss Rose! Maggie!'

Both she and Skinner looked up in surprise. The woman who waved to them was dark-haired. She was beaming and her eyes were shining with delight. She wore a brightly coloured top and jeans with a look of newness about them. Beside her in a buggy was a small girl, her hair in bright ribbons.

Maggie's eyes widened. 'My God. Lisa! Is that you?'

The woman rushed towards them, pushing the buggy as fast as she could. The drab, wan creature Maggie had met in Germany had vanished. In her place, the new Lisa Soutar was confident and effervescent.

'What the devil are you doing here?' Maggie asked as she reached them. 'What's happened?'

Lisa smiled. 'I've been looking for you. I rang your office and they said that you'd be here. I just wanted to find you and thank you.'

'Thank me? For what?'

'For waking me up, that's what. When you came to see me the other day, I was suddenly ashamed of the way I must have looked to you. And just talking to you about the curse and everything, I realised all at once just what my nana had done to my life. I decided there and then that I'd never do that to wee Cherry.

'Then when you phoned to tell me about the Bible, and what it was worth, the rest just fell away too. I thought to myself, "Bugger it, wumman, this is your chance to change your life!" And so there and then I packed up; I bought a plane ticket; I took my Bible from that bank vault, and I brought my daughter, and it, back home. Cherry and me, we're here for good. The Bible's here only until I can sell the bloody thing. As for Nana's warning, ah'll take my chance wi' the Devil! And as for the Witch's Curse, it's a good story, so maybe someone will help me write a book about it.'

Maggie threw back her head and laughed with delight. 'Yes, and Lisa, I know the very man!'

She paused. 'But what about your husband?'

'That miserable bugger!' she snorted. 'I have to thank you for that too. When you looked at the way we were living, when you looked at his fancy hi-fi stuff in the house and then at me in my shabbiness, you looked so bloody angry. I realised that I was angry too, only I'd been too feart to let it out.

'So as far as Corporal Davies is concerned, he can . . . well, saving the presence of wee Cherry and the gentleman here, do you know the phrase, "Piss up a rope"? All I have to do now is arrange things so that when I sell the Bible, he doesn't get a single penny from it.'

'Lisa,' said Maggie, 'it's a hell of a word to use about this, but you're magic!'

She stopped. 'But listen, I'm sorry. You've been thanking me. This is the man you should thank. This is my boss, ACC Skinner. It was him who sent me to see you, and it was him who uncovered the curse, and your tape.'

Lisa looked up at him, and her mouth dropped open. She looked suddenly sad. 'Oh, you poor man. You know, I still remember your wife like yesterday. She was so nice. I remember you too. What must finding that tape have done to you?'

Skinner smiled at her. 'I'm glad I found it, Lisa, for what it's done for you, and for what it's done to uncover more wrongs than you can imagine. It's a funny thing you know, but I believe that in this world, most things do turn out all right in the end. Even if sometimes it takes a few hundred years!'

Sixty-nine

Skinner's Round

'Team, could you do me a favour?' Skinner asked, as they stood on the first tee, at five minutes before 1 p.m. on the final day of the Murano Million. The crowd which gathered behind them was by far the biggest of the event.

'Name it, my friend,' said Darren Atkinson, with a smile, although his eyes were beginning to narrow as he gathered his concentration for the challenge ahead.

'Could you sign something for me? I can't let this week go by without having a memento of it.' He produced an event programme. 'Hah,' said Darren, 'a punter at heart!' He took the programme, signed it with a flourish, then passed it to Hideo Murano.

As the Japanese automobile heir and the millionaire singer added their signatures, Skinner said, 'I'm a punter indeed, skipper. I took your advice about going to the bookie's. So did my assistant, your stand-in caddy's fiancée. They gave us seven-to-two against you shooting sixty-three or lower. I've got fifty quid on you to do it. Maggie wasn't as sure though. She reckoned with Mario caddying the odds weren't long enough, so she only bet a fiver!' McGuire looked relieved by her lack of confidence.

Atkinson gathered the team together. 'Look, boys. This is crunch time. The team event's sewn up. We couldn't lose that if we tried. But in the individual event, I've got a million quid to secure, and I don't want to win it just by a shot or two. Bob, here, he's got something pretty big to go for too. He's in sight of the scratch amateur prize, and he could even shoot lower than one or two of the pros.'

Norton Wales cut in. 'So what you're saying, Darren, boyo, is that you'd like Hideo and me to keep out of the road of you two.'

Atkinson looked flustered by his directness. 'I don't want to be rude, but yes. That's about it.'

'Rude, man! Considering what's at stake, you've been magic all week. Don't worry about us. There's nothing in the rules to say we have to play, and we won't add anything to the effort, so for today I'll just be a spectator like that lot there. How do you feel, Hideo?'

Beside him, the Japanese nodded emphatically. He and Wales withdrew to the back of the tee, to explain the change of plan to their caddies, and to pay them for their shortest day's work ever.

For the fourth time, the announcer introduced the members of Team Atkinson. For the fourth time the professional and the policeman drove from the first tee. Skinner hit his best drive of the week, around 280 yards, and as close to Witches' Hill as he dared go. Atkinson's shot was majestic, all power and grace, soaring 320 yards down the fairway, leaving him the ideal approach to the flag.

Skinner and the champion walked together towards their drives, the huge gallery scrambling and scampering along the path to their left. As they passed the foot of Witches' Hill,

Atkinson saw the line of coloured tape inside the first circle of trees and bushes which roped off the hill, and the uniformed officers who stood at intervals inside the boundary.

'Why's that?' asked Atkinson, pointing to the hill.

'Oh we just want to keep any curious spectators off the hill after play, that's all. It's quite a historic site, after all. Or aren't you into history?'

The golfer laughed. 'No, not me.'

They reached Skinner's ball. He selected a four-iron and struck a safe, straight shot to the front edge of the green. It stopped thirty feet from the flag, making an opening par secure. Atkinson's feathered eight-iron was perfect. It rose through the still air, biting into the lush green five feet from the hole, backspin stopping it dead. Skinner shook his head. 'How you can do that with an eight-iron defeats me. I can hardly get my wedge shots to hold on the green.'

'Practice, partner. Practice for a lifetime, and the impossible will become merely the difficult.'

Atkinson's birdie putt never wavered, and they moved on to the second, a 385-yard dogleg hole which bent right around the hill even more severely than the first, with an area of rough on the left placed strategically to force players, in theory, to hit iron shots from the tee. Skinner's conservative shot left him further from the green than at the much longer first, but Atkinson took his four-wood from the bag and hit a high shot, with an early hip movement which helped it fade from left to right round the curve of the hill, bending like a well-struck free-kick in soccer.

They set off down the fairway. 'I don't mind telling you, Darren,' said Skinner. 'I'll be bloody glad when this week's over, and this whole circus has left my pleasant wee county.

This whole thing started with a murder, of a man I knew, and it's ending with something just as bad.'

'What, you mean Morton?'

'Who said anything about Morton, man?'

Atkinson paused. 'Well, he ducked out of the dinner last night, then he didn't show for breakfast this morning. I figured that you'd found Mr Nice and that he'd done a runner before you could arrest him.'

'Good guess, that. We've found Andrews all right. He's been a pain in the arse all week, but we've tracked him down.' Skinner stopped as he reached his ball. He looked at the lie and the line. 'Give me a three-iron, please, Neil,' he said to McIlhenney. Taking the club from his makeshift caddy, he hit another careful shot, which carried once more to the front of the green, a few feet closer to the flag than at the first.

'Good shot,' said Darren. 'Play to match par, not beat it. Pros play for birdies, all but the very best amateurs for pars. Remember that, play enough and you could get your handicap down to something near scratch.' His perfect tee shot had left him an approach of no more than 115 yards to the green. 'Wedge please, caddy.' He took the club from McGuire and hit an approach to the flag which finished even closer than the shot at the first. For a moment Skinner thought that it would drop into the hole.

As they moved on to the third, a 220-yard par-three with a green almost surrounded by bunkers, Atkinson was already two under par. He smacked his two-iron to the back of the long green, its widest point, leaving himself with a long putt but with his par secure. Skinner's three-iron was short of the green, but his thin chip ran fortuitously close to the hole to secure a third par.

They came to the fourth tee and surveyed the 465-yard hole, its fairway bisected 240 yards away by the stream which flowed from the murky Truth Loch. 'You know, Darren,' said Skinner. 'I can tell you now, I've spent a good part of this week thinking that you might be the ultimate target of whoever's been killing people out there. Anyone as good as you, and as successful as you has to have a host of enemies, and if one hated you enough to want you dead . . . well. I've known circumstances before when a series of crimes were committed to confuse us, and throw us off balance, while the real target is achieved.'

He shook his head. 'Not this time, though. Every crime committed this week has had a purpose, and very strong motives behind it. The strongest of the lot, actually: power and money. The only time we've been off balance this week was when Hector Kinture's mother sent that bloody silly note to the *Scotsman*.'

He fell silent as Atkinson addressed his ball and hit a towering drive, carrying the stream by fifty yards and taking a high forward bounce. He stepped up in turn, concentrating with all his might. His drive cleared the water also, and ran on to finish 300 yards out, his longest of the week.

They strode off the tee together. 'By the way,' said Skinner, 'the third note was dropped off in the early hours of this morning, at the *Daily Record* office in George Street.'

Atkinson looked across at him, with raised eyebrows. Skinner glanced back, with a sad look in his eyes, an expression of huge disappointment.

'You know, Darren,' he said, 'it was the way you treated poor Sue Kinture that started me thinking that maybe your feet had a touch of clay in them.

'I reckon you must have women throwing themselves at you all the time. But if you took those opportunities, they'd deflect your concentration from the main mission, to be Number One, and you wouldn't be quite the ruthless bastard that you are.' They reached the narrow stone bridge which crossed the stream. Skinner stood aside to allow Atkinson to cross first.

'Sue's a really nice lady you know. OK, she's married and she shouldn't have made eyes at you, but old Hector is no good to her between the sheets, and out of his frustration with his condition, he gives her a hard time now and again, so there's an excuse. But she didn't deserve what you did to her, screwing her brains out in her own house on the night of the PGA dinner, then cutting her virtually dead the next day.

'No gentleman behaves like that, Darren – yet that's your image, the first gentleman of golf. I was really disappointed in you, when Sue told Sarah, and Sarah told me.

'And then I realised.' He stopped at his ball, and hit an adrenaline-charged six-iron into the heart of the green. He handed the club back to McIlhenney. 'As I said, I realised what had happened to cause your change of heart.'

They stopped at Atkinson's ball. The champion took an eight-iron and hit a solid shot ten feet from the flag. 'Hope I'm not putting you off talking like this,' said Skinner. 'I've got a few quid riding on you after all. It's just that it's so much easier to tell you my story out here.' They strode steadily towards the green.

'We were discussing your behaviour towards Susan. It came to me that you changed towards her after I told you about the Keyman arrangement Hector had with Michael White, and that, because of it, he wouldn't need or want any new cash in Witches' Hill.

'I remembered that and I thought, "What a pity, Darren's not such a nice guy after all, shagging the poor lady just to get her to support him as the replacement investor in the venture, then dumping her when he finds that's a non-runner." And that's *all* I thought at first.'

He lined up his putt and sent it a foot or two past the hole, marked his ball and watched as Atkinson's ten-footer lipped the hole, drawing a gasp from the crowd, then swung a few inches past. The champion tapped in, slapping his thigh in frustration. Skinner said nothing, but rolled in his putt for a fourth straight par.

They walked across to the fifth hole, another par-three, but shorter at 170 yards than the third. The air seemed heavier than ever. Skinner glanced up. The clouds seemed lower, leaden and more threatening. 'Yes,' he said. 'That's all I thought at first. But then my nasty, dark, suspicious polisman's imagination went to work, and I started having the sort of thoughts that wake you up in the night.

'That's when detecting really does become like golf, Darren. After all the practice, a good golfer imagines playing the shot he's faced with, and then he plays it to make his vision reality. After all the teamwork, the good detective pictures in his mind the commission of the crime. Then he goes out to see if the evidence is there to colour in his outline. And when the really good detective goes looking, a guy like me, with a *really* nasty, suspicious mind, it nearly always is.'

Atkinson's back was to him, over his ball, as he finished speaking. His shot was majestic, a high seven-iron pitching over the flag. Behind them their massive gallery cheered, then groaned as the backspin this time took the Titleist back down the slope of the green. Skinner hit a five-iron. The ball caught the sole of his club and flew low. It pitched short of the green but ran on, finishing, to his and the crowd's surprise, slightly closer to the hole than the classic shot of the champion.

They walked from the tee together, as before. Skinner resumed his narrative. 'The first thought that came to me, as we bathed the baby one night, was "Why is Darren rubbishing this course quite so hard?" I mean it's brand-new, but it's well over seven thousand yards long, and to any normal human being, even a seasoned pro like Tiger Nakamura, it looks bloody difficult. Suddenly, among all the rubbishing, I caught a whiff of something unpleasant, and potentially, dangerous. I caught the scent of envy. And then, to add to that, I remembered something else. I wasn't able to confirm it until this morning, but once I did, that part of the story was pretty well firmed up.'

He fell silent for a while as they reached the green, as he watched Atkinson line up his putt across the difficult, slanting surface, and hit it, to stop two inches above the hole. The champion tapped in and stood back, applauding with the rest, as Skinner two-putted safely for his par. 'You're doing well, partner,' he said, coolly. 'Keep up the good work.'

'Thanks,' said Skinner as he tossed his putter to McIlhenney, and began the twisting walk to the next tee. 'Anyway,' he went on, 'as I was saying, another recollection had come to me. Last Sunday, Lord Kinture was telling me about all the people who wanted to invest in Witches' Hill. "Everyone and his brother *literally*" he said.'

'When I asked him again, this morning, he confirmed what I had guessed. He told me that, originally, you and your brother Rick had wanted to be major players in Witches' Hill. In fact you wanted to be the majority players, and to have sway over architecture, management and everything else. He said that you two realised that Witches' Hill had the potential to become the world's top golfing resort in the world's finest golfing country. He told me that you offered him all the development capital and your input on design, assuming that he'd jump at the chance.

'But he and Mickey White didn't want you or your money. They had their own, and their own ideas and plans for Witches' Hill. Lord Kinture said that when he turned you down, you and Rick were . . . "*incandescent*" was his word.'

He paused as they reached the tee, and looked down the narrow sixth fairway. 'So Darren, I added all that up in my nasty detective's head, and I was forced to a conclusion that I genuinely hate . . . that as well as Mafioso Mike Morton, another potential bidder, but a man who tends to pick fights in public with people who have crossed him, I've got two other people with just as strong a motive for killing Michael White.'

Skinner broke off, as Atkinson hit a careful three-wood to the heart of the fairway, away from any of the inviting bunkers. His own shot, a full drive, edged perilously close to a sand-trap on the right, but bounded just beyond its clutches. They marched off together once more.

'Where was I?' said Skinner. 'Yes, White. As I picture it, you and Rick saw him as the barrier to your involvement in Witches' Hill. You knew that Kinture needed his cash. So you reckoned that if he was dead, you and Rick could buy out his widow. You had the motive, you two, and your behaviour with Sue Kinture, plus your comment to me that you'd like to invest, proved that you had thought about it after the event. So why not *before* it?'

He paused and looked at Atkinson. The champion was

striding along beside him, head down, unsmiling, looking for all the world as if he was concentrating on his next shot. 'That brought me to the heart of it, Darren. Could I picture you, you of all people, as someone who would murder, who would take lives in pursuit of gain or ambition?

'And the terrible thing is, man, and it pains me, I can.' He shook his head.

'Hundreds, thousands of people, maybe more, have the motivation to murder. The questions which follow are, "Is it worth it?" and "Are they the sort of people who would kill for their own gain?" Whatever the answer to the first question, the answer to the second is almost invariably – and fortunately – a loud "No!"

'Premeditated killers, as opposed to the spur-of-the-moment domestic variety, are totally ruthless in their pursuit of an objective. They are totally determined. They are dedicated. They are mentally very, very strong.

'I've just described the qualities which go to make business tycoons, fighting soldiers, successful policemen and many others, including champion sportsmen. The difference between all of them and the sort of person who killed White is that they possess compassion. They have the conscience gene that's missing from the killer's DNA make-up.

'I've dealt with people like that, Darren. I can pick them out. My method's pretty crude, but I've never known it to fail. I choose my moment, and I just look into their eyes!'

They stopped at Skinner's ball. He beckoned McIlhenney towards him, and selected a wedge. His shot was high and sure, to the back of the green, not flirting with the bunker on its front edge, behind which the hole was cut. Atkinson, emotionless, called for his sand-iron, and floated a soft, delicate shot. If the putting surface had been a dartboard, it would have been a bull.

They approached the green and the champion looked stonily at the ground ahead. 'I've looked into your eyes, Darren. I did it again, just now. Every time you concentrate on a golf shot, and hit it, the real you is there to be seen. You can't hide it. I look, and I see ruthlessness, determination, dedication and strength. But I don't see a trace of compassion.

'I've looked in your eyes, my friend, and I believe. You could do it. You've got deadly eyes, Darren, the kind I've seen in dozens of interview rooms and, once or twice, in people standing over their victims. None of them have ever walked away from me.'

He lined his putt and hit it straight and sure, to the edge of the hole. Atkinson's attempt, from fifteen feet, stopped on the edge. Characteristically, he slapped his thigh, the only form of emotion he had shown since the round began.

They walked off the green together. 'I can read your mind as well,' said Skinner. 'You're thinking, "I'm all right. He can't prove a thing. I was in England when White was butchered, in the midst of a crowd at Bracklands when Masur was drowned, and at the dinner last night when Morton was set alight."'

Skinner looked quickly at him, sideways as he spoke. Atkinson's expression stayed stony.

'That's it, Darren,' the policeman said quietly. 'That's the last piece of proof, and all the confession I'll ever need. The fact that I told you about Morton, whose death is still a secret to everyone except my people, Lord Kinture, and Arthur Highfield, and you never even twitched . . . because you knew!'

They stepped in silence on to the seventh tee. Atkinson

looked down the length of the 575-yard hole, reached out a hand to McGuire for his driver and crashed out one of the longest drives that Skinner had ever seen. The ball carried for over 300 yards and bounced on for another fifty.

As he bent to retrieve his tee, for an instant the real Darren Atkinson looked up at Skinner. He spoke not a word, but in a flashing moment, his mask of affability was ripped away and a driven fury shone in his eyes.

The policeman stared back at him, unblinking, before turning away to concentrate his mind on the shot ahead. His drive was as straight as Atkinson's, but finished sixty yards shorter.

'It's right, though,' said Skinner as they jumped down from the slightly elevated tee. 'You do have alibis for each crime. But Rick, your brother, he doesn't.'

They walked in silence to their second shots. Skinner's three-wood approach left him fifty yards short of the green, but Atkinson's sweetly struck two-iron soared unerringly to its heart.

'You might not believe this,' said Skinner, on the move once more, 'but the fact that you and Rick are twins might have escaped me, but for my friend Henry Wills. He saw you yesterday, in the exhibition tent, and he thought you were Rick.

'Because he taught him, you see, at university back in the early eighties. He taught him history. In the tent, Henry called out, "Reginald". I turned, and you were there with Sandro Gregory, stepping off the Shark's Fin stand. But you didn't see us, or react to Henry's shout, and I thought nothing of it at the time.

'When Henry saw you later, from a distance, and learned

who you were, he thought he'd made a mistake. Of course in effect he was right. When he saw you, he really did see the face of his old student. But Henry's only good with faces, and he couldn't recall the name that "Reginald" used, so at that point, I didn't twig. I didn't make the connection until Morton said something about you and your doppelgänger brother. Even then it took me a while to say to myself, "Bugger me, they're twins!"

'I asked Arthur Highfield this morning. "Two peas in a pod," he told me. "Darren takes care of the golf, Rick takes care of the business with the same dedication. You hardly ever see them together," he said, "but when you do you can only tell them apart by their clothes and by Darren's big golfer's hands." Oh yes, Darren, and by one other thing. Rick's a smoker, according to Highfield.

'I haven't met your brother yet, but when I do, when eventually I choose my moment and look into *his* eyes, I bet I'll see the same thing there that I see in yours.'

Skinner reached his ball, and took his sand wedge from McIlhenney, who, with McGuire, was following just too far behind to be within earshot. 'With that,' he said, 'the jigsaw was complete. I saw the whole picture in my nasty detective's mind – a pair of murderous twins, ready to do anything in the pursuit of their objective. To be Number One . . . in everything.'

He chipped carefully on to the green, avoiding the direct line to the flag over a wide bunker, but making his par-five secure.

'It's quite a thought, isn't it?' he said as they walked on to the green. 'The Atkinson Twins, two psychopaths out to rule not just a chunk of some city, but the game of golf, both on and off the course.'

He stood back and watched as the champion's eagle putt rolled just past the hole, and joined in the applause of the gallery as he tapped in to go three under par. 'Keep it up, Darren,' he said smiling as he walked away, having completed his own par. 'I'm backing you to shoot sixty-three, remember.

'Anyway, back to poor old Michael White.'

'There you are, you and Rick, thwarted over Witches' Hill. Good losers, so Kinture and White think, for you agree to play in the Murano Million, and Rick signs M'tebe, Urquhart and Andres in as well. Rick even comes up and plays a round with Michael White, who shows him his private changing room, and tells him about his habit of bathing in his Jacuzzi, rather than showering, after each round.

'You and Rick make your plans. You know about the practice round last Sunday, because Andres is playing in it. So Rick leaves the tour event last Saturday . . . same day as Richard Andrews goes off to have his piles done.'

He stopped as they stepped up on to the eighth tee, from which the clubhouse was in sight once more. Atkinson ripped off another deadly accurate drive down the 430-yard hole. Skinner, following, played cautiously with a three-wood to avoid the meandering stream.

They fell in step once more, coming close to the skirting crowd, hearing their shouts of encouragement. 'Last Sunday, while everyone is out on the course, Rick just wanders in to the club. He hides in the starter's hut, over there.' As he walked, Skinner pointed casually towards the square building on the horizon.

'While he's in there, he smokes a couple of fags. Unusual fags. Last week's sponsors were dishing them out at the event, to those and such as those, but you can't buy them in the shops yet. He left a couple of stubs. There's nothing we can match on them, but they certainly cut down our list of possibles. Cut it down to one, in fact, since Andrews was having his arse examined in Surrey by that time.

'Eventually he sees the first match coming in and it's White and Cortes. He nips, unseen, into the clubhouse through the open door which is normally used only as an exit. He goes into White's changing room and through into the Jacuzzi.'

Skinner broke off to play his second shot, a three-iron which finished on the front edge of the green, then he and the champion, their caddies following a few yards behind, walked off towards another stone bridge across the stream.

'A few minutes later, White comes in. He puts his watch and stuff on the shelf, and he's hanging up his towel beside it when Rick smashes him on the side of the head. He drops like a stone. The blow might have killed him, but Rick makes sure. He's as big and powerful as you, and he heaves him into the bath, so there'll be no mess. Then he cuts the poor bugger's throat.'

They reached Atkinson's drive. The champion's wedge-shot was poor by his standards, but still finished only twenty feet from the hole.

'Can you imagine anything as callous as that? Of course you can, you helped plan it! While the rest are gathering in the bar, Michael White is left dead in bubbling water turned pink by his blood. It doesn't bear thinking about, but it happened.' Skinner shook his head, and shuddered.

'After he's done the business, Rick counts the rest in, then nips out by the door he used to come in. He takes White's wallet and wristwatch, in the hope that we'll assume it was murder associated with theft. Then he has his first piece of bad luck. He meets Hughie Webb, greenkeeper, nursing his Sunday hangover. Hughie, who's not too bright, takes him for you, and asks for an autograph. And Rick, desperate to be on his way, takes his grubby Gullane 2 scorecard and signs on the back, "Best wishes, Darren Atkinson". From the quick glance that I had back on the first tee, his signature's quite like yours. Maybe he signs some of your photos, for you, eh?'

He stopped to play his approach shot, striking it rather too hard, and knocking it twelve feet past the hole. But, after another birdie attempt by the champion had missed by a millimetre, he stepped up and knocked in the putt for his eighth straight par.

As they crossed to the tee of the 540-yard par-five ninth, which, like the opening holes, curved round Witches' Hill and back towards the clubhouse, Skinner said, reflectively, 'It's quite a story, champ. And you know, if you'd left it at that, at White's murder alone, I'd probably never have caught on.

'Hughie Webb's a lousy witness. He doesn't know whether it's breakfast or Easter, so even if I'd found that connection, I'd probably have assumed that he'd made a mistake and had met you on the Monday. It was only when I started thinking in the context of all three murders that I tied you in.

'If you'd just been a bit less greedy, a bit less ambitious. But not you and Rick. Suddenly you saw a chance to make the big jump you'd been dreaming about.'

They smashed two more crunching tee-shots down the ninth, but Atkinson's ball took a bad bounce and, to the groans of the gallery, was swallowed by a bunker 290 yards out.

'What you two want, Darren,' Skinner resumed as they walked on, 'is to make DRA Management, absolutely the number one, unchallenged leader in world golf management.

You told me casually that your ambitions extended to America. Now I see how strong they are. The fact that Mike Morton made a half-hearted attempt to lean on you a few years back probably convinced you that you wouldn't beat SSC by business means, and the whole of Asia knows about Masur's Yakuza connection.

'No, the game plan which the terrible twins drew up called for the elimination of the strong men at the head of SSC and Greenfields, each of whom held his business together. With them out of the way you'd move in. You'd sign up the top boys not just in Europe, but in the Americas, Asia and Australasia as well. You'd control the game. DRA would be Number One, worldwide.

'That's the plan. Suddenly you see a chance to put it all into practice in one sweep. Masur and Morton are both here. Even better, they're at each other's throats over Tiger Nakamura.'

Skinner's ball was only a few yards short of Atkinson's bunker. He thought about trying for the green but saw the sand lying in wait ahead, and hit a five-wood, leaving himself a thirty-yard pitch to the green.

The champion's ball was plugged wickedly in the bunker. Even with his strength and skill he was able only to coax it clear by a few feet, the ball landing in straggly semi-rough, only its top visible. Looking at the lie, Skinner expected him to select a mid-iron and to trust to his wedge to save par. But he was mistaken. 'Three-wood, please, Mario,' said Atkinson. To the astonishment of the gallery, Atkinson took the club and, from that position, fashioned the finest golf shot Skinner had ever seen. The ball soared away, on a right-left drawn trajectory, rather than the usual professional's faded shot, flying against the line of the curving fairway, flirting with the trees of

411

Witches' Hill, but plunging, as if wire-guided, into the centre of the green and rolling up to the very edge of the hole. The spectators in the small stand behind the green rose to their feet as one. The gallery around the golfers cheered wildly. As the ball came to rest, Atkinson glared across at Skinner with fire in his eyes, and his lips drawn back in a silent animal snarl.

As they walked on down the fairway, the policeman said quietly. 'That was a sort of answer, Darren, wasn't it? You know, it's as well you use golf clubs, not firearms. Otherwise I think I'd have to kill you, and I'd hate that.'

His tone changed and became conversational once more. 'As I said, I've encountered people like you two before. They've always perished on the sword of their own ambition. You guys have perished on your imagination. Just as no one else would have imagined that shot back there, so no one but Rick would have had the flair to fasten on that bloody stupid note by Hector Kinture's mother to the *Scotsman*.

'The trouble is, once I found something out, it was like a signature. And what I discovered was that Rick, as Henry Wills's student fifteen years back, had heard the vague, unsupported tale of the Witch's Curse.

'It was dismissed as colourful folklore by serious academics like Henry, but it stuck in Rick's mind, and when he read the old Lady Kinture's piece of nonsense in the newspaper, he had his brainwave. *"Blade, Fire and Water"*, the old curse said, and here you were, with your potential victims, at Witches' Hill.' He paused to allow the champion to stride ahead on to the green, smiling and waving to the cheering crowds, and to tap his ball in for a fourth birdie. Then he played his chip, safely, to the green, and walked on to secure his par.

'Four under at the turn,' said Skinner, as they stepped the

few yards to the tenth tee. 'We need five more on the back nine if Maggie and I are to pick up our winnings.'

'Don't worry,' said Atkinson, solemn and deadly serious. 'You're on a sure thing.'

'I'm firing him up,' thought Skinner as he watched another monstrous drive leaving the champion with the shortest of second shots to the green 390 yards away. 'The harder I go at him the better he's playing. The man's an animal. And he's pulling me after him,' he added as an afterthought as his own drive split the fairway, soaring out 300 yards to astonished applause.

Golfer and policeman resumed their side-by-side march, and their parallel duel. 'You shouldn't have let Rick do that, you know. The problem you had was that the first note had something about it. The old lady had seen the real Witch's Curse. You see, it was a sort of family secret. Eventually I saw it too, and it was clear to me that the second note had a different author, someone who'd only heard the story of the curse, not the full version.

'When we found Morton last night, I knew there'd be another. We had men outside all the newspaper offices this morning waiting for Rick, but he beat us to it.

'The notes kept us off balance for a bit. They took up resources. The one thing I never bought for a second was the notion that there might actually be a local coven intent on fulfilling the curse, but it was still a line that had to be investigated.

'And it all turned on itself in the end. While at first the note was no lead at all to Michael White's killers, eventually it turned into one, when you two decided to ape it. And when we got lucky again, discovering that Rick attended Henry Wills's classes, man, it pointed me right at the pair of you.'

They reached Skinner's ball. Again he took no chances with the sand on his left, or the waters of the Truth Loch on his right. He hit a low, punched shot, pitching the ball and sending it skipping on to the safe part of the green, making his par virtually certain. It had hardly come to rest, before Atkinson was ready. His ball almost split the flag as his sand wedge sent it spinning towards the hole. 'Five under, I think,' he said quietly.

The Truth Loch was even more in play on the eleventh hole, biting a chunk from the fairway and forcing even Atkinson to play it as a dogleg, taking iron from the tee. He and Skinner hit safe tee-shots, then followed with three-wood approaches. The champion's shot reached the green easily, while the policeman's was short but safe.

'So here we are,' said Skinner as they walked along the waterside. 'White's dead, and we're chasing our tails. Then Mike Morton does you a huge favour by picking a fight with Masur, right in front of me. It was such an inviting set-up that you just couldn't resist it. So there's Masur after the dinner, walking back, over there.' He pointed across the loch towards the outline of the ducking stool. 'He's even in the right spot. Rick comes out of the darkness. Probably Masur thinks that it's you, that you've decided to walk back too. He doesn't see the threat until it's hit him on the back of the head. He's out as he's tied into the chair. And even if he wakes up as he's lowered into the water, all he can do is struggle, as the water fills his lungs.' He paused, with another slight shudder.

'Next morning, the body's found, and of course we suspect Morton straightaway, as you planned. The silly bugger even compounds his predicament by going for a walk in the garden at Bracklands after dark and getting mud on his shoes!

'I have to admit, the murder of Masur was real creative thinking. *Not* your average assassination. And that was where it really started to go wrong for you, when you first over-reached yourself.

'Because the trouble was, it was *too* creative for Morton or Richard Andrews. They're old-fashioned Mafiosi types. Their way would have been to take the back of Masur's head off with a silenced .38, not something as flashy as that. I doubt if Andrews would have taken Masur off-guard, either.'

He stopped, concentrating hard on his third shot to the par-four hole. Abandoning caution for once, he took his wedge and surprised even himself by hitting his shot to within a yard of the pin. He raised his club to acknowledge the crowd's applause, and walked on to the green, marking his ball to allow Atkinson to claim a safe par before completing his own.

'Still, we had no choice but to treat Morton as our chief suspect,' he said as they walked to the tee of the 230-yard par-three twelfth. 'With Andrews unaccounted for, he was still the best bet we had.' He shook his head. 'Then Rick dropped that bloody note at the *Herald*, and I said to myself "Wait a minute!"

'The editor's a pal of mine, and he agreed not to use it. That didn't bother you, though. You weren't after publicity. You just wanted us to see it, without taking the chance of dropping it on our doorstep. You knew that Morton wasn't the murderer, so you saw the second note as a back-up, to forestall, you thought, any chance of us looking in your direction.'

He stopped as Atkinson lined up his two-iron and smacked the ball greenwards, over the guarding bunker, to land eight yards from the flag. Skinner's three-wood was high, so high that he thought for a moment, as he watched it against the now-threatening clouds, that it would drop into the sand, but, willed on by striker and crowd, it carried safely to the fringe of the green.

'You poisoned Bravo for the same reason, of course,' he said as they walked on. 'Right about here. With me on the scene as the perfect witness to an attempt on your life. I thought "What a stoic you are, Darren," as I watched the way you played on after it, as if you were in no danger. Which of course, you weren't, other than from me, eventually.

'Yes, that spiked drink was intended for poor old Bravo all along. I'd asked you about Mr Nice by that time, and you thought, "What a good idea to make the coppers think that he's after me as well!" A nice wee piece of insurance against the silly polis looking too hard at other people's motives for murder, including yours.'

He reached back and accepted his putter from McIlhenney as they reached the green. His ball was just off the putting surface, but the grass was even and he was able to roll his approach smoothly and safely up to the side of the hole, for a slightly fortuitous three. Atkinson's eight-yarder across the slope of the green was beautifully judged, curving down from the right to finish three inches behind the hole.

'Lovely putt, Darren,' said Skinner as they walked through a small coppice to the raised tee of the 565-yard par-five thirteenth, a monster of a hole with a narrow tree-lined fairway for the first 250 yards, opening out into a bunker-fringed hogsback. 'That must have been hellish difficult to read. But then you're at your best under pressure, aren't you?'

As he had done on the first three days, Atkinson took a three-wood from the thirteenth tee, avoiding the dangers of the hogsback. Skinner played even safer hitting a two-iron for accuracy, low between the corridor of trees.

'That was Rick at the side of the tee, wasn't it?' said Skinner as they walked on. 'Rick gave that wee boy the drinks, done up in his rain gear, in glasses and a floppy hat, so no one would recognise him and think they were seeing double. Of course you couldn't risk the spiked drink going astray. So you had that in your bag all along. The drinks that were handed out, so publicly, were clean, but you did a double shuffle with the bottles.'

He tapped Atkinson, convivially on the arm. 'Hey, maybe you dumped the spare one on the course. The bins are all emptied daily, but just maybe, if I used enough people to sift through the public refuse tip, I might get lucky and find something odd; a full, untainted bottle of isotonic thirst quencher, with your prints on it, and Rick's, and those of that wee boy. Doubt it, though. I'll do you the courtesy of assuming that you wiped it.'

They reached their tee-shots. Skinner used his two-iron again, clearing the hogsback and finding a flat piece of fairway 100 yards from the green. Atkinson put his ball thirty yards closer, with a four-iron.

'That was an awful thing to do to Bravo, Darren. He thought he was your pal as well as your caddy.

'It was an awful thing you did to Oliver M'tebe too, having his father kidnapped by those two Australians, just to put him off his game this week. That boy must be the goods right enough. They say he's approaching your class already, and that he'll be the next Number One.'

'Eventually,' said Atkinson, evenly. 'That's why we signed him up. But the time isn't here yet, Bob, not yet.'

'No, but he's enough of a threat now for you to do something about it. After all there's a million pounds in the pot this week. The biggest prize ever, and you weren't going to let anyone else lift it, were you, not even if you picked up your manager's thirty per cent as a consolation.

'So you had Mr M'tebe picked up. You hired those two Aussie caddies, guys you knew would be linked to Masur, not you, and they picked him up off the street, just like that. The South African police hadn't a clue where to look.'

The thirteenth green was on a rise, like the tee, and guarded by two bunkers. Skinner judged the distance carefully, and hit a full shot with his wedge. Polite applause from around the green told him that he had found the putting surface. Atkinson's feathered shot, hit with his third wedge, was a dream of a shot, all softness and touch. It followed the flag unerringly, and drew a roar from the gallery. The two strode up the slope to the green.

'Of course, pinching M'tebe's old man wasn't part of your grand design,' said Skinner as they walked. 'I wasn't really interested in who did that, until one of the Aussies let something slip. The Reverend was smarter than they expected. Just before he escaped, one of them used the name, "RA". At first, I assumed he meant Richard Andrews, but when all the other pieces fell into place, I realised that he didn't. He was talking about Rick Atkinson.

'That's when you shattered my last illusions about honour and the nobility of the human spirit, Darren. I mean, multiple murder's one thing,' he said, his tone filled with ironic sadness, 'but fixing a golf tournament, for God's sake! How could you?'

He shook his head and sighed, almost theatrically. 'Poor Oliver, poor Bravo. Reminds me of the old saying, about there being no greater love than that of the man who'd lay down the lives of his friends to save his own!'

Skinner's ball was indeed awaiting him on the narrow green as he crested the rise, even if it was fifty feet from the hole. He lined it up, thinking only of distance, and rolled it up, stopping it two feet to the right of the hole to secure, to his inner joy, his thirteenth par.

'So there we are, Darren,' he said, walking to the fourteenth, a relatively gentle 414-yard par-four, designed by the course architect to imbue a false sense of security into the unwary before the tigerish finishing holes. 'Two enemies dead, the tournament in your hands, the police protecting your life and limb, and Mike Morton, your last target, in deep trouble with us.

'But that gives you a problem. We're watching Morton like a hawk, in case Richard Andrews tries to make contact with him. Ironic, isn't it, we're treating Morton as a murder suspect, and by doing so we're protecting him from the real killers.'

He laughed as they stepped out on to the tee. Atkinson looked away from him down the fairway. He took his driver from McGuire and sent the ball an effortless 290 yards. Skinner did his best to copy the ease and smoothness of his swing, and was rewarded by a straight drive which carried around 240 yards but pulled up sharply on the fairway, running on only a further ten yards.

'You know,' said Skinner, suddenly serious, as they headed off once more, 'I'll have Mike Morton on my conscience for as long as I live. If I had kept him under surveillance, he'd still be alive. I couldn't see the whole picture at that time, yet it should have occurred to me that if Morton wasn't behind the two murders, and the attack on you, then he might easily be a target himself. But he shot his mouth off at me yesterday after-noon, and I got annoyed. I still wanted to speak to Andrews, if

419

only to close off that line of enquiry, so I gave Morton twenty-four hours without cover to produce him, and the threat of what would happen if he didn't. But in truth, the poor bugger genuinely didn't know where Andrews was!'

He paused, and looked sideways at Atkinson again. 'You must have thought all your Christmases had come at once, when you saw my people drive away from Bracklands. One day to go, and a clear shot at Morton, if you can get him on his own.'

When they reached it, Skinner's ball was sitting up nicely for his next shot. Once more, the flag was protected by a deep bunker, making a direct approach hazardous, and so he hit his five-iron instead carefully to the wide area of open green to the right. Even Atkinson fought shy of a direct attack on the flag, landing his soft eight-iron twenty feet away.

'It turns out to be pretty easy. Rick phones Morton, doesn't he? He tells him he wants to meet him in secret, last night. Maybe he says that he wants to talk to him about his company and yours co-operating now that Masur's out of the way.' Skinner was looking closely at Atkinson as he spoke. Beneath the mask of impassivity, he thought that he detected the faintest twitch of an eyebrow.

'Morton agrees to meet him. He says he'll skip the dinner. Rick says, "Good, let's meet where no one'll interrupt us. How about on top of Witches' Hill, just after dark?" Morton says OK, and he's a dead man.'

Skinner lined up his putt, lagging it almost perfectly once more, leaving himself an eighteen-inch tap-in. Atkinson stalked his putt like a tiger, in pursuit of his seventh birdie, but once again found only the lip of the hole.

'It was only when I stood on the top of that hill this morning, looking at what was left of Morton that the whole thing fell into place,' said Skinner as they walked from the green. 'I thought about his "doppelgänger" remark, I thought about Henry's case of mistaken identity, I thought about the second note, and I knew right then what I should have worked out yesterday. If I had, I'd have saved Morton's life.

'It takes a very special sort of person to plan and to do what your brother Rick did to Morton.' The policeman's conversational tone had gone, and his voice was hard and cold. 'I've only ever met one other man who could have done that. I breathed a sigh of genuine relief when he died. But now I've met two more like him.

'To lure him up there; to ambush him; to handcuff him to a tree; to pile the wood around him; to set fire to it; to stuff his handkerchief into his mouth to choke off his screams. And then, I guess, to watch him, as he writhed against the flames, until you were quite sure the job was done.

'Yes, you're very special guys, you Atkinsons. I'm looking forward to meeting you side by side.'

They had reached the fifteenth tee, 195 yards away from its small green, which sloped away so that only the top of the flag could be seen. Although only a par-three, it had proved the most difficult hole on the course.

'So how about it, Darren?' said Skinner, very quietly, so that only he and Atkinson could hear. 'This has been one-way traffic so far. I've shown you what I can see with my detective's vision. It's all logical, and to me it's all unanswerable truth, and maybe I can even prove it. So what d'you say? Underneath all that calm, have I got to you, you ruthless, murderous bastard?'

The golfer turned to him, with the animal look on his face once more. 'Sure Bob. I'm just scared helpless. Let me show you how scared I am.'

He turned and called to McGuire, the professional smile brought back as quickly as it had been banished. 'Four-iron, please, Mario.'

He took the club from McGuire, and hit a shot so audacious that even Skinner was amazed. Rather than playing the hole in the only way which seemed possible, by hitting safely to the back of the green and settling for two safe putts, he fired in a shot on a lower trajectory. The backspin seemed to make the ball sizzle off the club-face. The crowd sucked in its collective breath in suspense as it zoomed towards the target, to pitch, clearly, above the flag. Suddenly the gallery clustered on the viewing platform behind the green, roared its applause. 'Bugger,' said Atkinson quietly, after a few seconds. 'It hasn't gone in, they're not jumping high enough!'

Through the fifteenth, sixteenth and seventeenth, Bob Skinner, the rest of the onlookers, and the television audience across Europe, saw a display which was to be ranked by commentators as the finest burst of tournament golf ever played. Atkinson seemed to select shots which looked impossible, then to execute each one perfectly. The ten-inch birdie putt at the fifteenth was followed on the next hole by two six-iron shots, one from the tee, the next to within a yard of the flag. The 527-yard seventeenth was humbled by an impossibly long drive, a five-iron and a six-foot putt for an eagle, taking the imperious champion to ten under par.

In the face of this awesome, intimidating display, Skinner kept his concentration. He felt himself inspired by the unspoken challenge of this chilling man, and played the best golf of his own life, extending his string of successive pars to what was for him an unprecedented seventeen.

At last they stood together on the eighteenth tee. 'Looks like you're in the money, Bob,' said Atkinson, and Skinner alone caught the trace of mockery in his voice. 'A par up the last for a sixty-two, and this finishing hole; I mean it really isn't worthy of me.' He looked down the 472-yard par-four hole. The southern side of the Truth Loch made a jagged bite into the fairway, intimidating to Skinner. From the championship tee, anyone taking a direct line to the flag had to carry his drive 290 yards over water to gain the reward of a mid-iron approach. Nearer the tee to the left there was a second landing area, allowing the professionals a safer option of hitting a two-iron or three-wood. Closer still there was a third section of fairway which required only a 180-yard carry but left a second shot of around 300 yards to the green.

'You went on about me rubbishing the course, Bob, and by and large you're right. All things considered, most of it is pretty good. But this hole really is too easy for me. All I have to do is hit over the water and it's at my mercy.

'Well, not for me. If O'Malley can't design a decent finish for me, I'll create my own challenge.'

'I understand,' said Skinner. 'There's the rest of us, and there's you, Darren, or at least you and Rick. That's how you see life, isn't it?'

Atkinson looked at him, and Skinner caught in his eyes, as well as the deadly ruthlessness, something which he had seen only once before in his life, an arrogance, a belief in personal infallibility so strong that it seemed to engulf mere fanaticism and carry on to something beyond. 'Have it as you will,' he said.

He called out to McGuire. 'Four-iron, please, Mario.' The knowledgeable crowd murmured in surprise. Skinner, who had been doing his best all week to ignore the spectators' presence, looked at them over his shoulder, and saw for the first time among them, his daughter. A slight frown creased Alex's forehead.

He turned back to watch Atkinson, feeling on his face the first fat drops of the rain which had been threatening all afternoon. 'First landing area, Bob,' said the golfer quietly. He hit an easy gentle shot which soared high over the water to pitch softly in the centre of the first promontory. 'There, that leaves me three hundred to the green, and a bunker in line with the flag. No one could get on in two from there. A hundred quid says I get a birdie. Got the bottle for that, Mr Skinner?'

'You're on,' said the policeman, evenly. 'Neil, my driver please.' He lined up on the central landing area, swung smoothly and struck the ball as cleanly as he could. The distance across the water was 230 yards, but the adrenaline was coursing through his body and the ball cleared it easily. Its left-to-right fade was accentuated by a friendly bounce, leaving him around 190 yards to the green.

As Skinner walked from the tee, pulling on his new all-weather garment, Atkinson fell into step beside him. 'You know, Bob,' he said, with undisguised mockery. 'This story you've told me, it's really good. It flows along nicely, I have to admit. But a story is all it will ever be, 'cause it's got a couple of loose bricks.

'For openers, I remember quite well meeting that dozy greenkeeper – on Monday – and giving him an autograph. I was heading off to practice and I signed it in a hurry. Golfers are notorious among collectors; half the autographs we do are written on the march, so no two signatures look the same . . . apart from those on cheques. That's how it was with Webb.'

'At least that's what you'll say in court,' said Skinner, as they walked in step around the first curve of the Truth Loch.

'Exactly! And you know better than I do what a good QC will do to Hughie Webb in cross-examination. After five minutes he won't be able to swear what month it was let alone what day of the week. I don't fancy your star witness in the White case, mate.

'Tell you something else. I don't see Susan Kinture standing up in court. I'd have to say that she came to my room . . .' He looked at Skinner in mock outrage. 'My hostess, for God's sake . . . climbed straight into my bed, muttered something about not having had any for years, and set about me. I'd have to say that I told her next day that if she ever did anything like that again, I'd go straight to Hector.'

He slowed, as they approached his ball. 'Those are two problems you've got. Here's another. Masur only decided at the last minute to walk back to Bracklands, after he and Morton had their second barney. How the hell could Rick have known about that? There are a few claims of empathy in twins; you know, one experiencing the other's pain even when they're miles apart, but nobody in his right mind's going to suggest that they're telepathic.'

He stopped beside his ball, and knelt down to look at its lie on the soft, lush, velvety grass. 'Watch this, Mr Policeman,' he said, standing up. 'Driver, please, Mario.' McGuire looked at him in surprise, but Atkinson nodded in confirmation and held out his hand, snapping his fingers. Behind them the crowd murmured as they saw the white-bibbed policeman caddy remove the cover from the longest club in the bag, notoriously uncontrollable even from the best of positions on the fairway. Atkinson swung the driver experimentally.

Standing behind the ball he looked down the line of the 300-yard shot which faced him, nodding to himself as he planned it.

Skinner could picture the look in his eyes as he stepped up to address his ball, ignoring the rain, which was growing heavier by the minute. He swung with an unimaginable combination of power and finesse, thundering it away yet leaving the grass unmarked. The Titleist soared in its early flight out over the loch, heading, it seemed, far to the right of its target. Then, with a curve which defied gravity, it drew unerringly back in towards the green, pitching first on the fringe, then leaping forward to the flag. Skinner strained his eyes against the gloom of the afternoon, but was certain that he saw the ball come to a dead stop on its second bounce, looking for all the world to lie on the very edge of the hole.

The view of the spectators behind the rope barrier was hampered by the bunker which guarded the green, and by the distance itself. Some cheered, but others stayed silent, not seeing where the shot had finished, thinking perhaps that it had gone awry. In the stands beside the clubhouse there was a moment of stunned silence, as the crowds there in the distance took in the sheer enormity of Atkinson's blow. And then, as one, they leaped to their feet, some waving programmes or hats. It took a moment for the sound to travel back down the fairway, and then it reached them, crashing over them like a wave.

The champion turned back to the policeman. 'Impossible shot that, wasn't it? To bend a ball like that with a driver, to hit it that far, and then to pull it up with backspin. You're right, Bob. There's the rest, and there's me.

'A hundred quid, I reckon.'

'It'll be worth it,' said Skinner, 'for that shot. But what a pity that you don't keep your power-lust for the golf course. What a pity that you see people as you see golf balls, to be manipulated, and crushed when necessary, with the same level of feeling.'

They walked on, towards the next landing area, and Skinner's ball. 'Telepathy, Darren, you said earlier. Almost, but not quite. You ask me how Rick knew that Masur would be walking back alone to Bracklands, in the dark, and vulnerable?

'Dead simple, really. You've both got mobile phones. The latest digital GSM model by Motorola. They've got numbers in series, and they were supplied by a company in the South of England. They work internationally, so wherever you are, you can talk to each other. It *is* telepathy of a sort. One of you has a thought, and the other can share it seconds later.

'Remember the night of the PGA dinner? You were embarrassed when your phone rang. Embarrassed! You almost swallowed your tongue. That was Rick, calling you by mistake. That's not a guess. I know it. I've checked, you see. This is your world, Darren, but I've got mine, and there I can do things that *you* couldn't imagine.

'I know Rick called you during the dinner. I know you called him afterwards. I know you called him last night, after my detectives had left Bracklands. I know that he called Morton just a couple of minutes after that. If I'd had a wee bit more warning, I'd even know for sure what he said, and what you said to him. But the jigsaw didn't fit in time for me to do that.'

They arrived at the detective's ball. He looked down the line to the green. The flag was guarded by the encroaching bunker but, from the line of Atkinson's shot, he knew that the hole was cut well back from it. ' "Play the card, not the course", you told me. Best golfing advice I've ever had, and I'll never forget it. Let's see if I can finish in style. Eighteen straight pars and Skinner's round will be the best he's ever played.

'Five-wood, please Neil.' McIlhenney gave him the club, with a brief smile of encouragement. He lined up his shot, gathered his breath and his concentration and hit it, high and handsome as he had intended down the line of the flag over the bunker and to the back of the green. The applause of the crowd was less rapturous than for Atkinson's shot, but it was warm nonetheless. His chest swelled with pride. The champion joined him and they walked together towards the green, under the eerie, threatening, darkening skies, in the rain the intensity of which was gathering slowly but inexorably, to the breaking point of the storm ahead.

'I'll fill in the last part now, will I?' said Skinner. 'Where has Rick been all this week, to have been able to do all these things, to react as swiftly as he did to your two telephone calls, to take advantage of sudden opportunities to remove the only two guys who stood in the way of your ambition to make DRA Management the Number One force in world golf, with the Number One player at its head?

'Was he booked into a hotel near here? Hardly, not looking like he does, among all these golf fans.' He shook his head, and took from his back pocket a small white card, on which a few lines were scrawled.

'On August 1, a Winnebago mobile home – the compact version, not one of the big ostentatious jobs that stand out a mile – was registered in the name of DRA Management, number P 325 QRC. These things are popular among golfers, especially those who don't have wives. Arthur Highfield reckons this new one must be your fifth.

'Before that, last March in fact, a Yamaha trail bike, 125 cc, was registered in the name of Reginald Atkinson, number N 763 LRC. Arthur thought he remembered seeing a bike mounted on the back of your last camper vehicle.

'One of my guys got these numbers this morning through the PNC. Then he had calls made to all the caravan sites. We struck it lucky at Yellowcraig, outside Dirleton. It isn't a commercial site: the local Ranger Service looks after it, and the sort of people who go there tend to wear green wellies rather than golf shoes. The warden we spoke to remembers the vehicle. There's no register kept there, but his description matches the one we've got.

'It won't be there now, though.' Skinner's pace slowed as they approached the green. 'This is the really clever bit. Earlier on today, Rick had a call on his mobile. There was hellish interference on the line, but he'd just have been able to make out you, or rather a voice which through all that static he was certain was yours, telling him to drive the van to the course and to meet you behind the eighteenth after the tournament. Then the interference got too bad and the line went dead.

'He tried to call you back, but he got a pre-recorded message telling him that there was a fault with your phone.'

Skinner stopped, in the rain, and looked at the great golfer with a savage smile. 'I can't touch you, Darren. Not yet, at least. I'm sure that twins talk to each other on the phone all the time, and that would be your defence. But I can arrest Rick in connection with Morton's death, after that phone call he made to him. Then, after the motorcycle tracks in the mud at the foot of Witches' Hill, which my people found at first light this morning, are matched to the Yamaha, I can charge him with his murder.

'Who knows, maybe I'll find something in the Winnebago that'll be a perfect match with the dent in Michael White's skull, and in Masur's. But tough if I don't. Doesn't matter to me whether Rick gets three life sentences or just one. Either way, I'll make sure that the prosecution drops enough hints to the judge to get him a twenty-five-year minimum sentence.

'Now, champion of champions, your public awaits. Go ahead and take your applause, and your million quid.'

And so Darren Atkinson, as he had done so often before, strode alone on to the eighteenth green of Witches' Hill, to the roars of thousands of his admirers, waving and smiling, and hiding his real self from their sight. As Skinner followed him up the green to fading applause, he walked across to mark his ball where the shot of his golfing life, or anyone else's, had finished, two and a half feet from the flag.

Skinner glanced up at the leader board and saw, to his quiet satisfaction, that Oliver M'tebe, with a final round of 65, had finished a comfortable second. Then he bent down, marked his own ball, wiped it clean and replaced it, with the maker's name pointing directly towards the hole. As he paced out the distance, he glanced across at the silent crowd, and saw his daughter once again. For an instant their smiles linked across the green, and then he bent to his eight-yard putt. Keeping the head of the Zebra clear of the grass, as Atkinson had said, he stroked the ball. It rolled smoothly on its way, ten feet, twenty feet, its line two inches to the right, until, in the last two feet of its travel it curved towards the hole and fell in, for his first birdie of the day and a round of 71.

He punched the air in delight, as the crowd shouted, smiling and waving to Alex as he retrieved his ball from the hole and backed off, leaving the oval green to the champion.

The crowd fell silent in expectation, as Atkinson, now wearing a dark blue waterproof jacket, strode across the close-mown grass. He replaced his ball and looked down the thirty inches of his putt, satisfying himself that there was no swing or borrow that he did not see. He bent over the ball, and set himself for his sixty-first and last shot of the day.

The rumble of thunder which broke into the silence, although still some way distant, drew a gasp from the crowd. His concentration broken, Atkinson stood up to let it subside.

To Skinner, watching intently from behind, it was as if the man had looked into a mirror. The figure who faced him, standing behind the green, and whose puzzled eyes the golfer's met, could have been Madame Tussaud's finest work of art. Skinner had met twins before, but never any who were more identical than these. Height, build, hair-colouring, suntan, even their blue waterproofs; everything matched.

And then Rick Atkinson's expression changed, as he caught something in his brother's face, and completed the mirror image. The look in his eyes was cold, hard and furious as sudden comprehension dawned. It confirmed for Skinner, beyond any final doubt, the vision of the crimes which he had pieced together in his detective's eye. Atkinson began to back away into the crowd, but found himself restrained on either side, discreetly but effectively, by Andy Martin and Brian Mackie.

The crowd, oblivious to the exchange, fell silent again. The rain began to hammer down harder as Darren bent over his putt for a second time. He struck it quickly. The ball rolled true and caught the hole, but it was travelling too fast and spun round the lip, finishing on the edge but still on the putting surface. The crowd's groan could not drown out the sound of the champion's slap against his thigh. He reached over and tapped the ball into the hole to win the Murano Million. Their disappointment forgotten, the crowd rose, cheering.

Skinner walked across the green to his partner, unsmiling, yet with his hand outstretched. 'That was some round of golf, Darren,' he said quietly, 'given the conditions. Sixty-two, ten under par, in the final round of a tournament. But only you and I will ever know how good it *really* was.' He took his hand in a grip rather than a shake. 'Now come over here, before you go for your prize and get your reward. I want you to hear this.'

He eased Atkinson in front of him towards his twin at the edge of the green. As they reached him Alison Higgins stepped between them, her back to Darren. 'Reginald Atkinson,' she said, 'I am arresting you in connection with the death of Mike Morton. You do not have to say anything, but . . .' Rick's face was impassive as she recited the mandatory caution. He looked, not at her, but over her head at his brother.

'I didn't . . .' Darren began.

'I know. Keep it that way. Don't say anything.' Without a fuss, and without a single spectator being aware of the drama, he was led away by Martin and Mackie.

Atkinson and Skinner were left in the rain. Their two caddies stood on the far side of the green. 'I suppose those two stooges were in on the act,' said the golfer, nodding towards them.

'In on what act?' said Skinner. 'Think yourself lucky. You got a free caddy. Mario can't take a penny of that million of yours, but I'll have to pay the other bugger. Now come on, let's get our scores in and they can have the presentation. We should let the people get away home before the weather gets any worse. As well as that, Darren, having to let you walk free from here is sticking in my throat, so the sooner I'm shot of you the happier I'll be.'

He led Atkinson off the green. Behind them McIlhenney produced Skinner's big, bulging, rolled golf umbrella from its pouch down the side of his bag.

As they headed for the clubhouse, Skinner's way was blocked. 'I suppose I should say well done, Skinner,' said Everard Balliol. 'Damn fine round that must have been. Too damn fine for a seven-handicapper, but I suppose the company made the difference.' The taciturn Texan looked at him. 'We'll have a rematch some day, buddy. Depend on it.'

'Your place or mine, any time,' said Skinner, and resumed his progress to the clubhouse.

'You think you're getting away with this, Darren, and in a physical sense, you're probably right. Rick won't say a word to implicate you; I guess he'll claim that Morton threatened him. He'll get his twenty-five years regardless, but you'll still be a hero, not tarnished at all. You'll be able to headhunt someone to run DRA for you and build the business into something that'll let Rick live in luxury when he gets out. The grand design is under way, even if your twin will be over sixty before he can enjoy it.'

He paused. 'You know, ultimately people like you and he only care about yourselves. Rick won't shop you because he couldn't gain from it, that's all. Pretty soon you'll have got used to the idea of life without him. You'll build your empire. That's what you're thinking, even now, isn't it?

'Except that's *not* how it's going to be. Mike Morton's father, the old man of influence, is still alive. Masur's Yakuza friends, the boys in Tokyo, they're still around. And I'm here.

'I know the full story, Darren, and I'm going to make it my

business to see that they hear it too: all of it. Don't build yourself an empire, friend. Build yourself a fortress, because they'll be round to see you sometime fairly soon.'

Atkinson looked at him, weighing him up. 'That's bullshit. You wouldn't do that. You couldn't do it.'

Skinner stared back, with eyes like ice, and Atkinson saw him, saw all of him, for the first time. 'You haven't the faintest notion of what I could do, Darren. And you better believe that I *will* do just what I've said. I've told you, I've met people like you before, one or two of them, and none of them has ever got away from me.

'Neither will you slither away from what you and your brother have done here. You may think you have. But sooner or later, someone, Sicilian or Japanese, will come calling. Now's a good time to quit, partner. At the top. Because it's going to be impossible to stay there if you can't go out in public for fear of your life. DRA Management is finished. You're finished. My word upon it.

'Now, let's get these scores in and this presentation over with. Oh yes, and there's that hundred quid. Birdie at the last, remember? You owe me. I'm not letting you off with that either. See you outside.' He strode into the Recorder's tent and handed his signed scorecard to the Marquis of Kinture, who was acting in that capacity for the conclusion of his tournament, then turned on his heel and walked out again without a word.

Outside, beside the eighteenth green, where the crowds still waited for the presentation, Norton Wales and Hideo Murano had joined McIlhenney and McGuire, and the four were sheltering under large umbrellas from the steadily worsening rain. A girl in the sponsor's livery handed one to Skinner as he joined them. Beside them, a small presentation table had been set up in front of the stand.

Skinner's clubs lay at McIlhenney's feet, but McGuire leaned on Atkinson's huge bag. The ACC looked at it idly. Suddenly his eyes seemed to narrow, and he looked more closely. He looked over his shoulder and called, loudly, to Arthur Highfield, who, in a trenchcoat, was setting up a cordless microphone on the table.

'Come and take a look at this,' he said, pointing to the bag.

Highfield walked across impatiently. 'Count them,' Skinner ordered. The PGA Secretary counted the clubs in Atkinson's bag. Once, twice, a third time, his consternation growing by the minute. 'My God,' he said eventually. 'He's got fifteen clubs in his bag. One too many.' He looked at McGuire. 'Has anyone tampered with this?'

'It's never been out of my sight, sir,' said the Detective Sergeant, indignantly. Highfield groaned, and put a hand to his head.

'What's the penalty for an extra club?' asked Skinner.

'Depends,' said the official. 'Has he registered his score?'

'Yes, I left him in there doing just that.'

'Oh my God,' sighed Highfield. 'Then he's disqualified.'

'How embarrassing!' said Skinner. McGuire, McIlhenney, Wales and Murano looked as shocked as he. He thought for a moment. 'Look, Arthur, don't you think that the best thing you can do is to scrap the presentation and stand down the crowd.'

'Mmm. I think you're right.' He walked back to the microphone and switched it on. 'Ladies and gentlemen,' he called, and paused. A second boom of thunder, much closer this time, gave him inspiration. 'If I may have your attention please. I am very sorry, but it has been decided, because of the weather, that the presentation will take place indoors. I thank you for your attendance today and all this week and hope that you have enjoyed the wonderful golf which we have seen.' As he switched off the mike, Darren Atkinson emerged solemnly from the clubhouse. Highfield rushed off to meet him.

'Maybe we should make ourselves scarce till we find out what's happening,' said Skinner to Wales and Murano. 'My daughter's over there. I'm going to talk to her.'

He reached Alex as she stepped down from the stand, the hood of her oilskin jacket tied tight under her chin. 'Hi Pops,' she said, excitedly, easing herself under his umbrella for added protection. 'You were brilliant.' The thunder crashed again, shaking the ground. The rain tumbled down. Although it was only a few minutes after five o'clock, it was as if night was about to fall.

'When are you going to tell me what's happened?' Alex shouted above the downpour. 'That man Andy and Brian took away, that looked like . . .'

Suddenly Skinner felt a powerful tug on his left arm. He swung round, sending water cascading from his umbrella on to the figure before him. Darren Atkinson's composure had cracked at last. He stood there, almost glowing with rage, waving a golf club in the air.

'You bastard!' he screamed, waving the club. It was a Shark's Fin nine-iron, new and shiny.

Skinner smiled at him, and a feeling of satisfaction flooded over him. 'You didn't think I'd let you pocket the Million, did you Darren? How could I when you've let me down, along with everyone else who loves this game?

'As well as being a conspirator and a murderer by association, you've betrayed millions of people, me included, who made you their example. What you did to Oliver, as well as being illegal in every country I've ever heard of, was plain cheating. The lad deserves the Million, not you.'

'Damn your hide!' Atkinson shouted. 'You and your monkeys planted this club in my bag.'

Skinner shrugged his shoulders. 'So prove it.' The thunder crashed, hugely. 'It's just your bad luck,' he said, as its echoes subsided, 'that I'm at my best on a Sunday afternoon as well!'

Darren Atkinson snarled in impotent rage, spun round on his heel, and stalked away from the policeman and his daughter, the club grasped tightly, near the head, in his right fist. He strode down the fairway, the rain thrashing down on him in torrents. They watched him as he came almost to the edge of the Truth Loch, and as he pulled his arm back and above his head, to throw the alien nine-iron, the hated cause of his defeat, into its dark, storm-dappled waters.

The single shaft of lightning shot down from the darkened sky, cast like a huge jagged, shining spear. It found the route which it sought in the club raised up in Darren's hand. The golfer seemed to be consumed by it as it coursed through him to the earth below. He jerked and danced in its grasp, like the flickering black centre of a huge candle, its brilliant white light reflecting in the Truth Loch beyond and flooding Bob and Alex where they stood.

It vanished after a few seconds, but by then they were blinded. Against the dying sound of its accompanying thunder, Skinner heard his daughter scream, and felt himself tremble. He realised that he was still holding his umbrella and threw it from him, instinctively, as far away as he could. Again and again, he squeezed his eyes tight shut, as if to rub away the last of the searing light.

Gradually his vision returned, and he realised that he and Alex had been edging, hand-in-hand, down the slope, towards the centre of the lightning strike, tugged like moths towards the candle. He held her still, pressing her face against his chest to help her eyes recover, and to prevent her seeing, when they did, what lay before them, on the shores of the Truth Loch, in the centre of the charred circle, a twisted, melted thing in its hand.

Trembling still, Skinner looked on and whispered, '*And by lightning . . .*' to no one in particular.